Praise for
The Pirate Queen

"In *The Pirate Queen,* Patricia Hickman explores the question that haunts us all: 'am I enough?' Saphora Warren has all the trappings of the good life, yet is trapped in her own good graces. On the eve of her escape, she is forced by her own moral code to stay the course. Adrift in her emotions, Saphora learns to navigate her life from the inside. The words are poetic, the story is sublime; you will root for this good woman to claim the treasure we all seek—a life full of love. Saphora Warren is more than enough. And like a true Pirate Queen, she will steal your heart as well."

—LESLIE LEHR, author of *Wife Goes On*

"*The Pirate Queen* is a poignant, inspiring tale of finding faith, hope, and love in the midst of loss. Patricia Hickman, you owe me a box of tissues!"

—TAMARA LEIGH, author of *Leaving Carolina*
and *Nowhere, Carolina*

"*The Pirate Queen* drew me in from the first page and surrounded me. Hickman breathes life into her characters as they experience some of life's greatest joy and greatest sorrow. Through it all, Hickman reminds us the God of hope is in control."

—RACHEL HAUCK, co-author of *The Sweet By and By*
and author of *Dining with Joy*

"Patricia Hickman's *The Pirate Queen* took me by surprise. At the start, I thought I was reading a Southern-style Danielle Steel. Then I found I was settling into a one-of-a-kind family drama. Tender, compelling, outstanding. A book you'll want to share with your friends, your best friends."

—LYN COTE, author of *Her Abundant Joy*

"In *The Pirate Queen,* Patricia Hickman weaves together a rich story of forgiveness and grace. Her characters stole my heart, and I struggled and then cheered alongside them as their lives were refined and then transformed. Highly recommended!"

—MELANIE DOBSON, author of *Love Finds You in Homestead, Iowa* and *Refuge on Crescent Hill*

"Patricia Hickman's *The Pirate Queen* was so much more than I expected. She's a fine writer, so my expectations were high. She surpassed them. From the *Southern Living* photo shoot at the beginning to the final scene, I enjoyed each twist and turn in the plotline. An extraordinary tale of deep feelings and God's love."

—DONITA K. PAUL, author of The DragonKeeper Chronicles and *Dragons of the Valley*

THE PIRATE
QUEEN

THE PIRATE QUEEN

A NOVEL

PATRICIA HICKMAN
AUTHOR OF *PAINTED DRESSES*

WATERBROOK
PRESS

THE PIRATE QUEEN
PUBLISHED BY WATERBROOK PRESS
12265 Oracle Boulevard, Suite 200
Colorado Springs, Colorado 80921

All Scripture quotations are taken from the New American Standard Bible®.
© Copyright The Lockman Foundation 1960, 1962, 1963, 1968, 1971,
1972, 1973, 1975, 1977, 1995. Used by permission. (www.Lockman.org).

The characters and events in this book are fictional, and any resemblance
to actual persons or events is coincidental.

ISBN 978-1-4000-7200-2
ISBN 978-0-307-45909-1 (electronic)

Published in the United States by WaterBrook Multnomah, an imprint of the
Crown Publishing Group, a division of Random House Inc., New York.

WATERBROOK and its deer colophon are registered trademarks of Random
House Inc.

Library of Congress Cataloging-in-Publication Data
Hickman, Patricia.
    The pirate queen : a novel / Patricia Hickman.—1st ed.
        p. cm.
    ISBN 978-1-4000-7200-2—ISBN 978-0-307-45909-1 (electronic)
  I. Title.
    PS3558.I2296P57 2010
    813'.54—dc22

                                        2010005617

Printed in the United States of America
2010

10 9 8 7 6 5 4 3 2

To Jordan M., who reminds me how easy it is to love.

❧

And to our friends Judy and Del Arrendale. Judy, you
wanted another beach book. Hope you like this one.
Your friendship is a treasure; your prayers kept us afloat.

Well something's lost, but something's gained
In living every day

JONI MITCHELL, "Both Sides Now"

THE PIRATE
QUEEN

1

My shell is not like this, I think. How untidy
it has become! Blurred with moss, knobby
with barnacles, its shape is hardly recognizable
any more. Surely, it had a shape once. It has a
shape still in my mind. What is the shape of
my life?

ANNE MORROW LINDBERGH, *Gift from the Sea*

One might have observed that all of the right people had been invited
to the Warren estate for the *Southern Living* shoot. The certainty of
the Warrens' happy existence on Lake Norman was firmly set in the
minds of the departing guests. Undoubtedly, through the women
present, the affair's success spread off the estate and into the notable
neighborhoods. The party had ended, leaving the catering help to
stow away the perfectly selected china settings.

Saphora Warren pulled down the balloons, plucking them out of
the air and then inserting a straight pin into the latex. As quickly as
she dropped the dead latex remains, a teen boy she had hired to clean
up after the lawn party picked them off the ground. He had trolled
past her dock on his Jet Ski yesterday and, when he saw her sunning
on her boat's deck, had asked in vain for a cold beer.

Lake Norman's shoreline lapped at the Warrens' family boat in the
distance, the mast a cross against a pale pink manse located transversely

on the opposite harbor. One house sat like a relic on the Warrens' end of the Peninsula, a reminder of the older ranch houses standing before the year the lake was put in. It was unseasonably hot for late June. The warm brown water turned red along the clay-brimmed lawns.

Several of the guests had driven family boats across the lake, arriving early for the *Southern Living* lawn party. Had not Saphora's housekeeper, Tabitha, just led the women docking their motorboats and sailboats along the Warrens' dock into the guest room near the swimming pool to slip into garden dresses and brush out their hair, matted down after a morning of tennis? But here the afternoon had been spilled like sweet tea poured out, the ladies already gathering in clusters to kiss good-bye and float back to their pretty houses across the lake.

Saphora noticed she had forgotten to shave her legs. She pulled down the hem of her skirt as if she were straightening it at the same second Abigail Weed, the journalist from *Southern Living,* noted a few more descriptive details about Saphora's gardens, the patio containers holding gold black-eyed Susans that turned open faced to the sun. Saphora was popping the balloons so methodically that Sherry, her cook and personal assistant, ran from the kitchen out onto the paved patio yelling, "What in the world?"

"It's nothing," said Abigail, taking over, speaking for Saphora, and familiar enough with running *Southern Living* lawn parties like productions that she said to Sherry, "Sherry, can you help Mrs. Warren?"

Sherry took the straight pin from her boss like she would a child who might hurt herself. "Miss Saphora, aren't you the one to be doing that?" Sherry said, implying that Saphora should not do menial tasks like deflating balloons. But Saphora was not herself today, and that accounted for her giddiness.

Abigail put down her laptop that held the contents of Saphora's "life on the lake" and joined Sherry in killing the remaining balloons.

"This is some place, Saphora. You live in your own fairy tale," said Abigail.

"Bender planned it this way from the beginning." Saphora had not noticed before how the high hedged wall surrounding the estate and the trees of a similar height enclosed the house like an evergreen compound. Bender had commandeered the landscaping crew using words like "picturesque" and "palatial."

"Bender's your husband, Dr. Warren?"

"The plastic surgeon. Yes. He invented a procedure." She did not know why she told Abigail that without her asking. But it was the surgical procedure and its ensuing fame in the medical community that gave Bender the things he needed to order his life. He dressed like a prince, closet arranged like a Manhattan department store. He was tall and good-looking.

When Saphora had gotten around to telling Bender the call had come from *Southern Living*, he was dressing in a golf shirt for his Sunday morning game. He patted her as he sprinted out the door, telling her she was using up the magic from her lucky star. He spread envy, she was pretty sure, as he putted over the third hole. She imagined him mentioning the *SL* lawn party in a casual way, like doctors do.

This morning he had taken one final turn around the rear lawn, proud the house was selected for the *Southern Living* magazine spread. Practically speaking, a write-up about them could affect home value in a sagging economy.

Not showing up for the lawn party was his way of making himself elusive so that he would become the subject of the party's talk. Saphora knew her lines just as she knew Abigail would have fished around the subject of Bender's illustrious career until she acquiesced. So Saphora helped her cut to the point she was after. One last time. It was not that she owed him anything. Promoting Bender was a full-time habit.

"I heard about that award," said Abigail. "Back in the nineties, right? It's all over the Internet. You must be the envy of all your friends."

Saphora looked at the four remaining women still mingling on the patio. "I don't know." She smiled. A faint laugh fluttered out of her throat. She was not as fast as Bender with words. She would lie awake, and the right thing to say would come to mind. But too late. Her brain was about to explode from storing so many unsaid things. Thinking deeply rather than broadly presented so many lost opportunities.

Saphora was curious about Abigail's life in Florida. She imagined Abigail writing clever descriptive phrases about the photographs of the places where she had traveled. She made fast friends, probably had to with her schedule. Abigail was a woman who did not care whether her clothes were designer made or factory overruns. There was an attitude about her that Saphora defined as gypsy. A woman who lived to cull out the far-flung corners of the universe.

Sherry joined Abigail, and the two of them set to reopening the still-inflated balloons, sucking the helium out of them. Sherry sang, "La la la la." Abigail laughed. Then Sherry laughed until Mark Ng, the photographer, walked up on them.

"I've got to head back to Tampa," he said to Abigail.

"You're always the spoilsport, Mark," said Abigail. The helium was still constricting her vocal chords.

Mark hefted his camera bag and walked away from them. Saphora had never met a more somber young man. He did not like or want to keep any of the photographs using the lake as a backdrop, calling the lake "too brown to photograph." Saphora overheard him ask Abigail if it would be improper to colorize the lake photographs blue, but Abigail was a purist. "It's a lake, Mark, not the ocean." As soon as he walked away, she said to Saphora, "He's a coast dweller. He doesn't get lake life."

Saphora liked Abigail right from the start because of her secret admiration for cynical women. Abigail whispered sharp criticisms into her ear; she was good at assessing people on sight. That was evident as each Peninsula wife had arrived browned from playing tennis on clay courts. "There's one with plenty of time on her hands," she would say.

Abigail was good, however, at bringing people she liked into her circle. She took Saphora into her confidence at the outset, making Saphora feel elevated, as if she and Abigail were circling overhead, their communal laughter falling down on the mortals below.

The few remaining guests lined up along the courtyard quad to offer polite farewells to Saphora, but mostly to ogle Abigail, hoping against hope she would use her magical influence to pick their house for a photo shoot. But today was reserved: Pick Saphora Day.

One of the women was a naturalist named Erin Guff. She thanked Saphora for Bender's donation to her pet ecological fund.

Bender had not mentioned donating to Erin's charity.

"That husband of yours is generous to a fault," said Erin.

Her tone was affected. She was hiding something, Saphora decided.

Erin lobbied for environmental interests along the Outer Banks, like educating homeowners about how lawn fertilizer polluted the ocean. Saphora admired her activism if only because it seemed so daring. She admired anyone unafraid to confront and wished she could have that kind of boldness. But Erin's subversive tactics were not admirable.

Today Erin stood like a centerpiece among the other Peninsula wives. She wore a white strapless dress picked up in New York, not like the other women, who dressed like colorful birds from Charlotte boutiques. She looked away for a millisecond, long enough for Saphora to come to the conclusion that she had slept with Bender. Saphora should not have invited her to the party. Now that she thought about it, women had weakened Bender's character.

Erin turned to face her again. "I love you dearly, Saphora. You're a treasure." She said it as if she had found wings and flown between Saphora and Abigail.

Saphora let Erin kiss her cheek. But it left an itch.

Mark came alongside Saphora as she unthreaded a silk garland out of the trellis. "Thank you for letting us crash in today, Saphora," he said.

"Can you send some of the pictures to me?" she asked Mark. "I can pay you."

Mark's sleeve brushed her forearm. He packed up the camera but seemed to take his time. Stalling was what a man like Mark did when he wanted to linger around a woman. He awkwardly interjected idle chatter, unlike her husband, who was never without exactly the right thing to say. Saphora was terrible at flirting. She had once filled out one of those personality quizzes that assessed her flirting skills. She was in the one percentile of women who did not know how to flirt. Not knowing how to flirt seemed to make her better, less like Bender.

"Sure. Here's what it'll cost you. Tell me how you make your barbecue sauce," Mark said to Saphora. He winked, she was pretty sure. Very charming, an Asian man's wink. She walked alongside him toward the front gate. The back of his hand brushed the back of her hand. He was not so somber after all.

Saphora had not cooked one of the twenty or more dishes for the staged party. Sherry had whipped up the sauce in between cooking two other dishes. "It's the chili peppers," she told him, sounding more southern than usual, probably because Mark seemed to expect it from her. "And brown sugar. Sherry can tell you." She had a terrible memory for the details of what went into a sauce or any combination of ingredients that came together so perfectly as to draw admiration. Memory was not her strong suit. She could go downstairs for a cold cola, and the next thing she knew she'd be staring into the dryer trying to remember why she came downstairs. "Sherry's around here somewhere," she told him.

"Did I hear my name?" Sherry sidestepped Saphora, flirting above her boss's missed opportunity. She was African American, tall, leggy. The kind of woman who would turn heads if she could only afford the right clothes. But her voice was still so helium bloated that Mark turned away.

"I'll e-mail you, Mrs. Warren," he said. "Just so you know, you're the nicest hostess I've photographed so far."

Saphora hung on Mark's compliment and his gaze until he broke eye contact and headed through the gate for his car.

Sherry finished with the catering company's associate, who was responsible for packing up the remaining folding chairs. The last of the chairs disappeared into the delivery truck. Soon the lawn was clean again, although trampled.

Sherry said, "This is the best party we've ever had, Miss Saphora.

You impressed the fool out of those ladies from the Peninsula Club. Not a one will ever top this."

"Because of you, Sherry. You should take the rest of the day now," said Saphora, "for yourself." That should get her out of the way.

"But what about dinner? Dr. Warren, he's home by dark tonight, he told me."

"We'll warm up leftovers. You cooked plenty, enough for an emerging country."

"I am beat, for sure. I got to prop up my dogs."

"Go home and rest. As a matter of fact, take tomorrow off too. Paid, I mean. You deserve it."

She caught Sherry off guard.

Saphora walked her to the back entry where Sherry had parked her Kia. She helped Sherry into her car and told her to check in with Dr. Warren Thursday morning. Sherry continued to resist being brushed out of the house so quickly. "I saw your suitcase lying open on the bed when I was putting up your clean towels, Miss Saphora. You going somewhere?" she asked.

"Oriental," said Saphora, not looking directly at Sherry. The Outer Banks beach house Bender bought five summers back, in the coastal village of Oriental, had stood empty for all that time.

"You should have told me. I could have driven up a day ahead and stocked up for summer. You know how cobwebs take over."

"I'm in a stocking mood," said Saphora. "It's therapeutic."

"Not for me. It's just plain old work."

Saphora ran out of excuses. The late afternoon hour was swimming away, and she needed to get her cook and personal assistant out from under foot. "I left that bag of costume jewelry for you in the bathroom. Did you find it?"

Sherry was on to her. She kept her eyes on Saphora in a manner showing her unease with leaving her mistress to organize dinner. "I did. That's some of your good stuff. You all right, Miss Saphora?"

"Better than most." It was only costume jewelry; Sherry liked the junkier accessories. She looked good in bright costumey pieces that cheapened other women's looks. "This is your bowling night. Jerry is waiting for you."

"You know me too good, Miss Saphora." She took her time putting her pocketbook in the backseat, her apron in the passenger seat, folded too neatly for something she was about to put in the wash. She finally climbed into the car. There was a moment when she looked as if she was still conflicted over leaving.

"Have fun bowling," said Saphora.

Sherry closed the door and started her engine.

"Bye!" Saphora managed to get her sent off, down the drive and out the gate.

A food smell hung in the kitchen. It followed Saphora up the staircase and into the bedroom when she realized it was she who smelled like everything that had been cooked from four this morning on. The steamed clams and chili-soaked shrimp were for the time being a part of the fabric clinging to her skin. She peeled off the blouse and the woven silk skirt and slipped into the shower. The dual shower heads shot the water at her skin like tiny bullets. The bathroom mirrors steamed over so that when she stepped out onto the marble she could not see any of her face or the small dimples of cellulite pocking her buttocks. She cycled four days a week, but her body responded like an old pillow.

She stuffed the nine-hundred-dollar blouse into the dry-cleaning bag. She was leaving behind the expensive stuff, the part of her wardrobe she had passed through Bender's impeccable filter, and taking her everyday clothes. She wondered if she would ever see that blouse again. Benny Taylor's boy Eric would pick up the dry-cleaning bag Thursday morning after Sherry hung it on the rear kitchen door. Three days later, Eric would return the dry cleaning—her blouse, Bender's laundered shirts, and his golf pants. Sherry would whisk them upstairs to hang in the dressing room. Saphora shoved the blouse deep into the dry-cleaning bag as if she didn't care what happened to it.

She finished rolling up her comfortable traveling clothes to pack tightly and then slipped into the twenty-dollar jeans bought on clearance at Kohl's. Bender had rolled his eyes at her for slumming, as he called it. It was her happy rebellion to wear whatever she wanted. Saphora packed the Gucci suitcase with a few of her skinny clothes and some middle-of-the-road size sixes since she could possibly lose weight while living alone. Then she included the everyday clothes that actually fit. Maybe size eight would be her permanent state of being. *It's up to me,* she thought.

She looked around the Bender-sized bedroom for the last time. Tabitha had come Monday to clean. Saphora made the bed this morning, four hours after Bender got up at three to drive to the hospital. There was not a wrinkle in the bedding. She could flip quarters on the sheets. She opened the nightstand drawer. The items in the drawer were neatly segregated into a tray that held Bender's watch and wedding band at night. There were always batteries in the flashlight tucked into the drawer that Bender used when he routinely got up at two in the morning to relieve himself. A new set of golf clubs in the bag waited just inside the walk-in dressing room. A mini putter station lay five feet out from the dressing mirror. It took little time to remove any traces of herself. She wondered how long it would take for Bender to notice she was gone.

She zipped the suitcase closed and grabbed a ball cap she normally wore while running. She pressed it down over the two-hundred-dollar hairstyle Bender had called "perfect, so perfect for you, Saphora."

She rolled the suitcase onto the upstairs landing at the exact moment the front door opened. She assumed Sherry was coming back to remind her how to use the warming oven. She stepped up to the edge of the overhang, resting her hands on the balustrade to look down into the entry. But Sherry had not come back. Bender came through the front door instead of the back entry, where he usually parked the blue Lexus, the only car he willingly left out in the rain. His face was white as scallops, and his skin palely gleaming. His shirt was wrinkled, and he had not dressed for the hospital but was wearing a plaid shirt, like the kind he wore tarpon fishing off the coast of Florida. He looked to the back of the house, as if he were looking for her, or maybe for Sherry to mix up a martini in the middle of the day. Had he not said he had an important surgery scheduled with a client from the Peninsula? A nose job, wasn't it? Maybe it was yesterday. She couldn't remember.

"Good grief, Bender. It's not even four," she said in the quiet of the afternoon.

"Saphora," he said, breathless, as if he had been running. He was looking straight at her, but not as if he was at all perceiving her. He was looking past her. It was not like him. Bender was always direct. "I'm glad I found you," he said distantly.

She was thinking about the suitcase beside her on the floor. How to explain? She would send him into the kitchen for a beer and then hide the luggage. He would fall asleep halfway through the drink, and then she would leave. Nothing was keeping her from leaving.

"There's cold beer in the kitchen. Some leftovers. You like fried green tomatoes. I can't have any so you might as well," she said as if she had not already eaten two. Her pulse drummed in her ears.

Before she could rattle off the list of dishes she thought might entice him, detour him from his upstairs shower, he said, "I'm sick."

The sky was not yet darkening and would not for several hours. Not even a motorboat rumbled distantly from the dock.

"A glass of club soda then?" she asked, nervous, her thoughts spinning.

"Come down," he said, disappearing into the house.

She caught up with Bender after passing the mud room, where the photographs of their three children hung above the coatrack. The coatrack still hung eye level to a first grader even though their youngest boy, Ramsey, was now married and a dad.

Saphora had her first child because she was too young to organize her life around birth control. So she spent the first two years of marriage organizing her life around Turner. He was the biggest baby, her mother-in-law said, in four generations of Warrens. The Warren men came small into the world and then grew to be tall men. They were big earners and big spenders. Bender's mama had called her only son Bender the Spender. She had passed away two years earlier after a vacation in Austria. Bender had said women who married Warren men seldom lived long after their men died. They lost their purpose.

Turner had seemed like a lonesome little boy. If Saphora had known about temperaments back then, she would have known Turner was born to need people around him. She could have had twenty children and never filled Turner's need for companionship.

She had not thought of putting him in day school until after his sister, Gwennie, was born. Then the youngest came along, another boy whom his brother and sister called Ramsey, after a story that had been read to them in Sunday school. Saphora never told them the difference between Ramsey and Ramses. But the name had suited him the minute he opened his eyes—blue, never to turn another color.

Saphora read baby books and went to a parenting class at a church, where they tried to rook her into membership. Confidence in mothering came too late. But finally the three of her children were in school and then they were grown.

Turner married a girl from New York. She took him away from his Lake Norman nest and then sent him back. He was a charmer but not a good provider, and girls these days are smart to catch on. Turner kept his boy, Eddie, on weekends and summers. He called his boy Eddie because his ex named him Schuyler Eduardo Warren even with Turner at her side laughing and telling her she could not possibly mean it. She was not Latino. All of the Warrens debated the middle name privately. Saphora's sister, Emerald, said it was probably an old lover named Eduardo. But Emerald was prone to gossip out of turn.

Gwennie was an attorney who never married. Ramsey married a girl who kept him working long hours at a job anyone could do. Ramsey's first child, Liam, had the temperament to either blow up a building someday or else research incurable diseases. He tortured his brothers, twin boys, until they came running to Saphora, calling her Nana, a name Ramsey's wife, Celeste, selected when Saphora couldn't accept any of the pet names for Grandmother.

As Bender continued down the pass-through that led into the living room, Saphora was thinking about her children back when they were young and under her control. It was strange, as if the house had locked away the echoes of them running through the house calling out to each other, only to let them out at that instant.

Bender took the upholstered chair that faced away from the bookcases. He looked awkward in the chair, and that is when Saphora realized he had never sat down in that chair until now.

"You should have seen the *Southern Living* people, treating us like we were all Hollywood celebrities, snapping pictures of Sherry's food. I didn't let on that I was nervous."

She figured Vicki Jaunice might have noticed her anxiety when Saphora inadvertently dipped her shrimp into Vicki's sauce. That was when, for the first time, she decided Vicki had slept with Bender, the same as Bernie Mae Milton and Pansy Fulton.

Vicki had gotten her start in business when Saphora recommended Vicki's cosmetics business to all her friends. The home-based business had ballooned into a sizable basement office with six staff members. She should never have let Vicki get a foot in the door with her friends.

Bender opened a Red Stripe with one twist of the cap, without looking at it or her.

"Abigail says our house photographs like a castle. Isn't that good?" she asked. "She's the *SL* journalist." Had she told him that already?

Bender could not settle comfortably into the chair. He had put on the weight he often did in the winter but would take it off as soon as he could get active again in the summer.

"I've never noticed so many books in this room," he said.

"I should give some to the library. But they are, after all, our books." Saphora kept books from as far back as second grade. She could look at one spine and it was like a time machine, like the blue book titled *The Last Affair* given to her by a boy who kissed her out-side the boys' locker room. He had never asked her for a date. But he kissed her and then handed her the book. Whenever he passed her in the hallway, he winked at her.

"Have you noticed a change in me, say, over the past month?" he asked.

"You've gained weight, but then you take it off as you please," she said. He could gain weight, and women still thought of him as good-looking.

"I can hardly take the stairs. Then, dizzy spells. You haven't no-ticed me complaining of headaches?" He had a controlled tone, nor-mally, but his voice tensed. His long, manicured fingers lay on top of his stomach accusingly. "And nausea." He took a pair of eyeglasses from a case in the table drawer and carefully pushed them up his nose. Then he got up and, running his finger down a shelf of med-ical books, pulled three from the bookcase. He placed them on the end table and then sat back down in the chair. A faint moan came out of Bender such as she had never heard before.

"Maybe you are taking the stairs more slowly," she said. His ex-pectations of her were often passed off like a quiz. There were curi-ous other seasons of Bender, as she privately called them, where he went on self-assessment tangents. When he did, he swept her and the kids into the assessments too, over their weight; whether or not she had kept Turner, Gwennie, and Ramsey sweating long enough over a tennis game; or improving their math skills.

Lately he had focused solely on improving Turner, a relief to Saphora as it took the pressure off her to perform according to Ben-der's tightly regimented life.

"It just seems you would notice."

"Tell me what it is I should notice, then, and I'll try," she said, her voice strained, like piano strings stretched too far.

"That I'm dying," he said, so quietly that a flock of birds outside the window nearly drowned him out.

"Bender, it's a mistake," she said, knowing how he worried himself into illnesses privy to doctors. She quietly assessed the books beside him on the table, volumes she had saved from his first year at Duke med school. He ran his finger over the surfaces. Soft particles rose up in the glare of the lamp. "Tabitha should dust more often."

"I'll tell her," Saphora said quietly.

"I've gone to two different doctors."

"Bender, your health is important to you. It's not like you let yourself go like some people. You know yourself how technicians make mistakes. It was just last week one of your patients got read the wrong x-ray report." A doctor wrongly told a woman she had a tumor right behind her nasal cavity. "You're fine."

His hands curled over the ends of the chair arm so tightly that it seemed his fingers might go clean through the upholstery. "Saphora, you're not listening."

Bender had said before that she was not a good listener. She was feeling her oats still, what with her suitcase waiting upstairs. "I can't stand it when you're like this."

"It's cancer, of all things."

"I'm not listening to any of this."

He told her, "You'll have to call the kids." He pulled out a pad from the table drawer and the pen from his pocket. "I'm going to see Jim Pennington at Duke. He's the one to do this."

"Yes, of course." Jim had been Bender's best friend in med school. They actually met playing on the same soccer team. They remained friends over the years, occasionally socializing with the wives involved.

"You're making a list?" she asked. Bender's list making aggravated her only less than his flittering around with the Peninsula wives.

"I'll put the house up for sale," he said, "if you'd like. I can't imagine you knocking about in this place all by yourself." He kept scribbling, as if he were writing out a prescription.

"Sell the house?" she asked, feeling as if the ground beneath her shifted. It was like him to run back and forth, sneaking off for medical testing without telling her. But here he was making major decisions when the air in her ears was near to exploding. She wanted to yell at him. But she sat quietly. She was a good wife—that's what he had told a group of his men friends just last week. The doctors played cards out on the back deck Friday nights. She could hear how the conversation went from golf to a botched surgery by a doctor not from their circle. She had taken a swim and come back so she missed what got them talking about wives. But she had let his compliment slide off her as she was already entertaining the idea of running away.

"Gwen has the best head on her shoulders. Maybe she should tell her brothers."

She was the first girl in her class to pass the bar. Gwennie took her father's pressures on her in stride. Better than Saphora.

"I've been knocking about in this house by myself since we moved into it," she said, but he was busy working on the list. "You're jumping ahead of things, Bender. What is it you say all the time? Don't make decisions if you're too hungry, angry, lonely, or tired." Her emotions were beginning to tear away, though. She hated showing tears in front of him. He considered her weak when she did.

"Saphora, stop crying," he said.

She pulled open the door on the mahogany commode, where she kept the tissues.

"I want to die in Oriental." He took a medical journal into his lap. "If I have to die."

"Bender, the hospital is too far from there. Stop acting as if you're already dying." He was making her so mad she felt the urge to walk out on him. But she stayed in her chair as if he had tied her into it with ropes.

"There's hospice. And Duke is not that far. I'd like to leave in the morning. It's only three hours."

"It's over three hours, Bender, and that's a long drive."

He went on as though she hadn't said a word. "Sherry can help out."

"For goodness' sake, Bender! How soon?"

"Six months. Six years. Doctors never really know those things. We guess."

"What about our friends? We'll be so far out."

"We'll have them up as I'm able."

Saphora got him a glass from the cabinet and poured the rest of his beer.

"Call Sherry. She'll get the house ready," he told her.

"I gave her time off. She worked herself to death for this party you insisted I give."

"Call her back. I need her there. Better yet, have her come here tonight."

It was the opportune moment Saphora had waited for ever since Bender had appeared so suddenly in the middle of the day. "I'll call from upstairs. I need to compose myself."

She climbed the stairs, swept away by the urge to run for her suitcase and bolt for the door. The luggage was where she left it, behind the upper-landing balustrade. She wheeled it back into the bedroom. A tag from Nantes still dangled like a loose earring from the handle. She had gone to France two years ago, taking Gwennie to Europe for passing the bar. Bender had stayed behind in Lake Norman even after Gwennie had lost her temper with him for never joining them on a single vacation.

She stowed the luggage, still packed for Oriental, in the storage cubicle of her dressing room. She pulled up Sherry's telephone number in her BlackBerry. She scrolled past Gwennie's number, and then there were Ramsey's and Turner's numbers sandwiching Sherry's. Turner's next nursing shift would be starting come dinnertime. He took any shift to fill up the hours away from his son and the ex-wife who said she loved him but could not stay married to a man with Turner's low ambitions.

Gwennie would be the first to call her back. Saphora scrolled back up and called her daughter. She heard the forceful little recorded voice answering mechanically as if she needed to place the thought in the caller's head that she meant business. Saphora left a message to call her and then added, "This is rather serious, Gwen." Then she hung up and wondered if she had said too little by saying "rather serious." Gwennie would surely understand why she had not spilled out over the phone that her daddy was dying.

Saphora did not want to call Sherry after giving her the rest of Tuesday and also Wednesday off. Bender surely did not mean that he wanted to leave the next morning for Oriental. Her Oriental.

She walked out of the dressing room, stopping just short of the bedroom. Bender was pulling back the pale blue matelassé coverlet she and Gwennie had picked up in Nantes. He dropped his trousers over the footboard and slid under the coverlet. When he closed his eyes, he said, "When Sherry gets here, have her come upstairs. She can make my calls."

"Sherry's not home."

"Call her cell phone, Saphora. For Pete's sake, think!"

"Bender, she's gone off with her husband." She didn't tell him they were bowling but left it mysteriously unsaid. He'd not think bowling important enough. But she didn't want Sherry here tonight in the middle of their shock. "Rest yourself." Saphora walked into the bathroom, wounded by Bender's suggestion that she could not think on her own. Her telephone rang. It was Gwennie.

It rang thrice and then switched to her answering service.

Bender yelled, "Who was that?"

Saphora closed the bathroom door. She sat on the closed toilet lid. She pulled paper from the toilet roll, wiping her eyes. She could hear Abigail mysteriously talking as if she were circling again overhead. "You must be the envy of all your friends."

She said through a sob, "Envy's an expensive piece of real estate."

What a circus act we women perform every
day of our lives. It puts the trapeze artist to
shame. Look at us. We run a tight rope
daily, balancing a pile of books on the head.
Baby-carriage, parasol, kitchen chair, still
under control. Steady now!

ANNE MORROW LINDBERGH, *Gift from the Sea*

Bender had deep-sea fished from the time he left behind his mother's
house in Old Salem to take his premed classes until he had bought
the seaside house in Oriental. But his ownership of so much stuff kept
him working more and fishing less. Yet as Saphora stiffly packed his
suitcases upstairs the next morning, he was down in the garage drag-
ging out his rods and lucky hooks. Saphora pulled out the gently
used blue cap he said had brought him more good fortune than even
the boat he had dubbed the *Evelyn*. She turned abruptly, *thwhapping*
the cap against the door frame to smack the lint from it.

Because she brooded in a state of self-pity for too long, dissolv-
ing into tears, she hated herself all the more. She did not hear Turner
calling her name down the hallway.

He once told her that she had gotten so accustomed to tuning
him out—he was the most talkative of his siblings—that in order to
get her to respond after several attempts at calling her "Mama," he

would finally yell, "Miss Saphora," like one of the lawn boys, and she would turn and answer him.

So it was when he yelled her name into the bedroom, "Miss Saphora!" that she ran to the marble sink to flush her face with cold water. Because she expected Turner to be working a shift at the hospital uptown, she fully anticipated that a domestic had come up the stairs, sent on an errand from Bender.

She took so long at the sink, half hoping to be left alone to stormily finish Bender's packing, that when she came fully upright to dry her face, she yelled, "What in blazes?" finding Turner grinning at her from the open door.

"You're dressed, aren't you?" he asked, half covering his eyes, typical of Turner since he was always the one to come bounding in unexpectedly without a thought for privacy.

"Turner," she said, not fuming, as she might have done in the past. She had a strange craving for the comfort of his silly need for her indulgences. He kissed her like he had always done when greeting his mama. To hide her swarming fears at this point was hopeless.

"What has he done now?" he asked, not a hint of surprise about him. He had found her upstairs crying more times than could be counted.

Saphora allowed Turner to help her to the chair next to her bed.

"Is that Dad clanging around in the garage," he asked, "in the middle of the morning?"

"Turner, sit here next to me," she said, the empty chair next to hers still neatly covered with the new chair cover she had pulled over it to match the matelassé.

He took the seat but said, "You're scaring me, Mama." Turner's normally deep mellow voice was rising.

"Don't think you know, Turner. You don't." He was assuming, she realized, that his daddy had wounded her in that covert way of his. She dried her eyes and composed herself as soberly as she did when he was five and begging her not to make him attend kindergarten. "Your daddy's gone and gotten medical testing."

"Is that it? He looks fine," said Turner.

"He's not fine. Cancer's not fine." She knew he'd be stunned. "Can you believe it?"

Turner stared across the room through the open drapes, his never-quite-blue eyes fixed upon a sailboat that crossed the lake without any wavering of the mast, the water smooth and void of ripples. "Now Dad's got his rods lined up along the drive, tackle laid out," he said, not looking at her. "Is he selling his stuff?"

"He's going fishing, Turner," Saphora said, waiting for Turner to turn and look at her.

He finally did and then laughed, short and dry as if he could not laugh or cry.

"Fishing! Can you believe it?" She laughed with him, incredulous.

"He's going to be all right then?"

Saphora could not look at Turner anymore. She looked out the window. The sailboat had already passed.

"Why is your luggage out, Mama?"

"We're going to Oriental."

"He'll need treatments, won't he? What kind of cancer?"

"He's setting it all up at Duke to find out for certain. You know how he takes charge. Bender Warren will get the best of the best." The cocktail of emotions left her feeling inwardly emptied out. Resenting Bender had been a guilty pleasure. But she did not know what to make of her feelings right now.

"His prognosis is good then?"

"Not at all."

"He'll fight."

Saphora got up to fasten the lid on Bender's suitcase. "Will you call Gwennie? I left a short message but couldn't bring myself to leave that kind of news on her phone."

"You'll tell Ramsey then?"

"That's not an even swap," said Saphora. Ramsey was emotional. Nothing like his daddy.

"Gwennie will feel responsible, as if she's to blame." Turner sat with his face in his hands. He was always so open, not afraid to say whatever came into that head of his. "Maybe Daddy should tell Gwennie."

Saphora imagined Bender manipulating Gwennie's emotions all the way up in New York. "Never mind. I'll call Gwennie. You call Ramsey."

There was a racket coming up the stairs. "Who do I hear?" asked Saphora. The television blared downstairs, and Bender was in the garage.

Turner sat up. "I nearly forgot. That's why I came by. My sitter quit last minute. I've got Eddie for eight weeks. I was hoping you'd help." He looked apologetic. "That's before I knew about Daddy."

"Eddie's downstairs?" The television rumbled like a race car. Turner's son was addicted to electronic games. He spent most of his time with his hands glued to some controller or another, a lot to manage for a boy who wouldn't make his own bed. "Turner, we're leaving today. Can't you take him to one of those drop-off places?"

She knew why the sitter had quit after only a day. Eddie went through sitters like a gambler going through tokens. She imagined it was tough to get sitters for rambunctious eight-year-old boys.

"I tried. They're all filled up."

"That Presbyterian church downtown. They've got a child-care service. I'll find the number."

"He's too old for child-care service, Mama."

Bender came into the room. "Turner, I'm glad you're here," he said in a voice uncharacteristically gentle. Turner was without words.

"I told him," said Saphora.

Turner extended his hand politely to his daddy. "You'll beat it."

"I will. You know it," said Bender.

Eddie came bounding up the stairs, ramming into his grandfather. Bender grabbed him around the shoulder and pulled him tight. It was unusual to see Bender giving him any kind of affection.

"Eddie says his sitter quit, Saphora," said Bender. "Turner, how about you let the boy come with Saphora and me to the Outer Banks? You could always come up over the weekend and get him."

Eddie's head popped up, his body twitching with excitement. "Can I, Dad?" Eddie asked. "Please? Please? Please?"

Saphora was surprised he offered without consulting her. She would have enough on her hands just dealing with Bender and cancer treatments. She watched helplessly as Eddie's endless energy, amped up with anticipation, turned him into a human bottle rocket aimed at her well-adorned furnishings.

"Saphora, you don't mind. We've been saying we need to take more time with our grandkids," said Bender.

She had said that Bender needed to take more time with his grandkids. "Bender, I don't know. You're not feeling well. We're stopping first at Duke Medical." She looked apologetically at Turner. "I wish we could help."

"Eddie will be fine with us," said Bender. "Saphora, you're good with Eddie."

"I'm not really." She hoped she wasn't making Turner mad.

"I need this." Bender was not himself. He had never felt comfortable around children. He wasn't thinking clearly about convalescence or anything practical.

"What a relief, Daddy!" said Turner. "I'll be up on the weekend to join you and pick up Eddie."

Eddie set himself free from Bender's side embrace. In two leaps and a hop he was somersaulting over the bed, his sneakers planted momentarily on the matelassé coverlet. Turner nabbed him before he could go back the other way. "Not on the furniture, Eddie. Want to go fishing with Grandpa?" he asked.

"I doubt that once Bender starts his treatments he'll be fishing." Saphora was slowly realizing she was the only clearheaded Warren in the room.

"I will," Bender said, looking into Eddie's eyes. "I should have taken you out in my boat a long time ago."

Eddie's mouth came open. He was lapping up Bender's attention.

Saphora stopped thinking about her luggage, packed since yesterday. She also stopped thinking about Bender's suitcase now parked expectantly next to hers. She needed to stop Turner from dropping his life in her lap as he had done in the past.

Eddie bolted out of the room, shouting as he went, "Fishing with Grandpa! Fishing, fishing!" They heard his feet thundering down the stairs. "I'll get—" was the last they heard before the back door slammed behind him.

"Turner, I still think you're going to need a good sitter of some sort. Want me to call the Presbyterians for you?" she asked. "They might have referrals for older kids."

"I'll do that this week while you keep Eddie in Oriental. This is such a treat for him. I'll be down Saturday. I won't have to be back at work until Tuesday, so we'll all have plenty of time together." His eyes emoted a passing thought. He said to his father, "If we manage this right, I won't need a sitter at all."

"We'll work it out," said Bender.

"I have to finish up for the trip," said Saphora. She went into the bathroom, closing the door behind her.

◈

Turner had conveniently put Eddie's clothes into a grocery store bag. Saphora repacked them in one of Gwennie's college duffels. As she stowed it under the car seat, Eddie bounced a ball off the garage, calling out, "Score!" each time the ball smacked the gate, causing it to shudder and the latch to rattle. She tried to remember if slipping cold medicine into a soda was child abuse. Nothing to worry about. Once would not hurt. "I'll be right back," she said to Bender.

She went inside the house and ransacked the refrigerator. She found a Diet Coke wedged between a hunk of Brie and leftover shrimp. She made a mental note to have Sherry come clean it out before an unholy stench had a chance to form.

When she got back holding the spiked Diet Coke, Eddie said, "I'm not allowed soda pop."

"Just this once," she said. "Nana allows it every now and then."

Eddie drank it down as if he might never be allowed soda pop again.

"We're all packed," said Saphora.

Before Bender left behind Highway 73 for Interstate 85, Eddie fell into such a deep slumber that Saphora climbed out of her seat to check his pulse. The little blue vein in his right wrist pounded rapidly, the caffeine from the cola fighting the alcohol in the cold medicine. Saphora sat back in the front passenger seat. "I didn't intend on Eddie joining us. At least not until we had settled in. You know the house is going to be covered in dust and cobwebs. Eddie's allergic to mold."

"You called Sherry, didn't you?"

"She's off until Thursday."

"Saphora, she needs to come back to work. She'll like staying at the house in Oriental. It'll give her a sense of purpose to open it up for us."

"Bender, not everyone finds purpose in catering to your every whim." Almost as quickly as the words came out of her mouth, Saphora looked away from him to act like she had an interest in the passing cars.

"I don't like to talk on the phone while I'm driving, Saphora. Call her and let her know I need her."

He said it so nicely that peacefulness settled over her. It wasn't like him not to snap back at her when she was on a tear. "I'd rather open up the house myself," she said. "I might as well tell you that I'd been thinking of spending time there myself. I was going to open up the house anyway."

"You're lost without Sherry."

"I can cook if I put my thoughts into it."

"As of when?"

"I don't mind my own cooking, Bender."

"It's not like you to argue. You know you like having Sherry around."

"It's my mood lately." He was making her mad again. But with Bender's cancer between them, she chose her words.

"I always win, Saphora." He laughed.

The first time Bender said that was when she had decided to take classes at the local community college. She had learned to point and shoot a high-powered camera. She only needed a few more courses to build confidence and then start taking on clients. She photographed the outdoors very well. She mostly liked catching people with interesting faces in candid moments. She took trips into the city and out to the country to catch people living life, unaware. But Bender felt that Ramsey, being only a first grader, needed her at home for support. She had argued with him, and Bender had said, "I always win."

He never laid a finger on her. He didn't have to.

"Good grief, Bender. I'll call Sherry. Will you pull over and let me get some coffee? It's still early."

When Bender took the next exit and pulled into the parking lot of a convenience store, he handed her a five dollar bill. "Get some crackers for Eddie and sunflower seeds for me." His phone rang; another plastic surgeon calling. The news of Bender's cancer spread through the hospital system like a national emergency.

Saphora visited the coffee center to the right of the checkout stand. She waited her turn behind a truck driver. He talked to a friend through an earphone. He had driven all the way from Houston and was on his way to Charleston with a load of food for a pizza chain. She experienced a strange envy for his freedom. He passed Saphora and then, surprised to find her standing so close, excused himself.

"May I ask you something?" she said to him.

"Sure, go ahead," he said.

"What's it like traveling up and down the highway, being in a different city every night?"

"Like a gypsy."

"Is it lonely?"

"I'm not allowed to take on riders."

"I didn't ask that." At least, she did not mean to ask that.

He looked around as if someone might hear and then said, "I'd take you, doll, that's for certain."

Saphora could smell the faint whiff of man sweat that infuses cotton shirts when slept in. "I was curious about living like a gypsy, that's all. If you're finished pouring your coffee, I should get on with getting some for my husband." She had not meant she would jump in a truck with him and leave. Men had funny ideas about women, and they were all wrong.

He was duly put back in his place. He stepped aside as Saphora pulled out a foam cup for Bender's coffee. "He has cancer," she said as if she knew he waited for another word from her.

"Lots of people are getting that. Me, I'll take a good old-fashioned heart attack," he said. He went off, he said aloud, in search of barbecue chips and beef jerky.

When Saphora climbed back into the car, handing Bender a coffee and sunflower seeds, she said, "We should buy groceries outside Oriental. Except for produce. The farmer's market has plenty of local vegetables." Sherry handpicked locally grown vegetables. Not that he noticed. "Raleigh has a nice supermarket right off one of the exits."

Bender had reclined the driver's seat so far back he could fall asleep. "Sherry will take care of the food, like always. What did she say about me? Did you tell her yet? Maybe it's best to tell her about me in person." His eyes were still on the car ceiling. A ribbon of sweat above his upper lip made him look nervous. "The top of the car needs cleaning."

"Maybe I should drive," said Saphora. She had completely forgotten to call Sherry. But it was at that instant the phone rang and it
was Sherry. "Here she is, calling me back." She stepped out of the car
and walked around. Sherry had gone to the mall to add another set
of piercings to her ears. She was thanking Saphora for the bag of costume jewelry when Saphora said, "There's an emergency."

Sherry was so upset that she began spilling guilty confessions for
leaving too early.

"It's Dr. Warren, Sherry. He's come down with something. I'm
taking him to Duke for tests and then he's going to recuperate at the
house in Oriental," said Saphora. She finally gave in to Bender's anxious stare. "He needs you, Sherry."

"I'm leaving now for Oriental. How many days will you be
there?" she asked.

"Plan for a couple of weeks." Bender had never taken that much
time off from his practice. "It might be serious." Saphora felt dis-
honest for having said Bender had "come down with something."

"I'll throw together a few things and get on the road within the
hour."

A relief came over Saphora. "After you set up the house, maybe
you could take time for yourself down on the beach."

"That's how you are, Miss Saphora, worrying about others when
you need help," said Sherry.

Saphora named a few things for Sherry's grocery list. "Riesling
from Shelton Vineyards. They have it in the stores now." Oh, what
was the use? She had intended on living simply for once when she
had planned her escape to Oriental. "Keep it simple," she said and
ended the call. She looked through Bender's open window. He had
closed his eyes and fallen asleep behind the steering wheel. "Bender,

I'll drive." She shook him awake, enough to get him out of the car and into the passenger's seat.

She climbed into the driver's seat and adjusted it for shorter legs. Before she could tell him that Sherry was coming to open up the house, he had fallen back to sleep. Since she had to take Bender to Duke first anyway, Sherry would have the house opened up and aired out a day ahead.

A card of pills was in his shirt pocket. He had taken sleeping pills for as long as he had been taking surgical shifts. But the small yellow pills did not look familiar to her. She would look them up later. Whatever they were had the same effect on Bender as cold medicine on Eddie. She took a deep, cleansing breath and aimed the car for Raleigh.

She found a country music station but turned it down low so as not to ruffle Bender's intellectual sensibilities. Bender was pale. Beads of sweat formed just above the bridge of his nose between his brows. It was the first time she noticed that he truly appeared sick. She felt a sinking responsibility for what had happened to him. If she had noticed sooner, he might have gotten tested sooner. She had friends who confessed that they fantasized about what they would do if their husbands died. Saphora had not wished death on Bender. She had just imagined him far away, as if she could erase the place between the day she had met him and now.

The way he was acting was so not like him. Bender lived life happily on the perimeters of danger. Twice each summer he and other surgeons met in the gulf to tarpon fish. His last fishing excursion, he was the only man on the expedition to reel in a marlin. Then he started raft fishing, a sport that some of the twenty-something fishermen had sold him on. He caught a swordfish that might have pulled him under if his buddies had not rescued him.

Years ago he booked a wild game hunt, insisting that Ramsey and Turner accompany him. But Turner, loudly demonstrative, had gotten so afraid of the unfamiliar sights and sounds of the Serengeti that the guide had ordered them back to the compound. Before dawn, Turner had said, the sound of the Jeep's engine gunning woke them up. Turner worried all day when Bender had stayed long past the allotted time. But in he came at sundown, the cicadas screaming and Turner pacing. Ramsey cried so hard Bender yelled at him to act like a man. Bender and the guides hauled a dead lion out of the Jeep. Bender sent it off to his friend who did taxidermy as a hobby. Then he hung the head in his office at home. Saphora never liked going in there after that.

Bender slept until Saphora drove into the afternoon crawl of Raleigh's traffic.

"I was dreaming about you and the kids," he said.

The last time he had said that was when Turner and Gwennie were still in diapers. "What were we doing?" she asked.

"We were all out in a boat. But not Lake Norman. It was a different lake. People were loud along the shoreline, like in Mexico. Even louder. There was rock music, not our kind, but like the kids play nowadays. I kept trying to get us farther from the noise. But you kept saying how you liked the music. You didn't seem to mind it."

"I do like music."

"I just wanted things quiet."

"Maybe you shouldn't allow me in your dreams."

"Why do you have to say that?"

"Good grief, Bender! I annoy you as much in your dreams as when you're awake."

He frowned, then continued. "There was this old woman on the shore. She was staring at me. I kept steering the boat away from the shore. But then I would look up and there she would be again. She was following me. She had on this, I don't know what you call it, this white serape thing wrapped around her. She was all white—white hair, white serape, white shoes."

"Like an angel?"

"Not beautiful like you'd think. Very old and penetrating eyes. At least I don't think she was an angel."

"Did she like the music?"

"What difference does that make?"

"I'm hungry, Nana." Eddie had come awake.

"It is past lunchtime," said Saphora. "We'll grab a bite before we check into the hotel." She had gotten a room at the Embassy Suites. "I'll ask the hotel clerk to give us an extra bed."

"They've got two-bedroom suites. Get one of those," said Bender.

"They're triple the price, Bender."

"Eddie needs his own room. You know how he is. I've got to have my sleep."

Saphora drove to a restaurant off the interstate. "No good restaurants around Duke," she said. Bender lay in the car while she went inside, Eddie hopping through the door behind her. She requested a table. She waved Bender inside, and they sat down and ordered sweet teas. The wait staff was slow, irritating Bender. But she soon had Eddie fed and back in the car.

Bender called his friend Jim Pennington, the oncologist at Duke. When Saphora pulled under the overhang at the patient check-in, Jim was waiting for Bender. He was tall, his deep eyes warmly looking out from his dark African American face.

Bender got out of the car. Eddie started bouncing around the interior of the car, claiming he was a pro wrestler. Saphora was sorry she had left the cold medicine back at the house. Once Bender closed the door, she snapped. "Eddie! You can't lose it today, or else Nana will lose it."

He quieted down, surprising her. After she parked the car they both followed Bender and Jim into the hospital. Eddie was immediately interested in the gift shop. The window was full of stuffed green monkeys dangling from ropes, little green leaves glued on to make the display look like a jungle set. "No toys today," she said. Turner and his ex-wife had indulged Eddie with so many toys that his bedroom floor was no longer visible. It was a competition to see who could give Eddie the most stuff.

Eddie charged the gift shop.

Saphora had never had trouble standing up to Turner. She should have left him to figure out what to do about Eddie. She had never believed that his marriage was really over when his wife, Karen, had said it was over. Karen was not a good judge of character, so how could she judge when her marriage was over? Turner would never learn how to father if Saphora kept allowing him to drop off the boy.

Bender came around the corner looking for her. "Are you coming up?" he asked.

"I sure hope Turner drives in this weekend to take care of Eddie," she said. She followed Eddie into the gift store. "Eddie, stop touching everything. Let's go." She made sure Eddie was actually paying attention before turning to Bender. "I can't do this, Bender, and take care of you."

"Then call Turner," he said, the tone of his voice rising as if she were disappointing him. "He's a shift nurse. He can take hours or not take them."

Bender knew that Turner needed all the hours he could get. He also knew how to get his way even while agreeing with her.

By now Jim had come back and was standing in the corridor near the physicians' elevator, staring at them. He took out a key and turned it in a special lock that allowed him to call for the elevator. The surgeons' special getaway system only added to their sense of entitlement.

Eddie bolted away from Saphora when the elevator doors opened. "I get dibs to push the button!"

Saphora was sure her face was red as she passed by Jim, who held the elevator door open. Jim didn't seem to notice. He gave Eddie the floor number, then talked shop with Bender. "The pathologist I wanted came in on her day off to run your tests. She's the best at Duke. That makes her the best in the state," he said.

Eddie pulled a Blow Pop from deep in his pocket. He started to unwrap it, but Saphora took the sucker out of his hand. "Later," she said, stuffing it into her purse. Eddie locked his arms around his waist and glared at her.

"I'll speed up the test results for you," said Jim. "You all can head back to Lake Norman in the morning."

"We're staying at the house in Oriental," said Bender.

"We love that house," Jim said to Saphora. "Thanks for letting me take Jeanie and the kids there. That river is the Neuse, right?"

"Yes, the Neuse," said Saphora. Bender's friends knew more about the place than she did. She had not seen it since they had closed on the house.

Jim said, "Once they nail down the type of cancer you have, we'll talk about whether you'll need my help or a different specialist's."

"Isn't it lymphoma?" asked Saphora. Bender had said it, she thought. But then she realized he had not said exactly what it was.

"It's a brain tumor," said Jim. "Saphora, I'll let you know about his treatment in the next day or so. I'll keep you abreast of every detail."

Jim had so much warmth that Saphora teared up. She wiped the tears from her eyes.

The rest of the afternoon was spent in the cancer center's waiting room since Eddie could not sit at his grandfather's side during the blood work. That was another thing Bender had not thought about. Saphora could not sit beside him. That is when it occurred to her that Bender might have orchestrated the whole afternoon so that she would be watching after Eddie while he and Jim talked about their golf games.

She held back from crying this time. It was an acquired gift.

3

It is only with the heart that one can see
rightly; what is essential is invisible to the eye.

ANTOINE DE SAINT-EXUPÉRY, *La Petit Prince*

It was a clear day in spite of the hurricane warnings going out south
of the Outer Banks. The wake was high, and the sheriff's son had
posted undertow warnings up and down the Oriental Marina. Bender
asked Saphora to park at Tiny Beach. "I'd like to take a walk down to
the marina before unpacking," he told her as he got out of the car.

Saphora said, "You want me to walk with you?"

"Better stay with Eddie. He'd rather enjoy the sand."

Saphora frowned.

"Go ahead. Why don't you let Eddie out for a run."

Bender made Eddie sound like a little beagle.

A beach run might give Eddie a release after being pent up during the more than three-hour drive from Raleigh. Eddie grabbed
Saphora's empty drink cup to use as a sand pail.

Bender had already started his stroll down South Avenue by the
time Saphora got Eddie aimed toward Tiny Beach. It was really a
small patch of sand, not anything that could be called a beach. More
like a sandlot on the water.

She opened the car door and sat sideways behind the wheel. She
could see Eddie well enough. She glanced toward Bender, who was

walking past the pretty little houses populated by artists and retirees, he said, who each had their own story about how they wound up living in Oriental.

She did not move for the ten minutes it took Bender to become a quarter-inch blemish down South Avenue.

Eddie was building a cup-shaped castle foundation. A sea gull landed next to him. Sometimes children fed the sea gulls, enabling the birds and turning them into a nuisance for the tourists. Eddie filled the cup with sand and held it out to the bird, but as the sea gull hopped within a few feet, he hurled sand at it. The air was salted with spiraling feathers as the bird lifted, screeching.

Bender merged into a herd of couples taking sunset strolls. He walked as if he were not sick at all, taking long purposeful strides, and then disappeared.

The Neuse River was a body of brackish water lapping against the rock and brown sand beaches, spilling into the ocean where the town of Minnesott Beach took up. Because of the natural harbors and inland banks and the lack of tidal action from the ocean, Oriental was called the sailing capital of North Carolina. A regatta floated down the Neuse, the lead craft manned by teen boys shouting back and forth to keep their sailing rig ahead of the remaining twelve crafts in the race.

A boy who appeared slightly older than Eddie walked up on him. He showed Eddie his sand pail, specially shaped for expert castle building. Eddie looked back at Saphora as if waiting for his cue. He was a boy comfortable inside the safety of his family circle but who acclimated slowly to other children. Eddie was a budding narcissist as far as Saphora was concerned. Turner had corrected her once for analyzing Eddie.

"Invite him to play," Saphora yelled above the wind. Then she pulled her feet into the Lexus. The wind picked up, tossing her hair around her face like tentacles. Then it died down. Saphora returned to eavesdropping on the boys' chatter.

The boy sat down next to Eddie, giving him a shovel. He seemed intent on leading Eddie, coaching him and goading him until Eddie was filling the pail exactly as instructed.

The boy had thick black hair that hung in points around his thin face, such a mop of hair that it made his bony facial features look all the more wan. He could be a mixture of races, but there was a distinctive Asian look about him. He was so skinny he should not be seen without a shirt. His pale physique had darkened over the summer, camouflaging his rib cage. He had learned English in the South. His vowels had a southern roundness.

Saphora kept watching up the street for a sight of Bender until she was sick of herself for worrying over him. He had not seemed for an instant to think of what his situation was doing to her. He took it all in stride as if he were making out a list of what they would do on vacation—call Sherry, fill the pantry, stop at the town beach, and drive up to Raleigh for chemotherapy.

She turned on the radio in time to hear the hurricane had turned south and was headed for Cuba.

Eddie's mound was beginning to take on an identifiable castle shape when Bender appeared, walking up South toward them. The sun was going down. He carried a store-bought bag of shells for Eddie and laid them like an offering beside him.

Saphora's telephone rang. Gwennie had finally gotten her deposition behind her. She sounded distressed. Turner had gotten to her first. Saphora was glad not to have been the one to tell her about her daddy's cancer. Gwennie was headed to Oriental. She would arrive tomorrow morning.

"I'll pick you up in Raleigh then?" Saphora offered.

"Is he being hard, Mama?" she asked.

Bender's long Warren shadow fell across the road.

"He's back from a walk downtown. Here's the phone," said Saphora to Bender. She could hear Gwennie complaining to her for handing the phone off. She put the phone in Bender's hand. He held it for a minute, maybe for the sake of composure.

Saphora left him to talk to her while she coaxed Eddie off the little beach.

The Asian boy with the castle pail was taking a picture of himself and Eddie, the castle behind them. The boy held up one hand in a pose. He snapped the picture. "I do this everywhere I go. I've got a zillion pictures of me holding up my hand just like that in front of, well, everything. The Lincoln Center. A big Texas hat on a bull in Houston."

"Isn't that a 'Hook 'em Horns' symbol in Texas?" asked Saphora. She had seen the Texas Longhorn fans use the gesture at college football games.

"It is. But they don't own it, my mom says."

"Don't say that to a Texan," said Saphora, smiling. "You must travel a lot."

"My folks are semiretired." It was funny to hear him say it. "They adopted me even though I was seven. I've only been with them a couple years. We've gone quite a few places."

"Adopted?" said Eddie.

Before Eddie could say something rude, Saphora said, "They must be so honored to have you in their family."

"Tobias," he said. He put out his hand.

"You're so mannerly, Tobias. Your parents have taught you very well," said Saphora.

"You might know them if you're from around here. They have a house in Oriental."

"That's where we're staying," said Eddie. "My grandpa's house is right on the water. Look, it's up South." He pointed to the house. It had a pretty green roof and a porch with nothing on it. Saphora would dig around the garage for porch chairs.

"It's an old house, but I have my own room," said Tobias. There was a sense of isolation about Tobias as if he had learned to live on his own for most of his life.

"Eddie would love to have you over," said Saphora. She walked Eddie and Tobias back up to the Lexus, where Bender finished up his call with Gwennie.

She got out a pen and took down Tobias's telephone number. Eddie needed a diversion, a playmate. "Can I meet your folks?" she asked.

"They've gone for a walk," said Tobias. "They said they needed grownup time. I'm good with that."

"I'm tired," said Eddie. He handed Tobias his shovel. He got into the backseat without saying good-bye to the boy. He was likely still drugged from the cold medicine.

"I'll be sure he calls you, Tobias," said Saphora. "He's shy, but he'll get over it."

Tobias was just walking away when he turned and said, "Sometimes I'm sick. But I take medication."

"This is my husband, Bender. He's sick too," said Saphora.

Tobias shook Bender's hand. "Be sure to call," he told Saphora.

When he was gone, Saphora asked, "How did Gwennie sound? Turner told her your circumstances already, so she did know."

"Fine," was all Bender said. He followed Eddie back to the car.

Saphora looked up and down South trying to catch sight of Tobias's parents. Tobias was walking straight through the sand castle. The delicate turrets collapsed around his feet. He saw her watching and yelled, "I'd rather it come down on my terms."

It occurred to Saphora that it was a rather adult response, but she had heard of the occasional child who was an old soul.

It was at that point the sun finally set. The couples all along the road to the harbor stopped to watch. She had not shared, to her recollection, a single sunset walking down a beach with Bender.

୧୬

By the time Saphora drove down South Avenue, dusk was settling over the house, making it look like an old manor house in England. She had kept up the lawn service. The fence running the length of the backyard to the water was draped with flowering trees. Bender got out of the car and unlocked the padlock on the garage door. He would have a garage door opener installed soon enough and said so.

As they drove up, it was evident the house had faded under the continual coastal sun. Saphora would buy potted plants to place near the house if it seemed Bender wanted to stay long. She doubted that, assuming he would tire of trying to die in Oriental. He would want to head back to where his friends could come and see him once he realized he could not decide just to lie down and die.

The old garage door shimmied but then opened like a yawning old man. Saphora drove inside. Eddie jumped out onto the garage pad still holding the bag of seashells.

Saphora told him to brush the sand off before going into the house. She unlocked the door, and just inside there was a mud room. "You can wash the grit off your hands in the mop sink in the laundry room. Look around the house for a jar or a vase. You can pour your shells into it and start your collection," she said. "Careful you don't drop them." He was not accident prone like Turner, but she still sensed the need to chase after him just as she had Turner to keep him from hurting himself. She hoped Eddie would find a life faster than his father, who had gone from career to career until he found his place in nursing.

That was still a sore spot with Bender, who had planned lavishly for all three kids to attend expensive private colleges. Once Bender had nearly blamed Saphora for Turner's lack of drive. But she had pushed him until she was exhausted. Some boys just don't take to their raising, as Saphora's father once said of Turner. He had passed away two years earlier, leaving her mother, Daisy, a content widow. Saphora wondered if all the women in her family were happier alone.

She had not confessed to Bender her secret pleasure in knowing that Turner had found happiness in simple living. He liked his city flat, his Saturday night gathering of buddies at Ri-Ra in uptown Charlotte. Of her three children, she envied Turner the most.

Gwennie was her daddy's greatest source of boasting. But Gwennie possessed a nervous anxiety, a continual heaviness hanging over her that seemed to take the joy out of her journey. Ramsey was not happy in his job as an insurance adjustor, but his wife, Celeste, had a deep need for a bigger house and a nicer car. From the moment she had seen where Ramsey grew up, she imagined him being as big a success as his daddy. But the son of a surgeon hardly ever becomes a surgeon.

Bender pulled a tarp off some things they had stored right after they'd bought the place and stocked it for summer vacations. "Here are the deck chairs." He carted one out the open garage door. He returned and kept doing that until he appeared with one large blue dolphin chair.

"Where did we get that?" asked Saphora.

It was a heavy thing, and he had to use all of his strength to lift it. "I bought it for a song from a beach shop down in Wilmington. It is my chair, if anyone asks." He carted it out.

Eddie dropped the bag of shells onto the garage floor and ran into the laundry room.

"I'll get the bedroom ready first if you need to rest," said Saphora to Bender.

"I've got too many calls to make. Can you quiet Eddie down?"

The boy was singing in an elevated falsetto.

"He'll respond just as well to you," she said. She popped open the trunk. "Eddie, there's a garden outside. Go see if the birdbath needs water." She knew it would, and that would keep Eddie busy playing with the water hose.

Eddie disappeared into the house. He yelled out tribal noises from outside over a tire swing strung from the tree house. Saphora imagined once he got his bearings around the beach home he would spend most of his time out back.

"Don't get the luggage. I'll do it," said Bender. He was just about to pull out the largest piece when he slumped against the car.

"Bender, I'll do it!" said Saphora. She tried to help him, but he resisted and stood up on his own. He walked into the house, mad, muttering, but not so Saphora could understand. She was too tired to translate anyway.

Bender did not take to Saphora fussing over him. Even as a boy, his mother once said years before she passed on, if he had a fever he would get frustrated if she hovered. But he had always found comfort in allowing a hired servant to pay him all the attention he needed.

Saphora wheeled the luggage into the laundry room and then through the kitchen. The house had a dumbwaiter right next to the butler's pantry. She tucked it all into the elevator and sent it upstairs.

She opened the pantry. Sherry had not beaten them to the house after all. It wasn't like Sherry not to show up or call.

Bender had set up shop on the sofa and coffee table. "Let's don't go out for dinner, how about? All I need is coffee and a pastry. I don't want people talking about this all over town yet."

"Like anyone knows us, hon."

"There's still more testing, so what's the use anyway until I know more?"

"Aren't you supposed to radically change your diet?"

"Coffee and a pastry are therapeutic. Here's cash. Go down to that grocer's and get me some croissants and a bag of coffee." He pulled out his BlackBerry and started phoning his assistant, Nalia. He made sure she understood she was to expertly hand off his surgeries for the next two weeks to his partner, Sam Werther.

Before Saphora left again, she said, "Does that mean we're only staying here two weeks?"

He was already engaged in his business with Nalia but told her, "I told you already, Saphora. Don't play games. I'm too tired for them."

❧

Saphora was examining the fresh tortillas in the ethnic food aisle when Sherry called. Her five-year-old son had come down with chickenpox. He had been exposed through his cousins who had come in the week before.

"What exactly is it Dr. Warren has?" she asked.

Saphora hesitated between the black beans and pinto beans. "It's cancer," she said.

Sherry was quiet. Her son was crying in the background. Finally she said, "Knowing Dr. Warren's condition, I can't bring any diseases into the house." She kept apologizing until she was nearly crying. "They say pox can be carried in your clothes. And Malcolm's so sick. I've never seen him crying and clinging like this. I just couldn't leave him with his grandma."

"I'll manage. Truth be told, Sherry, I need to do something with myself. If I had you here doing everything for me, I'd be lost." She wanted to sound sincere so as not to place guilt on Sherry. She wasn't about to admit to Bender she was already feeling the pressure to keep the beach house as organized and efficient as Sherry would.

"I know how you hate cooking. This is awful," Sherry said, and then said it again. "This is awful."

"I'm not a bad cook. Why does everyone think that?" asked Saphora, laughing.

"Is he bad sick?" she asked.

"They did some tests at Duke. We'll know more in a couple of days. Don't worry. Bender is the comeback guy." It wasn't a total lie. Bender was known for his sporty zeal in his days playing on the semi-pro golf circuit. His happiest days had been at a tournament he won in Southern Pines. But he had gone on to lose the next tournament just short of the nationals.

Saphora was still holding a package of tortillas when she spotted a man tucking what appeared to be a can of oysters into his pocket.

"Hold on, Sherry." She managed to move in closer to see if his pocket was bulging. It was. She looked around to find the nearest clerk. But being in such a small town, she would be lucky to find one nearby in the middle of the afternoon. "I'll be fine, Sherry. I'll call you back," she said.

The man rounded the corner, disappearing out of her sight. Finally she spotted a clerk whose name tag read Bernard Newman. He was pricing yellow cake mix on the end cap. She hissed, "Bernard, come here."

When he did not respond, she hissed again. "Look, Bernard, over here!"

"You talking to me?"

"I'm Mrs. Warren, Bernard," she whispered. "There's a pickpocket in the store."

"Did someone steal your money, Mrs. Warren?"

"Not a pickpocket. I mean a shoplifter, Bernard. I just saw a man put a can of oysters in his pocket."

"Are you sure, Mrs. Warren? The only other customer in the store is a minister. I seriously doubt he'd steal a can of oysters."

"I just saw him, I swear, Bernard."

At that instant the oyster thief walked past Bernard. "Have you got any soup crackers?" he asked.

Saphora mouthed, "That's him."

The thief smiled at Saphora although he did not make direct eye contact.

"Do you mean oyster crackers?" asked Bernard.

"Sure, that's what they're called," said the man.

That had to be a ploy. There he had oysters in his front pants pocket and could not remember oyster crackers?

"Little round crackers? You sprinkle them over soup," said Bernard to the man.

"Do you have any?"

"Down aisle eight, Pastor."

The minister disappeared, the bulge in his right pocket still obvious.

Saphora asked Bernard, "Aren't you going to ask him what the bulge is in his pocket?"

"That'd be rude. Guys don't ask other guys things like that."

"I saw him do it, Bernard. He's stealing oysters." Now that she thought of it, it was the perfect crime. Who would accuse a minister of stealing and, of all things, something as high priced as oysters? "If you're not going to say something, I will," she said.

"Don't you think God takes care of things like that, Mrs. Warren? I mean, if he did steal it, shouldn't I give it to him anyway? Turn the other cheek?" He was playing her, it seemed, by the smirk on his face.

"He should know better, Bernard." She decided right then that she was going to confront the thief. She left her shopping cart next to the ethnic foods and brushed past Bernard and around the corner. She passed aisles five and six, and then seven, until she nearly ran straight into the pastor coming out of aisle eight.

"Excuse me!" he said.

Before he could walk around her, Saphora said, "Excuse me. I'm Saphora Warren."

Without waiting for any more details from Saphora, he said, "I don't think we've met, have we? I'm Pastor John Mims, the pastor at First Community Church down on Church Street. Call me Pastor John. Do you attend church, Mrs. Warren?"

"Sure I do." It had been a few years, but that wasn't the point. "It's just that I saw you put that can of oysters in your pocket."

"Oh!" He laughed. "It's this right hand of mine."

"You blame your hand for stealing?"

"No. It's paralyzed. I didn't want to push a cart around for two items. So I shoved the oysters in my pocket."

"You're paralyzed?" All color drained from her face.

"It's an old injury. I've learned to live with it," he said. "I'm sorry you thought I was stealing. I thought I was the only one in the store."

Bernard called from the checkout aisle, "You need any help, Pastor?"

"I'm fine, Bernard."

By this time Saphora was feeling flush. "I'm so sorry, Pastor. I feel like an idiot. Will you forgive me?"

Bernard was actually laughing. The nerve of him!

"On one condition," said the minister.

"Anything." And she meant that. She prayed the linoleum would split open and swallow her whole.

"Next Wednesday night we're holding a fund-raising dinner at the church for a children's fund. Will you come?"

"I promise. I know how to find your church."

"I'll look for you, Saphora," he said. He met Bernard at the checkout.

Bernard was smirking from behind the counter.

She mouthed, "You knew!"

She finished filling her cart and then waited behind a display of canned peaches until she saw Pastor John leave the parking lot. If she was lucky, he would forget about her and she would disappear into Bender's cancer.

4

When one door of happiness closes, another
opens; but often we look so long at the closed
door that we do not see the one which has
been opened for us.

HELEN KELLER

Gwennie's flight ran late. Saphora stopped for a coffee and then
parked in the pickup lane in front of the Raleigh-Durham airport.
Just as the airport cop looked about ready to ask her to take a lap,
Gwennie burst out the door lugging her bright red suitcase.

Her hair was swept up into a ball cap. She looked younger than
the last time she came home. She was either thinner or just bare faced
enough that Saphora could imagine her again as a twelve-year-old girl
playing soccer. Gwennie played sweeper throughout her high school
years for the Davidson girls' soccer team.

Saphora met Gwennie on the sidewalk and helped her with her
luggage. Gwennie hugged her, but it wasn't her usual quick hug, her
let's-get-on-with-things Gwennie hug. She held on to Saphora until
she was sobbing. Saphora relished Gwennie's sudden need for her,
never having wanted to let go of Gwennie from the day she packed
up her small car and moved to New York.

"I got you a coffee," said Saphora, drawing back to look closely
at Gwennie.

"You look terrific, Mama," said Gwennie, more quietly than her normal tone. "I expected you to be falling apart."

"Have you had breakfast?" she asked.

"You know I skip it," said Gwennie.

Saphora drove them to just outside the city limits, where she found an exit with a pancake house. "Well then, how about some comfort food before we head to Oriental?"

"If we're going to cheat, it has to be chocolate chip pancakes," said Gwennie.

Saphora agreed. Everything she said was making Gwennie cry.

Gwennie pulled off her ball cap. Her hair tumbled down to her shoulders.

"Your hair is red," said Saphora.

"Some blond, some red. I couldn't decide." She combed it out as she pulled down the mirror in the visor to apply mascara.

They parked and went into the pancake house, where they were seated in a corner with a loudspeaker playing country music overhead.

"Have you gotten settled into your new place?" asked Saphora.

Gwennie had talked about buying a Manhattan flat near enough to the office that she could walk or ride a bike. When a small two-bedroom condo came open, she had called saying she was praying that God would help her close on it soon. She'd started attending one of those downtown churches where the pastor looked as young as Turner and preached in sandals.

"I've got a view over Manhattan. I'm painting it on the week-ends." She opened her purse and pulled out cardboard paint samples. "See?" She handed them to Saphora. Then she turned on her telephone and showed her a picture of her kitchen and then her bedroom. Sitting at her kitchen table was a young man, blond and tanned.

"Anyone interesting come into your life?" asked Saphora.

"I've dated a few guys. No one interesting. The guy sitting here is from across the hall. Bill is infatuated with me. He's a plumber," she said, but then added quickly, "not that there's anything wrong with that. Don't look at me like that. He's one of those guys comfortable in a pickup truck. Dad would never approve."

"Dad's not going to be married to him."

Gwennie had always sought Bender's approval since she was four years old and playing in her first soccer league. Saphora complained that she was too young. She thought Gwennie would have more fun in a gymnastics center. But Bender wanted all of his children in team sports to hone them for the real world.

Saphora wondered if Gwennie would have wound up in a stiff Manhattan law firm if she had started out in ballet slippers instead of a jersey. She somehow thought she would have.

They finished up their breakfast and got back onto the interstate for Oriental.

"Your dad got his call from his doctor friend at Duke this morning, Gwennie."

"Turner told me Daddy's getting a second opinion."

Bender was in the shower this morning when Jim called. He turned off the water and asked Saphora to hand him the phone. One arm came up onto the ceramic wall in the shower, his forehead resting against his arm, when Jim told him the tumor was the size of a peach.

"The tests in Davidson were right. There's no new news," she said.

Gwennie assimilated into a working mode. She pulled out her calendar and wanted to know the dates of his regimen so she could figure out when she could come back.

"His surgery is tomorrow."

Gwennie said, "Then it must be pretty advanced." When Saphora did not answer her she said, "This is devastating."

It was hard seeing her cry.

෬

Saphora lost herself in her thoughts on the drive back to Oriental.

She was making a mental timeline of when it seemed that she and Bender had taken different paths. Bender started cheating when Saphora was pregnant with Turner. He justified it by saying that she was not as interested in sex. But Saphora wasn't disinterested in sex. Bender was just so—she didn't know what it was, but he did not know how to woo her. The courtship had ended with the "I do's."

One night she could not get Turner to take to his feeding. She sat rocking near the only picture window in the apartment. The moon cast such a bright light that Turner came wide awake. He was such a giggly baby anyway. Saphora had attributed his early sense of humor to a high IQ. He played tricks, causing the milk to flow from her nipple and then drawing back and laughing when it sprayed his face.

Bender got up in the middle of the night to check on her and the baby, or so she thought. Instead, he wanted her to come back to bed with him. She told him the baby wasn't finished eating yet. He was mad, as if she were using Turner as an excuse.

"Bender, it's not an excuse. If I put Turner in his crib without eating, he'll not go back to sleep."

It was things like that, Bender had said, that let him know she wasn't interested in him.

Saphora was not sure how many women he had consorted with

over the years. But it had been at least two years since he had touched her. The other wives in their circle of friends comforted Saphora, saying it was best she look the other way. But she had become obsessed with believing in something besides settling.

When Saphora pulled up the drive, Eddie was playing Frisbee in the front yard with the new boy he had met on the beach, Tobias. The boy had not waited long to drop by. A blue bike leaned against the house.

Saphora took one of Gwennie's bags. Eddie was not accustomed to Aunt Gwennie, so he looked at her more as a curious stranger than a relative.

"Eddie, go and hug your aunt," said Saphora.

"He doesn't have to," said Gwennie. She dug through a bag and pulled out a box. "I brought you a present," she said.

Eddie bounded for her, hands extended. He opened the box as if he did not already have more stuff than he needed back in Charlotte in his room, each item representing a guilty pang from his mother or father for the separation Eddie lived between.

"It's a bug holder," said Gwennie. "Like, you catch a bug in the net, then drop it into the holder so you can watch it or feed it. One of the little bug house walls has a magnifying glass to watch it up close." She shrugged, more for Saphora's sake. "It looked educational."

Saphora coaxed a "thank you" out of Eddie and then said, "Take it to the backyard and share it with Tobias."

Eddie took off without an invitation to Tobias. So Saphora told the boy, "Go ahead and join him. I'll bring you lunch so you can have it up in the tree house. Pizza or something."

Tobias was much calmer than Eddie. He walked up to Saphora and put his arms around her.

Gwennie said she was surprised a young boy would pay so much attention to an adult. She introduced herself to him.

"I'm Tobias. My parents live about ten blocks away. I called first and Dr. Warren told me how to get here. I'll go and play with Eddie. I'd love lunch in the tree house, Mrs. Warren," he said. "Pleasure to meet you, Gwennie." He tracked Eddie to the backyard.

"He's awfully mature," said Gwennie.

"We met him at the town beach when Bender made us stop so he could take a walk."

Gwennie followed through the front door. Bender had set up an office in the downstairs room he called a library. He pored over a procedure manual.

Saphora volunteered to take Gwennie's suitcase and bag to the guest room opposite the study to give Gwennie time with her daddy. But she left the door open and could conveniently hear them.

"There she is," Bender said, an old wooden desk chair squeaking as he got out of it. He had always greeted Gwennie differently than the boys. She was his Gwen. There was an elevated intensity all over Bender as if he might break in two at the sight of her. She had not always brought out the best in Bender when she was a teen. But Bender admittedly had not ever been good at relating to young people. Once she had gotten her bachelor's degree in tow and was well on her way to law school, Bender gained a sudden vocabulary for praise in her presence.

Saphora picked up the suitcase and then the bag and set them on the bed. She opened the drapes covering the french doors while Gwennie sobbed next door. With the extra light in the room, the fine silt was visible that had coated the table surfaces over the seasons the house had been closed up. She wanted Sherry to come and see to everything after all. She went into the guest bath and pulled a hand towel out of the closet. It took only a couple of minutes to dust the furniture. But as the afternoon sunlight hit the surfaces, she could see her fresh swirls in the wood top. She pulled out a glass full of seashells from the upper closet shelf. She placed them on top of the smudged table surface.

Eddie shrieked from outside.

She ran to look through the glass doors. He was only reacting to Tobias, who had beat him to the top ladder rung and was climbing into the tree house.

Gwennie appeared in the doorway. "You look like you did the night I pulled my first tooth," said Gwennie, "wincing at the sight of blood." Crying aged her in a good way.

"I've never seen you so sentimental," said Saphora. "I like it." She handed her a box of tissues.

Gwennie closed the bedroom door. "Daddy looks fine, Mama. I don't know what I expected."

"Surgery and chemo will change how he looks. So enjoy today." The tabletop did not shine in spite of the steady rubbing she was giving it. How her housekeeper made old tables look new again was beyond her.

"I'm glad you brought him here. It'll keep him out of the office so he can properly mend."

"I think he didn't want his colleagues to see him looking like a patient."

"Daddy said he wanted Jim overseeing his treatments."

Saphora knew what Bender had told her. But in spite of the distance between them she still knew him better than he knew himself.

"You probably haven't been in much of a cooking mood. If you help me, I'll make pizzas for the boys and something healthy for us," said Gwennie.

"I don't care if it's healthy."

"I'll make both."

The afternoon moved slowly for Saphora. The boys took their pizza up the tree house ladder. Bender joined Saphora and Gwennie for pizzas and salad but seemed relieved that Gwennie was in such a talkative mood. It was like her to rattle along in waves of what had been accomplished, especially in front of her father. She had closed on the condo and paid off her car. Of course, now she was afraid she would have to trade in the car because none of them were built to last. It was a soothing inventory of all things Gwennie.

"You've done something to your hair," said Bender.

That surprised Saphora so much that she said, "That's nice you noticed."

"I notice when my daughter's changed her hair," said Bender. "That color suits you."

Gwennie reddened under his approval.

"I just meant it's not the usual thing you talk about," said Saphora.

"That's nonsense. I can make personal observations. What are you implying? I can't coalesce like you, Saphora? I realize I don't ramble on like you women are prone to do," he said. Looking at Gwennie he added, "Present company excluded. But I need the comfort of daily talk just like everyone else." His voice was growing in volume. "Does that surprise you too, Saphora? That I'm just like everyone else?"

"Daddy," said Gwennie.

"I'm tired." He said to Saphora, "Forgive me."

"It's not important that you're like everyone else, Daddy. Don't give it a thought," said Gwennie. "You're not like everyone else. You're you. Mama is, well, Mama."

There was a distinction in the way Gwennie alluded to Bender's uniqueness followed by the sort of tone that asserted that Saphora was exactly like everyone else; it stabbed Saphora even more than Bender's comment. "Do we have to compare me to anyone?" she asked.

Bender laughed as he once did right after they were married. It was a laugh he had inherited from his father, who had often gotten Bender to laugh at his mother for some comment he felt proved she was less than intelligent. It was very off-putting.

"I'm going to leave you two to catch up. I'll wash dishes," said Saphora.

"You and Gwennie stay and talk. I've got to finish my reading," he said, getting up from the table. He turned and looked at Gwennie and said, "I'm sorry. It's the pressure of tomorrow that brought out the worst in me. Not your mama." His cell phone vibrated, so he took it out and said, "I'll be. It's Sam the Hammer." He left the table.

"Who is Sam the Hammer?" asked Gwennie.

"Minor league pitcher for the Tigers," said Saphora.

"Dad knows a baseball player?"

"They fish and play golf together." There was a rumor that Sam Hammersley was being scouted for the Cleveland Indians.

Bender held up his hand as if Saphora and Gwennie were talking too loud. He disappeared into the library.

Saphora did not want to respond childishly to Bender, so she fell quiet. He had a history for bringing closure to an argument without apologizing. She used to imagine scoring a winning point. But what was the use? She sat silent. "You don't have to do the dishes," she said to Gwennie.

"I want to," Gwennie said. She went outside to collect the boys' lunch leftovers.

Saphora stood over the sink. She battled the strangest array of thoughts. She defined it as a mixture of guilt and anger. It was not a new emotion. It was an old resurrected hybrid of emotions she had come to know during the first ten years of their marriage when she could not for the life of her figure out how to win an argument with Bender. His negotiation skills were nearly at a genius level. Even when he brought the matter to a close, there was a nagging cloud hanging over Saphora that said even though his tone had gentled, he used a codified language that only alluded to his need to get on with the night so he could fall asleep listening to Bread.

She revisited the conversation to the point where she had set him off. Then she got angry with herself for having said anything at all.

She looked through the window over the sink and found Tobias hanging upside down out of the tree looking straight at her. He was like a lucky charm for her emotions. She laughed and that set him to clapping his hands as if it had been his intent all along to bring her out of the doldrums.

He tried to pull himself up, but his tiny abdominal muscles would not respond. Gwennie went up the ladder and helped him slide up into her arms. Then he climbed back down onto the ground.

By nightfall Tobias had gotten on his bicycle and gone home.

Eddie said to Saphora, "Tobias told me that his father said he could win the prize for the most pills taken in a day. He had to take more, so that's why he had to leave."

Saphora couldn't figure out Tobias's illness.

Eddie manipulated Gwennie until she gave in and joined him in a violent video game. The goal of the game was to cut off the opponent's head and then win another pail of green goo that gave the victor more power over his enemy. Gwennie's sorceress kept losing her head. That meant she had to use her potions to restore her own head. By the end of the game, Eddie had taken her castle and all of her servants as slaves. Eddie shouted when his monster changed the sorceress into a whining cat. The game was over.

Saphora stowed the last of the leftover pizza and salad in the fridge, then excused herself. Bender had taken a sleeping pill early on and was snoring quietly in the upstairs bed. Saphora slipped on a pair of white terry slippers she had bought recently and absent-mindedly tucked into her suitcase. She pulled a sweater over her head and walked out onto the balcony. Suction from within and without snapped the door closed behind her.

Night had fallen over the Neuse River. A lighthouse was blowing light across the ocean beyond the hillocks of marsh grass. Saphora swished leaves off the deck bench seat and found solace sitting quietly with no one to ask anything of her.

She could nearly see the house next to them through the fog. The tree-lined fence separating the houses blocked much of her view, but she figured that had been the intent of whoever had erected it twenty years ago. It had come with the house and was one of the features Bender liked, the privacy of a fenced backyard barricaded by deep water. No one to bother him.

Even the night noises were comforting. But then a not-so-distinguishable faint sifting sound began from behind the next-door neighbor's backyard trees. *Sift. Swish. Sift. Swish.* She figured it wasn't any sort of insect rubbing its legs in the night air. Maybe a raccoon. Then she decided not. She sat up to see if there was a light on in the house. A rouge of candle glow seeped through the top of the windows in back of the house. The swishing noise persisted. It might have been something mechanical, but the rhythm was too crisp and uneven, not any kind of noise a machine would make.

Saphora sat for an hour on the balcony, her curiosity causing her to sit guessing until she decided that it sounded like a shovel cutting into the soft, sandy loam. But the house was not near enough to the beach or the riverbank to pick up the activity of clam diggers or even teenagers building a pit for an illegal bonfire.

Finally the digging stopped. A door closed. Despite her curiosity about the digging, Saphora was even more curious about the occupant. Whoever had rented out the summer house had taken up a spade to dig by moonlight. Why on earth a neighbor would take to digging after midnight got her so curious she subconsciously got out of her chair to lean over the balcony railing. No hint of a human presence came through the trees. The next morning she would finagle a way to introduce herself.

The house next door had gone completely dark. There was nothing to watch except the half moon. She sat under it until the cool wind chased her indoors. The door faintly whined at the hinges.

Bender's eyes opened, cat's-eye slits widening under the hairline of moon falling across his face.

She froze in the doorway. "I'm sorry if I woke you up," she said.

"Don't apologize." He did not take his eyes off her or look away as had been his custom for many years. "You look pretty standing there like that, the moon on your hair." His voice was so thin that Saphora realized he had startled awake. Before he dozed off again he said, "But you have always been the prettiest of all the wives." Then his eyes closed, and he fell directly asleep.

Bender had once asked Saphora to join him in a pact: only one of them could take a sleep aid in case the house caught fire. He had seen too many burn victims in his operating room. Besides, the kind of sleeping pills Bender brought home from the hospital made him nearly comatose. She watched him sleeping and then took her place beside him as she had done for twenty-seven years.

She fell asleep as the puzzling sifting sound started up again.

5

With a new awareness, both painful and humorous, I begin to understand why the saints were rarely married women.

ANNE MORROW LINDBERGH, *Gift from the Sea*

Bender lay in the hospital bed with the blinds pulled closed. He looked too big for the bed, awkwardly pulling at the pale green hospital gown. Getting him to wear it took the genius coaxing of a nurse forewarned that he was a bona fide god complex–affected surgeon.

Jim came in to check on him and talk to him about the side effects of the chemo if indeed the therapy was needed. "It's good to talk about chemo and prepare for the possibility of it," he told Bender and Saphora. "Then if you don't need it, no big deal." But Jim felt chemo was the viable avenue and made good on his promise to keep Saphora honestly abreast of Bender's diagnosis. He showed them the gels from the CT scan. The tumor had shown up in his cranium, a small shadow that looked like a tiny moon gliding over earth. Jim left to meet up with the surgeon who would perform Bender's procedure. He had promised Bender to observe and assist during the surgery.

After Jim left, two nurses prepped Bender for the procedure.

Saphora sat beside him, offering ice chips, although he complained of hunger pangs. The wife seated next to the patient in the bed opposite them doted on her Latino husband, whose dark eyes softened each time she smiled and pushed more ice into his mouth.

Bender stared stiffly at the golf tournament on the overhead television. He kept switching the channels back and forth between the tournament and a tennis match.

"Ramsey is coming," said Saphora. Their youngest son, hearing about his daddy's diagnosis, had bought a ticket into Raleigh-Durham.

"He doesn't have to come," he said, still not taking his eyes off the tournament.

"Of course he's coming," she said. "You'll dry out. Eat this."

"Saphora, just hand me the cup. I can feed myself ice."

The Latino's wife glanced up at Saphora. She was a white lady who spoke in a quiet voice but laughed uninhibitedly. There was a faint mixture of sympathy and humility in her eyes, eyes that seemed to participate in everything she observed.

Gwennie came huffing into the room. She had taken the stairs in lieu of the elevator. She had used the exercise ploy as her excuse for avoiding elevators most of her adult life. But Saphora knew her fear of them.

"Eddie went to stay the afternoon with his new friend, Tobias," said Gwennie. "I met his parents. The husband looks old enough to be Tobias's granddad. The mom looks a lot younger than him, but what do I know?" She set a stack of freshly bought magazines on Bender's tray and kissed her daddy.

It was the first time he took his eyes off the television. "Hold on to this," he said, handing her his phone. "If I get any calls, just plug them into the message center on my laptop."

Jim reappeared, flanked by two OR nurses. "No phone calls for a few days, Bender," he said. "Gwennie, shut that thing off."

Gwennie froze between the power of two stiff-necked surgeons. Finally Saphora took the phone. "I'll take care of it."

Bender was wheeled out of the room. He was about to disappear behind the two automatic doors into the OR center when Saphora was overwhelmed with emotion. He looked helpless lying there, drifting off against his will into the sedation and under the management of a surgery crew not his own. Saphora leaned over the bed rail and kissed him lightly on the forehead that would soon be minus the thick blond forelock that had distinguished Bender from so many of his friends with thinning hair.

The last emotion to register on his face was indistinguishable to everyone looking at him except Saphora. He had seldom registered fear, but there it was in his eyes just before they closed.

An hour later she sat outside the surgery center holding a pager until Gwennie coaxed her down the stairs for a late lunch.

The cafeteria was dressed up like a Fourth of July parade. Red, white, and blue streamers festooned the common areas, linking the various buffet lines like veins. Helium balloons floated cell-like above the cash registers. Saphora had completely forgotten the Fourth and said so to Gwennie.

"It's two days away. We can watch the fireworks on the water in Oriental. Turner will be in town, and Eddie's never been to the Croaker Festival," said Gwennie. "We'll take him, and it'll help keep our minds off things."

"Ramsey is coming too. But Celeste is staying home with the kids. I told him to tell her not to worry." Celeste tended to feel guilty about everything.

Gwennie put an apple on her tray next to the pasta dish. "I don't know that it's a bad idea. Those three kids of hers are out of control. But then I know nothing about kids. I'm too impatient." Gwennie wasn't patient with Celeste either. She said, "Celeste does that counting thing with her kids. 'Okay, Liam, I'm counting to five and then you'd better do what I say.' The instant I would get Liam alone, I'd say to him, 'Listen, kid, do it on one or you're toast!'"

"Celeste told me she couldn't figure out why her kids were scared of Aunt Gwennie."

"Fear is akin to respect, Mama. Don't confuse the meaning."

"Now you sound like your daddy."

"I realize I don't need kids of my own," she said.

"Gwennie, I can't wait to see what kind of mother you'll make. Don't minimize all children under Celeste's definition of family. She's got Ramsey believing that if he so much as even thinks about a career change, he'll wreck his kids' college funds."

"College! Liam's what, five?"

"Liam is seven. Celeste has an exacting sense about saving money."

"Celeste has an exacting sense about leading Ramsey around like a poodle," Gwennie said over her shoulder as she led the way to a table on the farthest side of the cafeteria.

"He does seem cloistered by Celeste."

"I know my brother's not perfect. But he was the fun brother, the one who always knew what to do on a boring Saturday. Celeste has killed my baby brother and replaced him with a trained circus act."

"He did always struggle with discipline," said Saphora. At first, it had seemed Celeste was good for him.

"That was Turner. Ramsey was a natural B student. That's not a failure, Mama. My phone's ringing," said Gwennie. She covered her pasta with a napkin. "I'll take this outside. Signal's awful in this place."

The sandwich Saphora had picked off the deli line was untouched. She cut it in half and then in fourths. Finally she wrapped it up in her napkin.

"Impossible to eat the day of their surgery." A woman seated across from her spoke. She was the Latino husband's wife.

Saphora felt elated to see a familiar face. "How do you eat during something like this?"

The woman introduced herself as Linda Valdez. "It's my husband's second surgery. We both lose weight when Emilio goes under the knife. Try eating smaller portions more often. Tell yourself you're just eating a snack. It's better than adding starvation to stress."

Saphora gave Linda her name. "How long has your husband known about his cancer?"

"A year. They gave him six months, but Emilio's not giving up. We have five kids. He's not going to leave us behind, he says. He says God wouldn't dare bring him into heaven complaining."

"Bender just found out. We don't know the prognosis yet."

"Chemo is hard on them."

"He hates to lose his hair. But he told his doctor, Jim Pennington, 'Shave it all off for the surgery and get it over with.' I hate every step of it."

"I wish I could say that after a year, you're a pro at fighting cancer. But each day brings a new battle." She got up and came to Saphora's table. She took a seat beside her. "Don't think I feel sorry for myself. Emilio and I have never known this kind of love before. You'll know soon enough what I mean."

Saphora was getting better at holding back her tendency to fall into a crying jag. But after several tears slipped down her face, she finally just let go and cried in front of this stranger. Linda might have assumed her tears were all for sorrow. It would have taken too long to explain that the day Bender told her about his cancer was the day she had planned to leave him. Linda would think she was a terrible wife. She said, "My daughter is coming back. I don't want her to see me like this."

"It's good for her to know you're not an iron woman. You don't want to teach her to live ashamed of her emotions. A daughter can know her mother is less than perfect. She'll be stronger knowing the truth." Linda said it effortlessly, like a woman well practiced in opening up her life for the whole world to see.

In her next leg of life, she would request an outlook like Linda's. She dried her eyes and smiled for Gwennie.

ଚ୍ଚ

The first time Saphora's hospital pager went off was to tell her that Bender had not yet gone into surgery. Three hours later, the entire surgical team had gotten ready in order to proceed. That left Saphora and Gwennie waiting until midnight, when he was finally wheeled out of the operating room into recovery.

Before Saphora reached the recovery room, Bender was shouting, "Where's Saphora? Bring her to me!"

Gwennie ran slightly ahead of Saphora but then stepped aside to allow her to pass and enter the recovery area, a sort of wide, open room cordoned off only by curtains.

Three nurses, including a big male nurse, maneuvered Bender onto a bed. But he was putting up a fight. The smallest female nurse stepped back to let her male associate try to gain control of Bender's troubled waking state.

Bender's eyes met Saphora's. "There she is." His words were slurred from the sedation. "I thought I'd lost you." His eyes closed. His grimace showed anguish uncharacteristic of him.

"He's a little groggy. That's normal," said the male nurse.

Saphora took Bender's hand. "I'm here, love," she said. She had called him "love" in their early days as a couple. Seeing the suffering in his eyes brought back something tender inside her. Maybe it was self-comforting.

Bender tried to get up again, turning on his side and exposing his bare backside to the smaller nurse who stood at the end of the bed. Gwennie laughed nervously as the nurse pulled the sheet over him. He sucked in deeply when the sheet covered his mouth and nose. Saphora took over the post of calming Bender down, adjusting the sheet and talking evenly.

Gwennie plopped down in a corner of the room and pulled a magazine in front of her face.

"Bender, you're coming awake," said Saphora. "You're in Duke Medical. Get your bearings, love." He was dependent, thrashing to come back in the world as if he were being born again. His head was taped with gauze tinged red. In spite of what he asked of Jim, only part of his head was shaven. His blond curls made a halo around the bandage. Blue circles were forming around both his swollen eyes.

Jim walked up beside Saphora. "We found what we were looking for. It was a mass the size of a lemon." He said to Bender, "We'll talk about your treatment in the morning." He left Bender's bedside but continued to make eye contact with Saphora. She followed him out of the room.

"He's going to have a walloping headache for a week or so," Jim told her out of Bender's earshot. "If I were you, I'd hire a nurse who'll come to your house. You know Bender. He'll be a handful to manage. I'll recommend an agency."

Saphora knew the surgeon song and dance before delivering the prognosis. She was ready to get to the bad news. "What's his prognosis, Jim?"

"Depending on his will to battle this thing, he could have six more months. I know you, Saphora. You'll make them count."

She struggled to talk for the minute it took Jim to locate a box of tissues down the hallway and bring it back to her. "He wants to convalesce in Oriental," she said, still trying to maintain her composure. "So I'll need to find a nursing service near there. Is that possible?" She stammered around until Gwennie ran to her side, as if she could somehow give her the ability to talk again.

Jim bent to hug her. His voice was somber. "I'll find you a good home health nurse near Oriental," said Jim. "The best I can find. We're going to give him a light sedative to sleep through the rest of the night. You and Gwennie might as well go to the hotel and get some rest. Be back here about midmorning, and I'll meet you in his room to powwow with you and Bender."

"I'll drive us to the hotel, Mama. I called Tobias's mom, and she says the boys are sleeping, not to worry about Eddie."

Saphora revisited the thoughts that dogged her the day of the *Southern Living* party. Now she felt a strange elation coupled with guilt. She had wanted to leave Bender, but she had not wanted him to leave. Not like this.

"Have I been a good wife?" she asked Gwennie.

"Don't do that to yourself, Mama," said Gwennie. "No one can say you haven't."

6

I'm not afraid of storms, for I'm learning how
to sail my ship.

Louisa May Alcott, *Little Women*

Saphora let Tobias in the door. He circled around her, saying quickly,
"Morning, Mrs. W." He and Eddie played together nearly every day
for the first two weeks in Oriental following Bender's surgery. Whenever Saphora drove Bender to Duke, Eddie stayed behind with Tobias
and his mother, Jamie. Today Saphora told Jamie she should drop
him by. He kept Eddie busy outside, away from video games. His
adoptive mother was younger than Saphora, his father more the age
of a granddad, as Gwennie had said.

It was overcast but rain was not predicted. "They're no trouble,"
Saphora told Jamie. "They'll stay out in the tree house all day."

Jamie doted on Tobias. She never overstayed her welcome, just
staying long enough for a pleasant visit. She made the days spent in
vigil over Bender less burdensome. She was one of those highly pos-
itive women who never had a bad thing to say about anyone. Saphora
wanted to be like her.

Jamie said, "It's good that Tobias has made a summer friend. I'm
indebted to you." She let herself out.

While at the hospital Saphora had called and ordered a leased
patient bed. Finally, midmorning, the rental company's setup guy

arrived. He recommended she install Bender's sleeping space in the library. The energy to take the stairs evaporated under the rounds of chemotherapy coursing through his circulatory system. Bender could look out across the backyard and the Neuse and see the way the rain swept down the river, waving like women's skirts.

Bender got off the sofa and dressed himself in the library's bathroom. Then he immediately sat in the rocker next to the hospital bed.

Saphora washed berries and placed them around a plate, a cup of hot grits in the center, an egg on the side. He liked butter, but not today.

He told her, "Tomorrow I'm eating in the breakfast room. Could you not overcook my eggs?"

"You said that yesterday," she said. "Hospice is looking for a nurse. Nothing yet. But they'll find one. We're just so far out." She wasn't going to bring up the fact that they would not have this problem in Davidson.

The doorbell rang. Saphora gave him his medical journal. "I'll be back," she said. She left the library and walked to the front door. When she opened it, her surprise caused the visitor on her front porch to laugh. "Pastor?"

John Mims was holding a white envelope. "Mrs. Warren! I looked for you at the fund-raiser. We missed you."

"My husband's recovering from surgery," she said, although she knew she had forgotten her promise to Pastor Mims out of convenience.

"I'm so sorry." He politely composed himself. "I heard the news Monday, just yesterday."

"How did you find me?"

"Bernard."

"Oh. Of course." The curt grocery store clerk was also a covert neighborhood spy. She waited for a moment, thinking he was just dropping by a calling card.

But the minister was well versed in making his intentions known in as few words as possible, his serious eyes examining her.

Finally she said, "Want to come inside?"

John followed her into the two-story living room. "Nice digs, Mrs. Warren." Judging from his age, he was a product of the Jesus movement of the seventies.

"It's an old place. We should sell, but Bender thinks we need it for taxes."

"I hope you keep it. We like new folks coming to town for the summer. Oriental's pretty quiet through the winter. Summers, we come to life."

"I'd like to have some time out in the village. We haven't been sailing or anything," she said.

"Dr. Warren's doing better, I hope?"

She thought about Bender kneeling over the toilet puking up dinner last night. "Better, I guess," she said. "How did you come to know about his cancer?"

"Same way I found you. Bernard. He's like the town post office. If it comes through Oriental, it comes through Bernard."

If she wanted privacy she'd have to find another grocery store.

"I can visit with the doctor today if he's up to company."

Pastor Mims meant well. But Bender's interest in religion was piqued only when he breathed a prayer on the ninth hole to speak a bit of magic over his handicap. She was forming the words that would hopefully get him headed back out the door and on to more profitable pursuits when Bender appeared at the entrance to the library.

"Saphora, it's all right. I'm needing some company. Reverend, if you'd like to come and visit me, can you come back here? Best view in the house," said Bender.

Saphora was still holding the coffeepot. She tried not to look so open mouthed at Bender's invitation. So she asked, "Tea or coffee?"

"Coffee for me," said Pastor Mims.

Saphora followed Mims as far as the kitchen. He wandered into the library while she got out an extra cup. She was more than curious about Bender's invitation to John Mims. She carried the coffee to the minister, who had taken the chair across from Bender. Then she excused herself to set up the cutting board on the marble buffet.

Just as John Mims greeted Bender, the library door closed.

The telephone rang. It was Turner wanting to talk to Eddie. He told her he would be up Friday. Saphora went to the back door, opened it, and called Eddie down from the tree house.

Turner had come up the last two weekends. He had still not secured a sitter in Charlotte. But now that Eddie had found such a good friend in Tobias, Saphora did not have the heart to pressure Turner into taking him back home. School was starting in a few weeks anyway.

Ramsey was also coming for the weekend, but this time he was bringing Celeste and their three boys. Ramsey confessed to Saphora that he had to explain to his children who their grandpa was. When they visited Lake Norman in the summers it was mostly Saphora who had spent time with them out in the sailboat.

Celeste had been Bender's excuse for not being around, staying late at the clinic when they had visited them in Davidson. He said her nervous talking made him want to gag her. Her temperament had worn on Bender so much that he had made himself scarce, much to his detriment, since Ramsey's children had almost no remembrance of him at all.

Bender's voice was still too faint to hear through the closed library door. She laid aside the squash and onions, scraping the vegetables into a bowl and stowing them in the refrigerator. Finally she opened the door to the library and said, "Sherry is finally coming up. Her son is over the chickenpox, and her mother is watching him."

Bender was so intent on whatever he was telling Pastor Mims that he kept talking as if Saphora had not opened the door at all.

She closed the door and then faxed a grocery list to Sherry. She couldn't wait to see her. Once she drove in—she had promised by noon—Saphora would not lift another finger. The fax machine started grinding and jittering. She shut it down and made a new list on her BlackBerry. Sherry was most likely on the way to Oriental anyway.

Sherry was her savior, but she felt guilty about that. Truth be told, if Sherry did nothing but stand beside her and prop her up, that would be fine. She loved her just for the comfort she brought her. Somehow, though, she was a buffer between Bender and her. With Sherry minding the everyday chores, he would stop complaining about the food and work out his demands with her. She had a calm way with him, asserting her will and taking his complaints in stride. Then she would go and retreat into a romance novel without another thought for Bender's obsessive temperament.

It occurred to Saphora she was hitched to Bender's circus through years and years of habit.

Finally, a phone text flashed that her list had been successfully sent to Sherry. Saphora had gone as far as she could go. She would go into town for the afternoon. She had not sailed since arriving, exactly what she had planned to do in the first place. Renting a boat was easily done downtown at the Oriental Marina.

She decided not to tell Bender where she was going. Sherry could tell him. He was becoming so dependent on her. Who was he, after all, to run her ragged like she was another of those nurses who fluttered around him at the clinic, doing his bidding?

Pastor Mims finally came out of the library, closing the door behind him. He was looking pleased with his visit. "Dr. Warren's resting," he told her. "He is a surprisingly spiritual man."

"Oh, for Pete's sake!" she said, taking the chopping knife and dropping it into the sink.

Pastor Mims quietly said, "You take care, Mrs. Warren. I'll show myself out."

His last look at her was one that she had seen before from Bender's friends when they sensed tension between them. Pastor John looked so intelligent, but Bender was smooth. He had won over another convert to his Bender cult. She imagined them all gathered to pay tribute to him, and that is when she realized that Bender had been building a case for himself, as if the Almighty could not see what she saw.

It occurred to her he'd even been nicer to her since leaving Davidson. She wanted kindness from him, but for other reasons. Whenever she would see a couple quietly talking in a café, touching, and the husband gazing into his wife's eyes as if he could disappear into them, be lost in love with her, she couldn't help but feel a pang of something. Nothing as harsh as jealousy. Just a pang of wanting to feel something that others seemed to feel, a love that swallowed her up in completeness.

Bender's followers would all gather for his funeral and say the things about him that he had scripted and planted in their thoughts. Then she would stand up in the middle of them and start naming the women who had fawned over his special qualities. Perhaps that is exactly what she ought to invite from the funeral guests; she'd ask each of his girlfriends to stand and recount what Bender had done for her behind closed doors.

Yes, exactly! Pastor Mims would say a prayer and then give her the floor. She would roll out the list like she was reading off the groceries for Sherry. "Erin Guff. Vickie Jaunice. Bernie Mae Milton. Pansy Fulton." And while each woman was standing up and running out of the church, Saphora Warren would finally be getting the last word.

She sat down on a stool and buried her face in her hands. *What is wrong with me? I'm turning into the very thing I hate. God, help me!*

⁊⁊

Sherry promised she would see to Bender. She had stopped in Raleigh and stocked up on groceries. When Saphora pulled away from the house, Sherry was out back feeding Eddie and Tobias pigs-in-a-blanket. She would finish up Saphora's squash dish and feed it to Bender for lunch. Saphora felt tension releasing from her shoulders.

Saphora stopped at the mailbox and was about to pull away when she saw the next-door neighbor getting his mail. She pulled up slowly and stopped. She brought down the car window and smiled, neighborly. "I'm your neighbor, Saphora," she said.

He was startled but acknowledged her. "I've seen you out with your boys playing."

"Oh. That's my grandson, Eddie, and Tobias. Tobias lives a few blocks from here."

"You're a grandmother? That's surprising."

She had heard before that she looked too young for grandkids. But she appreciated it coming from a man who looked twenty years her junior. "My three are all grown. I have four grandchildren," she said.

"I'd heard my house was next to a surgeon's house."

"Your house?"

"For now."

"I didn't know it had sold."

"I used to rent it, then one day decided to buy it. Is he your husband?"

"Bender's a plastic surgeon and, yes, he is my husband." She knew not to act surprised that he knew. She'd learned already that Oriental was too close-knit for privacy.

"I'll keep a look out for him. That's an interesting name. Bender."

"His mother gave him her maiden name." She realized she was divulging a lot while he was saying little. "Your name, though, is a complete mystery."

"I'm sorry." He laughed, sliding the mail under one armpit. "Name's Luke." He pushed his auburn bangs out of his eyes, then followed by adjusting his glasses. He looked over the tops of the wire frames rather than through them. He was good-looking like Ramsey, but his eyes reflected a tincture of higher IQ.

"Are you a summer resident or all year?" She hoped it wasn't stepping over the line to ask.

"I live here. I'm local now, bought this place just last month. My wife wanted this house."

"I'll try and come over to meet her," said Saphora.

"I'm a widower." He slid the envelopes into the other hand. The fact that he was moving back toward his house told Saphora that standing out in the hot sun baking was not in his plans for the afternoon. "Well, it was good to meet you. You take care."

She waved and pulled away, thinking it was such a strange thing for a man to buy a house for his wife after she had passed away.

Before she arrived downtown and parked near the Oriental Marina's dock, she remembered the shoveling sound going on that evening she had been sitting on the upper deck. But solving that mystery wasn't the kind of question to ask a man she had just met.

⟶

Saphora took her sailing lessons on Lake Norman eight years ago. The sailing master told her it was her second nature to sail. Bender had promised that when they moved onto the lake sailing would be a shared activity. But he had also agreed to see a counselor with her to try to improve things between them. The psychologist he chose was a golfing friend who was passive to Bender's aggression. They went twice and the doctor declared Bender a healthy balance of male spirit and sensitivity.

Saphora took the first sailing class alone. After that she navigated their small craft, the *Evelyn,* around the lake with her best friend, Marcy, who had moved into a condo in uptown Charlotte after her divorce.

Marcy's job as a rug broker took her away so often that the only time Saphora had taken the sailboat out all summer was when Turner came by on the weekends. The Tuesday that Abigail Weed had descended on her back lawn with the *Southern Living* crew, Marcy was in Indonesia. She had invited Saphora to join her. "Be spontaneous," she had said. But Saphora was secretly fantasizing about her own getaway. It was a practical plan to move into a place she and Bender already owned. She planned it so she'd make no waves until circumstances dictated differently. It occurred to her that the fact she had planned to make no waves was exactly why it was never a plan in the first place.

She stopped in at a harbor café and ordered a fish sandwich to go. When she arrived at the dock, Captain Bart Larson, the dock master, waited for her in his lawn chair. He held an open umbrella, she assumed to block the sun that was beginning to beat down.

"Mrs. Warren, there you are," he said. "Aren't you a pretty sailor."

She was happy to hear him say so.

He was tanned from floating in and out of the harbor carting tourists around the islands and the eastern shore. His white brows made a ledge over his eyes. He seemed to be having trouble getting around.

"I had a stupid accident," he finally told her. He was holding a cane with the other hand. "I was fixing my daughter's roof, and the whole ladder came down with me. Once you break a bone at my age, it's hard to get back what you lost."

She shared concern and then asked, "What am I taking out today?"

"*Miss Molly.* She's mine. Not a rental. Small and skinny like you. But you look salty to me, as if you can manage her."

Saphora followed him to the sailing rig, a Herreshoff design, he told her; the *Miss Molly* bore the angular sails found on old Chinese rigs. She was an older, small, all-wood craft bearing a deep enough bow to cut a path through the roiling river wakes.

"There's a storm coming in tonight," he said. "I figured you'd want to reef your own sails."

There were no clouds. The blue canopy was everlasting from the north to the south.

"There's time on the way," she said.

"Old sailors reef first. That's why they're old."

"I know. I'll do it now."

He laughed. He seemed like a man who didn't mind her having a little fun with him.

She got into the boat and hooked up her halyards. The sails raised into the sky. She did wonder why he gave her his own boat. But she was, after all, going it alone. The *Miss Molly* must have been the only one-man vessel available. "Just a three-hour tour," she said. "The weatherman's calling for clear skies, though." She had listened to the radio driving over.

"The weatherman's wrong." He was known, Bernard had told her, for superstitious beliefs, following the Farmer's Almanac, planting beans by moonlight. A romantic old soul.

"I put a fishing rod in the cabin."

She had stipulated that she wanted to fish. "Exactly what I need," she said. She paid the deposit and untied the dock line. If the weather held until Saturday, she'd invite Turner and Ramsey to take a boat out into the open sea. She doubted Gwennie would join them, but if given the choice of staying in the house with Celeste or sailing, there was a good chance of getting Gwennie aboard.

"I'll have a houseful of company Saturday. Can you reserve a bigger rig for me?"

He checked his schedule. "A cruiser."

"I'll take it." Ramsey and Turner and their boys would be crew enough.

There was a nice wind, so she sailed on a beat up the Neuse. She tacked alongside the wind that pushed her toward the sound, close hauled, and then changed tack, zigzagging until she was running windward. She let out the sail fully, and *Miss Molly* sped windward, bow toward the Pamlico Sound.

She let her thoughts blow away along with the wind that blew back her hair. She left behind the marina and the problems with Bender. Focusing on navigating the boat elevated her spirits. She realized she had been living under an unfair regimen. There was no doubt that she would take more days for herself and take advantage of Sherry's time in Oriental. Where was it written that a woman had to silently submit to a life that did not acknowledge her for her worth?

Captain Bart had left her the chart for locating the South River. She sailed in on a tailwind and dropped anchor in one of the coves. Navigating a massive river alone was a chore, though. The Neuse was less predictable than the waters of Lake Norman. She'd be glad to relax and let her sons take the helm Saturday. Ramsey would love it. He had taken to sailing quicker than Turner. He said it was a way to meet girls confident in their abilities. But he talked like that to sound superior to Turner, who did not care an iota. Still, she had sailed alone today on strange waters, and somehow the strangeness had enveloped her with a new sense of worth. But had she taken too long to seize a small slice of autonomy? Was her whole life a waste? Even her daughter had managed to cut ties from the suffocating requirements of being a Warren and find her own personal space to simply be Gwennie. She was always a smart girl, even when she could not escape the Warren harness.

Gwennie fell in love the same summer that Turner took to sailing. Saphora took her to the yacht club for dinner and a swim, where she met a young college student named Paul Stalinsky. He was not there because of his family's membership in the club but because he had taken a job as a lifeguard at the club pool. He started coming around the house often, taking out a borrowed boat. He motored right up to the Warren dock, sounding one of those awful horns. Gwennie would go running out of the house and down the back lawn to meet Paul for a boat ride. But Bender discouraged her relationship with Paul. He was a smart student and athletic. He attended UNC Wilmington and would go back in the fall. But when asked about his future plans, he was too ambiguous for Bender. He told Paul that he needed to end a summer romance that was going nowhere.

Gwennie sat out on the porch crying, refusing to go to bed until sometime after midnight and promising to never forgive her dad for sending Paul off the premises.

That summer had held the promise of the kind of memories that draw most families back to the water for more adventures. But each one of them, Turner, Ramsey, and Gwennie, had come up with excuses for not accompanying their parents when Saphora had planned their first trip to the house in Oriental. Not wanting to travel without her kids, Saphora cancelled the trip. That was why the house sat void of a visit by a Warren. She never tried to plan a trip to Oriental again.

She suffered a quiet ache even though Marcy had told her that most older teens did not enjoy the company of parents; that was why so many went off on group trips together.

Saphora cast her line. She then placed the rod in the frame and locked it in. The *Miss Molly* bobbed in the wake of the charter that motored by. She fished and sat wondering why she had not insisted on her children coming with her that summer to Oriental. She was the mother and they the progeny dependent on family support of

summer activities. Now Bender's cancer brought them all to Oriental the summer she had decided to mend there in isolation. It seemed
like fate had propelled some mystic, psychic wind, drawing them all
back against plans, against dreams, and deposited them all here in answer to a mother's prayer. But did God really care about a mother's
unspoken desires? Had God really heard her silent prayers all these
years? Did he hear prayers at all?

ରୁ

She had not meant to fall asleep. But the lack of any bites, the slow
undulation of the rig riding the swells, and the radio broadcasting
faint sonatas lulled her into an afternoon stupor.

She did not know how long she had slept when the first raindrop
hit her square between the eyes. She startled out of the captain's chair.
The sky was dark, not any sign of sunlight. The radio was crackling.
Captain Bart was on the shortwave trying to locate her. She made for
the cabin and checked in. "I'm on my way back," she said. She
checked her watch. "I'm late." It was an hour past the time she had
promised to pull back into the Oriental Marina.

"Do you need assistance, Mrs. Warren?" he asked.

She felt harebrained to have him so worried. "I'm headed back.
No worries. I'll be back at the dock in an hour."

The breeze blew over the port, much to her relief. She tacked,
beating into the wind. The rain let go. She was mad at herself for
dozing off. Weird, but she was feeling an unjustified resentment of
Bender. He had never joined her sailing even though he joined friends
often on fishing expeditions. He had even ordered the *Evelyn* deliv-
ered to the Oriental Marina for a couple of men's fishing excursions,
both times without the wives.

She was drenched and mad that she was fighting this storm alone. Two sailed a boat better than one, but long ago she had learned to do things on her own. Independence wasn't a bad trait in an age of shifting circumstances. But marriage was supposed to be a two-person tour.

She and Marcy had once plotted for their independence. Marcy's husband, Jackson, was much older than she was, just as Bender was six years older than Saphora. They both presumed they would out-live their husbands. Marcy said the two of them should move to the Outer Banks and live out their days traveling, not cooking, and cer-tainly not catering to men who ignored them. To everyone's shock, though, Jackson drew the affections of a young woman who would settle for no less than all of his attention. She wanted more than a relationship on the side. The best he could do for Marcy was pay for her condo in uptown Charlotte.

Marcy was so devastated that she could not bear to stay at home while the Realtor measured the house for the listing. She stayed sev-eral nights with Saphora, Sherry mixing up the martinis and Saphora keeping tissues on the ready.

Marcy had a master's degree in business. Running her husband's printing company had provided her with managerial skills. She could take care of herself when it was all said and done. But their scheme to escape the responsibilities of Lake Norman's elite circles of spoiled men and eager younger women took a sharp detour. Marcy's new career obligated her to travel most weeks outside of Lake Norman, leaving Saphora short one best friend and one unrealized scheme. So with torrential rain streaming down her arms and legs, Saphora was mad at herself and Bender. She was mad at Marcy and Jackson. She might as well be mad at God, who seemed to be raining on her. "How about a little relief?" she shouted.

The wind and rain beat Saphora in the face. She kept tacking but the waves were swelling. The small craft struggled in the roiling water. The mainsail was flapping. Saphora shakily trimmed the sail and headed down the Neuse. The water was calmer inland, but the storm increased in intensity. So much for prayers. Her drenched knit clothes hung on her by the time she spotted the lights of the harbor.

When she pulled into shore, Captain Bart was beside himself. He hobbled toward her waving his open umbrella. "Woman, I thought you'd drowned yourself!" He helped her onto the dock and then wrapped her fingers around the umbrella handle. "You look drowned."

She threw her arms around him apologetically, grateful to be on land again. Captain Bart kept nudging her toward the overhang of the marina.

Several couples milled around inside the motel, looking out the wall of plate glass windows at the storm, nice and dry while watching her being helped to safety. She pulled off her sopping wet hat and then smiled as if she had enjoyed sailing home in a storm. Several women inside clapped, and one put her fingers to her mouth and whistled.

"Go on inside. Your fans are waiting," said Captain Bart. He tied off the boat and hobbled back to his yacht, muttering about women and sailing.

7

Just don't give up trying to do what you
really want to do. Where there is love and
inspiration, I don't think you can go wrong.

ELLA FITZGERALD

Saphora bought a windbreaker, some dry pants, and a knit sailing-motif top and changed into them inside the tourist shop's dressing room. By the time she warmed herself with coffee in the café and then drove home, the only light on in the house was the kitchen's. She pulled into the garage and entered the house through the mud room.

Sherry was cleaning with bleach. "This house has not been touched since Dr. Warren bought it," she said. "What was that, a half decade ago? If you ask me, you ought to put a property manager to work, keeping it rented out and the housekeeping up on it."

"I could kiss you, Sherry," said Saphora, throwing her arms around her and glad to be back on solid footing again.

"What happened to you?"

"I don't want to talk about it." She pulled a towel out of the laundry basket sitting on the floor by the range. She dried out the damp ends of her hair. "Is he asleep?"

"They must be keeping him on some kind of dope."

"Eddie?" Saphora called out.

"Those are not the clothes you left wearing. You got caught out in the rain, didn't you?"

"I sailed home in a storm."

"Miss Saphora, that's not like you at all. You okay?"

"A little hungry."

"I'll make you an egg sandwich."

"Where is everyone?"

"Eddie and Tobias, they're up in Eddie's room. Tobias got himself a new baseball card. They got flashlights and they're looking at his collection under a sheet tent. I helped them make it so they'd not use good sheets."

"How long's Bender been out?"

"That man's so sedated, he's been out two hours. I did get him to eat. He's got his medical books all around that hospital bed. You think he'd be tired of reading nothing but medical books."

"He's working on the cure for brain cancer."

"I feel sorry for him, looking so weak and helpless like that. But don't tell him. He don't like pity," said Sherry.

It occurred to Saphora that Sherry was telling her things about Bender as if she knew him better than Saphora did. Had she been doing that so long that Saphora just accepted it as part of the arrangement? Had he even asked about her? "He wasn't worried about me?"

"Asleep since nine, like I said. I told the boys to try and go to sleep by eleven. But it's summer. I know how my son likes to stay up summer nights, so I've given them their space and all that."

She was such a good soul. "I know it's not easy being here, Sherry."

"My mama loves keeping Malcolm. Besides, in the morning I'm taking a walk along the beach and finding me a chair where I can read my novel. You need me, you just page me."

She cooked Saphora's favorite guilty pleasure, egg and tomato on toasted homemade bread—egg lightly fried in olive oil, a sprinkle of sea salt, then a big slice of tomato from the farmer's market, served as a sandwich with the bread she had baked that afternoon.

"I'll take it upstairs," said Saphora. Sherry followed her. She got out the breakfast tray and set it out on the deck. Then she moved the rattan rocker outside. "Your other chairs are soaked," she said. She lit a candle and placed the sandwich plate on the tray. "The moon looks as big as Saturn," she said.

The Neuse was churning out a ways from shore, like arms reaching to twist it like a sopping wet towel.

"I'm fine now, Sherry," said Saphora.

"I'm down the hall if you need anything." She hung out on the balcony for a moment, standing in the open bedroom door. "I know it's hard leaving him downstairs and you up here. But I know men. I'm sure he'd move over, make room for his pretty woman."

"Maybe so," said Saphora. She told Sherry good night and then secluded herself out on the deck. The Neuse pushed the rain on past Oriental's swelling banks toward the sound. She would take Eddie and Tobias bank fishing in the morning after pancakes.

Sherry was a good wife and mother. Her husband, Jerry, raked in a small salary repairing engines for a Nissan car dealership. Sherry invited him along every year for the Warrens' Christmas party. He was a lanky black fellow, a little shy around the Warren men's boisterous storytelling. Their son, Malcolm, looked like both of them.

Not living under the Warren roof gave Sherry a different perspective about them. She did not seem to notice the distance between Bender and Saphora, inserting herself into the gap between them naturally, as if it were a part of the job description. Or maybe she knew more than she admitted. It could be that her comment about snuggling up next to Bender was her way of trying to salvage what had been dead for many years. Sherry was an expert enabler, of that she was certain.

A pinging sound caught Saphora's attention. She thought it was the clanging of a bait pail down on the river. She finished the first quarter sandwich, dripping with yellow yolk. The sound continued and was too curious to ignore. She got up and leaned over the balcony. It was coming from the next-door neighbor's yard again—that shoveling sound. It had to be the man she had met this afternoon. Luke, wasn't it?

Eddie and Tobias were two windows down. If she called out to Luke they would stir and possibly come running down the hall, excited by late-night commotion. She sat back in her chair and started another quarter of the sandwich.

Whatever Luke was doing, he certainly waited late to start. The rain had softened the ground, which could be why he decided to plant so late. Maybe he was like Captain Bart, planting beans by moonlight.

She lost interest in the sandwich. The egg had gotten cold. She got up and went inside, where she pulled on dry cotton socks. The next thing she knew she was tying on her running shoes and slipping down the hall. Sherry's light was off, and the boys had fallen so quiet that they were either sleeping or feigning sleep.

She crept down the staircase and across the floor to the kitchen. Sherry had locked up the house. Saphora unlatched the french door and felt a breeze licking her bare calves as she walked into the night air.

The dampness left in the air smelled like air-dried laundry. Not even the mosquitoes had ventured out yet following the storm. The

moon was bright as daylight, so she could see to walk around the boys'
bicycles and soccer ball. The tree limbs dripped rain onto her scalp as
she inched toward the gate at the side of the house. A bullfrog made
the only definable sound besides the tailwinds tangling in the trees.

Near the gate Luke's shoveling was without question. Even a faint
male groan was discernible as he pushed the tip of the shovel into the
newly dampened ground. She tried the latch on the gate. It was
rusted and resisted the pressure she put on it. Finally it squeaked and
opened, clanking free.

The sound of shoveling stopped.

She did not open the gate immediately. Now she was feeling like
a kid trying to see into the neighbor's business. She had just about
decided to turn and run back across her lawn when the gate opened
slowly but wide, Luke standing in the middle. Saphora gasped.

"I thought I heard something," said Luke.

"I feel like an idiot," she said. "I heard a noise, then the next
thing I know, here I am sneaking into your yard."

"I've wondered if this gate was ever opened."

"Since I know it's you, I won't disturb you," she said.

"You're not disturbing me," he said. He clearly held a shovel in
his hand.

"I've heard of planting by moonlight," she said. "The ground
should be nice and soft."

"It's not as easy as it looks," he said.

"So you are a gardener," she said.

"I'm sorry if I was bothering you. I work all day in my studio
making pottery. I don't have time to do much else unless I do it at
night," he said.

"You're an artist. You should show me your pottery sometime. I collect pieces." By that, she meant she had bought two pieces with the intent to begin collecting. But her idea had fallen by the wayside. "Who knows but what I've bought your work," said Saphora.

"I'll show you," he said, "sometime."

It was evident to Saphora that Luke was not inviting her over at this late hour. She apologized again for disturbing him. "I'll see you then," she said. She closed up the gate and locked it shut.

She was under Eddie's tree house when the sound of shoveling started up again. The moon was full. It had to be beans he was planting.

❧

When Saphora woke up, the smell of pancakes was already coming up the stairs. Sherry had an odd sense about her, always a step ahead of Saphora. Saphora slipped into a pair of shorts and a tank top and headed downstairs.

Eddie sat next to his grandfather, eating pancakes and laughing at Tobias. "Morning, Nana," said Eddie. "Tobias is trying to make me believe pirates are in the neighborhood."

"It's fun to believe," said Saphora. "I need coffee. Sherry?"

Sherry pointed to the empty cup next to the coffeepot. "You were up late."

"I couldn't sleep."

"You saw him, didn't you, Mrs. W?" asked Tobias.

"Who, Tobias?"

"The next-door pirate," said Tobias.

"Is there more syrup, Sherry?" asked Bender. "I heard you up last night too, Saphora."

"I took a walk," said Saphora.

"You met the pirate," said Tobias. "You talked to him through the fence."

"Luke's not a pirate," said Saphora. "Is this a game?"

"He digs every night," said Tobias. "For treasure."

"Luke's a gardener. Some people believe if you plant by moonlight, your plants will grow better," said Saphora.

"Who's Luke?" asked Bender.

"The next-door neighbor," said Eddie.

"If he gardens by moonlight, wouldn't that be odd?" asked Bender.

"I can see him from the end window," said Tobias. "He's not planting. Just digging."

"You don't know," said Eddie. "Nana, he doesn't know."

Saphora had not been able to see Luke from her window. The tree blocked her view. "You can see Luke from Eddie's window?" Of course, Eddie's room was on Luke's side of the house directly over the library, where Bender slept.

"Every night I've stayed over. He digs with a shovel. I can see him come out of his house and then he digs in the far corner. I watch him plain as day," said Tobias.

"You think he's digging for treasure?" asked Bender.

"He's planting beans," said Saphora. "And he's a nice person. Not strange."

Sherry brought warmed syrup to the table. "My grandmother used to plant by the moon's phases. I didn't think that meant she had to actually garden at night."

"Captain Bart gardens by moonlight," said Saphora.

"He's a very strange man," said Bender. He pushed away from the table. "He once told me he practiced nude gardening."

"How do you know Captain Bart?" asked Saphora.

"I've sailed from here, Saphora. You know that," said Bender.

Eddie and Tobias laughed. Eddie spit milk back into his glass. He repeated, "Nude gardening," and then Tobias echoed it. Eddie was laughing in spasms, snorting and sucking milk in and out of the glass.

"Your grandpa's making that up," said Saphora. Captain Bart was not the type.

"Time for your meds, Dr. Warren," said Sherry.

"I'll take them in the library," said Bender.

Saphora got up to offer help.

"I can manage it," said Bender. He filled a glass with water and excused himself to his forced asylum.

Saphora froze, her offer dismissed and she feeling objectified.

Sherry stood between Saphora and the library, a pained look on her face. "I'm sorry," she mouthed, noticing how hard Saphora genuinely tried to help him.

Saphora was quick to bring attention back to the boys. "I'm offering two extra seats on the riverbank for a front row to fish," said Saphora.

"We're playing video games," said Eddie.

"I'd rather fish," said Tobias. He got out of his chair and took his half-eaten pancake to Sherry. "That's all I can eat," he said.

"You eat like a little bird," Sherry told him.

"I need to call my mom. Maybe she'll let me stay if you mean we'll fish," Tobias said to Saphora.

Eddie was disappointed.

"You can play video games anytime, Eddie," said Saphora.

He showed his exasperation by shoving his ball cap back onto his head. "I'll fish. It's boring, but I'll fish," he said. Tobias was not going to be a boy Eddie could rule over.

"Don't forget to be back in two hours, Tobias. I promised your mother you'd not miss your next dose of meds," said Sherry.

Saphora let the boys set up the lawn chairs on the shoreline, spacing them for optimum room. She didn't want one of them snagging her or each other on a hook.

She didn't bother putting on her waders or boots. The river was running too fast for wading. She gave each boy a rod and reel and a packet of bobbers. "Eddie, you show Tobias how to tie on his lure." She walked farther up the bank and tied a trout fly onto her string. The river was brown and murky after the rain. She made two casts, finally hitting the hole she had spotted. A flicker on the line, and she balanced her feet on the bank. The end of her rod quivered and then a tail was in the air.

Eddie was shrieking and running up the bank toward her.

"Don't distract me!" she said, laughing. She and Marcy had made a couple of trips along the mountain streams in the past two spring seasons with not a single bite from the trout. Those fruitless trips must have increased her odds for this fast strike.

She wound the reel softly. She had always felt the feminine touch was the best strategy for waiting out a big rainbow. The trout was pretty and green, no doubt camouflaged for a season under the dark green river water. He fought her every time she pulled him a little closer to the bank.

It took a half hour of patience. Three men down the shoreline came up to watch, a hunting dog lapping alongside them. As she pulled the pretty boy out of the water, Eddie scooped it into the net. He was shouting so loudly he set the dog to barking.

"We need another one this size," said Saphora. "Go and catch one for Nana, Eddie." The fish was at least two pounds. She reached into the fish's mouth and slowly pulled out the bright gold hook.

Eddie dropped the trout into Saphora's basket. He skidded back down the bank, although he did not look quite as confident. He had never reeled in a keeper. He swore there was a fish the size of his leg that hid down in the marsh grass. He talked about it so much that Bender had named Eddie's mythical fish Big Indifferent.

Tobias did not follow along after Eddie. He wanted another look at Saphora's trout. She opened the basket, keeping watch for the species' tendency to try to beat its way loose again.

"You're not a girlie girl, are you, Mrs. W?" asked Tobias.

"If by that you mean I'm a manly girl, not exactly true. I'm closer to girlie, Tobias. I buy too many shoes just like the other girls."

"My mom would never reach in a fish's mouth and take out a hook."

"It's cruel to leave it in."

"She wouldn't want to hurt it, so maybe you could tell her. Could you show my mom how to fish?" he asked.

"Is that so she'll take you?"

"If you'd show her."

"I'm glad to, Tobias, if she's interested."

Tobias's mother had not been by often, what with him riding his bike down to the house. "Maybe she would come over for dinner," said Saphora.

Tobias was clicking the handle of his rod, releasing his lure into the water and then bringing it back up. "She's picking me up today anyway."

Saphora brought her line out of the water. "Tobias, I've never asked you about your illness. That would be nosy. But I don't want you to think it's because I don't care."

"Can you call her when we get back?" he asked.

"Maybe your mom and dad would like to help us eat this fish tonight," she said.

"It's just her. Daddy's gone back to Wilmington. For work, he says."

"Then you'd better catch us some more fish."

Tobias returned to the spot just a few yards from Eddie. His thin frame made his eyes look exotic. He was thin, yes, but she would not have thought him sickly.

Tobias cast his line awkwardly into the water. Then she came alongside him to show him how to reel and then recast. "If you don't want to talk about your sickness, Tobias, I won't ask," she said.

Tobias looked down where Eddie was dropping his line. "Do you care if I play with him?"

"Of course not. Whoever would say such a thing?"

"Thanks, Mrs. W. I'm careful not to make anyone else around me sick. I don't know how I got born with what I have. But it makes some people mad."

"Ridiculous! Look, your bobber just went under. Reel, Tobias!"

8

While I know myself as a creation of God, I
am also obligated to realize and remember
that everyone else and everything else are also
God's creation.

MAYA ANGELOU, *Wouldn't Take Nothing
for My Journey Now*

Tobias was giddy all afternoon waiting for his mother to show up.
His father was semiretired in Wilmington, working in computer software, and had gone home, leaving Jamie and Tobias to stay at their
beachside cottage. Eddie was relieved as he subsisted lonely and without cousins until Friday.

Jamie sat beside Saphora out on the lower deck. The radio was
blaring since the boys had turned it up loud. Saphora was about to
turn it off when Jamie told her, "Wait. That's my favorite song."

Saphora turned it down but not off. "I know this song."

"Joni Mitchell. She was amazing," said Jamie.

Saphora was trying to recall another of that singer's songs when
Sherry came out and announced, "We have Bass à la Tobias and
Trout Saphora. Plus a lasagna if you don't like fish."

"I still can't believe Toby caught a fish," said Jamie.

"He reeled him in with hardly any help," said Saphora.

Eddie was melancholy about Tobias's conquest since he still

had never brought in a fish. So Saphora said, "Eddie will catch the next one."

Bender came out, dutifully carrying a casserole dish. "Stay around too long and Sherry puts you to work." His hair was growing out since the surgery, and he had long ago ditched the ball cap. His smile had returned too, especially in the presence of women.

Jamie kept worrying over Tobias staying up in the tree with Eddie. "I hope he doesn't stay over too much, wear out his welcome."

"Not at all, Jamie. He keeps Eddie occupied. Eddie's an only child, so it's good to have a friend around to remind him he's not the only fish in the pond," said Saphora.

"Toby's had such stomach problems. Has he complained?" asked Jamie. "I worry about him being exposed to dirt, to dirty water, to other sick people. All I do is worry."

"Hasn't complained to me. We like having him around. Let him be a boy."

"Are you sure?"

"Of course! Do you have any other children?"

"No. We'd intended to, but...we..."

"No need to explain," said Saphora.

"Tobias wasn't really planned."

Saphora raised an eyebrow. "How does that happen?"

"Well, one night we saw a special TV show on adoptions. You know they're out to manipulate your emotions for a worthy cause. Mel's got such a soft spot for needy creatures, that is, as long as I take care of them afterward. He adopted a rescued Pomeranian from the pound. Of course, I'm the dog walker and feeder. The day Mel walked in the door with a skinny boy, though, I nearly died."

"He didn't ask first?"

"Mel called it a temporary situation. His friend had met Tobias when his company sponsored a group of foster kids at a Christmas party. That was when he met Tobias. He was quite taken with Tobias. But the friend's job took him traveling so much that he couldn't seriously consider helping Toby."

"So he called Mel," said Saphora.

"It was love at first sight, at least for me. We kept Toby just for the weekend. It was his birthday. His caseworker said she always tried to place her kids in a temporary home at least on the day of their birthdays."

"Sneaky, isn't she?"

"Very."

"How's the Pomeranian?"

"You'd think he and Toby had grown up together. When Toby's down here with Eddie, Fang sits and stares out the window all day long watching for him."

"Fang?"

"He has this crooked tooth right in front. Mel says it gives him character."

"Tell Tobias he can bring Fang with him to see Eddie."

"I wouldn't do that to you. Fang's getting old. He has to wear a bellyband now for doggie incontinence."

"They'll be putting a bellyband on this old girl one of these days."

"You don't look a day over thirty-five."

"Sherry, give this woman extra helpings," said Saphora.

Sherry called Eddie and Tobias out of the tree house.

"I could use an extra mate or two Saturday, Jamie. Would you and Tobias like to join us sailing?" asked Saphora.

Eddie came running up onto the deck. "Tobias is on the floor of the tree house, Nana. He says he can't get up."

Bender climbed up into the tree house and brought Tobias down.

Tobias talked quietly to Bender, answering his questions. Bender took him inside and laid him on his hospital bed in the library. Tobias was so limp Jamie gasped at the sight of him. He never stopped smiling.

Saphora thought it might have been a habit of his while waiting to get adopted; always make them think you're happy.

Bender had seemingly forgotten about how weak chemo had made him. "Look into my flashlight," he said.

"I've seen lots of those," said Tobias.

Jamie admitted to Saphora, "We've had three scares this year, but he always comes out of it. Tobias is resilient like that." But she was nervous and paced the whole time Bender asked Tobias about his symptoms.

Bender felt around the boy's lymph nodes. Then he asked, "Tobias, have you had an accident? By that, I mean a bathroom accident?"

Tobias looked away, as if embarrassed to answer.

Saphora told Eddie, "Wait outside with Sherry."

Sherry led Eddie out of earshot and then closed the library door behind them.

"Dr. Warren, he's got a doctor he sees on a regular basis," said Jamie. "You don't have to do this."

"I've got a bathroom right here where we guys can go and clean up," said Bender. "Ladies not allowed, right, Tobias?"

Tobias looked happy to know the women were being thrown out of the room. He allowed Bender to help him off the bed. Then he and Bender disappeared into the large bathroom that serviced the library.

Jamie was too surprised to protest. Saphora was surprised too. Bender had not had his nose out of his medical books since Jim had told him cancer was a certainty.

The plumbing in the old house rumbled. The shower was warming up.

"I'm sorry we've disrupted your meal," said Jamie.

"No need to apologize," said Saphora, keeping her voice low and considerate. Jamie had said she was a worrier. Saphora understood worrying and did not want Jamie to feel as if she were a bother. "We know Tobias is sick. He never misses taking his meds. Sherry's up on his medicine schedule as much as Bender's."

"You've got enough on your hands just looking after Dr. Warren," said Jamie.

"Tobias would never have let you or me take him into the bathroom for a shower. Bender's got the doctor's bedside manner, and he's a guy. This couldn't have happened at a better place," said Saphora.

"You can see why I could never take Toby out on a boat."

"Tobias seems like the kind of boy who wouldn't take to your treating him like he's too frail to do anything. You know, he asked me to teach you how to fish today," said Saphora.

"He thinks that he never gets to do what other kids do. But we've had such bad luck just giving him a little independence." Jamie was standing outside the bathroom door now, listening.

"Let's go up and get some of Eddie's clothes for Tobias."

Jamie hesitantly followed Saphora upstairs. Saphora opened a bureau beside the bed where Eddie slept and pulled out several pairs of shorts. "Look through these. I know Tobias is smaller around the waist, but he'll be fine for the night. It'll do him a lot of good allowing him to finish eating that fish he caught and then catching lightning bugs with Eddie."

"You're taking this all in stride," said Jamie.

"I wasn't a perfect mother. But I did learn from my mistakes. Tobias is dying for some normalcy. He wants to be treated the same as Eddie or any other kid without his illness."

"He must have told you about his AIDS then?"

"No, but what does it matter what he's sick with?" Saphora did not show surprise.

"Does Dr. Warren know?"

"He's a doctor. He'll figure it out."

Jamie took a pair of Eddie's khaki shorts and a T-shirt. "I'm glad Toby found you and Eddie on the beach that day, Saphora."

Now that Jamie had brought it up, Saphora thought how serendipitous it was for Tobias to have picked them out of the other families out walking. "I'm glad too," she said, equally glad that she and Jamie were becoming friends.

"It's like angels guided Toby to Eddie," said Jamie.

Lately Saphora had thought the opposite, that fate was playing one mean trick on her after another. She could have used an angel or two driving away that storm. But now that she thought about it, it seemed as if an angel had come upon her that day on Tiny Beach, dressed like a thin, dark-haired boy looking for a friend.

ॐ

Jamie took Tobias back to their cottage. Bender sat quietly on the lower deck rubbing mosquito repellent on his arms and legs. Sherry and Eddie had gone into town for ice cream right after dinner. They took down orders and promised to return with some for Bender and Saphora.

Saphora lit a couple of candles to take outside and then joined Bender. He was holding a cigar to his nose and smelling it, eyes closed.

"You don't smoke," said Saphora.

"Sometimes I do, Saphora. Occasionally after a golf game my buddies and I would hit a martini bar—one that allowed cigars. This is one I've had for a while. I'm just smelling and remembering."

"If you smoke it, I won't tell Jim."

"If I won't clog my arteries with fried fish then there's no point in ruining my lungs with a cigar." He dropped it back into his shirt pocket.

"Tonight, with Tobias, that was incredible how you took over. It could have humiliated him. But you were...amazing, actually."

"I understand what he's going through. We guys have to stick together." He looked out over the dark river. There was nothing to see except the moon behind a cloudy haze. He seemed to disappear into the dark void.

"Bender, look at me," said Saphora.

"I'm looking," he said, calm, like a man thinking over his life. "You're still beautiful after all this time."

She took in the compliment, considering he said it with such earnestness. "I don't think I've ever told you that what you do is important. You give your patients back their lives after they've been through horrible accidents. All those burn victims. You help them find their dignity again." She was fishing around so much that his countenance changed. He was even more attractive when his eyes softened and a slight smile appeared. He made her smile too.

"It means a lot to hear you say it. We don't always say what we should say."

She gave his comment some thought. "I think it's because I feel like a watcher."

"What does that mean?"

"I watch you, but I'm standing outside your world." She didn't know how to explain it. "I don't have access to your world." That didn't come out right either.

"I give you everything I've got, Saphora."

Again, he equated material things with love. "All I've ever wanted is to know you love me."

"Everyone loves you, Saphora. Why don't you know that about yourself?" he asked.

"Is that what you think I'm talking about? Some issue with low self-esteem?" She was careful not to raise her voice. "Everyone loving me isn't the point. This is about you and me."

"You want me to tell you I love you. But there's no end to telling you. You're not easily satisfied, Saphora. You're no picnic."

"Should there be an end to telling someone you love them?"

"I just mean that you seem to need it more than the average person."

"Only because there's such a deficit of hearing it, Bender."

"Now I'm cold-hearted?"

"Bender, I didn't mean to get us off on the things that upset us." She wanted to do whatever it took to get him to stop looking disappointed in her since it would only make her mad at him again.

"I love you. Can you believe that?" he asked.

"Am I enough?"

"That is a silly question."

The slamming of car doors brought Bender up out of his chair. He picked up one of the candles and blew it out and then the other. "I'm going inside to have one scoop of vanilla ice cream. Nothing on the top, no chocolate or cherries. I'm down to that now, Saphora. Not a good sherry or a vodka and no cigar. God or this awful existence finally has me cornered in a dark place where I can't have any of the small luxuries that give me a moment of pleasure. That ought to be punishment enough for the night."

"I'm not punishing you." She could not say anything else to him. She was stuck on the idea of God cornering him.

He went inside.

All she had intended to say was how heroic he was to come to Tobias's rescue. Now here she sat outside, alone and racked with guilt, while Bender joined Eddie for ice cream. She wondered if he was realizing what a treasure he had in Eddie, or his children and daughters-in-law. He still seemed to see them all as an extension of his collections, like trophies. She had failed again at trying to explain the empty ache she had felt for longer than she cared to admit. Cancer had made the ache deeper instead of bringing them back together. If she told this to any of her children or her friends, she would be judged as being petty in the middle of her husband's trauma, when all she was trying to do was recover some of the lost conversations they had missed over the years.

If I could have one wish, she thought, *it would be to experience a whiff of the joy behind Tobias's smile.* It had to be the fact that he had come from a rootless life, whatever that meant in a foster care system, to now being rooted in his adoptive family. Perhaps he was so grateful to be connected to a family that he could forgive his dependence on medicine that kept him among the living.

If she could get beyond the empty feeling of marriage to a man who did not know how to love her, she could grab hold of a little of Tobias's joy. Always the obstacles.

"Nana, come inside for ice cream." Eddie stuck his head out the french door, a rim of chocolate mustache outlining his mouth. "Can you have some or will it make you fat?" he asked, having heard her turn down dessert most of his life.

"I don't care if it makes me fat, Eddie," she said. "Give me chocolate and nuts and cherries, all of it."

She ate the cup of ice cream, lapping up Eddie's silly stories and even tolerating Bender's absorption in a golf game on television. She wouldn't let Sherry clean up the ice cream mess and instead sent her out of the kitchen to read or whatever she wanted to do.

Bender fell asleep on the couch. She turned off the television and covered him with a blanket. Eddie kissed his grandfather so hard that Saphora was surprised he did not stir at all.

"He's taken his medication, Eddie. He'll see you in the morning."

"I love you, Nana," said Eddie.

"I love you too," she said. But it was his sincerity that broke open some of the emotions she had tamped down. "More than I can even tell you." She hugged Eddie until he told her she did not have to get so mushy.

He went upstairs to bed without complaining.

She was not the least bit sleepy, being overwrought with dark chocolate decadence. The moon drew her back outside as if she were an ocean tide.

She could not get Tobias out of her head. He left behind a residue of his delicate self wherever he went. At first she thought it was his dependence on the kindness of strangers that caused those around him to pause and be thankful for their good health. Then it came to her that it was his humility.

Luke was out shoveling again. Of course. There was a full moon.

9

Out of the welter of life, a few people are
selected for us by the accident of temporary
confinement in the same circle.

ANNE MORROW LINDBERGH, *Gift from the Sea*

The artists drawn to Oriental's warm shores had at some point in
years past gotten the idea that tourists needed evidence of the existence of the Oriental dragon, a town myth. So in strategic locations
around town, brightly colored giant dragon eggs sat perched in nests.
The signs placed near the large stones disguised like eggs and painted
in all kinds of mural motifs declared the spots were a natural nesting
ground for the Oriental dragon.

In spite of the brilliant marketing ploy, Oriental attracted more
sailing and yachting aficionados who had chanced upon its busy harbor than tourists lured by its humble publicity campaign. The town
residents liked the fact that Oriental was a best-kept secret. The boat
owners making up the sailing community loved its cozy, welcoming
harbor and the lazy lull of its downtown streets.

In front of each shop or café were bike racks full of bicycles for
people to ride and then leave at the next shop or café they visited. The
town provided the bicycles to encourage the locals and tourists to put
more bikers than drivers on the quiet streets. Saphora walked across
the street to Ida's B and B and borrowed a blue bicycle deciding, for

the time being, not to occupy her thoughts with Bender. The act of pedaling down South to the marina lessened her worries, swapping them for the lightness of soul she felt through the simple act of carrying food home in a backpack. She could disappear into the simple pace of Oriental and pretend she belonged to these gypsy types who lived part of the year sailing navigational routes down the Atlantic coasts, summers on the Gulf.

She came upon a farmer's market under an outdoor tent. A local vendor wearing a straw islander hat manned the rows of folding tables. The tables were ornamented by bins filled with homegrown tomatoes and crookneck squash. He poured a bucket of green beans into a cardboard box. Walking up and down through the aisles, Saphora took in the smallness of the display. It wasn't masses of vegetables like the bulk produce sold in large supermarkets. It was all that this man had grown from his home-based garden to produce this small, potent, natural bounty. He washed a tomato and handed it to her sliced in half. She thanked him and ate it warm. Its strong tang, superior to bland supermarket tomatoes, made her picture her mother, Daisy, bent over a container garden. "I'll take six," she said, and he bagged them.

He set out local honey and she took a jar.

Out front a sidewalk guarded by garden containers paralleled the two-lane downtown road. Beyond that the village harbor serviced fishing boats coming in and out. Captain Bart was greeting customers. Sea gulls serpentined overhead waiting for dropped fish. She asked herself what had taken her so long to come to Oriental.

In the next tent a half block down, two men wearing expensive blue-and-white windbreakers reclined in lawn chairs behind a table filled with fresh fish. When Saphora approached the table, one sat forward, happy to see her.

"What's the fresh catch?" she asked.

"It's all fresh," he said. Grocers back home all claimed the fish was fresh when asked, too. But she trusted the local boys' claim here along the coast. "How's the tilapia today?"

"Almost out of tilapia. We've got salmon just off the boat. Some swordfish and tuna steaks."

Gwennie was coming in tomorrow, catching an early flight. She would want the tuna steak. Sherry shared her tastes. Saphora picked out two tuna steaks for the women and two swordfish steaks for herself and Bender. Eddie would eat corn dogs.

"Do I know you?" he asked.

"My husband, Bender, and I are here for the summer," she said. "We have a house on South."

"The big blue house with the green roof. Is that the one?"

"Yes. But it's my first time here."

"Glad to meet you. I'm Reed Holt and this is my brother Lane." Reed wrapped up the fish and bagged it for her to tuck into her backpack.

"I've heard about a fishing tournament Saturday," she said.

"Yep, the annual tarpon tournament's kicked off by a kids' parade down this street in an hour," said Lane. "A couple of vendors will be frying fish."

She thanked him. She would try and rally Eddie and Tobias. There was time to get the fish home into the refrigerator and pick up the boys. The last thing she needed to get was a couple of onions. The farmer's market had sold out.

She rode the bicycle back up South and swapped it for the Lexus. The grocer's was a little too far for biking on a short schedule. She drove to the grocer's and spotted the yellow onions. She bagged one up and was just about to meander toward the checkout lane when she heard, "I think you must be following me." Pastor John Mims stood grinning and pinching an obviously ripened tomato.

He startled Saphora, but she kept the surprise from her face as much as possible, attempting a normal-looking smile. No use hiding.

"I'm glad I saw you. Did Dr. Warren tell you about tonight?" he asked.

"Not a word," she said. So far she was not lying to Mims. Bender's highly realized sense of self-possession had followed him from Davidson. Cancer had not simplified him but made him more complicated than even their first three decades together.

"The ladies' quilting group is holding a silent auction and bake sale. Bender didn't tell you about it?"

"He wouldn't, Pastor." She would be honest with him. "Bender's not into bake sales and such," she said. Bender was plying the minister with promises he did not intend to keep.

"The doctor said you'd be good for a pie. He didn't tell you?"

"I haven't baked since we hired Sherry. And she cooks to suit Bender. He doesn't eat pie." She couldn't tell whether or not Mims was kidding.

"That's a shame."

"It's nice to see you, Pastor."

Before she could escape, he stopped her again. "Mrs. Warren, you don't have to bring anything. I was just trying to find a way to invite Dr. Warren out of the house. He says he's not been out much since starting his chemo."

"I doubt he'd come. He's already got Sherry cooking dinner for tonight."

"Sure, but if you can make it, it's at six o'clock. There's one silent auction item that's a vacation to the mountains. They expect it to be a hot ticket. But someone like Dr. Warren could give them a run for their money."

"I'll tell him," she said, slipping away from the minister to the checkout lane.

Bernard sat on his stool as he must do for hours on end all day. "Mrs. Warren, I saw you confronting that crooked preacher. Want me to have him arrested?"

"Not today, Bernard," she said. "Next week is jail-the-minister week." She paid and left.

ڽ

When she pulled into the drive, Eddie was spraying Tobias with the garden hose. Tobias ran off the concrete into the grass. He made a big deal of stopping Eddie at the source, clamping a section of the hose in two. Eddie pumped the nozzle twice and, finding it dry, tossed it down, running at Tobias.

"Eddie, come and get the groceries," said Saphora.

Tobias beat him to the car and threw open the back door.

Wanting to keep the two of them from tangling like feral cats, she said, "Both of you grab a bag and then run into the laundry room to dry off. Then I'll take you downtown to a parade."

"I wanted to go swimming," said Eddie.

"The parade!" said Tobias. He had a strange way of agreeing with adults. He carried the produce sack one-handed through the open garage door.

"Is there a pool, Eddie?" asked Saphora.

"The motel pool, Nana. The next-door neighbor said his cousin works there and would let us in," said Eddie.

"When did you meet the neighbor?" she asked.

"This morning. Luke was out cutting grass and messing around."

"Just be sure you ask the owner."

"Luke said he'd vouch for us to his cousin," said Eddie. "He's already called ahead."

Luke seemed reliable enough. "We'll see. Hurry or we'll miss the parade."

By the time she got the two of them on bikes and headed downtown, children were lining up with their wagons and bicycles. Each kid had decorated a bicycle or a wagon with a dragon theme.

Eddie and Tobias found a spot on the curb beneath a shade tree. Saphora left them to watch the children pass while she slipped into a jewelry store. The owner had been hitting estate sales. Saphora found a pair of antique earrings the color of the lake. She bought them and then went back outside, where she found Eddie spitting on the walk.

Eddie had turned his back to the street. "This is dumb," he said. "Swimming's a better idea."

"I shouldn't swim, my mom says, unless she knows," said Tobias.

There was a sadness about him that made Saphora say, "I'll call her if you want to go. Can you swim?"

"Took lessons. I can race," he said.

Bender called. Saphora stepped away to take the call. She was exasperated to hear that he had decided to go to Pastor Mims's silent auction and bake sale. "Did he call you? Because I saw him at the grocery store, and he was really pushy about the whole thing." She was surprised to hear that Mims had not called. Bender had placed the event on his calendar after promising the minister he'd go. He said, "I told Sherry she was off for the night."

"Without asking me?"

"She's been cooking day and night since she got here," he said.

"I like to know is all."

"Now you know."

"Eddie and Tobias want to swim," she said, not at all interested in taking time out of her evening for a church event.

Bender told her she could take them and still have time to come back and join him. "He's a minister, Saphora, who came by to see a complete stranger. He got me thinking about some things."

"What things?"

"Things."

"Whatever."

"I figure I can show my gratitude. It's a small request he's making."

She could not figure out Bender's odd behavior. She sighed and then said, "I'll be back in an hour."

"There's the motel where Luke's cousin works," said Eddie when she turned back toward the boys.

The motel was only two blocks away.

"I see it. Let's head on out then," she said.

Eddie was stuffing his shirt into his backpack. She called Jamie, who was hesitant to let Tobias go. "You can't keep sheltering him," said Saphora, keeping her tone respectful. "Besides, I'll be poolside. Stop worrying."

Eddie raced Tobias to the front parking lot. It was a small resort pool under the management of a riverside mom-and-pop operation.

Eddie and Tobias had put their swimsuits on under their clothes. Eddie had planned on swimming all along.

Tobias stayed on his bike for so long that while Eddie went in to square things with Luke's cousin, Saphora returned for Tobias. "Tobias, did you forget something?"

He sat like a small bird, looking up at her. Finally he slipped off the blue bicycle and popped down the kickstand. He followed her through the marina gate.

Eddie had already made an impression on Luke's cousin, who introduced himself as Wayne. Eddie had never been inclined to negotiating, so Saphora was not only relieved but pleased that she and Tobias were greeted with such enthusiasm.

"Luke called and said you might drop by," said Wayne. "Mrs. Warren, you can sit under that umbrella over there. We have beers and soda pop in the cooler."

Wayne was a very short man, graying around the temples. He wore a beach shirt like tourists wear down in the Keys, and his feet had tanned in the shape of his blue flip-flops.

Several mothers sat around the pool while their children jumped in and out with foam noodles and plastic inflated sea horses.

The shade of the umbrella gave Saphora a respite from the hot afternoon sun while she relaxed.

It seemed that one of the mothers was watching her. She smiled at the woman, thinking they might have met in Lake Norman.

The woman turned away but then got out of her chair. She approached Wayne at the beverage hut. Wayne leaned out of the window; his dark sunglasses hid his eyes.

The woman turned and marched back to her lounge chair without a drink.

It had not been a minute when a shadow appeared next to the umbrella shade. Saphora smiled up at Wayne. "The boys are having a nice swim. I'll have to thank Luke for calling you."

Wayne hemmed and hawed around so much that Saphora thought something awful must have happened. "What's wrong?" she asked. She checked her phone to see if Bender had called.

Wayne knelt next to her chair. He whispered, seemingly embarrassed to speak. "Mrs. Warren, the women across the pool have lodged a complaint. I think they're just nosy. But I have to ask you about the skinny boy you brought to the pool."

"Tobias? Has he caused a problem?" She couldn't imagine it. Tobias had been a dream to be around.

"Is Tobias adopted, by any chance?" he asked.

"I don't see whose business that is," she said.

"One of the women said there was a big stink up at the RV park last month. A couple brought in an adopted child. He had AIDS. When they asked the boy to leave the pool, there was a big scandal. They published the boy's picture on the Internet. That woman thinks she's ID'd Tobias as that boy."

"ID'd? Like you ID a criminal?"

"I don't mean it like that, Mrs. Warren," said Wayne.

"AIDS isn't passed through swimming, Wayne."

"People get nervous, Mrs. Warren. It's dumb, but you know how folks can be."

"This isn't the sixties, Wayne."

"They're paying guests, Mrs. Warren."

"I'm glad to pay you whatever you want."

"Don't make me have to ask you to take the boy out, Mrs. Warren."

By now the two women had come to their feet. A small crowd gathered around them. They each took turns calling their children out of the pool. It was like a scene out of a civil rights movie. Saphora got out of her chair. She stared down the woman who had first reported Tobias.

Eddie was so busy diving for nickels he did not notice that Tobias moved slowly toward the shallow end of the pool, away from the guests staring at him. He stopped Saphora, who was halfway down the pool's patio. "Don't say anything, Mrs. Warren," he asked. "It just gets worse when you do."

"We can't just let this go, Tobias," she said.

"I don't want to get you into trouble, Mrs. Warren." He picked up his towel and left the pool area.

Eddie came up holding two nickels. "I found them!" he yelled. He searched around the pool's ledge. "Where's Tobias?" That's when he saw the group of adults standing and staring at his grandmother. "What happened? Nana, where's Tobias?"

ை

"You should have seen them, Bender! It was like Rosa Parks being asked to give up her seat on the bus," said Saphora.

"Did Tobias refuse to get out of the water?" asked Bender.

"Not at all. He's such a sweet kid. They were all staring at him like he had leprosy. I told him he didn't have to get out of the water. But he did. He came and put his arms around me, as if he had to comfort me." Saphora was still fuming. "He told me, 'I don't want to get you into trouble.' Like he wasn't going to let me take his punishment. They were treating him like a criminal."

"Where is he?"

"After that, he was humiliated. He asked me to drop him by his house. But I couldn't just drop him off. I took him inside and told Jamie what happened. She took it in stride. I was mad as bats and there she sat, serenely taking it all in. She made pizza for Tobias, and they planned to watch a movie. Is this the way it is now? We all just lie down and let people roll over us? What happened to the sixties? What's happened to us, Bender?"

"Are you saying they're teaching Tobias to be passive?"

"I just can't stand this. Don't you think the boy should stand up for himself?"

"He's sick, Saphora. That's a lot of balls in the air already. Now you want him to add activism to his happy little act."

"Who then? Someone's got to do something," she said.

"We're about to be late."

"Oh, hang the church bake sale! Like any of them care what's happening right out their front door."

"It'll do you good to get your mind off Tobias. I'll drive," said Bender.

Sherry sat Eddie down for warmed-up spaghetti. "Bring us back chocolate pie, all right, Dr. Warren?"

"I thought you were off for the night," said Saphora, picking up her purse.

"I'm still in charge of the kitchen, right, Dr. Warren?"

"And I'm not. I got it," he answered.

"Bring us a pie, though," she said.

"Will do," said Bender.

Saphora lacked the resolve to sweep the incident out of her thoughts. She fumed all the way to the church.

Standing at the church door with an irritating grin on his face, Pastor John handed a silent auction bid ticket to Bender. Saphora hardly looked at him. She could not get the picture out of her head of Tobias climbing out of the pool as if he had broken the law. He had not shed a single tear.

Several tables displayed baked goods along the outside walk, luring the hungry and the curious, filling the church gym with people who wandered in from downtown. Bender immediately slapped down a ten to hold a chocolate meringue pie.

He moved table to table, picking up objects like handmade

pottery and home-canned salsa. It amused Saphora to see him taking an interest in a conventional community project. He took out his pen, the one he used to write out prescriptions and keep his golf score. He bid on a dinner and two symphony tickets and then the vacation package to the mountains.

Saphora said, "What's gotten into you?"

"It's all in fun, Saphora." He picked up a quilt and examined the fabric and stitching.

"But this is something only enslaved husbands do. This isn't a Bender Warren activity. You're the man who makes fun of men who are dragged into church by their wives."

"This isn't church, actually."

"But it's prosaic. You run from prosaic."

"The incident with Tobias has soured you, Saphora. Take a breath. Look around you."

"What is this, some new enlightenment that comes with brain cancer?"

"Maybe. A man can change."

She felt as if someone had slipped into the house, pulled out the old Bender, and slid a new man into the old Bender suit.

Two tables away she was almost certain she saw one of the women who had shunned Tobias at the pool. But then she wasn't sure. The woman looked too agreeable. Saphora said, "If you're going to win the mountain trip, you'll have to ante up another twenty. Make it more than an incremental difference. Run off the wannabes." She took his pen and increased his bid by twenty dollars.

"That's the spirit! Now let's go and wait to see if anyone is watching. You know the competition's just waiting for us to walk away," he said.

"That's why you up it so much. Two dollars will only tempt them to keep trying." She had organized enough silent auctions to know the ropes of winning a bid.

Bender returned to the symphony tickets. "See, ten people have filled in bids behind mine. We've got to think of a new strategy." He found Pastor John in a corner eating a cookie. "John, what time does this thing end?"

"In an hour," said Pastor John. "Oh, I see what you're up to. You want to slide in at the last minute and win your prize. What is it you're trying to win?"

"The mountain trip and the symphony tickets," said Bender.

"You're up against the Flanigans. They're financially solvent. Michael Flanigan owns half the shrimp boats out in the harbor. They'll be hard to beat," said Pastor John.

"I hate to lose," said Bender. "Any suggestions?"

"Act as if you don't care what you win. Hover around other bids. Place a few more bids at the other tables so as to throw the Flanigans off." John pointed them out casually so as not to draw attention.

"We can beat them, Bender," said Saphora. "They're amateurs."

"I smell blood," said Pastor John.

"Is this addictive?" asked Bender.

"Not sinful, like bingo," said the minister.

"Saphora, you go to that table, the one with the quilts. I'll go to the opposite side of the room and act interested in the pottery," said Bender.

"I'm interested in the pottery," she said, thinking it might be Luke's work. But Saphora strolled over to the quilts, making a great show of selecting one. It was blue and white and expertly stitched. It would add some color to the plain master suite. Just as she had penciled in the bid, the Flanigan woman stood right beside her looking over the bid list.

Pastor John nodded in such a knowing way that Saphora was beginning to feel overcome with confidence. She also felt ashamed of herself for having judged Pastor John. She had not seen Bender enjoying himself this much in so long that the auction was worth the time spent in foolishness. She placed another bid and then casually joined Pastor John at the cookie table. "You've done a good thing, Pastor," she said. "I've never known a single minister who could make an impression on Bender. It's like watching a miracle."

"You never know what God is up to. I thought that the afternoon you fingered me for stealing oysters."

"I'm an idiot sometimes."

"Don't ever say that, Mrs. Warren."

He was exactly the opposite of the man she had judged in the grocery store. "Look, there goes that Flanigan fellow upping Bender's bid," she said.

"Honestly, Mrs. Warren, I hated to tell your husband, but I've never seen Flanigan lose."

There was so much she could have said about Bender. But the minister's curious opinion of him was too much of a novelty. At the close of the auction, Bender would have everything he had set out to get.

As Saphora went out to the bake sale table to pay the balance for Sherry's pie, a bell sounded from inside. Pastor John's secretary was calling the auction to a close.

Saphora worked fast. She picked up some canned beans and bought a potholder. After all, it was for a good cause. When she went inside she could not find Bender.

Pastor John spoke into a microphone attached to a squeaking public address system. He called out the auction items one after another,
a woman handing him slips of paper as fast as he could read them off.
Finally, he came to auction item number twenty-two. Saphora looked
up, spotting Bender. He was talking with, of all people, Michael
Flanigan. Knowing him, though, it was only another strategy.

Pastor John announced, "The winner of an evening of dinner
and a symphony goes to…Michael Flanigan!" The couples packed
into the church hall erupted, applauding. Everyone in town knew
him. Saphora knew Bender had given that to him to appease him.

Finally John called out the number that most people had been
waiting to hear. "Number fifty-eight. A mountain vacation at the
Chetola Resort."

The room fell quiet. It irritated Saphora that Bender was still in
the back of the room quietly conversing with Flanigan.

Pastor John's microphone screeched. Then he exclaimed,
"Michael Flanigan again! Michael, you won the mountain vacation!"
Pastor John held out the prize to Flanigan.

Bender shook Flanigan's hand and gave him a pat on the back.
He walked him up to the front of the room to claim the prize.

John announced, "Saphora Warren has won item seventy-three,
the blue wedding ring quilt!"

Saphora waved her ticket in the air while everyone applauded.
She returned to the registration table to pay for her bid and pick up
the quilt. She checked the ledger. There was the final bid in Bender's
handwriting.

The remaining items were announced, and the attendees started
moving toward the front door while the women's committee members began breaking down the booths.

Bender thanked Pastor John for the invitation. Saphora headed out the door, put out with Bender for losing all of his bids.

On the way home, Saphora pulled out the quilt she had won. "I wasn't about to let that Flanigan woman win. Obviously you weren't either."

Bender stared placidly ahead.

"Are you upset at all?" she asked.

"The church needed the money. I didn't really want to win. I was just upping the money to keep Flanigan bidding. He can afford it."

"I don't believe you."

"I know."

She looked at a small package between them. She picked up the familiar-looking box and then opened it. "These are the symphony tickets and dinner out."

"I bought them off Flanigan. He didn't need them, and I told him you'd like to go when we got back home."

"You bought them for me?"

"Unless you'd rather not go."

"No, I'll go. It's just a surprise, that's all."

Bender kept smiling. *It could be a ploy,* she thought. He had never done anything without an ulterior motive. "Thank you," she said.

It was quiet between them on the drive back. But not unpleasantly quiet.

10

Normal day, let me be aware of the treasure
you are.... Let me not pass you by in quest
of some rare and perfect tomorrow.

MARY JEAN IRION

Bender took his meds and went to bed.

Saphora pulled the old comforter off her bed and replaced it with
the wedding ring quilt. The majority of the fabric was some shade of
blue, except for the oyster white rings. She replaced the pillowcases
with blue cotton covers and tossed the old throw pillows on a closet
shelf. There were some blue pillows left up on the shelf. She arranged
them on the bed. The room looked like a different place.

The empty area over the headboard needed some framed art. She
would look around the downtown shops for something nautical, like
what hung over the Sailing School's fireplace.

She slipped into a pair of yoga pants for sleeping and a T-shirt.
She pulled back the linens and was getting ready to turn on the TV
to find a late-night movie. But the moon outside seemed to be telling
her that TV was such a spoiler when the river was running past. She
opened the balcony door. The wind sent the tree leaves into faint,
shuddering spasms. She opened the door wider and sat on the edge
of the bed to hear the night sounds. And yet the frogs were quiet. The
silence created a tension in the air that made Saphora pause.

Sherry had left chai tea on her nightstand. She poured a cup and then took it out onto the balcony to drink. Some women sipped, but Saphora always drank deeply, so much so that her cup was quickly empty.

She walked to the balcony's edge. Finally, the sound of the river was in its place and there was a small frog chorus down along the banks.

Luke puttered around his backyard. She could see his flashlight beam gyrating above the fence. No surprise that it sounded like he was digging again. She put down the cup, listening until she decided that curiosity was enough reason to put on her leather flats. Before she could question how shallow she was to spy on Luke, she was tip-toeing downstairs and then outside, standing at the gate. Through a crack in the gate, she could see a shop light illuminating the spot where he worked.

That was when Bender's light came on in the library. If he looked out and saw her, he might ask for an explanation. There was no single explanation for what she was doing snooping around the neighbor's fence. She pushed up on the lock. The gate opened and she walked through. She found a place to squat and hide behind a bush.

Luke stood over a hole, wearing a knit cap, perhaps to keep the hair out of his eyes. However, the warm night air did not warrant a winter cap. He looked very nearly grim in the light of the lantern. He had clamped a metal light onto his back fence, and an oil lantern hung on a kind of hook like the ones used for hanging hummingbird feeders.

He took off his eyeglasses and cleaned them with his shirttail. Plaid suited him.

Saphora moved slowly toward him without coming out of the

shadow of the trees. She stayed hidden behind a large photinia. There was a faint smell of magnolias. Tourists tended to bring them to plant and make their seaside home like their mountain home.

Luke might have cooked out on a grill for his dinner as there was also a faint cloud of burnt charcoal and lighter fluid.

He shoved the tip of the shovel into the hole. It went down at least a foot. He was digging a serious hole, possibly for a tree, Saphora decided. She looked back at her house. Bender's light had gone out. Eddie was still up. The light through his window on the side of the house shed a dim yellow cast across his blinds, probably the lamp left on while he conquered a video monster.

She moved in for a closer look. That's when she startled Luke's cat. The animal bolted out of the shrub, hissing like cats do when their privacy has been invaded.

Luke came up from looking into the hole. When his cat tore past him, he scolded her and then returned to digging. Then he stopped and jerked the flashlight up and aimed it within a foot of where Saphora crouched.

Saphora didn't know what he was looking around to see. The light was so bright that when it fell across the photinia, Saphora thought he had spotted her. But he was too intent on returning to his hole. There was no tree nearby or any sort of plant with a root ball that might fit into such a large hole.

Luke looked down into the hole. Then he took the tip of the spade and tapped all around inside the hole, a strange ritual. "You can either stand there all night or come and help," he said.

Saphora looked beyond his digging place to see who Luke might be addressing.

"Mrs. Warren, is that you?"

She came out of the dark and said apologetically, "It's me. Did I scare you?"

"Just Johnson."

"Johnson?"

"My cat."

"I can help, if you need it," she said, nervous and embarrassed that she looked nosy rather than helpful.

He picked out a second shovel from a utility cart and gave it to her.

When she took her place on the other side of the hole, he said, "If you don't mind, there's another hole I need about two feet back from where you're standing."

Saphora stepped off the distance; but after marrying Bender she had decided to never agree to anything without full disclosure. "Are we planting something?"

"Just let me know if you find anything."

The ground had been saturated. She saw the water hose running the length of the fence. The sandy soil was soft, so she got at least a half shovelful out of the first try. She dug until she heard a sharp clink against the tip of her shovel. The sound did not escape Luke's attention. He came alongside her and helped dig. As she lifted out shovelfuls and dropped them alongside the fence, he got down on his knees and grubbed out the sifting soil around her spade.

Finally she pushed downward on the top of the spade with her toe and lifted, but the shovel resisted. "I've hit something. Don't know what," she said.

Luke ran and got a small hand spade. He dug around the object until he could get his fingers around it. "You've brought me luck, Mrs. Warren."

"The suspense is killing me," she said. She had never had any luck with any games of chance or the state lottery. She dropped the shovel and fell alongside him. She paused, looking at her nails. So much for the manicure! She dug her nails into the soil.

Luke pulled on the object. She dug around it, loosening it while he yanked. After a dozen hard tugs, he pulled it out of the ground.

"Whatever it is, it's coated in mud," said Saphora.

Luke turned on the hose and blasted the object. Then he held it up as Saphora aimed the flashlight at it. "It's an old roller skate," he said.

"Is that important?" she asked.

He tossed it aside. "Not to me." He was so let down that he extinguished the lantern and then sat on a bench at the edge of his garden.

"If I knew what it was I was looking for, I could be of better service." When he did not answer, she said, "You know treasure hunters use Geiger machines or something, don't they? Have you thought of using better equipment?"

"It's getting late. I don't want your husband worrying, Mrs. Warren."

"He's practically comatose on his cancer drugs, Luke."

"Cancer? How long has Dr. Warren known?"

"Longer than me. A month. I don't know for sure."

"He kept it a secret?"

"Until the day of my *Southern Living* party. He figured he couldn't go it alone after that."

"Why do they do that?" He talked under the full light of the moon. He picked dirt from under his nails, saying, "They don't want to worry you. It's like they want to be strong, protect you from the pain as long as possible." He sounded glum, as if all of the sadness flooded the land from the river to the spot where he sat, pouring into the hole of his life.

"Don't they know it's worse to not share the news?" she said.

"That's it. But you shouldn't feel guilty, Mrs. Warren. I carried enough guilt for me, Mabel, and the whole Weston clan."

"Was that her family?"

"Mabel Birch from Jackson, Mississippi. My family is the Westons. I never would have thought I'd marry a cheerleader."

"Why not?"

"I had my nose in a book since age four. Won the Virginia state science fair in the seventh grade."

"Class nerd."

"Thanks, Mrs. Warren."

"I'm fond of nerds. My daughter, Gwennie, was like that. Always scholastically driven. She made cheerleader just to prove she could do it, but then turned them down flat."

"Mabel was head cheerleader."

"Gwennie would have taken over, that's for sure."

"Mabel always had a cause. We rented this house year after year. We called it our summer place even though it was a rental. But I was too stubborn to buy it for her. She wanted it so she could volunteer to baby-sit turtle eggs or keep watch for rare birds. She would have taken Tobias right into our house. That's how I got Johnson."

"So you know about Tobias?"

"My cousin's an idiot."

Saphora did not know how to answer.

"Is he all right?" he asked.

"You know kids. They act all right for our sake."

"Wayne's a gutsy kind of guy. Catches those big fish, marlin, tarpon. Caught a kingfish once, hours on end he sat in that hot Atlantic sun reeling and fighting the fish until he pulled it on board. But he wouldn't know anything about what a kid like Tobias goes through. He was just taking care of business. That's Wayne for you."

Saphora couldn't share Luke's sympathy for Wayne. "I should get back."

"You tell Tobias to hang in, all that."

"I'm sorry I couldn't be more helpful." She got up.

"Mrs. Warren, you're a great lady." He came to his feet. He bent to kiss her.

It was only a cheek peck. Still, it left her flushed from the chest up. "I've got to go," she said. She nearly tripped getting through the gate.

She had trouble opening the french door because her fingers were caked with mud. Finally, she gripped the knob two-handedly and pushed the door open with her hip. Electronic sounds of fighter knights and raging dragons filtered downstairs from Eddie's room. He needed to turn that love of adventure toward a good book every now and then. But Turner was so overwhelmed working long hours just to pay day-care costs he never thought to sit Eddie down before bed to read to him.

"I thought I was dreaming." Bender's voice startled Saphora.

"Bender, you're up."

He lay stretched out on the sofa. "I wake up most every night. The same drug that puts me to sleep startles me awake. I hate nights because of it. I heard a noise. I turned off my light to see outside. You were going through the neighbor's gate."

"It's only Luke."

"Oh. What's on your hands?"

"Helping him dig a hole." She put her hands behind her, even though she had nothing to hide.

"Lunar gardening, I guess," he said.

"I don't know much about him. I'm sure he's affected by his wife's death. Why do you look so strange?" By that she meant it was as if he were looking at her for the first time.

"I'm admiring my wife. Is that all right?"

She was still flush from digging.

"Jim says I should watch so I don't get eaten up with regret. Seize every minute, he says. Try to make your wishes come true."

"Like what?"

"Every cancer patient makes a wish. I wish I'd done more for you."

"You're tired."

"If I had, instead of you traipsing through the neighbor's fence for companionship, you'd have come to me."

His epiphany should have made her feel flattered or justified. But he was only annoying her. "Luke's not my outlet for companionship, Bender."

There was a silence during which neither Saphora nor Bender engaged for about a minute. It was exactly the kind of minute that married people usually used to gather up ammunition so they could lob words like Eddie's knight hurled magic goo at the dragon. But Saphora only wished for something between them besides tension.

She moved closer to get a better look at him. He had used the walker, obviously. It was beside the couch. His head lay against the sofa pillow. His eyes closed, like one of his animals shot down in the Serengeti. Saphora helped him settle more comfortably. "Let me help you." She took him by the shoulders and helped position him into a reclining position, his head falling into the sofa cushion. She covered him with the afghan. He was snoring so fast she thought he was kidding around. It was an attractive quality; it made him like everyone else.

෨෨

The only way she could fall asleep was to bend their rule and take a sleeping pill. Sherry was right down the hall anyway. So she did and slipped away into that deep nonawareness that comes with prescription sleep aids.

The next morning Sherry had to wake her and bring her strong coffee.

Saphora did not bother to change out of what she had slept in before coming downstairs. She found Eddie at work on a bowl of oatmeal. Sherry was coaxing him. "Throw raspberries into it," she said, "for vitamins."

Saphora poured her own juice and sat across from Eddie. She could see the top of Luke's fence beyond the tree house. Whether or not he had returned to digging holes, she didn't know. Bender's words and the fact that he was sitting and waiting for her to return from Luke's place made her feel as if she had betrayed her husband. Even if that was not exactly it, Bender had stirred up a mixture of emotions that deflated her.

"Where's Dr. Warren?" she asked Sherry.

"I'll see about him," said Sherry. She had not been gone a half minute when she came out, wide-eyed. "Miss Saphora, you'd best come."

In the seconds it took her to cross the kitchen into the library, she could only think of how Bender was so close to opening up to her the night before and how she could have responded differently. But she had lived most of her married life between guilt and regret. When she followed Sherry into the room, she found Bender sitting on the side of the hospital bed. He looked frail. His arms were thinner since beginning the chemo. He buried his face in his hands. On his pillow lay all of his blond curls, downy as if a goose had nested there overnight.

Sherry told him, "I'll take care of all that, Dr. Warren. I'll put it all in a bag and get you a clean pillowcase." She was trying not to cry, but her voice broke. "I'm sorry, Miss Saphora. I'll pull myself together."

While Sherry went for cleanup materials, Saphora stood stunned at the sight of Bender without hair. She tried to comfort him. "We knew this was coming. You know bald heads are back," she said. "All of the young men shave their heads now."

"It's all right," he said. "You don't have to think of the right things to say." He had lost every bit of his hair. His eyebrows, even his lashes lay like kitten hairs on the pillow.

She offered him coffee.

"Just hot tea is all," he said.

She went into the kitchen, where Sherry rummaged through a drawer for a plastic bag. She was wiping her eyes over finding Dr. Warren in such a state. "This is so sad, Miss Saphora. I can't believe this is happening."

"We can't do him any good falling apart," said Saphora. She took the kettle off the burner and poured hot water into the teapot he had brought home one winter from Austria. It was the color of the Austrian sky, he had told Saphora. Now it was the color of her mood.

"It's just so hard to watch him lose a little more of himself every day."

"You gather up his hair, and I'll bring him his tea."

Saphora was about to break open, and Sherry must have realized it. She grabbed on to Saphora, and the two of them stood there with Dr. Warren's tea brewing while they held on to one another. There was no script for what to do next.

"What do I do with his hair?" asked Sherry.

"Take it out to the trash bin in back of the house so he'll forget about it."

"You think he'll forget about it?"

"Just get it out of his sight."

Sherry drew back her shoulders like she was about to go in and clobber Dr. Warren's cancer. She walked into the room, holding out the plastic bag and not showing that she had been crying.

Eddie came up behind his grandmother. He wrapped his arms around her and said, "Sherry was crying, Nana. I saw her. Is it Papa? Is he dying?"

"Eddie, don't think like that."

"Can I go in to see him?"

"Good idea. Get the breakfast tray and put some of those berries on a plate. Maybe he'll eat for you," she said. A minute later she pulled the bags from the tea and put the pot on the tray Eddie had found.

Eddie led the way, Sherry opening the door for him. "Papa, eat," said Eddie. When he saw his grandpa's slick head, he glanced down at the floor but kept walking toward him, carrying breakfast.

"Eddie's brought you fruit, Bender. What do you say?" asked Saphora.

"I'll try, Eddie."

Sherry cleared away the lost hair from his pillow. Saphora replaced the pillowcase while Eddie wobbled around like a little Pinocchio, balancing the breakfast tray on the end table.

"What do you think about Papa's new hairstyle?" asked Bender.

"Very cool," said Eddie, barely above a whisper.

Saphora watched Eddie, his forced smile, the way he stood awkwardly in front of Bender. She had seen Turner stand in a similar manner. He could put on such a show for his friends, but in front of Bender he quietly stood as if under an obligatory spell, awaiting his father's dispensation. Bender did not dole out compliments regularly.

"Dr. Warren, you want something else?" asked Sherry. "A sandwich? Or I could make a breakfast pizza."

Bender's hand trembled as he lifted the spoon to his mouth. "I didn't hold down the last pizza," he said. "Better feed me like you would a helpless baby." He dropped the berries back into the dish.

Self-pity did not look good on him. It took only a glance from him for Saphora to realize that he wanted Eddie taken out of the room before he broke down.

"Eddie, I think you should go into the tree house and straighten it up," she said. "Tobias could visit and it's a mess."

Eddie walked out quickly and Sherry followed.

Saphora said to Bender, "Gwennie's coming today. You should try and shower, put forth your best foot, all that." She felt her lip quivering, so she bit it until it nearly bled.

"Today's Friday? How did I lose a day?" He lay back onto his pillow. The rims of his eyes were outlined in the color of Eddie's raspberries. "I don't want Gwennie seeing me helpless. It'll kill her. Help me into the shower, Saphora."

"I'll get the water ready. You come along on the walker. It's good practice," she said.

She got the water misting up the stall like a steam room. Bender made it as far as the door, but then he stopped as if his soul hovered between the ceiling and the floor. Saphora helped him to the shower. "It can't help your equilibrium to lie down all day. Try and stay up," she said.

"I feel weak. Good Lord, am I dying already?"

"Dizziness is just a symptom of, you know, drugs and all." She was grasping for an explanation. He shouldn't see her afraid. "Here's what I'll do." She helped him undress as she said, "I'll help you clean up." She pulled off his shirt.

"That's the best news I've had all day." He hobbled into the shower.

"You hold on while I scrub," she said.

He let her take over. Then he smiled and looked younger doing it. "Here I look like an old man and you're as youthful as the day I married you," he said.

He had not told her she looked young in so long he surprised the wits out of her. She joined a gym years ago, but he never said he noticed when she firmed up or, busy with running after the kids, had to let herself go.

She poured soap into a loofah. "This is rough. Maybe too rough. If your skin is too sensitive, I can use something else."

His skin did look thin, like the skin of a premature baby. Saphora half expected to see his heart beating through his chest. He used both hands to brace himself against the tile. "It's fine." Then came the tears, coming over the rim of his emotions like a waterfall. Bender had not been a man to cry, so it was painful to see him letting go. But strangely comforting, as if he were turning into a mortal in plain sight of her. Maybe the Bender of the Serengeti was never a real person after all.

11

And what guarantee have we that the future
will be any better if we neglect the present?
Can one solve world problems when one is
unable to solve one's own? Where have we
arrived in this process? Have we been success-
ful, working at the periphery of the circle and
not at the center?

ANNE MORROW LINDBERGH, *Gift from the Sea*

The last thing Gwennie told Saphora was not to pick her up from the airport Friday afternoon. She wanted to drive in and have time to think, she said. She was one of those girls who thrived in isolation. That was why she could spend hours poring over court records or writing up a dissertation as if the whole world waited expectantly for her to release it.

But knowing that Gwennie planned to arrive at two fifteen left Saphora with too much time to pace and watch out the front windows. She cleaned up the formal living room and then the guest room so that she could work with the blinds fully opened to the front drive. A car pulled into the drive, and her heart nearly stuck in her throat.

"What are you cleaning for, Miss Saphora? I cleaned those rooms yesterday," said Sherry.

"I think Gwennie's here," she said.

"Eddie asked Tobias over. That's his mother's car, isn't it?" she asked.

Saphora pulled back the faded curtain. "It's Tobias."

Eddie ran upstairs. He was still wearing only a pair of tattered race-car underwear and a T-shirt. "Tell Tobias I'll meet him in the tree house," he said.

Sherry met Tobias at the door. Saphora ran to answer the kitchen phone. Jim told her he had given their phone number to a home health nurse. Saphora took down her information and told Jim she would call her if Bender worsened. Between Sherry and her, the two of them had managed his cancer as good as any nurse. She was getting the hang of it but knew that any day her stint would be over.

When she came back to see if Tobias had eaten lunch, Sherry was smiling so big she looked near to bursting. She was holding the door open for Gwennie, who shouldered her things in an overnight pack. Sherry laughed as Gwennie threw her arms around her mother.

"Gwennie, you're too thin, but look how beautiful you are!" Saphora was near to crying again. "Come in and see your daddy."

"Is he upstairs?" asked Gwennie.

"We fixed him up a bed in the library so he can watch the boats pass."

"I'll leave you to visit. Girl, it's good to see you. I like that red in your hair," said Sherry.

Gwennie planted a kiss on Sherry's cheek. "Here. It's from a little jeweler's in Manhattan. They make their things so pretty and no one piece like the other."

Sherry accepted Gwennie's box and tore it open right then. "A pearl bracelet." She held it up for Saphora to see.

"Gold. Delicate little pearls," said Saphora.

"And one diamond. Your birthstone, Sherry," said Gwennie. "The pearls came from Hawaii. You said you always wanted to go."

"Now you're making me cry," said Sherry. "I'll wear this to church."

"Wear it for everyday," said Gwennie. "Mother's always saying she saves things for special days. But don't wait." She shifted the small throw pillow she carried under her arm. She had traveled with that pillow since she was in college. It was a pillow her daddy gave her when she graduated high school. It said, "Love is forever."

"This girl's gone and got some wisdom since we saw her," said Sherry.

Gwennie pulled out a big brown sack with rope handles. "For you, Mama. Open it."

"I don't need anything but you here," said Saphora. "But I'll open it." She snapped apart the red ribbon that tied the handles together. "It's our wedding picture!"

"I had it blown up and framed," said Gwennie. "Turner slipped it out of the house and mailed it to me."

"You'll not believe this. This matting matches the quilt I just put on my bed," said Saphora.

"There's my girl." Bender had gotten up out of the bed and walked into the foyer, using his cane. Saphora had helped him dress in a woven shirt the color of peaches.

Gwennie looked at her father, his somewhat withering frame standing under the last of the afternoon sun as it poured in from the overhead window; his bald head caught the light.

"Got a new hairdo for you," said Bender.

"I love you, Daddy," she said. She went to him and hugged him, but gently as if he might break into a thousand parts.

"I need a real Gwennie hug," he said. "I've waited all day."

Saphora helped her with the shoulder bag while Gwennie hugged her daddy.

"Let's take the party back into the library," said Saphora, worried he might slip on the polished floor.

"I need some fresh air. Let's go out onto the deck," he said.

Saphora stepped out of the way. "Gwennie, will you do him the honors and walk him out?"

There was no use arguing once he got back a portion of his strength. He took long purposeful strides as if he had not just spent the morning hanging on to Saphora for support. He was looking so rejuvenated it seemed as if, during the time they all spent laughing and hearing Gwennie talking about her life in the Big Apple, for just those moments, there was no cancer.

"There was this big shark took my bait out in the Atlantic," said Bender. "Let me tell you about that day, Gwen."

Saphora was relieved at the effect Gwennie had on her daddy. He sat forward, holding those long fingers of his out like baseball gloves, using his hands to talk like he had always done. She could not take her eyes off him. Give him a listening ear, and he turned on the sparkle. She remembered the first time he had asked her for a dance at a street festival in Charlotte. The air was so dense and humid it felt like a giant breathing down her collar as she and Marcy waited for their dates to show up.

She and Marcy were supposed to meet two frat guys from their biology lab for drinks. The guys ran late. While she and Marcy got in line for hot dogs, Bender and his friend Jim were looking for the beer stand. Marcy invited them into line. Jim took his time about noticing Marcy, so it didn't bother her to tell them that they were waiting for dates. Competition might have been the reason Bender moved in and asked Saphora to dance.

He danced with her, meandering them through the uptown mob of people, moving her farther away from Marcy and their dates. Bender could dance and converse without missing a step. The first thing she liked about him was the sound of his voice. He had only a slight southern turn to his syllables. He was smooth, and she was carried up in his charisma. He was not afraid to kiss her that night either when he walked her back to her car. He pulled her close and pressed his forehead against hers. She remembered what he said just as plainly as she could recall other important things, like her childhood address.

"Mama, did you say you rented a boat for Saturday?" asked Gwennie. "Mama?"

Saphora opened her eyes. She had drifted so deeply into the past that Gwennie's voice startled her. She answered Gwennie and then could not help but revisit the memory she had just left off when she was recalling their first kiss. It was right after he told her, "I don't want this to end."

⁂

By eight o'clock, the summer night brewed under the dying heat of the day. Turner pulled into the drive first. A half hour later Ramsey and Celeste parked out in the street. Turner let them in. Liam, Ramsey's oldest child, hit the entry rug and then leaped, his wheeled sneakers squeaking across the polished floor. His twin brothers followed him, yipping like Chihuahua pups. Arnold and William were three and still running around in diapers the size of bowling bags.

Gwennie helped Sherry put out a stack of plates on the deck tables. Sherry said to Saphora, "Did I tell you your sister called?"

Emerald was Saphora's younger sister. The two of them grew up complete opposites. The years became another excuse not to stay in touch. So she wasn't surprised it had taken weeks for Emerald to check in about Bender.

"I'll call her later tonight," said Saphora.

"She's flying in tomorrow," said Sherry.

"We don't have the room."

"Your mother bought her a plane ticket."

"That's just like her," said Saphora. "I don't have the energy for Emerald and all this company too."

"She can have my room."

"Where will you sleep?"

"I've been meaning to tell you. I need to head back to Davidson." She said it as if Saphora might yell at her. "I've been cooking all day. Your freezer is full and ready for every meal through Tuesday. Even made up burritos for all these boys you got running around. You can fry as chimichangas or microwave them."

"Sherry, you can't mean you're leaving this weekend, not with all this company."

"Mama says Malcolm's missing me something fierce."

"If you don't mind, I'd rather you bring him back here. We'll tell Emerald to get a hotel room," said Saphora. "My sister should have planned better."

"I'll come back Monday. That'll give you all family time. Miss Lacey can sleep in my bed. I will bring Malcolm back with me, though, if you're sure you don't mind."

Saphora was trying to imagine managing everyone plus Emerald. Her sister was a walking bucket of tears. "Can Jerry just come up with Malcolm tomorrow?"

"I'm sorry. I promised to be at Malcolm's game tomorrow night." She waited for Saphora to acquiesce. When she didn't, Sherry said, "I'll cancel and stay."

Gwennie said, "Not and miss your son's game. Mama, I helped Sherry plan the meals. I know exactly what to do. All we have to do is warm the food, make a salad." She said to Sherry, "You pack and head out in the morning. I'll pick up Aunt Emerald at the airport."

"You're sure?" asked Sherry.

Gwennie gave her mama a look of disapproval.

"I'm being selfish. I'm sorry," said Saphora. She knew that Gwennie was sacrificing to even pick Emerald up at the airport. She tolerated her even less than she did Celeste. Saphora could already imagine Emerald standing at the foot of Bender's bed and sobbing over him. Her sister had been depressed since age six.

☙

Sherry and Gwennie put out two kinds of enchiladas on a buffet service and wheeled it onto the deck.

Celeste was exhausted after wrestling with her three on the plane. "You would not believe," she said, walking into the middle of them. "Liam tried to crash the cockpit. The flight attendants had to bribe him with cookies to get him back in his chair. I told him if they called airport security on him, I'd just have to let them take him away."

Gwennie left them for the harbor of the kitchen as if she might say something she would regret.

Ramsey got up and ran off the deck, seeing Liam following Tobias and Eddie up the tree without his shoes. Arnold and William brought up the rear of the cousins' troupe, dangling off the tree ladder's bottom rungs.

Celeste glanced toward Ramsey, then turned back to Saphora. "I guess you heard Ramsey's up for a promotion."

Saphora's life had been wrapped up in all things Bender. Ramsey had not told her a thing since he had gone into insurance anyway, though. He lived in his father's shadow, nothing high enough to announce.

Ramsey was back in the deck chair now, listening to Turner talk about one of his patients. He looked uneasy, as if he might bolt from his chair. Celeste had drilled him to stay on the boys like a bird dog.

"The insurance company's opening a new branch, and he's being considered for the lead manager job," said Celeste.

Since Ramsey had gotten his MBA from McColl at Queens, Gwennie had made it known to Saphora that the entry-level insurance job was beneath her brother's talents. Perturbed at anything Celeste said, she turned away. "Sherry, I'll get the picante."

"Margaritas, anyone?" asked Sherry.

"Exactly what I need," said Celeste. "I'd give a left kidney to have you come and live with us." She laughed after every other sentence.

Saphora followed Gwennie back into the kitchen. Gwennie leaned on the marble countertop, seething.

"She's not really said anything all that bad, Gwennie," said Saphora.

"I know. It's everything about her that makes me want to gag her. Her nasal voice. That laugh of hers is driving me nuts. The way she says, 'Ramsey! Ramsey!' as if he lives to do her bidding. I can't stand to see him in Celeste's jail."

"If you don't let it go, you'll say something you'll regret," said Saphora. But she had to admit that Celeste wore her down to a nub.

"I got three orders for margaritas," said Sherry, running back into the kitchen to fill her tray again. "Any more takers?"

"Not for me," said Saphora.

"I'll take one plus hers," said Gwennie.

❧

Knowing that Emerald was coming in on top of a houseful of family members set a different tone in the house. The guys gossiped around the breakfast table the next morning.

They were all going out in the boat for the three-hour tour, much to everyone's great relief.

Eddie was driving them crazy. "When are we leaving for the boat?" He said it for the twentieth time, Saphora was sure.

"When will you all get back?" Gwennie wanted to know. "Over three hours in the car with Aunt Em is my badge for the weekend. The rest of you sailor boys have to take a turn too."

"She's not that bad," said Ramsey.

"Just melancholy, Gwen," said Bender. He had once been Emerald's worst antagonizer.

"Do I know her?" asked Liam. Being Ramsey's oldest made him the most inquisitive.

"You'll be back before us, Gwennie," said Saphora. "Tell her she can rest in my room until we're back at the dock. But tonight we'll have to put her up in one of the B and Bs. There's Ida's B and B right across the road."

"What's wrong with Aunt Emerald?" asked Liam, shouting above the adults.

"One brick shy of a load," said Turner.

Celeste tried to redirect Liam's attention. "Have another bowl of cereal."

"She's odd, like those women you see sitting in remote coffee shops crocheting and talking about their lap dogs with other women who sit crocheting and talking about their lap dogs," said Turner.

"I have a lap dog," said Celeste. "I'm not crazy." She laughed.

"Aunt Emerald's crazy?" asked Liam.

"I didn't say that. Don't repeat me, Liam," said Celeste. "Go wash out your bowl."

"I'm still hungry. If Aunt Emerald's crazy, why do they let her out?" asked Liam.

"Not that kind of crazy, you dope!" said Eddie.

"Quirky, Liam. Forget about it," said Celeste.

By now Eddie was fully awake and tired of picking at his orange slices. "I like Great-Aunt Emerald. She's fun."

"There you go," said Saphora. "Emerald is fun, Liam. Now stop talking about her."

Liam was a sponge, soaking up everything the adults had to say, only to squeeze it all out again at inopportune moments.

"Nana, can Tobias come on the boat?" asked Eddie.

"What if he gets sick?" she asked.

"He won't. I'll make him swear." Eddie was begging.

"I'll call Jamie right now. It's up to his mother," said Saphora. After the swimming pool incident, Jamie had gotten more protective of where Tobias could go.

"He won't get sick," said Eddie. He sounded worried. But Eddie was a born worrier.

෨

Captain Bart sent a text message to Saphora. "Clear skies all day— thought you'd like to know." Turner drove them down the street to the Oriental Marina. Captain Bart waited on the dock.

Ramsey brought Liam and left the twins with Celeste. That was all for the best, Saphora decided. Liam argued with Eddie. He wanted to be first man on the boat.

"They quarrel like brothers," said Turner.

"Like us, you mean?" asked Ramsey. "We were good kids."

"Didn't I hear Jamie say she'd bring Tobias?" said Saphora out loud to herself.

"Ahoy, mates!" said Captain Bart. He had his cane but didn't seem to be relying on it this time. His morning coffee was in a mug that said USS *Titanic*. "Had your breakfast?"

"We ate before coming," said Saphora. "But I brought a picnic for later." She had put some of Sherry's fixings in a picnic basket.

Ramsey hauled a cooler of drinks and beer from the car trunk.

"Brought you boys something," said Captain Bart. He fished something out of the pocket of his windbreaker.

Eddie said, "I like your hat. Can my dad wear one?"

"Just my ball cap, Eddie," said Turner. "We yachters don't stand on ceremony. We wear what we want."

"Got some pirate tattoos for you both," said Captain Bart to Eddie and Liam.

"Stick-ons," said Liam, not at all impressed.

"I'll take them," said Eddie, "for me and my friend Tobias."

"Give me mine!" said Liam.

It came to Saphora that Jamie first told her she would keep Tobias home. Then Jamie called back. Tobias was giving her what for, telling her that he wanted her to treat him like other kids. She caved in. But there was no sign of her car in the lot.

Saphora imagined Tobias on board with his weak stomach. "They have those tattoos in all the shops, Eddie. Go on and give Liam one, and we'll buy one for Tobias."

Eddie halfheartedly gave up the tattoo to his cousin.

"I've got bags of them. One for you too," said Captain Bart. He pulled out another tattoo and offered the Jolly Roger to Saphora.

"Nana's a pirate queen," said Eddie. "Tobias calls you that, Nana."

Turner laughed.

"Tobias thinks the next-door neighbor's a pirate," said Saphora.

"We watched you and Luke next door digging late one night, under the moon," said Eddie. "He kissed Nana."

"Not that kind of kiss!" said Saphora. Eddie made it sound like something it wasn't. "He thanked me for helping him with a chore."

"Mama, you were in the neighbor's yard digging at night?" asked Ramsey. "And kissing?" he asked, laughing.

"He's a grieving man. And very young. Lord knows what you all would do if you were in his shoes," said Saphora.

"Time to shove off," said Captain Bart. He kept the schedule like an English nanny.

"All aboard, everyone," Saphora said.

Eddie was the first on board. Turner led him to the mainmast while Saphora ran down the dock and untied the dock line.

"Where you headed?" asked Bart.

"We'll go to Luken's Cemetery," said Saphora. "Old Town. I know that route now."

Ramsey took the wheel. He put on a captain's hat. Liam stood beside him, holding the wheel with his daddy.

A shout went up from the dock. Jamie waved, standing behind the open door of her car. She was honking her horn while Tobias yelled, running up the dock and waving his arms like a little squid. "Wait, I'm here!"

Jamie stood down from the dock on the walk. She shrugged at

Saphora and held up her cell phone. "Have him call me." She looked fresh and happy to see him try out boating.

Eddie said, "Hey, you didn't chicken out!"

"I wouldn't," said Tobias. He came aboard.

Eddie whooped and startled the sea gulls hitchhiking along the stern. He pulled another pirate tattoo out of the bag and gave it to Tobias.

Ramsey steered them toward Pamlico Sound. Saphora showed him the chart points toward Old Town. She sat on deck facing fore, not far from Turner and Eddie.

"Put on your pirate tattoo, Nana," said Eddie. When she closed her eyes and did not answer, he kept saying it until she sat up and moaned.

"Eddie, leave Nana alone," said Turner.

"It's all right." She pulled the tattoo out of her pocket. "Where do I put it?"

"On your arm, like a sailor," said Eddie. He was hoarse from giggling.

"You won't see it there. I'm wearing a jacket." She bent and peeled it back and then pressed it onto her calf.

That sent Eddie into spasms.

Tobias dragged a chair next to Eddie. He put on a big pair of Mafia black sunglasses. Then he started pouring on sunscreen so thick that Saphora got up and squatted next to him. "Let me help." She took his lotion and squeezed some into her hand. As she took his thin left forearm, she noticed that she could see nearly every vein inside his arm. His skin was so pale, like a fish floating upside down on the surface of the water.

"Other arm," she said.

He gave her the arm, surrendered to a woman he had known only a few weeks.

Not about to be left out, Liam pushed his chair next to Tobias, beside where Saphora squatted.

"Next, shoulders and back." She could feel every spinal stem down his back. "Eddie, I'll do you next and then Liam."

"We need to get some meat on your bones, boy," said Turner.

"He has AIDS, Daddy," said Liam. He was grinning as if happy to finally beat Eddie to the announcement. "What is that anyway?"

It was as if Liam had announced that he had just put away his toys and lit a dynamite stick.

Ramsey came up out of his stupor in the captain's chair. He was looking over the top of his sunglasses at Tobias. "Liam, why did you say that?"

Liam pulled his feet up off the deck and tucked them close to his body.

Saphora imagined the boys had been up in the tree house when Eddie blurted it out to Liam as if he knew everything in the entire universe.

"He must have heard that somewhere. Liam, it's not nice to say that," said Turner to his nephew.

"Why did you say that?" asked Ramsey.

Tobias's face was without any expression. His eyes were hidden behind the sunglasses. "Do I have to go back to the dock, Mrs. Warren?"

"Of course not, Tobias," said Saphora.

"Mama, what are you doing?" asked Ramsey.

"I'm getting a tan," said Saphora. She used the tanning lotion on her exposed calves, doctoring carefully around the Jolly Roger so as not to tatter the edges.

"He can't have AIDS. That's not possible," said Turner. He had a nervous laugh.

Tobias was so accustomed to adults talking over his head that he sat still, perched on the edge of his chair, staring down at the deck.

"What's going on? Someone tell me. It's a joke, right, Liam?" asked Ramsey.

"Sure, a big joke," said Tobias.

"Liam, come back over here," said Ramsey. "Help me steer."

Liam sat up but did not jump up. He was torn between his daddy and his friend.

Saphora poured more lotion into her hands. She rubbed it on her nose and into her cheeks. "I want everyone to calm down and talk about other things."

"You can't get it by touching me," said Tobias. He was trying to curry a little favor with Ramsey behind that stretched smile of his.

A lost butterfly alighted on the stern. It was white with black spots.

"You don't have to explain yourself, Tobias," said Saphora.

"So he really has it?" asked Turner.

"Why is everyone acting so weird?" asked Eddie. "Liam has a big mouth." He was batting back tears, fighting an emotion he could not explain.

"Shut up!" Liam exclaimed. "You told me."

"We should have been told," said Ramsey. "These are our kids, Mama."

"Tobias is my friend, Uncle Ramsey," said Eddie.

"What do you think, Ramsey?" asked Saphora. "That this little boy is going to breathe and you'll get it out here in this wind? I'm not kidding. Let's talk about something else."

A sea gull was screeching like a crazy hawk. It dropped down from the sky, dive-bombing the cruiser. It snatched away the white butterfly and was gone.

୧୬

South River wound through the Outer Banks like a twin ribbon to the Neuse, emptying out at Old Town. Saphora picked a spot where they could weigh anchor, and Ramsey parked the craft in the deep-water lagoon. Saphora got out the fishing poles from below and gave one to Eddie and Tobias. Tobias was cheery.

"I'm sorry that we're idiots," said Saphora.

"I can tie on my own lure. I watched you do it," said Tobias. His fingers worked the line around the lure, a popper that might attract a bass if the boy would impose some patience on his line.

Ramsey had fallen quiet, pouring all of his attention on Liam— not a bad thing, in Saphora's estimation. She hated the way young parents wound their lives around busyness and competitive activities instead of sharing from themselves. Fishing broke out of loud culture and forced the attention on the simplicity of seducing small, elusive, submerged creatures. Ramsey worked with his boy on improving his wrist action.

Once Tobias dropped his line, Saphora helped Eddie pick out a lure. "There could be some trout still left out here in these waters," said Saphora. "Use this furry black one. It'll look like a juicy bug to a trout."

Turner kicked back in the shade of the mainmast with his ball cap over his face. He was snoring already.

An hour passed and only Ramsey had caught a fingerling. He threw it back. "This spot is fished out."

"I'd like to take the raft inland," said Saphora.

"I'm starving," said Liam.

"There's sandwiches down below." Saphora was hungry too.

"Let's take a sandwich on the raft," said Tobias. "I'm going with Mrs. Warren," he told Eddie.

"Any other takers?" she asked.

"What time is it?" Turner came awake. "Did I burn?" Still in a stupor, he was rubbing his arms for signs of a sunburn.

"We're going below to have some grub," said Ramsey. "You're not burned, big brother. You fell asleep in the shade."

"I guess it's just you and me, Tobias," said Saphora.

Turner lowered the raft into the water. Saphora climbed down the ladder and steadied her feet as she climbed into the craft. She told Tobias, "Climb down using both hands. Eddie, you bring us two sandwiches and two cold sodas."

"Can I drive it?" asked Tobias. "It's a small motor. I know how."

"Let me show you a few things first. Then I'll sit fore of the raft and tell you where to go," said Saphora.

Eddie came galloping back across the deck. "Liam stuffed a whole sandwich into his mouth. He looks like a puffer fish." He jumped onto the ladder and climbed down. "Uncle Ramsey put your food and drinks in a bag." He handed the bag to his grandmother. "Here, Tobias, I'm giving you this." It was Bender's water bottle. Eddie had adopted it, and now he was giving it to Tobias.

"You sure you're not coming with us?" she asked Eddie.

"Daddy?" he asked. "Can I?"

"You stay here with me," said Turner, self-consciously avoiding eye contact with Tobias. "We need some father and son time."

"Hand me two rods and reels and the small tackle then," said Saphora.

Turner handed her two sets over the stern. "Here's your tackle box," he said. "The signal's weak on cellulars this far out, so don't stray on us."

"If we're not back in an hour, send a posse," she told him, still suffering pangs on account of Tobias.

Tobias held up the Wake Forest water bottle. "Thanks, buddy." He strapped on his backpack. "I brought fruit, Mrs. Warren. Dr. Warren told me that if I'm ever lost at sea, I could live a long time on apples and oranges."

"He told you that? We're not going to get lost, Tobias."

The South River floated like a pond in some places. Tobias figured out the small motor's workings as fast as a racetrack grease monkey.

The landscape was part riverbed, part marshland.

"There's an old cemetery out this way," said Saphora.

Tobias was overly eager to navigate. Finally he aimed the dinghy straight down the middle of the river. "It's a riot!" he kept saying. It wasn't a phrase she had heard from any of her grandsons. But Tobias said it whenever he gunned the small motor. "It's a riot!"

Saphora laughed each time. "Take her over to that old dock. There may be some fish under that old wood." It was also a good place to drop a line and eat a sandwich. She opened the sack lunch.

"Were there soldiers that died out this way?" he asked.

"Why do you ask?"

"You said there was a cemetery."

"Could be. There's one story says the plague hit here back in the last century. The survivors had to leave, so they resettled farther down the Neuse. Some think that's how Oriental got started."

"The plague. What was it?"

"A terrible disease. Everyone died of it. Now wet your line."

Tobias squeezed a sinker onto his line and then let her fly. The lure slapped the water and dropped dead into the green stink of the marsh. He held the rod between his knees and stripped off his black windbreaker.

Saphora gave him the sandwich. "It's ham. Hope that's all right," she said.

"I like ham. I like everything. Unless it's yellow."

"What's wrong with yellow?"

"Yellow is the color of one of my meds," he said like an old doctor.

"How much medication do you take?"

"Sixteen different kinds. Some of it tastes so bad I throw up. So I have to keep taking it until it stays down."

"It's not fair."

"You've got a bite," he said.

The tip of her rod bent toward the water's surface. She jerked the reel and set the hook.

"You always catch a fish?" he asked.

"I think you're my lucky charm," she said, preparing to wrangle her catch.

"My mom told me that too."

A pretty green trout flipped into the air.

"You've got to be patient with this guy," she said. "Trout can out-smart humans."

Tobias put down his rod to watch. "Don't let him go, Mrs. Warren. We'll make the others jealous they didn't come."

"That's right. They were too interested in eating."

"It's me, Mrs. Warren. I know that. I've seen it before."

"Don't say that," she said. She reeled the trout toward the raft. It had a lot of fight in it. She gave it some line and then started reeling again.

"I don't keep a buddy long."

"Eddie's your buddy for always."

"Sometimes I get mad about it. But what's the point? What am I going to do? Yell at my dead mom for giving me AIDS?"

"This guy is not going to come to us easily," she said. For a second, she thought she had lost him. Then he flipped into the air and slapped the water before submerging. "Did your mother know you were sick?"

"I don't know. She was passing through town. She stopped long enough to have me and then dropped me off at the hospital's emergency room door. She left me in a hamburger sack. The nurses told that to the cops, so the McDonald's baby is what the newspapers called me."

Saphora was trying not to laugh. But Tobias heard her and then he laughed. "My dad always asks if I came with a side of fries."

Saphora finally laughed out loud.

"Great guns, Mrs. Warren!" he said, standing up in the raft. "You lost him."

Saphora came up too, reeling up the nothingness of an empty hook.

Tobias looked disappointed and flopped back into the raft.

She asked, "When did your mama pass away?"

"A month after I was born. A nurse kept up with her. She didn't take good care of herself."

"That has nothing to do with who you are," she said.

"I'm who I decide I'll be. That's what my mom says."

"What are you going to be when you grow up?"

"A wrestler."

She laughed.

"Or a businessman like my dad."

"First one sounds more glamorous."

"I know."

"Your line is moving," she whispered.

Tobias came up out of the raft. He set the hook as if he were catching a whale. He yanked hard.

"I think you outsmarted my trout," she said.

"I'm bringing him in," he said. "I caught him, I caught him!"

Sure enough, it was the big trout. Saphora said a quiet prayer: *Give him this one wish, God.* She had not promised God anything, like she normally did when things went south. She had not even asked God to save Bender. It wasn't for lack of caring. Her prayers in the past few years seemed to be hitting a brass sky. She felt she had not known how to pray until right now.

Tobias reeled and waited and continued as if he had the patience to fight the trout all day. Finally the fish was beside the raft, its gills flapping in and out from the fight.

Saphora brought the net under him and lifted him into the boat. "You did it."

Tobias beat his chest and whooped so loud a crane lifted from behind the marsh grass. "Wait'll Eddie sees him!"

"It's time to head back to the yacht."

"Will Ramsey leave and take Liam home because of me?"

"I'll talk to him. Stop worrying. You're with me, Tobias. And that's all the invitation you need."

Eddie and Liam waved from the yacht. Eddie howled and that set Tobias to howling like a wolf. Liam laughed until Ramsey called him away from the stern. Eddie climbed down in bare feet. "Hand me him, Tobias. I'll pack him on ice."

Tobias did not want to let go of his fish. He had held it in his arms all the way back to the yacht.

"Let him help, Tobias," said Saphora. "Eddie, tell Turner to get the camera. This one's a good twelve-pounder."

"Daddy!"

Turner was waiting with the camera when Saphora pulled the ladder up behind them. She felt proud of Tobias but also of Eddie, who would not let his uncle spoil the day.

"Daddy, take our picture," said Eddie. The fish was big enough for the two of them to hold.

"You boys grin," said Turner. "That's got to be the biggest trout any of us've caught out in these waters."

"Mrs. Warren caught him first," said Tobias. "He's a caught-twice fish."

"Is that true, Mama?" asked Turner.

"We think so," she said.

"Now, Mrs. Warren, you get in the picture with us," said Tobias.

Saphora posed behind Tobias and Eddie. She held out her calf, turning it sideways to show off her Jolly Roger.

Ramsey headed them back to the marina. They passed a long regatta of boats headed back from the tarpon tournament. There was not a cloud the whole way back. The water rippled in the sun beyond the yacht, like pearls being cast behind them. It was a perfect day.

12

When each partner loves so completely that
he has forgotten to ask himself whether or
not he is loved in return, when he only
knows that he loves and is moving to its
music—then, and then only, are two people
able to dance perfectly in tune to the same
rhythm.

ANNE MORROW LINDBERGH, *Gift from the Sea*

Emerald was sunning in the front yard in a deck chair when Saphora
pulled up with Eddie and Tobias. Gwennie had helped Aunt Emerald check into a room at Ida's B and B. She could walk back and forth
from the inn to the house.

"Look at you," said Emerald. "Skinny sister. And you with a
cook and living the life of Riley!"

Saphora hugged her. "You're here early. How did Gwennie get
you here so fast?"

"I rented a car. When they announced the flight would be delayed, I called to tell her not to bother coming, not knowing if we'd
be cancelled and all. The man next to me said most flights were coming in later and later. Why do you think that is?" She didn't wait for
Saphora to answer. "I mean, with all the craziness going on, now
we've got this to contend with. Like it's not enough."

"You look well," said Saphora.

Emerald grimaced. "I've not been well. But I said the minute I heard Bender was dying that I wanted to see him alive."

"Is Grandpa dying?" asked Eddie.

"Oh foot! Shut me up!" said Emerald. "Now don't listen to me, Eddie. I'm just going on."

Ramsey and Turner pulled up behind them in the drive.

"Grandpa's fine," said Saphora. She already felt the knot of tension that Emerald brought to every gathering. Saphora led them all back inside.

Gwennie was frying Sherry's burritos. She frowned from the stove.

Saphora said to Emerald, "You take this remote and find you a TV show to watch, sister." Then she joined Gwennie in the kitchen. "Has she been hard to deal with?"

"The world's coming to an end is all," said Gwennie, but not so Emerald could overhear. "To hear Aunt Emerald tell it, you might as well pull the covers over your head and die."

"She said in front of Eddie that Bender was dying," said Saphora. "Did she mention how long she was staying?"

"A week."

"We'll all be dead by then."

"Ida's is expensive. When Celeste and Ramsey leave Sunday, we may want to move Emerald into their room," said Gwennie.

"Bender would rather keep her in the inn, I'm sure."

Eddie walked in, sent on a coffee run by his grandpa. "Are you talking about Great-Aunt Emerald? Grandpa just told her she could stay in the house with us Monday."

"There goes that theory," said Saphora. She tore wet lettuce while Gwennie dropped the burritos into a skillet of hot oil.

"Aunt Celeste wants to know when dinner's ready," said Eddie. "Arnold and William are driving her crazy, she says to tell you."

"Put these chips out on the table, Eddie," said Saphora.

When he got out of earshot, Gwennie said, "Does Celeste ever lift a finger to help when they come to your place?"

"Well, usually there's Sherry. But I don't remember that Celeste has ever helped with anything."

"She makes Ramsey do her work. I even heard her tell him to tie her shoes. She was too tired to bend over."

"She has put on weight since having the twins."

"I just want to shake Ramsey and say 'Wake up!' She's going to end up like those people whose family members have to wheel them around with canisters and drip bags attached by tubes."

"She thrives on attention. Maybe her mother spoiled her."

"Don't you know that story?" asked Gwennie.

"What story?"

"She was an asthmatic as a kid. Her mother wouldn't let her do a thing for herself. She had three sisters, but they all had to do the chores while she sat in a rocker watching and expecting them all to wait on her."

"They must have a lot of affection for her," said Saphora.

"They never talk."

"Let's stop talking about Celeste." The noise level in the living room had gone up twenty decibels since Emerald had arrived. It caused the boys to run up and down the stairs competing to be heard. Celeste was laughing above the dull roar of the other adults. Emerald was telling some sad story even though no one was listening.

Saphora mentally escaped as she sliced the cucumber. She remembered the day she had packed up her suitcase and decided to run away to Oriental. She was halfway down the cucumber when she recalled how she had envisioned the quiet river running past. She had imagined she would write her thoughts in a journal until her life made sense, like she had pictured it would be before she had met Bender Warren. She dropped the cucumber slices into the salad bowl like poker chips falling. Then she dropped in the diced tomatoes like little pairs of dice. She wanted doubles, but life gave her snake eyes.

"Eddie dropped the tortilla chips and now he's crying," said Gwennie.

Turner was standing helplessly over Eddie when Saphora came into the den. "Turner, the dust pan's behind the refrigerator with the broom. You go and get that. Eddie, stop crying."

"He's such a sensitive boy," said Emerald. "He'll make a good man someday. They grow up so quickly." She appeared to be searching for a reason to tear up, but the sentiment was not making the connection.

"For Pete's sake!" said Saphora. "At least turn off the TV. You're all yelling over it."

No one could find the remote control even though Saphora distinctly remembered putting it into Emerald's hand. Saphora turned off the set manually.

"So nice of you, sister," said Emerald. "We were just talking about the time I got mumps. Remember how you teased me?"

Bender was staring into his coffee cup. He seemed to be absorbing the noise. Saphora thought he actually liked the racket for once. He did not have to think about cancer when his ears were filled with screaming boys and in-law complaints.

"Dinner's ready," said Gwennie.

Eddie and Tobias raced ahead of Liam to the dining table. But Celeste was already seating the twins there. "You boys take your food outside to the patio," she told Eddie, Tobias, and Liam.

There were not enough chairs for everyone. "Not to worry," said Saphora. "I'll take my meal on the stool at the bar in the kitchen."

"But we want you in here," said Emerald.

"You won't notice I'm not there," said Saphora. After she said it, she thought it sounded like self-pity. But in reality she felt a peaceful calm as she left them for the kitchen.

Gwennie brushed past holding the platter of chimichangas. "Deserter," she whispered.

෴

It was when the boys had finally surrendered to sleep, the twins in front of the television set and Eddie and Liam passing out together on Eddie's bed, that Saphora got out of bed to enjoy the quiet of the house. She listened from the patio for the toads. But stillness had swept across the river neighborhood. There was a gentle sound coming from Luke's yard. It might have been a laugh. Luke had a hearty laugh, but this one was softer, nearly seductive.

Saphora could not sit for long wondering what was going on over the fence. She crept downstairs and out the back. The moon was big, like a giant deep-sea creature illuminating the ocean of lawns dotting the riverbanks. There was that laugh again, but it was not Luke's laugh for sure. Saphora found the gate open.

Luke was seated on a concrete bench, one of those ornamental types sold from yards through the southern countryside between Raleigh and the Outer Banks. One gloved hand rested atop his spade's handle.

The young woman's back was to Saphora, but she could see even in the dark that it was Gwennie.

The sight of her shocked Saphora so much that she gasped. Gwennie jerked around and Luke came to his feet.

"Mama?" said Gwennie.

"Mrs. Warren, do join us," said Luke. "We're having a talk about relatives."

"There's no shortage if you need me to loan you a few," said Saphora. She was still stunned to see Gwennie sitting across from Luke in the Adirondack he had made from scrap lumber. He had told Saphora that in confidence. "I feel like I'm interrupting."

"Luke's an artist," said Gwennie.

"I know," said Saphora. "He made that chair."

"And the bench. The pottery in his garage and a lamp in his bed-room," said Gwennie. "He gave me the mini tour."

"Did he? How nice." She was thinking how silly she was to feel oddly jealous. It had taken some time for Luke to open up to Saphora. But here Gwennie wandered in and he spilled out his entire life to her. Until now, she had enjoyed keeping Luke to herself.

"Luke's invited me to go deep-sea fishing with him tomorrow," said Gwennie.

"There goes my kitchen help," said Saphora. But before Gwennie responded with some guilty confession, Saphora said, "That's nice of you, Luke. And you've known one another what, five minutes?"

"One day, six hours, and twenty-seven minutes," said Luke.

"I wandered over here last night," said Gwennie. "Luke has this obsession for digging holes."

That was the troubled side of Luke that worried Saphora. But his obsession did not seem to bother Gwennie.

"He made me pancakes this morning," said Gwennie. She had not taken her eyes off him. "It was after you all took off when Aunt Emerald called to say her plane was going to be late so she would be renting a car. He found me sitting on the back deck reading."

"Reading a law book," said Luke. "She looked lonesome and bored. So I made her my famous pancakes."

"Famous to who?" said Gwennie, laughing.

Saphora was amazed at the bond already forming between them, and he a poor artist. Gwennie would drop him as soon as she was back in New York surrounded by legal eagles.

"Gwennie's headed back home Monday," said Saphora.

"She told me. I'll have to text you when I finish that piece you like, Gwennie."

"It's a gorgeous vase," said Gwennie. "He's staining it with peacock colors. Take a picture with your phone and send it to me."

"Peacock colors. That will go with your black and tan décor," said Saphora.

"It needs livening up," said Gwennie.

Then the talking stopped for a moment, Luke looking at Gwennie as if he had more to say but holding back.

Finally Saphora, taking her cue, broke the silence. "I'm up too late. I'll go back and leave you two to finish your talk."

As soon as she left, she heard them bantering in a way that sounded familiar. It was like the night Bender had taken her to Lake Norman, where his friend's parents docked a boat. That was the night he told Saphora that he would own a house on Lake Norman. He gave her a bracelet that his grandmother had left to him. Saphora wore it even now. It had been a night just like this night. Bender was talking about the life he wanted—with Saphora in it. That was the moment he had moved her like a chess piece into his world. She allowed it so freely, as if she would always love being a part of the perfect puzzle that Bender was piecing together for himself.

But Luke was no Bender. She imagined the shock he would get

if he got too close to Bender Warren's attorney daughter. Luke was easy to talk to and laughed so spontaneously that Saphora laughed along because he made her feel good. Luke held the moment hostage, squeezing every bit of zest from it, except when he returned to his obsessive digging. Then his whole countenance turned to brooding. That would be the side, she thought, that would drive Gwennie back to New York, even more than his spartan existence or his hermit's life on the Neuse River.

Gwennie was too smart to fall for a man like Luke. For some reason, that made Saphora sad.

☙

"Saphora, are you awake?"

Saphora was dreaming. Or so she thought when she heard Bender's voice early on Sunday morning. She opened her eyes. Bender was standing over her bed. He had not tried to climb the stairs since he had started chemotherapy, but here he stood. "Is everything all right?" she asked.

He had put on a shirt, most likely crisply ironed by Sherry before she took off for Davidson. He buttoned the cuffs, but with a little clumsiness. "I thought I'd go to church. Will you drive me?"

Saphora sat up. "You're going to church?"

"Don't act so surprised." A smile came out of his face like that of the young man she had kissed down on Lake Norman.

"What time is it?" She looked around for her clock. But with the summer stretching before her, she had not turned on the alarm clock all of July.

"A little after nine. Church starts at ten-thirty. You've got plenty of time."

He was serious. He expected her to get up and dress and drive him to church. "Which church?" she asked.

"John Mims's church. He asked me politely to come." He finished with the cuffs. "I thought I'd go."

By the time Saphora had dressed, putting on a skirt and blouse she had not worn all summer, Bender was sitting, finishing his coffee while reading a newspaper. He was as ready as when he first woke her. "You look nice," he said. "I like you in a skirt. Nice legs, Mrs. Warren. Sexy tattoo."

She laughed. "I forgot. I'll have to wash it off."

"No time. Besides, your skirt covers it. Nearly, anyway." He caught her look of uncertainty and said, "Pastor John won't care."

Bender followed her out to the car in the garage. "I'll get the garage door," he offered. Just as the garage door shuddered open, Gwennie stuck her head through the laundry room pass-through. "Where are you two going?"

"Church," said Saphora as if they went every Sunday.

"Daddy, are you all right?" she asked.

"I'm good, Gwen. I thought I'd take your mama to church."

Gwennie was in her old university sweatshirt, the sleeves cut out. Her bangs were strewn across her forehead, the back hairs of her head sticking up in a faintly waving mass. She looked nine again. "I wish I'd known. I would have gone with you."

"I didn't even know until an hour ago," said Saphora. Before she climbed into the driver's side, she said, "Did you enjoy talking with Luke last night?"

"I did," Gwennie said without divulging any more information.

Bender stopped short of getting into the car. "Our neighbor Luke?"

"Our neighbor," said Saphora. "Get in."

Bender got into the car, passenger side. When she closed her door, he asked, "Is she seeing Luke?"

"She saw him in the backyard last night."

"You know what I mean. Are they dating?" he asked.

"Luke's a good man."

"I'm not passing judgment." He buckled his seat belt. "But now he's after both my women."

"He's a fast one, that Luke. They've not dated. But he's taking her deep-sea fishing today."

"It could be a date. To Gwennie, a date of sorts," he said.

"She's a good judge of character," said Saphora.

"Gwen's the greatest daughter a daddy could have." He sounded like he was resigning himself to things he could not control.

Gwennie waved them off while bringing down the garage door.

He adjusted his seat back and closed his eyes. After a few minutes of quiet, he said, "She looked different, didn't she? There's something different about Gwen."

"Maybe there's just something different about you, Bender."

"It's possible."

"You never go to church."

"Saphora, I'm not the bad guy." He said it nicely.

"But you never talk about God."

"I don't, do I?"

"It's the last thing you'd think about," said Saphora.

He checked his watch. "Mims said there are two services. We're attending the second one."

She found First Community Church right up from the marina. There were a lot of people piling into the small building, threading through the ones leaving the first service. She figured Pastor John had knocked on a lot of doors to get his parking lot filled up.

Coming out the door was Tobias, followed by Jamie. "Dr. Warren!" he yelled. "You come here too?"

"It's my first time," said Bender.

Jamie kissed Saphora and said, "Pastor Mims is such a good teacher. You'll like the sermon this morning."

"Have you been going all along?" asked Saphora.

"It's our summer church. I'm glad you came." She led Tobias down the street.

Pastor John greeted people as they walked under the long canvas awning to enter the sanctuary. He was taken aback seeing Saphora and Bender coming toward him. "It's nice to see you here," he said to Bender.

"Fish aren't biting. Needed something to do," said Bender, smiling.

"Pastor John, it's good to see you," said Saphora. "He got me up early to bring him here."

"It was her idea," said Bender.

"You're both so very welcome," said Pastor John. He continued greeting and shaking hands.

Once they were inside, the old building's musty smell was overcome by the people who greeted them. There seemed to be a lot going on in so small a place. Two ladies were signing up members for group studies. A smiling man offered them coffee at a table filled with a variety of flavors. He asked them if they were new.

"First-timers," said Bender.

"If you fill this out and give it to me, I have a nice gift bag for you," said the greeter.

To Saphora's surprise, Bender took a pen from the man and filled out the card. He gave it back to him and accepted the gift bag, a pink one he promptly passed off to Saphora.

They continued down the hallway, following some directions from the man. Photographs of mission trips were affixed to bulletin boards.

Bender found a seat in the back. Saphora accepted some materials from a woman in jeans who greeted them. Then she sat next to Bender.

Along the floor in front of her, the carpet showed signs of some upheaval. Old wooden pews had once made impressions on the carpet. Cushioned chairs took the place of the pews now. Saphora remembered going to church with her mother as a girl. The pews were affixed in her mind as the one thing that made her so fidgety. It seemed this church was working to become a more welcoming place. Bender was being drawn right in, brain cancer scaring him from behind, Pastor John smiling and opening wide his doors before him.

"There's coffee out in the lobby." A woman who sat in front of them turned around in her chair. She stuck out her hand. Bender shook it and then Saphora.

"Thank you," she said. "I'm Saphora."

"May," said the woman. "You're new."

"Just here for the summer," said Saphora.

Pastor John took his spot on the platform, as poised as any man of religious ilk, and placed a Bible on the lectern. He made some humorous comments.

Bender shifted back and forth. He seemed uncomfortable.

"Want to go out for the coffee?" asked Saphora.

He shook his head and said nothing. Then his hand came down on hers. He clasped her fingers. He was crying. A box of tissues sat right under May's chair. Saphora got him one.

First Bender whimpered, a noise unlike any she'd ever heard from him. Then he leaned over, his head coming down into Saphora's lap as he collapsed.

⁓

It took an ambulance twenty-five minutes to come for Bender that morning. Pastor John had stepped right off the platform. He got some of the women praying.

As Saphora was climbing into the ambulance, one of the attendants was looking curiously at the Jolly Roger on her calf. Her mind was swarming with her husband's pallor, so it was a strange thing to notice. She sat next to Bender and took hold of his hand. He was eerily still and as white as a beach. He looked dead.

"I think he's had a seizure, ma'am," the other attendant working over him told her.

"Bender, can you hear me?" she asked. But he was in another place. She talked to him and rubbed his hands. She talked right into his ear while an attendant set up a drip. "Bender, don't you give up now." She did not know how many times she said it. But while she had felt awkward in knowing what to say to him up until now, the language was all suddenly so clear. "I love you, Bender," she whispered. "Don't leave me."

⁓

Bender's crisis brought the whole Warren clan off the waters of the Neuse River and into the uncertainty of a good-for-nothing cancer scare. Jim met Saphora in the Duke ER. By afternoon Bender was moved into a room in the cancer wing, where a team of specialists started the testings that follow in the wake of a cancer patient's collapse at church. Jim told Saphora this could be the final stage. Gwennie bustled into the room where they had placed her daddy. "Mama, what's going on? The waiting is driving me crazy."

Saphora held on to Gwennie until Gwennie sobbed. She had never been a girl to cry openly. But she could not contain it. Neither of them could. Gwennie said, "I told Celeste to feed the boys and drive them here later. I think she listened."

Ramsey came running up the hallway and into the room. "I'm here, Mama. Celeste is parking the car."

Turner ran in right behind him. They were standing at the foot of the bed when Saphora said, "Let's step out." When they followed her into the hall, she led them to a nearby waiting area to sit and hear the news. She told her sons, "He's not responding to anything."

Gwennie quietly joined them, sitting on the arm of Turner's chair.

Jim came into the hall. Saphora introduced him to Gwennie, Turner, and Ramsey. Jim said, "I'm glad to find you all here. He's had a stroke, Saphora. It will be a few days before we know how much brain function's been affected."

Because Turner had to leave by six o'clock, Ramsey felt the worst for also needing to leave so abruptly. But he had already booked their flights out for Sunday night. They had packed already and brought their luggage and kids in tow. He sat with his head in his hands. "Celeste brought Emerald along," he said. "I figured she could ride back with you, Gwennie."

"I'll see to her," said Gwennie.

Bender's predicament had softened them all, even toward Emerald. The sound of running was heard from the end of the hallway.

"I think your family's here, darling," said Saphora to Ramsey. She walked down the hallway to quiet the grandsons and greet her sister.

Emerald complained, "I could not sit alone worrying back in Oriental."

Saphora led them back into the hospital room, where Emerald took it upon herself to sit at Bender's bedside. The brothers nervously traded chitchat about work while Gwennie went downstairs to make calls. Turner was good about asking the nurses medical questions and then translating the answers for Saphora. But the sun was going down, and it was inevitable that Saphora would have to say good-bye to Ramsey and Turner and their families. Ramsey and Celeste took their good-byes out in the hall. Saphora told Ramsey, "I'm just glad you were here. You got to see him spry and surrounded by his grandsons."

"It's not over, Mama," said Ramsey.

Turner hugged him and each of his sons.

Eddie and Liam held on to each other, laughing like boys do when they're afraid to show emotion.

"I don't want it to be," she said. She had cried all the way through Sunday. Now even saying good-bye to Celeste was painful. She kissed Celeste. The twins were hanging on to Saphora's legs as if they were being wrenched from their mother.

"Your daddy's bringing you boys back," said Saphora. "Aren't you, Ramsey?"

"Soon," he said. But Celeste cast her eyes away. It was the cost of airfare that weighed in part on their decision to travel home, and Ramsey had to be back at work.

"I told Daddy I'd be back next week or so," said Ramsey. "I think he heard me."

"I believe that," said Saphora.

"Gwennie said she has to go back tomorrow," said Celeste.

"She does, but she has all kinds of airline miles. She'll use them if need be and get herself back here," said Saphora. It was so hard having children scattered all over the country, like seeds in the wind. "I'll keep you updated by phone, Ramsey," she said.

Liam hugged Saphora until it hurt both inside and out. "I'll see you soon," she said.

"Nana, is Papa dying?" he asked. He was red eyed, as upset as Eddie, who was the closest to Bender of all the grandsons.

"Liam," said Ramsey, "let's go." He herded the boys toward the elevator.

"I'll walk them out," said Turner.

Celeste sobbed and then was gone.

Saphora dreaded going back into the hospital room, not just because Emerald was no comfort, but because Bender had not responded to any stimulus, not even when Gwennie had spoken into his ear and begged him to open his eyes. Seeing him lying still and not giving out orders and managing the world left a giant vacuum inside Saphora.

She found Emerald sitting beside him, talking as if he heard her. "They say they can hear us, you know," she told Saphora. "I've been telling him how I bake brownies."

"Why that?" asked Saphora.

"I couldn't think of anything else."

"You can go for coffee, sis. I'll take a turn," said Saphora.

"Did you see them off?"

Saphora took the seat next to Emerald. "Liam was sad as could be."

"My grandson Clay looks a lot like that one," said Emerald. "He's grown now and in community college."

"Mother called," said Saphora. Late Saturday night her mother called to ask if Emerald was driving her crazy. "She's coming too. Just as Gwennie has to leave."

"You'll not be alone, I grant," said Emerald. "It's not good to be alone when you're gripped in such misery. When Alan left me, and then Tom gave me such pain—you know he smoked pot—I sat for days on my couch. The TV played night and day."

"Don't cry, Em," said Saphora.

"You know I can't stop," she said. Since she was very young, she could cry on command. Emerald could cry when everyone was laughing and cracking jokes.

"I need you to pull yourself together."

"But crying, they say, is like cleansing the heart." After all these years, Emerald had found a justification for her continual crying jags.

"Then yours is spotless as a newborn."

Emerald had built herself up as the family mourner. "I think it's my gift."

"You'll need more tissues then. That box is empty."

"I'll get some from the nurses' station," she said. She stopped at the door and then walked out, her bottom lip quivering.

Saphora took Bender's hand. "You're cold, love." She pulled the blanket over his hands and up to his neck. "I'm sorry that I left Emerald in here so long. She wants to help but doesn't know how. I hope you could hear your children telling you how much they love you. Eddie's so sad about this, Bender." She talked right along. Emerald might be right about him hearing what was said. But then he might be free-floating in some place between earth and space. "Gwennie's staying another day. She thinks she can breathe you back to us somehow. She's got that determination to get her way, you know." She pressed a tissue to her lips to stifle a sob.

Gwennie was taking Bender's stroke harder than either of the boys, even Turner, who was as emotional as a woman. She had talked at great length to Jim and then gotten all kinds of ideas off the Internet. That worried her even more. She read that a brain cancer patient's chances of survival were lessened if he started having strokes. "Bender, you've got to try," Saphora said. "There are things we've left unsaid to each other." She put her head down against the side of his bed. "We can't leave us like this."

He made a noise like a cat bringing up its just-licked fur. But the lashes that had started growing back did not flicker.

"I never said I was sorry. I know I have a part in our disintegration." It seemed odd to say it out loud, but then she felt better. "That is where we're left if you don't come back," she said. "I don't want us to part like two leaves on the water." That had been a poem he had read, had it not? Or maybe she had heard it in one of those awful dramatic movies played over and over in the afternoons. "We're like so many of those couples we know. I don't want us to have lived and then be left with things we should have said." She was starting to feel more alone talking to a lifeless version of Bender.

"I found an entire cabinet of tissues," said Emerald, bolting through the door, arms loaded.

"Six boxes is a lot."

"Oh, Saphora, you've been crying too. Look, tears on the sheets."

"Give me a box then," she said. "Come and sit by me, Em. Tell me about Tom."

13

Do you really want to look back on your life
and see how wonderful it could have been
had you not been afraid to live it?

CAROLINE MYSS

"But your flight doesn't leave until tomorrow," said Saphora. "And it's late."

Gwennie's suitcase sat by the door. They had decided against staying in a hotel and had driven back late to Oriental.

"I'm needed in New York. My client's fighting to hang on to the only business he's ever known. A competitor has swooped in like a bandit and applied for a patent on the software my client developed." She was putting in a second earring when she said, "I'll be back, Mama. Daddy won't even know I've gone." When she said it, the resentment at her daddy's situation bled through.

"Emerald thinks your daddy can hear us," she said.

"Maybe he can. If that's right, then he's more blessed than we are."

"I'll call you if there's any change."

"I'm coming back Friday night."

Saphora threw her arms around Gwennie. "That's what I need to hear, when you're coming back."

"It's that Luke, isn't it?" asked Emerald, who was coming down the stairs.

"I don't know what you mean." Gwennie would not look at her aunt.

"What is this smile, Gwennie? Is Emerald right?" asked Saphora.

"He's a summer thing, that's all," said Gwennie.

"He's a grieving man, Gwennie. Please don't make him one of your things you tuck into a temporary part of your life," said Saphora.

"I should know not to date a man my mother knows better than I do."

"I'm not saying that I know Luke all that well," said Saphora. "But he's not a summer fling kind of guy. You know that, Gwennie."

"Luke and I are friends, is all. Don't make it more than that," she said, her impatience evident in the way she aimed her suitcase at the front door.

"But look how you're smiling every time you say his name." Saphora thought Luke's effect on her was sweet. But still, she worried for his heart. Gwennie thought commitment was calling her stockbroker twice a week.

"I've got to go. I got the last seat on this flight, and knowing Northwest, they've overbooked."

There was a knock at the back patio door.

"There's your summer fling as we speak," said Emerald. She was still perched on the staircase, giving her a bird's-eye view through the patio glass.

Gwennie ran to the back door as Luke was opening it up to her. "Luke, I was coming over to say good-bye," she told him.

"I couldn't wait," he said.

Gwennie stepped outside and closed the door behind her.

"Oh, she's completely smitten," said Emerald.

"Poor Luke."

"Eddie told me Luke's digging for treasure in his backyard," said Emerald. "Don't you find that strange, given his circumstances?"

"Luke doesn't divulge all that much to me, Em."

Luke took Gwennie's hand and led her off the deck, as if they could hide from Emerald's nosy curiosity. Emerald slowly climbed the staircase until she said she could see the tops of their heads. "He's got her in his arms," she said, as if reporting. "I wish I could read lips. He's saying something, what is it?"

"Emerald, come down. Gwennie wouldn't like you spying on her." Saphora came up on the bottom stair step. "What are they doing?"

"Oh, now that's a kiss."

Saphora ran up three more steps. Gwennie's back was to them as she stood down on the lawn beyond the deck. Luke was holding her so close that she finally collapsed on him, crying.

"Summer fling, my foot!" said Emerald.

"Poor Gwennie," said Saphora.

"Poor Luke," said Em.

⟳

The next morning, Emerald must have decided that Bender's cancer could be crushed with all-purpose cleaner. She sprayed it on every kitchen surface and then went to work on the library baseboards. She was leaping to reach the library's arched doorway when the doorbell rang. She stopped long enough to let Tobias in the house. He ran to the back patio door, out onto the deck, and then back inside. Every Monday for the past few weeks he had counted on finding Eddie waiting for him up in the tree or out in the garage airing up his bicycle tires.

"Eddie's gone," said Saphora. "I told him to call you." Eddie had looked sad at the mention of telling Tobias good-bye. "He's coming back, probably next weekend. He's got school coming up, and his mother wanted to buy him some school clothes."

"He didn't call. What about Liam?" asked Tobias.

"All gone," said Emerald. She raked the top of the doorpost.

"Where's Dr. Warren?" asked Tobias.

"Tobias, come on over here," said Saphora. She seated him at the breakfast bar in the kitchen. "Dr. Warren's gotten very sick. He'll have to stay a long time in the hospital."

"Mom told me she heard he got sick at church," said Tobias. "But I thought he was, you know, throw-up sick."

It was probably all over town that Bender collapsed in church.

"He left church Sunday in an ambulance," said Saphora.

"I've ridden in ambulances," he said. "He wasn't afraid, was he?"

"He slept the whole way."

"When did you ride in an ambulance?" asked Emerald. She got down off the stepstool and put it back in the pantry.

Saphora did not want Tobias to tell Emerald about his illness. "Who hasn't ridden in an ambulance?" she asked.

"I've ridden six times, maybe more," said Tobias.

"You haven't!" said Emerald. "I once rode in an ambulance with my ex. Heart attack, he thought, but no. Just anxiety. Blamed it all on me, then served me with divorce papers." Her voice was getting tinny, like it did before she started to cry.

"Tobias, you know you can come here all you want, whether Eddie's here or not. If you're going up in the tree house, though, just let one of us know," said Saphora.

"I was born sick," said Tobias to Emerald. "Liam probably told you. He tells everyone."

"That you're doing so much better," added Saphora. "Emerald, why don't you take your cleaning project into the bathroom next to the library? I'm sure it needs attention. Sherry won't be back for a few days."

Saphora had finally reached her with the news, poor thing. She was sobbing and promised she would stop in at Duke on the drive back.

"I knew there was something peaked about your eyes. I'll bet you've got leukemia. Poor little boy," said Emerald.

She was tuning up for a squall when Tobias said, "I don't have leukemia, Miss Lacey."

"What then? Scoliosis? No, that's not what I mean. What do they call that thing I'm trying to remember?" Em was mixing up her diseases and conditions. But that was Em.

"HIV, ma'am."

"What is that? You don't mean AIDS," said Emerald. She came out of the library still toting the maid's caddy. "Saphora, does Bender know?"

"He's a doctor," said Tobias. "He knows everything."

"You can't mean it. But what with Bender's cancer, isn't that taking a risk?" asked Emerald.

"He's fine, Emerald. Talk about something else," said Saphora.

"I'm going back to my house," said Tobias. He hugged Saphora and was even polite to Emerald. "I'll come back when Eddie's here," he said. He left through the front door. A moment later, he rode past the front window on his bike.

"Really, Saphora, I understand your need for tolerance and all, but Bender's very susceptible."

"Emerald, this is how it is. Tobias is a guest here whenever he decides to come over. Please don't talk over his head as if he's not here or ask him about his illness," said Saphora. She was up to the ears with Emerald's commentary. "Bender likes Tobias. He makes him happy when he's around. If you understood anything at all about health, you'd know how important Tobias is to us."

"Again, you're choosing someone else over me," said Emerald. "But it's always like that. I'm the last person on your list. Any excuse, and you shuffle me out of your life like refuse."

"I'm not shuffling you out of my life. It isn't that, and you know it, Emerald. If you'd just stop and listen, I wouldn't mind explaining these sensitive matters to you."

"Like I'm a five-year-old. Is that what you mean?" asked Emerald.

"More like when you bury your head in the sand, you can't see the world around you." Saphora had not meant for her resentment against her sister to erupt into a full-blown squabble. "I do it too, Em." She had done well to hold her tongue up until this point. "But Tobias is a little boy born sick. Does it not come to you, without any prompting, that he needs a little sensitivity?"

"I only say what I say to show I care." Now she was blubbering so much she was hard to understand. She dropped the caddy onto the kitchen countertop. "I'm not lifting a finger to help in a house where I'm so disrespected. That's what I do, allow myself to be used. It's my plight."

Emerald would not fly back to Chicago until Thursday. Saphora would count the days.

❧

Later in the evening, Saphora ate her dinner upstairs on the bedroom patio. Emerald took to sulking so much that it made being around her all the more depressing. Saphora left an open container on the stovetop for Emerald to find and warm over.

She got to the lukewarm corn on her plate, moving it around

until it tasted more like the peas. Bender's phone vibrated on the nightstand. She picked it up but the number did not identify the caller. Bender had missed thirty-seven calls. She had not gotten that many calls in a year. Come to think of it, not one neighbor from Davidson had called to check on her or Bender, at least not on her phone.

The river was down since it had not rained in over a week. A flock of geese had landed in the backyard and ratcheted up the noise so much that Saphora yelled to shoo them. The birds were running back and forth to the water's edge. She set her plate on the patio table and then closed her eyes. When she opened them, she found she had fallen asleep and night had come. She could hear Emerald shuffling around below her on the lower deck. Her sister had lit a candle and turned on a country radio station. It was playing too loudly, but Luke would be the only one to hear it.

The moon was a sharp crescent hanging over the river as if it had been dropped accidentally and precariously dangled over the Neuse.

The light came on across the fence. The gate opened slightly and Luke said, "Saphora! Emerald! Come over. I've got something to ask you."

Saphora groaned. She was not ready to share a conversation with Emerald around. Emerald was surprised to know Saphora was on the upper deck looking down on her. She turned quietly. "Saphora is coming, Luke. I'm going inside," she told him.

"It will only take a minute, Emerald," he told her. "You come too."

Saphora turned off Bender's phone completely and dropped it into the nightstand drawer. By the time she slipped on shoes and made it down to the lower deck, Emerald had already met Luke inside his fence, probably to avoid eye contact with her sister. Luke waited inside his gate. He said, "I've made something. I need your opinion." He led Saphora and Emerald into his garage. The lights were bright from above and below. He had strung lights from the rafters and then clamped more lights onto the wall joists. His pottery projects took up one side of the garage, leaving the other side for his small car. "This is what I made for Gwennie." It was the vase she had told Saphora about. It was big enough for a hotel lobby, tall enough to sit on the floor and still be waist high on Luke. Around the shoulders of the vase were ornately fashioned scrolls and embellishments. He had mixed pots of stain and lined them up next to the vase on a stand.

Luke turned a spotlight directly onto the vase. The embellishments were small fish undulating around the vase's widest perimeters. "Gwennie loved the idea of a fish motif. She told me she saves bowls of seashells and starfish."

"Since she was really young," said Saphora.

"I found an ancient fish pattern and used that," he said. "It's Native American."

"What are those lines going down the vase?" asked Saphora.

"Native Americans believe the soul travels south after death. So the lines represent the journey from life to the afterlife."

"It's beautiful, Luke," said Saphora.

Emerald was still angry with her and did not seem to want to comment right after her. But finally she said, "It's the prettiest thing I've ever seen. Gwennie will love it. I love fish too," she said. "When do I get my vase, Luke?"

"You know her tastes, Saphora. What do you think of this blue green stain?" he asked. "I'll contrast it with a bronze, a flourish of gold, and then I'll use a walnut-tinted stain blended from the bottom up."

"You've got impeccable style," said Saphora.

"I'll have to ship it. She'll never get it home on a plane."

"Her birthday's in three weeks," said Saphora. "Perfect timing."

"It's Gwennie's birthday? That's like her not to tell me," he said.

"She's not given it a second thought," said Saphora.

"My Tom starts planning his birthday the day after the last one," said Emerald.

"Given the fact she's had her life caught up in everyone else's business, she'll be elated you're sending it just for that," said Saphora. "She's coming this weekend. She knows you're making it, though, right?"

"She's not really seen it. Not like this. I'll tell her I had to start over. I'll put out another piece that I'm working on. It's not as beautiful as this one," said Luke.

"That is a thought," said Saphora. "The last thing she'd do was look around for it if you used another one as a decoy."

"I can hide it at my cousin's motel," he said.

Saphora did not comment.

Emerald said, "I'm headed back to the house. But thanks for including me in your project for Gwennie." There was still that wounded child in Emerald who was slinging arrows Saphora's way. She left the garage and closed the door behind her.

"Is Emerald all right?" asked Luke.

"Just a little testy. I made her mad," said Saphora. "She thinks I've got it in for her."

"Gwennie says she's sensitive." He lifted his brows and made her laugh.

"She got like that when she was young. She didn't have the highest IQ between us. Then our father was a doctor and our mother was a college professor." Saphora remembered how so often it seemed as if Emerald was asking to be picked on. It was as if it was her way of drawing attention to herself, even if it was negative attention. "She didn't aspire like the rest of us."

"She's a really nice lady. She seems tender," said Luke.

Luke was kind to notice Emerald's good points. But she could not bring herself to compliment her when it seemed so false. "Your vase is not like anything I could go and buy. I might commission you to make one for me."

"I have some sample books. You can look at them and let me know if any of my past pieces appeal to you."

He made her a chai tea, and she went through all of his large notebooks. He kept photographs of his work dating back ten years.

"I like them all," she said.

"Find your favorite. It will say something about you."

"This small one looks like a river stone."

"Is that your favorite?"

"For some reason, yes."

"You're an earth mother."

"Not according to Gwennie."

"You make sure everyone in your circle is well fed, nurtured."

"That's a ploy so I can get them all out of my hair."

"Or you love deeply."

"I wish I could see what you see."

"You see life minimized down to its most basic and honest equations."

"Such as?"

"Believing that time will give you the answers you seek."

"You got all that out of my picking out a vase?"

"And observation."

"Luke, if I may ask, how is it that you see love in me? When I look in the mirror all I see is a critic and a cynic."

"Maybe your inner critic is working overtime. If I didn't shut that guy up, I'd never finish a single piece of pottery." He pulled out a worksheet and wrote a note about Saphora's pottery selection. "You have more control over those inner voices than you realize."

Grief must have its benefits. Wisdom spilled out of Luke like an artesian well.

"There's a dance downtown this Thursday. Gwennie won't be back, and I'm sure she would like it if I got her mother out of the house," said Luke.

"You're inviting me to a dance? What makes you think I can dance?"

"Everyone can dance."

"Where's the dance?"

"Down at the town hall. It's Salsa and Salsa night."

"I don't know anything about salsa dancing. Bender and I are old rockers."

Luke turned on a CD in the player next to his box of tools. The music was soft. He turned to the left and then the right. "I'll show you the steps." He demonstrated a basic salsa movement. Then he took Saphora in his arms. He was comfortable with intimacy. He talked just as comfortably looking straight into her eyes as he did across the room.

"I'm clumsy," she said.

"No apologies." He showed her another move. "Just follow me as I do it."

She placed one hand in his and the other around his back. She remembered when Bender was lean and fit like Luke. He had taken her dancing in uptown Charlotte at a small dance club. She practiced dancing privately for several days leading up to their first real date. Bender had moved like an athlete. But Luke moved more gracefully. Saphora felt his hips leading hers. He spun her away and then back.

"Mrs. Warren, you've been keeping yourself in that house cooking and cleaning for too long. You are a dancer, madam."

He turned up the song. The rhythm was driving. She could see the shop lights around the garage spinning as he turned her around.

"We're coming to the finale, Saphora. I'm going to spin you out and then back and then I want you to trust me. Drop backward over my arm."

She did as he asked. He moved her out and then back next to him. Her arms came free, and she lifted them up overhead as she arched back over his arm. She could feel the strength of years of pottery making in his forearm as he held her up effortlessly.

"You're wonderful!" he said. He helped her straighten up.

She imagined Bender holding her that night at the dance. He had pulled her close and kissed her. But what was the name of the song? She could not for the life of her remember. It was crowded out by too many other details collected in daily living. Saphora opened her eyes and realized she had nearly put her lips on Luke's. "I'm sorry," she said.

"You're missing your spouse," he said. "I understand exactly what you're going through." He stepped back from her and turned off the song. He was so amiable, putting her at ease. "Thursday night. Sevenish. Come over here and I'll drive us."

"Maybe I shouldn't," she said.

"You're completely safe with me, Saphora. Of all people, I'm the one who should be escorting you around. Gwennie would want it."

"It would look like I'm out on the town while my husband is in a coma." She shook her head. "Thanks anyway. Good night, Luke." She left Luke's creative womb of a garage. When she crossed the lawn, Emerald was sitting on the lower deck again.

"I heard music," she said.

"You were hearing things," said Saphora. She went upstairs, flush from dancing with Luke.

14

We grow primarily through our challenges,
especially those life-changing moments when
we begin to recognize aspects of our nature
that make us different from the family and
culture in which we have been raised.

CAROLINE MYSS

Emerald made two pots of coffee while waiting for their mother, Daisy, to arrive.

It took a lot of planning to please Professor Daisy; a White House planner might be overwhelmed attempting to please her.

Emerald had been on the outs with her mother since she had gotten pregnant before college. But Daisy learned to overlook Emerald's indiscretions when she fell in love with her first grandchild. No one knew whether or not he looked like his father since she had kept his name a secret. The man who eventually married her gave Tom his name but never fully his devotion.

Emerald, who had trouble enough juggling her own changing expectations, took up next with a house painter. When he struggled to stay off the sauce, she moved out of his little house by the railroad tracks and went to work for a lady who sold knitting supplies. Emerald started sweaters she did not finish, scarves that lay on her closet shelf still tied to the skein. But she learned enough skills to navigate the knitter's language and help the customers find what they had come to purchase. Emerald's boss promoted her to the head manager of the Spin-A-Yarn shop, a loft business in downtown Chicago.

While Saphora put together a lunch of tomato bisque and field greens, Emerald sat knitting in the place warmed by Bender the past few weeks. "I'm making a wall hanging for your bedroom upstairs, Saphora. Blue and beige. Do you prefer a rose border or seashells? Wait. I know already. It should be seashells."

"Mother wants me to take her straight to see Bender tomorrow morning. I called the nurses' station. There's been no change," said Saphora. She was comforted Emerald was not shooting bullets every time she looked at her. She was quick to forgive.

"I remember when Daddy was comatose," said Emerald. "I kept talking over him until Mother made me quit. She thought it was annoying him. But if it snaps them out of it, then what does it matter?"

"Bender told me a million times that his father died in his sleep. He said the Warren men are blessed to live until they just go to sleep. I always thought Bender would go like his daddy," said Saphora.

"There's no way to know. I wonder if I'll go like Mother's mom and sisters. They all had accidents. That sounds like a curse when you think about it."

"The Horn women all died of cancer, Emerald," said Saphora.

"Grandma got up in the middle of the night, fell, and cracked her ribs," said Emerald.

"But that was a complication. She was dying of cancer." She doubled the bags, making stronger tea. "I hear a car in the driveway."

Emerald picked up the pace, knitting faster.

"I'll get the door then," said Saphora. Daisy was already waiting on the doorstep by the time Saphora got there. "Mother, here you are. You should have let me pick you up." She hugged her mother, even though Daisy was not a hugger.

"I never thought the ocean would look so brown. Hello, lovie," said Daisy.

"That's the Neuse," said Saphora. "It does empty out into the ocean though."

"Oh, the Neuse! I knew that."

Emerald sat with her back to them, knitting on the sofa.

"Emerald, are you helping your sister?" asked Daisy.

"I'm making Saphora a wall hanging." Emerald got up and awkwardly hugged her mother. She started to look into her eyes about the same time Daisy looked past her.

As much as Saphora had wished for Emerald to leave, she was now glad, for she filled up the silence with her endless supply of words. Daisy was, at her core, as reticent as Saphora. Saphora imagined the two of them running out of things to say after the first hour of catching up.

"Bender's bought you a beautiful house on the water," said Daisy.

"Two," said Emerald.

"I've seen the Lake Norman place, Emerald. I was with Saphora when she decided to buy it." Daisy left the den and joined Saphora in the kitchen. "Do you have any broccoli, Saphora? At my age I'm putting it in everything now."

Saphora opened the refrigerator and checked inside the crisper. "There's no broccoli. I can pick some up later today though."

"Don't trouble yourself. I can do it. Emerald," she said as if she was irritated, as if her daughter's knitting was in the way of more important things, "why don't you make the drinks?" Next she inspected inside Saphora's refrigerator herself. She checked for fresh lemons and asked if she had a jar of lemon curds. Saphora had not seen lemon curd in the pantry since the *Southern Living* shoot. Daisy said, "How about I do the shopping for us?"

By nightfall, Daisy marshaled Saphora out of the kitchen. "I'll take care of dinner. You get some rest," she told Saphora.

Emerald moved her knitting out onto the deck. Saphora joined her outside, saying she wanted to watch the sun go down. Emerald said, "Mother takes over my place too when she comes over. Although I haven't seen her in years. She thinks my house is too small for stay-over guests."

"I'm glad to give up kitchen duties," said Saphora. She was feeling out of energy, running back and forth between the house and Duke. "She's not so bad."

"First you'll think that. Then it goes to her head. You'll see."

"I'll admit I get put out with her too," said Saphora. But the day before she was beginning to feel put out with Emerald. She tried to imagine herself knocking about in the house all by herself. "Do you like living alone, Emerald? Is the quiet deafening?"

"I keep the tube on, you know, hospital shows and the like."

"But what do you do with your time? You can do anything you want, right?"

"My son's never been a good decision maker. It seems I'm always bailing him out." She started a long story about her son and his tendency to move from job to job.

Saphora decided that Emerald never really understood what Saphora meant when she asked her a question. She had heard it said that it was easier to live through someone else than to become complete yourself. But in trying to do that—live for herself—she had gotten a whole houseful of people who needed her attention. Emerald had been given the opportunity to become whoever she could be, and yet all she did was enable her son. Saphora felt bad for continuously judging her sister. Maybe she explained herself so poorly that Emerald only heard part of what was said. "Emerald, I'm just curious is all. I'm not talking about your son. I'm asking what you do with your life now. What is the meaning of life for you?"

"He's really needy, Saphora. He is my life."

"But if you keep getting him out of his problems, then he'll never learn to do things on his own," said Saphora. "Are you saying that you don't have a purpose if your son doesn't need you to fix his life?"

Emerald put down her knitting. "Are you getting mad at me again?"

"I'm not. But don't you wonder if there's something more for us than bailing out our kids?"

"I don't know what you mean."

"Look at Mother. She's going to set the table, put out the food. Then she'll pout because no one lifted a hand to help. Of course, we could try to help and she'd run us out."

"She's not going to change," said Emerald.

"That is what I'm trying to say." She finally had it in her mind how to say it to Emerald. "I don't want my life to stay like this. I'm afraid of turning into her."

"Is that what you meant? You don't have to worry. You're not going to turn into her."

"You don't know. I might."

"Saphora, this is the way women talk when they're under stress. You wouldn't be talking like this if you and Bender were back in Lake Norman living life as normal."

"It wasn't normal, Emerald. I'd never go back to how things used to be."

"You are such a goof! I'd give my eyeteeth to have your life."

"Bender's not an easy man to live with. I was just a fixture in his well-ordered world." She was taking a chance, spilling her guts to flighty Emerald.

"He loves you. He told me."

"When did he tell you?"

"The night before he went into the hospital. He's in love with you, Saphora. You mean everything to him."

"Bender said that?"

"I wouldn't make it up."

Emerald would make it up though. If she thought she could make Saphora happier with a twist of her words, she would do it. Words meant nothing to her, true or not. They were just words. Emerald would take something as small as a nod of approval from Bender and stretch it into whatever she thought would improve what was said. It was her way of feeling included.

"You missed a stitch, Emerald. Look, there's a gap in your row."

She held up her knitting. There was the hole. "Oh, what's the use?" Emerald laid it aside.

ര

Gwennie called at bedtime to tell Saphora that she was finally making headway for the sake of her client. Saphora told her Luke had asked her to the town dance. "I turned him down. It wouldn't be right."

But Gwennie already knew. "You should go, Mama. Daddy would like to know you're not holed up brooding over him."

"I don't know."

"Go. It makes me feel less guilty because I can't be there."

"Should I?"

"Yes, go."

"How many times has Luke called?" asked Saphora.

"Once. But we've texted back and forth every day."

She hoped Gwennie was really coming back on Friday.

☙

Saphora helped her mother settle into the guest room where Eddie and Tobias had pitched a sheet tent as they spied on Luke digging in the backyard. The house took on a different music with them gone and Mother pacing up and down the hallway and brushing her teeth as she made a to-do list for the next day.

In spite of Mother's finicky habits, she had gone to bed and left the kitchen light on. Saphora went down the stairs and across the den. She was reaching for the kitchen light switch when she noticed the library door left open. She had not invited her mother into the room. But she knew she had a love of reading and would help herself to a book or two. She turned on the library light as she walked in. She found the room just as it had been the morning Bender had gotten dressed for church. There were his medical journals in a stack on the nightstand. He had left a magnifying glass out on the desk. But the middle drawer of the desk was ajar. She was about to close it when she opened it instead. She had never remembered Bender as one to keep a journal. But there, bound in green leather, was a journal. She pulled it out to examine it. It was slightly worn at the corners. That was a surprise.

She settled into the upholstered chair next to the desk where Bender had read before bed the few weeks they had stayed in the house. She held it closed next to her, her mind exploring their shared past.

She opened it to the first page, half expecting to find a story about one of his lovers. But it was a passage about Turner.

> Saphora has been in labor for twenty hours. She is so
> pale that I can hardly stand to look at her. I found this
> journal in the hospital gift shop. I'm writing in it to keep
> from losing my mind. She's not in any danger. But there
> is something so fragile about her, seeing her laboring to
> bring our first child into the world. Even that scares me
> to death. The world is not a place for children.

The staircase creaked. Mother was coming downstairs, probably for her nightly glass of baking soda and water. Saphora closed the journal although she wanted to finish reading it. She grabbed a book from Bender's nightstand and put it on top of the journal to carry it out. She shut off the light and met her mother in the kitchen.

"Saphora. I thought I saw a light on downstairs. Oh, you're reading."

Saphora said, "Might as well use the library."

"A Bible," she said.

Saphora looked down at the book she had grabbed off Bender's nightstand. She managed to not look surprised that she had picked up a Bible. "Oh, this. Pastor Mims gave it to Bender, I guess. Never know when you might need a little help from above, Mama."

"Sure, sure. Well, good night then."

"I'll see you at breakfast and then we'll head for Duke," said Saphora.

She got herself back upstairs. She locked her door and climbed straight into bed. The room was a pale blue in the glow of nothing but her reading lamp, like the night was all around her. She laid the Bible beside her and it fell open. Out slid a bookmark, meaning that Bender must have marked it. Or else Mims had done it for him. Ministers were sneaky like that, leaving things around for people to find, like those annoying people who leave little tracts on the sinks in public bathrooms. She did not know how many she had dropped into the trash can out of sheer willfulness.

A scripture was underlined in green, though, as if Bender had found something he liked and then grabbed the only pen he could find—a marker left behind by one of his grandsons. Saphora read it out of curiosity but also partly comfort. Just imagining Bender propped up in bed marking up a Bible comforted her. He was a man who had kept distance between himself and anyone who might try to look somehow beyond Bender the plastic surgeon. It was like finding an unlocked door.

He had marked a place in the book of Psalms:

You have taken account of my wanderings;
    Put my tears in Your bottle
    Are they not in Your book?

It was a mystery the way he had marked it. There were lines beneath it and then an arrow pointing toward the bottom of the page. Saphora held the page under the reading lamp to make out his notations. He wrote:

Is this literal or a metaphor? Would He keep vigil over
my pain so meticulously that he would preserve my
tears? And what book?

And then in bold lettering, *Ask Mims!*

Saphora turned page after page and found more markings and notations. Bender had been reading it, apparently for hours on end. When he would find himself at the end of his own human reasoning, again he would write, *Ask Mims!*

Saphora put the Bible beside her pocketbook and turned out the light. She lay in the dark listening to nothing at all. Even Luke was not digging. The river creatures had fallen quiet as if the earth were taking a big pause. As if waiting for her to notice that all these years, in spite of her occasional prayers, she'd neglected a part of herself— a connection to God. Maybe the soul needed to be tended the same as the mind or the body. Or else what was real crowded out what could be. Those matters seemed real to Mims. And while facing cancer, real to Bender. She must admit, cancer does make the heart look above earth for answers.

She closed her eyes and a phrase fluttered through her thoughts like a note dropped into her mind by Bender—*Ask Mims!* After she returned home from the hospital, she would pay the minister a visit.

୭ଠ

The smell of her mother's Good Morning muffins came up the stairs Wednesday and awoke Saphora from a dream about Bender. He was young again and paddling a small boat across Lake Norman. Only there were no houses anywhere along the banks, just a mist rolling down the slopes and surrounding him. He stopped the boat in the middle of the lake and then looked straight up at Saphora as if she were a disembodied spirit looking down on him. Then the scent of muffins came at her senses and she sat straight up in bed.

She did not make an effort to dress but went down in her sleep shirt and slippers. Emerald and her mother sat buttering and eating muffins. It was a quiet circle, the three of them eating breakfast without the need to jump up and fill a coffee cup or leave with breakfast half eaten to drive a child off to school.

The morning was like a gift to all three of them, at least in Saphora's estimation. But Emerald stared sadly through the patio doors and out across the Neuse, unable or unwilling to allow a moment of joy to seep in. Her mother sat tabulating her checkbook balance. Neither of them seemed aware of the miracle of eating muffins without interruption.

"Mama, will you drive us to Duke? I've got some reading to do," said Saphora.

"Of course," said Daisy. "Emerald, will you go too?"

"I'll stay behind," said Emerald. "I don't know why I'm so weepy this morning. Saphora, why do you think?"

Saphora knew it was a loaded question. One misstep and Emerald's sensitive comportment would topple into pity. "You're merciful, I guess," said Saphora.

"There's nothing wrong with her, Saphora. Don't coddle your sister. Emerald, you know you've got no reason to cry. It's Saphora going through a crisis, but you've got to take it and make it yours."

"You're horrible," said Emerald, so quietly that she surprised even Daisy.

"Emerald, you should take the small boat out a ways," Saphora said, inviting her to look through the window at the boat that Eddie had been using. "Borrow my rod and reel. The fish have been biting even late morning. Whatever you catch I'll fix along with dinner."

"Be productive, is what your sister means," said Daisy.

"I just mean go and have some time to yourself," said Saphora. "Mother, can you be ready in a half hour?"

"Five minutes," said Daisy.

Saphora dressed quickly and took Bender's Bible off the night-stand. Daisy waited at the bottom of the staircase. Beyond the deck, Emerald got the rod and reel out of the storage shed. She pulled the line out a ways and stared at it as if she was not exactly sure what to do next.

"She'll work it out, Mother," said Saphora. "When we get back, will you please try not to be so hard on her?" Saphora asked as kindly as she knew how. "Her plane leaves early tomorrow. Let's find good in Emerald." She gave the keys to Daisy and led her out to the garage.

Only two cars passed them on the road out of Oriental and into New Bern. Saphora played Beethoven in the player. Daisy was com-pletely enthralled with the tracking device. "At least I won't get us lost."

"I won't let you, Mother." Saphora opened Bender's Bible. She wrote down some of his notes in a notepad.

"I've tried reading it. My friend Jan, she loves her Bible group," said Daisy. "They're all the rage now. I don't see the attraction."

"Bender left some notes behind for a minister friend. He must have been on a quest."

"If it gives him answers in the midst of cancer, I'm all for it," said Daisy.

"It's not answers. He's asking questions," said Saphora.

"Like what?"

"Like this one. The scripture says, 'Consider it all joy, my brethren, when you encounter various trials.' Then Bender's note says, 'Is that kind of joy possible? How can I know it?'"

Daisy was strangely without comment.

Saphora took down his question in her notebook. "Then on the next page is the scripture about loving your neighbor. Bender asks, 'How will I know when I have that kind of love? Can I cause it to be true by something I do? Or does God put it in me?'"

"He's on a journey," said Daisy.

Parking decks surrounded the sprawling Duke campus. "Let's park below and then we'll be closer to the basement tube," said Saphora. She helped her mother find a single space open at the farthest end of the deck. They walked into the hospital and down the tube. A small tram zipped back and forth for those who did not want to walk. Saphora led her onto the elevator.

The cancer wing buzzed with activity. A high-profile senator had checked in for operable cancer. The paparazzi press corps were not allowed past the lobby just outside the elevator. When the elevator door opened, the journalists were attentive only long enough to see if some celebrity was stepping out from the elevator.

An attendant stopped Saphora and asked for her identification. When she finally got clearance for herself and her mother, the nurse told her, "Your husband's room is right next to the senator's."

Guards were stationed next to the senator's door. Daisy was goggle-eyed over the press corps and the security. "How is the senator?" she asked the guard. He did not answer. A caterer pushed a cart around them, and the guard allowed her to pass.

"Did you see all of that?" asked Daisy. "Fruit, belgian waffles, and jams. Brunch for a king. That's our tax dollars at work, thank you very much."

The door to Bender's room opened. A nurse recognized Saphora. "Mrs. Warren. Sorry for all the noise. Senator Weberman's just checked in and brought his entourage with him."

"How is Bender?" asked Saphora.

"No change. Have you met yet with a neuropsychologist?" asked the nurse. "He can give you answers."

"Jim is scheduling one," said Saphora. "Dr. Pennington, I mean."

Daisy asked, "How about I go for coffee, and we'll sit with Bender for as long as you want?"

"Vanilla latte, skim," said Saphora.

Bender's room was dark. She opened the blinds and let in the noonday sun. But it woke the patient in the bed next to Bender. He let out a yawning sigh and then brought his bed up. His head was bandaged from surgery. He said, "Who's there?"

"Mrs. Warren. I'm visiting my husband," said Saphora. "Is the light too bright?"

"The light's all I can see," he said. "My tumor's affected my eyesight. I'm Mort."

"Saphora."

Bender's eyes were swollen closed, dark around his lids and under his eyes.

"My wife just left. She's tired of hospital food. So am I," said Mort.

"My mother's gone for some coffee. You want a coffee? I can call her."

"I'll pass. Coffee's not coffee anymore. It's all that flavored stuff and burned coffee beans. Diner coffee. Now that's coffee."

"I like diners," said Saphora.

"Mary's bringing me back a club sandwich if she can find one."

"The only restaurant around here is Italian, I'm afraid."

"That's okay. Sorry about your husband. I talk to him when no one's around. You never know."

"You talk to him?" That was comforting.

"He doesn't answer. But I don't mind," said Mort.

"I'm glad. I think he can hear us," said Saphora. She opened her purse. "I'm going to read to him, if you don't care."

"I'd like that." Mort closed his eyes.

Saphora read the passage about the tears in a bottle. Then she said, "I don't know what it means, love. But I'm glad you left behind your notes. I like reading them."

"I know that scripture," said Mort. "My mother used to talk about God saving our tears in a bottle. It must be from Jewish history. My mother, she was Jewish."

"God must have a water tower for mine," said Saphora.

"How long has your husband been sick?"

"A month. He was doing so well."

"It's not over till it's over," said Mort. "The tears you think you've wasted on cancer, they're not wasted."

"You don't really believe God saves tears, do you?"

"I think he counts them."

"Why would he do that?"

"That's when he's the most attentive."

"How do you know that?"

"He hangs out around human suffering."

"How do you know?"

"Look at where Jesus went. Where there was pain, there was Jesus."

"But you're Jewish."

"Just on my mother's side."

"Then he must be at the hospital a lot. You think he's here beside Bender?"

"Of course."

"Do you ever feel him?" she asked.

"I started out just talking to him, like he's a regular guy. With due respect, he's, well, God and all that. But then one day, he was just there."

"Did he say anything?"

"Not out loud. But I felt him with me, like he was there listening to me."

"What was he like?"

"Love like I couldn't describe. You try it. Just get alone someplace and talk to him. See if he shows up. What would it hurt?"

Daisy came in through the door backward, pushing it open with her rear end and holding out two coffees. "The line was as long as California," she said.

"Mort, this is my mother, Daisy."

"We're talking about God," said Mort.

"People do that in hospitals," said Daisy. "Have you ever seen an angel?" she asked.

"Not me," said Mort. "I don't think I'd know. Like the scriptures say, you might be entertaining angels unaware. I'd be unaware."

"But he says he can feel God," said Saphora.

"I did right after my husband died," Daisy said. She had a story no matter what was brought up. But she had never mentioned this one. She said, "At first I was mad at him for leaving me all alone. Then one day when I was really steamed and lonesome, I cleaned out the refrigerator of anything that reminded me of Bernie. I was throwing out anchovies, and suddenly it was like someone was standing behind me. I turned around and no one was there."

"Maybe it wasn't God," said Mort.

"Who then?" asked Daisy.

"Bernie's shadow, mad at you for throwing out perfectly good anchovies," said Mort.

15

What is right for one soul may not be right
for another. It may mean having to stand on
your own and do something strange in the
eyes of others.

EILEEN CADDY

Reverend Mims was pleased as could be that Saphora wanted to meet
him at the Marina Bistro for breakfast. He was done with his chores
of straightening the chairs and offering assistance to the infirm for the
week. He told her, as a matter of fact, that he was going straight to
Duke after he met with Saphora. That gave her as much consolation
as knowing praying Mort was rooming with Bender.

Saphora kissed Emerald good-bye. Her flight was leaving at
noon. She had finished a small square of the blue wall hanging after
all. "I'll ship it to you when it's finished," she said. "It's a patchwork
of our family." She held up the blue knitted square. She had woven
purple yarn into the center, creating a design of three female figures.

"It's got three women in it," said Saphora, finding nice things to
say about a wall hanging that Emerald might never finish. "Is that
you and Mother and me?"

"Us three. But I'll make the rest a surprise," said Emerald. She
kissed her and wheeled her luggage out the door while Saphora
locked it. "You must be going back to Duke."

"I'm going to meet a minister."

"About Bender?" asked Emerald.

"I guess so," said Saphora.

"Have him say a prayer for me. I get so under the weight of things," said Emerald.

"Em, you don't have to," she told her. But then, it was Em's way. She wouldn't be Em without her clouds overhead. She offered, "I'll drive you out and get you on the main road. Then you just follow the map I laid out for you." Saphora helped her put her luggage in the rental car trunk.

Emerald followed Saphora and then turned right. Saphora watched Em until the shade trees enveloped her. Saphora turned left and then right into the tiny marina. A row of blue bicycles parked in the bike rack surrounded one nice, lean black racer, the only bike locked into the rack.

Pastor Mims walked out of the bistro and waved. He held a bike helmet under his one good arm.

"Is that your racing bike?" asked Saphora. She imagined that riding with one paralyzed hand had taken some practice.

"It's mine. I'm training for a charity ride."

He led her to the back of the restaurant where he had already reserved a table for them with the view of the water. He asked the waitress to bring him a large juice.

Saphora pulled out Bender's Bible. That made the pastor grin so big that Saphora turned red, as if she were one of those women who carried Bibles into public places to make some kind of statement. "I found this in my husband's room." She opened it to one of the places he had bookmarked. "Bender wrote out some questions in his Bible. I had this idea in my head that if I asked you the questions, I could read the answers to him."

"He'd like that, Saphora. But I don't claim to have all the answers."

That made her like him even better. Saphora ordered an egg biscuit and coffee. Then she said, "There's a verse that talks about God saving tears in a bottle and writing them in a book."

"A psalm of David."

"Okay."

"It's a song book. First off," said Mims, "the Psalms are songs that came out of real people's struggles. This one was written by the shepherd boy who became a king. David's story can be read in second Samuel. If you read from that book, you'll find David was being chased by his enemies. He wrote the songs for his people to use to thank God for his persistence to see them through attack after attack from their enemies."

"But what does this mean, that he saves our tears in a bottle? Is the Bible always literal?"

"No. Within the context of this song, it's a metaphor."

"What can I tell Bender?"

"God is watching over him, so close that he sees every tear that Bender has shed." Her silence left him to respond, "Saphora, maybe you should try praying before you read the scriptures. Then ask God to show you what he's trying to tell you."

She read the scripture again. Then she said, "He sounds like he's trying to, I don't know, get his mental mind-set right."

"Partly. There's a metaphor in it."

"About God? About him being close by? I met a man who says he can feel God near him."

"It's possible. Although I don't always feel God close by."

"You don't?"

"No."

"How do you go on doing what you do then?"

"The same way a tree grows. When God is silent, he is maturing me. My spiritual and emotional roots grow beneath the surface of my life." He must have read her pensive expression when he said, "Then other days, seemingly out of the blue, I feel him again. Some like to call that a time of refreshing."

She closed the Bible. "But, Pastor John, I never feel him close by."

"Faith is believing what you can't see. Sometimes that means you can't feel anything either."

"If I could have a prayer wish, I'd like to feel him. Is that a selfish prayer?"

"You can talk to him about it. I don't think it's selfish. It's a reasonable request from a searching woman."

"You've made me feel better."

He had been kind and patient to address Bender's questions. "Can I help with anything else?"

"If you don't mind." She had not said this to anyone ever. But she hoped that by saying it, she'd be free of some of the burden she had felt these past few years. "Is it wrong to think I might have married the wrong man?"

"Why do you think that?"

"He's given me a lot of grief. I know he's not going to confess that to you."

"I can't tell you what he's confessed."

"Can you give me a hint?"

He laughed so hard that she laughed too. Then she said, "I know. It's private between the two of you."

"That Sunday when you brought him to church?"

"His one and only time in church, yes?"

"He left behind a card. You know those visitor cards you were handed coming in the door."

"He did accept it," she said.

"He wrote a note to me. It said, 'I want to talk to you, Mims, about Jesus, your church, and my cancer.'"

"He was looking for answers," said Saphora. "I thought so."

"That's normal for his condition."

"I'm searching too, Pastor John."

"You keep doing what you're doing—looking for answers. God hasn't left you all alone, Saphora. There's more to say, but today let's just leave it at me answering what you've asked."

"My head's full of a lot of questions."

"God knows those in advance of your asking them. He is that close to you, Saphora."

She started crying as if the whole Neuse River was running over the banks and out through her soul.

ᕤ

Tobias was waiting on the porch when Saphora pulled in. He got up and grinned as she walked toward him. "I've been riding around bored as all get-out. Could I climb up the tree house?"

"You should have rung the doorbell. My mother would have let you in." Now that she thought about it, it was probably best he had waited. "I'll get you a cold Coke," she said, letting him in. "You stay in the tree or you can play inside. Just let your mom know."

"I told her. She knows I'm here."

Daisy was watching an old movie. She sat on the sofa clutching a box of tissues.

"We've got company," said Saphora.

"Oh, hello, friend of Eddie's…ah," said Daisy, "I guess?"

"Mother, Tobias," said Saphora.

"I miss him so much I'm bored to death," said Tobias.

Saphora got out two canned colas and gave one to Tobias. He went out the back onto the deck and then climbed up the ladder.

"I had hoped to see Eddie myself. I want to hug Turner so hard I might hurt him," said Daisy.

"He got bad news. Someone quit at the hospital, and he has to take a weekend shift."

"But Gwennie's coming, isn't she?" Daisy asked.

"I believe so. The young man next door's taken a liking to her. Luke. He's an artist." Saphora turned down the volume on Daisy's movie.

"Artist? If he's not rich, he must be an extraordinary guy to be of interest to Gwennie."

"I don't think it will last. But he sure is moony over her. Poor guy."

"The last thing she'd do is get serious about an artist. What's he do anyway, paint portraits?"

"Pottery."

"That's worse, isn't it? Like those people who travel around hawking their wares at food festivals. I'm not knocking it. I'm just saying." Daisy sat forward, having trouble hearing her movie. She picked up the remote and increased the sound again.

The telephone rang. It was Jamie. She was sitting out in the driveway. Saphora invited her inside. When she opened the door, Jamie looked like someone had kicked her in the stomach.

"Is Tobias here?" she asked.

"He is, but he told me you knew he came here."

"He left upset. He was playing down at the marina. He tried to get some other boys interested in a kickball game. But one of them told the others not to go near him, that he had AIDS. There was a girl there who started screaming. Tobias was embarrassed. I'm just weary of seeing him wounded."

"I'm sorry as can be," said Saphora.

"The last thing I wanted was for it to be all over town, but now that's a hopeless wish. When I brought him here for the summer it was so he could get away from the crazies."

"I don't know why kids are so cruel," said Daisy. "Why would they think a little boy has AIDS anyway? Like kids know what AIDS is. He should have told them to get lost."

Saphora's first thought was to try to stop Jamie from answering. But then she reasoned that she and Jamie had become friends because Jamie didn't have to hide Tobias's sickness around her. "Mother, this is Jamie, Tobias's mother. She adopted him. He does have AIDS."

"I don't believe it," said Daisy.

"He was born with it," said Jamie.

"From his mother? Is that how?" asked Daisy. She turned up the movie another decibel.

"That's enough. Jamie, you don't have to say anymore," said Saphora.

"She drifted city to city," said Jamie. "She could have gotten it a lot of ways. I don't even know if there is a grave anywhere. She had a sister who saw to her after she passed. Toby handles it like an adult."

"But he's been playing with Eddie," said Daisy. "You know it's different in every country. I saw a whole special about it."

"It is different in every country," said Jamie. "A different cocktail of meds is used to treat it everywhere it has spread. But it's not a danger to children playing with a child who has the disease."

"I'm sorry. I didn't mean any offense," said Daisy.

Jamie managed to show her some understanding. "None taken." She said to Saphora, "We were going to the dance tonight. But now I'm sure Tobias is going to want to pack up and head home."

"I'm going to the dance." Saphora surprised herself saying it. "You have to bring him, Jamie."

"I'll talk to him."

By the time Jamie coaxed Tobias out of the tree, he was not at all agreeable to attending. Saphora promised him, "There will be so many there, and all new people to meet. I wish you'd come, Tobias."

"Maybe just drop in," he said. "Before we leave Oriental for home."

Saphora kissed him and gave him a hug. "You are such a grownup sometimes, Tobias."

She saw them out. Then she sat out on the deck until she could hear Luke shoveling. She yelled, "I've decided to go to the dance."

"I know. Gwennie told me," he said through the fence. He could not be seen at all. But a little dirt was thrown into the air, the tip of the shovel rotating and swinging back to earth. And then it was dark.

༄

Saphora was thinking about Gwennie Thursday night when she was deciding what shoes to wear. She admired women who could dance in heels. Gwennie danced in them as if she were wearing house shoes. But Saphora could hardly walk in them, let alone dance. She picked out a pair of soft leather flats. She put them on and then danced a few steps in front of the vanity mirror. She looked like a grown woman trying out for the high school cheerleading squad—the train had already come and gone.

The doorbell rang. She pulled on a black cotton-knit top and the earrings Bender had given her two birthdays past. She got to the front door, and there was Luke looking as if his cat had died.

"What's going on?" asked Saphora.

He walked past her into the house. "It's Gwennie. She says she's having problems with her client. She's not coming this weekend."

"She's not told me that," said Saphora.

"She will."

"I'll talk to her. You know Gwennie's under a load at work."

"I know. But I think she'd come if I weren't here waiting for her," said Luke. "Now I'm ruining things for you."

"Don't say such things."

"She's a free spirit. I'm a threat to her freedom."

"Luke, you've just met. Don't take it to mean more than what she's told you," said Saphora, turning on the outside light.

"I'm going to call her and tell her that she doesn't have to worry about coming here. I've got an art show to attend in Louisiana." He was no longer hearing anything Saphora said. "I'll call her now."

"Wait, Luke!" He was right about her, of course. But she could not stand to see him so dejected. "She just doesn't move quickly, that's all."

"I understand Gwennie. That's why I can't get her out of my head—and please don't tell her I said that. It's been three years since my wife died. It took me nearly that long to come out of my fog and finally buy this house, so I understand moving slowly. And I'm not the type that expects her to rearrange her life around me." He was talking as if he had a list of things to get out. "But I know she needs to come home this weekend for your sake and her dad's sake. So I'm going to Louisiana. Once she knows, she'll be here with you. You watch and see if I'm not right."

Poor Luke. Here he had the perfect opportunity to ask more from Gwennie, but instead he let her off the hook.

"All right. You go to Louisiana. But let me tell her. She should think you're too busy to call her again."

He opened the door for Saphora. "I like that idea."

&

The Captain's Quarters was a small bar and clubhouse for the yachters and sailors who docked along the Oriental Marina. Colored lights were strung across the front landing and along the roof's eaves. Two torches blazed on either side of the open doors. It was a few short steps from the Marina Bistro and only a few blocks from First Community Church.

The hall held only about a hundred or so bodies, so the line to get inside was already out the door and down the landing. The social calendar in Oriental was a little spare compared to most coastal communities, making Salsa and Salsa night a hot ticket. Luke introduced Saphora to the couples in front of and behind them, the Mettingers and the Shepherds.

"Good to see you out again," said the Shepherd woman to him. Her name was Faye.

"Saphora's my neighbor," Luke told her.

"We've been relentless in trying to get Luke out of that garage," said Faye.

"Her husband's very sick. At Duke," said Luke.

"Oh, you must be the plastic surgeon's wife," said Faye. "How is he?"

"Have you met Bender?" asked Saphora.

"I was at church when he got so sick. You looked scared. I would be too. I'm glad Luke dragged you here." Faye turned to Luke. "You did a good thing, Luke."

"I apologize. I can't remember much about who I met at church," said Saphora. But Faye did look familiar. "I'm sure we messed up Pastor Mims's whole day."

"He shortened his message. But that's not necessarily a bad thing," said Faye.

"Ha-ha!" Her husband, Mike, was lighting up a cigarette.

"I heard about that," said the Mettinger woman behind them. She called herself Sassy—one of those cute names that stick on little southern girls like glue and then follow them into adulthood. "Let me tell you, there's no better pastor than Mims. We weren't even regular attenders, and he had a ladies' group bringing me soup when I was so sick with the flu."

"Now Sassy heads up the ladies' group," said her husband, Joe.

"Pay it forward. Isn't that what they say?" asked Sassy.

"Pastor Mims has been there for Bender," said Saphora. "He's not like any preacher I've ever known."

"My ears are burning." Mims came walking across the landing from the bistro.

"They're talking about you, Pastor," said Joe. He got out of line and shook his hand.

"I came down here for soup. They make it for me when I don't want to cook," said Mims.

"I was wondering if you were coming to the dance," said Sassy. "You ever kick up your heels, Pastor?"

"Once did."

"You ought to come and give us ladies a spin around the floor," said Sassy. She was laughing.

"I've not had my study time this week," he said. "I'd best get back to the books." He smiled at Saphora. "You look beautiful, Mrs. Warren."

"Pastor, thank you for all you've done. I know Bender and I have cut into your time," said Saphora.

"My time is yours, Mrs. Warren." He excused himself a little awkwardly and continued walking down the street toward the house where he lived.

"Between Luke and Pastor Mims, it keeps me busy just trying to find women for the local bachelors," said Sassy.

Luke turned his back to Sassy and stepped closer to the club's door.

"Faye, tell me how long you've lived in Oriental," said Saphora. She first got Faye and then Sassy talking about what led them to the Outer Banks. Sassy was making Luke feel awkward, as if he were the odd man out. Turner was just like him, hated to be dragged into singles talk led by married people. Luke was not much older than Turner but seemed to share the same bachelor's sensibilities. He had successfully kept Gwennie a best-kept secret from the local wags.

Luke talked to another artist from town. Sassy and Faye occupied themselves with two other women interested in starting a card group.

Saphora rested against the railing, waiting for their turn to go inside. Pastor Mims continued walking down the street, the dark over Oriental's quiet streets swallowing him whole. She wondered what had brought him to the small thoroughfares of Oriental. He was articulate and had a quick wit. He had a charm about him. She even had to admit he was good-looking and could have gone anywhere. But he stayed here shepherding his small flock along the Neuse, as if they were the most important people in the world. Then she thought about

THE PIRATE QUEEN 219

his one paralyzed hand and how it was the first thing she noticed. She saw him in such a different light now. Come to think of it, she had not ever known a minister as well as Pastor John.

It was a curiosity how Bender's cancer caused her to see everyone up close, like she was seeing each living soul under some psychological microscope.

Finally the line progressed and they were inside. The band was playing "Brava." The head vocalist coaxed dancers onto the floor. "Grab a partner. Any will do."

Luke asked, "Want to dance before it's too crowded?" He brought his left arm up, his large hand covering hers. She brought up her elbow and it "kissed" his, as he had taught her to do during the garage dance lesson. He used his hips to move her back and then forward. He smelled like clay and shampoo. That must be the way of things with a pottery artist. He spun Saphora. She laughed, and then it was Bender taking her into the street the night of the uptown dance. He was so good-looking. She was lucky, so lucky that night, she thought. He gave her every dance. He didn't have to do that. There were other women from campus willing to dance. But he reserved every dance for her.

She thought about how small her expectations were back then. The list for finding Mr. Wonderful was short: number one, he should be a good dancer, and number two, be wildly rich. Bender, whose life was summed up in the activity of ambitions rather than the depth of his character, was all she knew because he was all she had planned to know.

Now she could spot trouble in a person after a few minutes. But she had not passed that gift on to Gwennie, who would pass up Luke for a shallow piece of suit and slick-backed hair.

"You look millions of miles from here," said Luke.

"I'm thinking about Gwennie," said Saphora.

"Makes two of us," he said.

"I just feel like she has grown up with some misconceptions about life and family. But it's too late to twist back the parenting lens and help her with a right perspective."

"You've done her proud, Saphora. Don't beat yourself up."

"I appreciate that, Luke. But growing up with everything at your fingertips can blind you." The dance ended and Luke found a table, where he pulled out a chair for Saphora. A giant margarita glass in the table's center was filled with salsa.

The Mettingers danced past. Sassy laughed in glee and winked at Saphora. Luke was so popular that they were treated like a fashionable couple. Or maybe it was the fact that they were spotted as mismatched, he the young and good-looking eccentric artist and Saphora his older sympathy date.

The extra chairs at their table filled up with the couples they had met outside on the landing. Next to them, several families had brought along their preteens for a father-daughter and mother-son dance. A server swiveled table to table enticing the guests with tapaslike skewers of southwest chicken and vegetables and bruschetta.

A small shock of black hair threaded through the dancing couples. Finally Tobias emerged, so somber that he looked sad. Jamie followed him, relieved to have found Saphora. "I made him come," she said.

Saphora said, "Here's a chair, Tobias. I've been saving it for you."

Luke said, "I hear there's a dance for parents and kids tonight."

"I'm not dancing," said Tobias. "Mom, don't look at me like that."

"I can show you a move that will wow the girls," said Luke. He coaxed Tobias out of his chair and led him several feet away to practice.

"He's ready to go home to Wilmington," said Jamie to Saphora. "But honestly, bringing him to Oriental has brought him to life. Eddie's been such a good friend. He doesn't have a friend like Eddie back in Wilmington."

"If I could, I'd wave a wand and make him well," said Saphora.

"I'd do the same for Dr. Warren," said Jamie, never completely losing sight of Tobias. "How is he?"

"No change."

"Don't give up," said Jamie.

"I know. Same to you."

All at once, Jamie's pleasant smile was gone. Her eyes narrowed and she said, "Don't look, but that woman from the motel pool is here. She's got her eye on Tobias." Jamie's voice was strained.

Saphora looked anyway. "That's not her, is it?" Tobias must have spotted her in town after the swimming pool incident and pointed her out to his mother.

"I think so."

"He can come here if he likes, Jamie," said Saphora. She got up out of her chair. She found Luke bent over, his hands on his knees while he explained a dance move to Tobias. She interrupted, saying, "Excuse me, but I'd like the first dance before all the girls line up and steal you away."

Tobias's nerve had not improved, even with a lesson from Luke. "I don't know."

"Give it a try," said Luke to Tobias. "Mrs. Warren's not so bad. She won't step on your feet or anything."

"Not too bad! Tobias, one dance with me and you'll never go back to those younger girls," said Saphora. She pushed herself between Tobias and the woman from the motel pool. Jamie was right about her.

The band played a slower tune, "Return to Me."

"Good, Luke showed you the box step. You've got it right. Good for you," said Saphora. She lowered her head so that he could spin her around. There was a little more room on the dance floor than when she and Luke had been dancing. Tobias seemed to relax. How she loved to hear him laughing! What a rapturous pair of eyes he had! As brown as pudding.

"I used to dance to this song with Dr. Warren," she told him. "It's from my parents' day."

"I'm sorry he's in a coma," said Tobias.

"Me too."

"He's the nicest doctor I've ever met. Even nicer than my pediatric doctor. And *he's* nice!"

"He likes you too."

"Why is that woman staring?" he asked. His feet got out of sync with the rhythm. But then he picked up the beat again.

"Because we look so good," said Saphora.

"I'd better get out of here," he said. "I know who she is."

"Tobias, just keep on dancing," she said. She spun again. Then she realized that the couples around them had stopped dancing altogether. As a matter of fact, several of them stared at Tobias.

Jamie came out of her chair. She was looking at her son as she had other times when she wanted to apologize to him for other people's sorry behavior.

Luke stood next to Jamie, arms crossed in front of him. His eyes reflected a helpless inner pain.

Tobias said, "You're a good dancer, Mrs. Warren. I'd dance with you again, but I have to go." He said it in such a humble tone of resignation that Saphora was even more pained that he showed such grace under fire. Her ire was on the rise, of that she was certain.

Jamie had strapped on her handbag the size of luggage, the one filled with the chemicals that kept her boy alive. She met him quickly on the dance floor. "Let's go," she said.

"I can't let this go on," said Saphora.

"I'll call you." Jamie did not look up but kept her mother's vigil over Tobias. She would have walked him out at that instant, never looking into the eyes of her son's circle of accusers, except that Saphora quietly stepped onto the stage. She asked the band leader for the use of his microphone. He acquiesced and handed her his mike, stepping away, still holding his electric guitar. "I guess this is one of those elephant-in-the-room moments," she said.

The band leader gestured for his drummer to stop playing.

"I mean, it's one thing to be sick, like my husband. But it's another thing to be a leper. I mean, cancer, well, that's a heroic way to die. But how dare this little boy come into the world and into our lives with something as unheroic as AIDS. Tobias, don't you know you're supposed to be invisible?"

"How cruel," one lady said.

"That's what we're asking of Tobias, isn't it?" asked Saphora.

Tobias had the sort of look he had the day Bender had led him into the shower, the look of a boy accustomed to living with having his dignity stripped from him on a daily basis. Humiliation was as natural on him as the smell of clay was on Luke.

"Tobias, you surely didn't expect to make friends here, did you? We pick and choose our friends here, don't you know?" said Saphora.

The woman from the motel pool pushed her way through the

crowd, an obvious move to slip quietly away. She was muttering something to her spouse and was nearly out the door when Saphora called out to her.

"Just a moment, ma'am," Saphora said to the woman. "Yes, you, ma'am. Before you leave, I think you need to know something about this little boy you stigmatize under your misguided fear."

The woman froze as if Saphora had cast a spell of paralysis over her.

"Tobias is smart and fun to be around. He's a darned good fisherman and, around here, that means he's in the club."

Laughter rippled through the crowd. A big man Saphora recognized from the fish stand downtown gave Tobias a hearty pat on the back. Saphora continued to speak about Tobias and how meaningful his friendship was to her and her grandson Eddie. As she spoke, the countenances around the dance floor changed from confusion and fear to kindness and understanding.

"Could it be," Saphora asked, "that we've been given a treasure in the Tobiases placed here among us? What will we tell God we did with his treasure at the end of our lives?"

A girl who had been sitting with her father next to Saphora's table came out of the crowd. She walked up to Tobias and held out her hand. "Want to dance?" she asked.

Tobias wiped his eyes. The girl handed him a tissue. She was blond, slightly taller than him. But he looked into her eyes as if he were twenty-one and would live forever.

The band leader started a song a cappella. Saphora's mind was awash in a strange euphoric memory. To her surprise, it was the first song to which Saphora and Bender had danced the night of their first real date. It was, of all things, a Joni Mitchell song, "You're My

Thrill." Somehow the song had wound around the injuries and the assaults that pocked her past and found its way back to her. The keyboardist picked it up on the next stanza, and the brass players came to their feet while the rest of the musicians joined in. Other couples joined Tobias and his pretty young partner in the dance.

> When I look at you I can't keep still.
> You're my thrill.

Saphora was overwhelmed with the strangest sensation pulsing up from the past. She remembered why she had fallen in love with Bender, of all things.

16

It is important from time to time to slow
down, to go away by yourself, and simply be.

EILEEN CADDY

"Louisiana? What's in Louisiana?" Gwennie sounded like she had a
cold, but the Manhattan connection was not always clear.

"Louisiana as in New Orleans or wherever it is Luke's gone for
the art show," said Saphora. It was Metairie, but that was nearly New
Orleans. Her feet were soaking in a tub, still sore from the rash of
dances that followed her talk-of-the-town speech last night.

"That doesn't make sense, Mama. He was expecting me in town."

"He said he didn't have to tell you that he wasn't going to be here
after all. You canceled first."

"If that's true, then why wouldn't he just tell me?" she asked.
"Not that I care, Mama, I'm just saying it's strange that you're delivering the news."

"I'm guessing, Gwennie, but it could be he didn't want to tell you
in the first place. You made it easier. Luke knows, like you know, it's
not going to work between the two of you." The salt water stung the
tops of her blistered toes.

"He told you that?"

"Not in so many words. Luke's a very private man, Gwennie.
Why would he tell me? Besides, he had so many dance partners last

night, I only saw him that first go-around on the floor. I did hear him asking a twenty-something lifeguard to watch his cat for him." She paused for the length of time it took Gwennie to hold her breath. "After that, we spoke only in passing. I caught a ride home early with Tobias's mother and left him to stay up late with his friends down at the marina."

Gwennie was stewing so much that the crackling noise coming over the phone sounded like it was coming out of her.

"Gwennie, can I call back? My feet are in a world of hurt."

"Who cares about feet at a time like this?"

"Like what?"

"Luke's gone off and not even told me, Mama."

"Does that matter?"

"It's just a courtesy. He should have paid me the consideration of telling me that he was leaving."

"I told him I'd let you know. Isn't that good enough?"

"Obviously he thought so."

"If I'm going to make it to Raleigh this afternoon, Gwennie, I've got some things to do," said Saphora. "Want me to call you from Duke after I check in on your daddy?"

Gwennie was so quiet Saphora thought she had hung up.

"Call me," she said, and hung up.

Daisy had left on a morning flight. The kitchen was reorganized to the point that Saphora had to rummage to find the oatmeal. But finally there it was behind the olives. Daisy had alphabetized the pantry, bless her heart.

The whole house seemed to sigh with her gone. Saphora took breakfast out on the patio. The tree between her house and Luke's was full of birds. The Outer Banks had over six hundred species.

They all seemed to land at once in a sort of communal morning song, irritating Saphora. Luke's gate was ajar. She took another bite of oatmeal. Then she got up and crossed the dew-soaked backyard, wetting her once-white scuffies. She was about to close the gate. But she had never walked up to Luke's gate without going inside. He had not asked, but maybe he had left the gate open on purpose. Maybe he wanted her to check on his place in his absence.

The lifeguard had not yet come for the cat. The old yellow tabby, Johnson, lazed under the drooping evergreen.

"Are you being looked after, Johnson?" she asked. She walked across the backyard, past a koi pond. The koi were all gone. Birds of prey could not resist the sight of a beautiful, exotic koi supper. Luke had not possessed either the strength or the vision to restore the pond to its former splendor. She walked around the fountain, a likeness of a young girl that had stopped burbling some time ago. Water had stained the child's cheeks like tears.

Saphora walked past the door that led into the garage where Luke holed up night and day pouring his grief into his work. She looked through the small garage window. It was too dark to see anything. She walked past the arsenal of garden tools Luke used every night looking for an elusive treasure. The shovel handle was worn smooth from use. The spade stuck to the handle only because it was rusted on tightly.

Saphora carried the shovel back across the yard. She would replace it with a new shovel at least. Not everything in Luke's yard had to be wasting away.

Patches of newly sown grass sprang up from the circles now filled with soil. She counted them on her way out. Ten, fifteen, twenty-two, twenty-eight. Plus two more under the tree. If he had dug a hole per night, Luke had been digging holes for a month.

Gwennie had come along at just the right time, just before Luke slipped down forever into one of his holes.

☙

Daisy had cleaned the house so thoroughly there were no chores left to be done. By noon Saphora battled restless thoughts. A storm moved across the state right down the interstate between the Outer Banks and Raleigh. She put off driving to Duke until after lunch.

She pulled out Bender's fishing albums, poring over photographs of him standing next to a mako shark he had snagged in the mid-Atlantic. He was so full of himself that he was flexing an arm muscle as if he had conquered the poor beast alone. Jim and two other surgeons had assisted with bringing it in. It was only eight feet in length. He had talked about the fight the fish had given him and how, upon hooking it, the mako had jumped out of the air just feet from the boat.

Lightning undulated, threading through the clouds above the river. The water was churning like it had the day she had navigated the Neuse alone. Saphora closed the drapes.

The den was dark, so she turned on the table lamps. She left the album open next to a cup of black coffee. There it sat as if poured for Bender. Next to it were two cookies, his favorites. She took the coffee and cookies to the sink and put it all into the garbage disposal.

Today was her first day fully alone in the house. She had imagined how she would eat what she liked, read without interruption. She would listen to Wagner—Bender thought Wagner was overplayed and often turned it off as if Saphora was not in the car.

Saphora got out a juicer and made a drink of fruit and soy milk. Then she made a waffle for lunch. She topped it with fruit, no syrup. She opened the curtains fully and watched the storm moving over the Neuse as she listened to the London Symphony Orchestra. She remembered the tickets Bender had won at the silent auction, tickets they could not share. Had he predicted his own health crisis, yet lavishly spent money on the gesture?

A couple of tears clouded her eyes. She wiped them and then stuffed a bite of waffle into her mouth. Her lips were salty. The taste was berry and tears. Thunder rattled the window glass. She worried that Luke's cat had not been picked up by the lifeguard. She hoped the cat had found the crawl space under Luke's house a dry refuge. The lawn chair Eddie had used for fishing lifted like a kite and was pitched into the roiling water.

Saphora put the dishes in the dishwasher. She had discouraged Sherry from driving back since none of the kids were coming for the weekend. Now she wished she'd let Sherry join her anyway, Sherry who inserted herself into every conversation, filling the air with laughing and silly storytelling. But it was pleasant noise and better than the deadness of the empty house. The storm outside only made the quiet of the house more explicit.

She had wanted nothing more than the house to herself. But now that every detail was perfectly ordered as she first imagined, it was not what she had predicted.

The rain was driving sideways, pelting the house. She looked out across the deck. The sky was entirely black now. Saphora closed up Bender's fishing album. She opened his diary. Then she took the Bible that Pastor Mims had given to him as if somehow she would magically open it and something important would fly out and comfort her. She felt like an old woman with her knitting and her Bible. She opened it anyway. No one would know.

ର୍ଯ

It was on the way to Duke, the rain-soaked interstate drying in the sun, that Gwennie called to say she was flying in before midnight that very night. Just as Luke had said. She had gotten nearly the last seat on a flight from New York to Raleigh that was cheaper than any flight she had ever booked in advance. "So it's silly not to take advantage," she told Saphora.

"Of course," said Saphora. "I'm glad you're coming. I'll already be in Raleigh. I'll pick you up then?"

"All right," said Gwennie.

Saphora was glad she'd at least have Gwennie knocking around the house all weekend. She had Luke to thank for that.

Senator Weberman's security guards were stationed, like before, out in the hallway. They sat eating a late afternoon meal of the better food from the catering company. Saphora was about to enter the room when a nurse came out from behind the station. "Mrs. Warren, I'm glad to see you."

"Is there any change?" asked Saphora.

The nurse, a Chinese girl by the name of Kew, looked around the station, making sure it was only the two of them. "Actually, I was changing his glucose this morning, and I could have sworn his eyes opened."

"Did he say anything?"

"I'm not sure about it, Mrs. Warren. But I thought I saw a movement out of the corner of my eye. Then I turned and he was still, like always." She meant well; she was a young nurse who had learned English in the South. Her accent was as pert and pretty as any Carolina girl's.

"I'll sit with him until after dinner, Kew. Then I've got to pick up my daughter from the airport. If I brought her over tonight, would that be all right? Visiting hours will be over."

"I'll see what I can do," said the nurse.

Good. A people-pleasing nurse. She would be a cinch to manipulate. Saphora thanked her and walked right into Bender's room. She was sick to death of the antiseptic smell of hospital rooms. Convalescing should smell like garden soil, she thought, or cherry candles.

She sat right down next to Bender's bed as if she might make his eyes flutter open, like Kew had said. She got down next to his ear and whispered, "I saw Reverend Mims about your questions. He told me some things." She sat back and thought how foolish it might appear to others to keep trying to wake Bender from his coma. Who cares, she would do it anyway.

She pulled his Bible out of her choke-a-horse-sized handbag. "Here's the way it is, Bender. I don't have any idea how to figure out your questions about God or heaven. I guess you might be wanting to find answers right about now what with your situation and all. I don't want to give you the wrong impression. I don't have the answers either. But this is how it was told to me by Reverend Mims."

She opened the Bible to where Bender had circled the part about God saving his tears in a bottle. She turned to make sure she was not disturbing the man who had been moved in next to Bender. Mort was gone. The new patient was either so doped up he was out of it or else floating like Bender between the hospital floors and heaven.

"Pastor Mims says that back in the ancient days people considered water precious. Giving up tears was like a sacrifice for their loved one. So saving tears was sacred. I don't know about all that, but I've shed a lot of tears for you, Bender." Mims had talked to her for as long as she asked questions. She paused as if giving him a moment to think about what she was saying. "I shed tears long before now, like all of the nights your place in our bed next to me was cold and empty.

Truth be told, Bender, I've filled up gallons of tear jars for you. You'd think I'd be all dried up by now, but instead…" She stopped, feeling like the Neuse was bursting through her walls again. She started crying but covered her mouth as if he might wake up and tell her to get ahold of herself. Then it came to her that if the ancients believed tears were sacred, then maybe there was something to it. She sobbed in the quiet of the hospital room with Bender still, her tears falling on his upturned hand as if he were catching them to carry around with him as he hovered between the hospital floors.

ᛡ

Gwennie's flight was fifteen minutes early, she said, since a New York tailwind had blown her plane south on a summer coastal stream. She kissed Saphora, but instead of heading straight for the luggage carousel, she said, "Mama, I brought someone with me, a friend from the office."

A tall man about Luke's age appeared from behind her as if Gwennie cued him to step up and make some grand New York attorney's entrance. "Mrs. Warren, I work with Gwennie at Bart and Ludstrum." He was a loving Italian man, kissing Saphora's cheek as if they had met from the long past.

"Gwennie, you didn't tell me," was all Saphora could think to say.

"I know. It was last minute. This is Mario. He works litigation at B&L."

"Are you working on a case this weekend?" asked Saphora.

"Of a sort," said Gwennie. "He's just broken up with his girlfriend. Truth is, I found him staring out his window at the New York skyline this afternoon."

"She felt sorry for me," said Mario.

"But I thought your flight was full," said Saphora.

"Mama."

"I'm sorry. It's just a surprise," said Saphora. "Mario, we're working through this situation with Gwennie's daddy."

"I won't be a bother, Mrs. Warren. I can even get a room at one of the inns," said Mario. "I've just got to get the weight of this week off me."

"He only needs a place to take a walk and clear his head. I called and, boom, we found a seat that was canceled," said Gwennie, not taking her eyes off Mario.

"Boom!" said Mario. "Here we are."

"You can stay with us." Saphora said. "There's room all over. I've got the whole house to myself. So you're not dating then?"

Gwennie looked at Mario and laughed as if the two of them shared some secret. "We're not dating. I'm just his shoulder to cry on this weekend."

"She's been wonderful, Mrs. Warren," he said. "Southern women are so sympathetic."

"I'm sure," said Saphora. She helped Gwennie find her suitcase.

"I'll get the rental car," he told Gwennie.

❧

Once they congregated in the hospital, Mario set up shop in a waiting area as if he could run an office from anywhere. He had his laptop open, a latte perched in his cup holder. His black polo shirt was open all the way as if he felt completely at home in their company. He took out a headset and then said, "The two of you go ahead and catch up. When I turn on music, I can't hear a thing."

"I'd like some time alone with Daddy first, Mama, if that's all right." Gwennie went up the elevator alone while Saphora sat in a chair across from Mario.

Saphora liked Mario well enough. He was a likable sort. But she had imagined finally having Gwennie all to herself for the entire weekend. But wasn't it like Gwennie to handle the whole issue of Luke with a good-looking Italian diversion?

Mario rested his thonged feet on the magazine table. "All she's talked about is her father. They must be very close."

"Bender dotes on Gwennie. She was the only real athlete out of all three of our children," said Saphora. He did adore her if for no other reason than the shelves of trophies next to his in the library. "The boys tried out for a few teams. But everything Gwennie set her mind to, she tackled. She's a lot like her daddy."

"My father loved me for my accomplishments too," he said.

She hadn't exactly said that, but he was perceptive to notice. Or maybe just experienced. "Were you an athlete?"

"Tennis and golf. State champion, national junior PGA tour."

"Your girlfriend must be sorry you broke up with her."

"Evie broke up with me. Wasn't willing to wait on my career. Now she's interested in a senior partner at another firm." He looked like a whipped pup. "I've heard he's married."

"It's a sad state of affairs, the way girls go after men in high places."

"Does anyone fall in love anymore, Mrs. Warren? I'd like to know."

"It's easy falling in love, Mario. It's staying in love that boggles the mind," said Saphora.

The elevator door opened. Gwennie came out, looking as if she would bean the next person who talked to her. "There's some Chilean nurse on duty who barely understands English. She won't let me in because visiting hours are over."

"Want me to try and get you in?" asked Saphora. "I know of a nurse who will help."

"I'm too tired to fight the forces. We'll just have to drive back tomorrow."

Saphora looked out the large window. It was the time of night when the sky is so close to midnight that the trees look like they're floating in milk. Her eyelids were heavy, so she told Gwennie she'd have to drive them back home.

"Let's get a hotel room," said Mario. "I'll pay and that'll be my treat to you ladies for taking in a stranger."

"Mario, I'm going to take you up on it," said Saphora.

"Deal," said Mario.

"So what were you two doing?" asked Gwennie. "Solving the world's problems?"

"She's coaching me in matters of the heart," said Mario.

"My mother?" asked Gwennie. She was tired. Sarcasm pierced through her usual diplomacy.

"Sure. Where do you think you got all your brains?" he asked.

∾

The next morning, Gwennie was able to get right in to see her daddy. Saphora and Mario joined her. Kew was raising his bed and opening the window drapes, letting in the morning sun. "There you are, Mrs. Warren. I heard your daughter got thrown off the floor last night," she said. "If I'd been here, I'd have given them what for."

"Kew, if I may ask," said Mario, "can you tell me about his brain patterns?"

"Sure. He's got the vitals of a man half his age, strong heart. But his brain is quiet as a butterfly."

"What do you know about brain patterns, Mario?" asked Gwennie.

"I was premed before I figured out that my sympathy was better suited to litigation," said Mario.

"Litigation requires no sympathy," said Gwennie.

"That's me. Mr. Coldheart," said Mario.

"I don't believe that," said Saphora. Nor could she believe that she was already taking up with him. "I mean, I guess if you're a litigator, you do have to hold people out at arm's length."

If anything was evident, it was that Gwennie did not need an exact duplicate of herself. But she would be the last to admit it.

Gwennie held on to Bender's hand for about the length of time he might have held on to her when, as a little girl with the flu, she begged him to sit by her bedside. But restlessness and a blocked cell phone signal soon overtook her patience, and she was ready to head for Oriental.

The drive back was as clear as if yesterday's storm had never come. When Gwennie was not on her phone with her assistant, Mario was talking to her as he drove the rental car right behind them. The two of them wrangled office staff around their cases from a distance as if they were duke and duchess of all things legal. Gwennie had girls otherwise off for the weekend holed up in her office looking through old cases as if their lives depended on whatever it was they had to find. Mario was no different. But where Gwennie captained them around in the same way her father ran a surgical team, Mario negotiated with charm, or so she seemed to indicate.

While Gwennie had Mario on the phone, Saphora said, "The two of you should go into business together. You work your will like two CEOs."

"Us?" said Gwennie. "You should see the senior partners working us through their slick little schemes," said Gwennie. She laughed at Mario on the phone. She told her mother, "He says, 'Don't let us fool you. We're still just the office flunkies.'"

By the time they pulled into the drive, Gwennie had tilted her seat back and fallen asleep. Saphora had to wake her up.

Gwennie sat up, rubbing her eyes and smoothing her hair. "I feel like I took a sleeping pill," she said. She finally got awake enough to walk around the back of the car and pull out her luggage. It was about then that Luke's cat started howling from next door as if it were caught in a trap. Gwennie left her suitcase inside the garage and a few moments later came back holding Johnson close to her. "Poor soaked kitty. He's been left out in the rain. I thought you said Luke had left someone to care for him, Mama."

Mario walked up, his belongings in a single backpack. "Him? Gwennie, Johnson's a she," he said. "Look. She's had kittens." He pulled back the cat's belly fur to show her two rows of swollen teats.

"Johnson, you're a mommy," said Gwennie. She patted the feline's sagging tummy.

It was about that time a car drove into Luke's driveway. The lifeguard Luke had asked to see to his cat jumped out and ran all the way around the back of his house, disappearing behind his gate.

"You'd best go and let her know she's got a lot of pet sitting on her hands," said Saphora.

"I'll give her a piece of my mind," said Gwennie. "Johnson could have been swept out to sea, for all she cares."

"Go and give her the cat," said Saphora. "Then help her hunt down Johnson's kittens."

"I can do that, Gwennie," said Mario.

"I'll do it," said Gwennie. "I know my way around his place."

By the time Saphora put Gwennie's suitcase in the downstairs guest room, Gwennie was back inside pacing in front of the patio doors. "She's awfully young. What is she, some high schooler?"

"She's not much younger than you. Working on her MBA," said Saphora. "Why? Does that matter?"

"Who is Luke?" asked Mario. He joined Saphora in the kitchen.

"Luke and Gwennie have dated," said Saphora. "Didn't she mention Luke?"

"Mama, Mario doesn't care about my private life," said Gwennie. "Did you say Luke danced with that lifeguard? She's a cute girl for her age. How would you know about her MBA?"

"I overheard it said, is all," said Saphora.

"Gwennie, is this the artist you mentioned over the copy machine?" asked Mario.

"We're just friends," said Gwennie. She opened the refrigerator and pulled out a liter of club soda and a tub of hummus. "Are we cooking?"

"Gwennie, why do you care if Luke danced with her?" asked Saphora.

"I don't care. I'm just curious."

Mario leaned against the island, crossing his arms. "Gwennie, bringing me here was the last thing you needed, wasn't it?"

"What are you talking about?" asked Gwennie.

"It was your idea to bring me here. Is this why? You wanted to use me to guard your feelings against Luke?" he asked.

"Mama, are you putting these thoughts in Mario's head? You have a strange habit of working your will over me in ways even I can't understand."

"Gwennie, your mother didn't say anything at all," said Mario. His Brooklyn accent was getting more pronounced along with his growing irritation.

Saphora noticed that Gwennie's knit top was spotted with cat footprints. "You should change out of your clothes and then stop complaining about Luke's lifeguard girlfriend," she said.

"Girlfriend?" Gwennie walked out and left Saphora and Mario in the kitchen. She locked herself in the guest room.

"Has she ever been in love before?" Mario asked.

"You think she's in love with Luke?"

"She's been floating around the office with that glazed-over look all week. Now I know why," said Mario.

"Good to know," said Saphora.

"Stop talking about me," Gwennie yelled from the guest room.

"She'll be miserable to be around all weekend," said Saphora to Mario. "You sure you're up for it?"

"It'll give me someone else's misery to worry about instead of my own," said Mario.

He's a smart Italian boy, Saphora thought.

17

You may encounter many defeats, but you must not be defeated. In fact, it may be necessary to encounter the defeats, so you can know who you are, what you can rise from, how you can still come out of it.

MAYA ANGELOU

Mario said his mother taught him to cook because his father was so helpless when she married him that she could not bear to see her son standing like his daddy, staring into the refrigerator, not knowing what to do next. Mario picked through Saphora's refrigerator crisper and her spice cabinet. He told Saphora she had the makings for a somewhat Italian meal. He would make dinner for them.

Gwennie had changed and was washing out her top in the kitchen sink. She held it up in front of the sunlight streaming through the kitchen window. Pin lights sifted through tiny claw marks around the arm holes. Johnson had pawed it into oblivion. She threw the mangled top into the garbage.

Mario pulled out an orange bell pepper and a red one, laying them on the cutting board. He sliced them into long, skinny strips and then cooked the peppers in olive oil. He got Gwennie to mince a garlic clove, seemingly to get her mind off the cat-sitting lifeguard.

Saphora poured one-half cup of white wine into the skillet over the peppers and garlic. Next she added some chicken stock. Mario's peppers and garlic gathered up around the wine and chicken stock like the vegetables were dancing in an undulating circle.

"How is Tobias, Mama?" asked Gwennie.

"I think he's looking for new friends. But that's the way of it for him," said Saphora. "I don't know if Jamie is going to want to bring him back to this town again or not."

Gwennie told Mario, "He's the boy I told you about."

"I remember," said Mario. He was beating a chicken breast half to death with a mallet.

"Have they gone back to Wilmington?" asked Gwennie. "I was hoping to see him one last time."

"They're here for at least this weekend. I invited them to the dance Thursday night. But when Tobias walked in, you would have thought the bubonic plague had walked into the room," said Saphora.

"I don't get it," said Mario.

"Is there any way to get Jamie to stay?" asked Gwennie.

"It's a summer home for them, like us," said Saphora. "Plus, Tobias has school." She thought about how people came and went, to and from the Outer Banks, never taking root in each other's lives. "I wonder how many kids like Tobias are expected to stay in hiding during the years they'd otherwise be out living life."

"I'd like to know," said Gwennie. To satisfy her curiosity, she printed facts off the Internet after dinner while Saphora explained to Mario how to make mint juleps. Gwennie laid the printout on the kitchen bar. "Why is it so secret if so many kids have it?"

Saphora got a call right then from Turner. After updating him on his father's condition, she got off the phone and told Gwennie, "Turner's wrangled time with Eddie for the weekend. He's bringing him tomorrow."

"Eddie's my nephew," Gwennie told Mario. "He's friends with Tobias."

"I'll invite Tobias," said Saphora. "He's been missing Eddie something fierce." Besides, she thought, she was missing Jamie and Tobias just as badly.

⁊⁊

Eddie had gotten taller in just the short time away. He wore a thin-striped, red and white T-shirt that Turner had bought for him, he said, because it was a pirate shirt. Eddie threw down pancakes like all he had eaten since he was back at his mother's were frozen breakfasts. "Nana, is Tobias coming?" he asked.

"The last thing Jamie told me was that he would be over this morning. Please stop fidgeting and eat," said Saphora.

The doorbell rang and it was Tobias. Jamie came in too. She was glad to see Gwennie and Turner back. Mario took over as the pan-cake flipper. He made smiling pancakes. Then he took on Eddie's challenge of making one like a penguin. That one he scraped into the garbage disposal.

"I'll have one, Mario," said Jamie. "Might as well. I haven't cooked breakfast since Mel went back to Wilmington. Tobias eats like a bird."

"Did you tell me when you were going back to Wilmington?" asked Saphora.

"Tomorrow," said Jamie. "We're packing up now."

"I'm heading out too," said Mario. "Tonight, the red-eye to New York."

"You didn't tell me," said Gwennie.

"My ex-girlfriend called. She couldn't get me at home. It was good for her to find me gone," said Mario. He gave Tobias a hot cake.

"We're all leaving you," said Jamie.

"I wish you could stay," said Saphora. "Eddie just got here, and he's so lonely with no other kids around."

"Tobias has clinic Friday. He hates it, but they've got to check his levels," said Jamie.

"Are there a lot of children there?" asked Saphora.

"A hundred kids," said Jamie.

Saphora sat, mouth open.

Eddie followed Tobias up the tree. Tobias had nearly made the fort his own in Eddie's absence.

"Is this the rest of his life? Really? He has to live like this?" asked Gwennie.

"What else is there for him?" asked Jamie.

"I guess I thought he'd do better with modern medicine and all," said Gwennie.

"It keeps him alive. I'm grateful for that," said Jamie.

"He's supposed to go around hiding his face. That's not right," said Saphora.

"I'm sorry he's had some misunderstandings here this summer," said Gwennie.

"He tries to takes it in stride," said Jamie. "But, Saphora, you were wonderful the other night. Gwennie, you would have been proud of your mother."

"What did you do?" asked Gwennie.

"Nothing that spectacular. At least, not compared to you, Jamie. I'm glad he's got you."

Jamie gave Gwennie and Mario a summary of all that transpired at the dance.

Saphora was uncomfortable with taking accolades considering what she had done was something anyone could have done. So she turned her back to the party and opened the curtains to watch the boys. Tobias was hanging his head out of the tree house opening. He was laughing while Eddie pulled on him from above. Tobias's baseball dropped out of the tree like a fig.

That was when an idea came to Saphora. She was mulling it over when Jamie jolted her back into the present. "Earth to Saphora."

She turned facing Jamie, clasping her hands in front of her, and said, "I was just thinking, I'd sure like to do something for Tobias. Something he'd like."

"Tell her no way," said Gwennie. "My mother can scheme like no one's business."

"I'm too intrigued," said Jamie. "Give it to me, full throttle."

❧

Marcy was flying back from Nepal. She called Saphora as soon as she landed in Dallas. "I'll be back in North Carolina tomorrow. Is Bender hanging on?"

"He's at Duke" was all Saphora could say about that. "Tell me what time you get in. I'll meet you at the airport," said Saphora. "Sherry's not here. You can have her room."

"Are you sure? I don't want to put any more pressure on you," said Marcy. "But I miss you awfully. And I'd like to see Bender."

"I'm glad you're coming home, Marcy," said Saphora. "I've been lonesome without you." They hung up and Saphora announced, "Marcy's coming. I'm going to the airport to get her tomorrow."

"Oh, there will be partying now," said Gwennie.

"Who is Marcy?" asked Jamie.

"My mother's best friend forever. They've been friends since college," said Gwennie.

The afternoon rushed past. Jamie called Tobias in and told him, "We've got to finish closing up the house, Tobias." She stroked his hair sympathetically. "We'll have to tell everyone good-bye."

Tobias looked put out, like all kids do when summer's doormat is being pulled out from under their reverie. Tobias told Eddie good-bye until next summer. Eddie was trying hard not to show emotion, but when they hugged, he wiped his eyes with the back of his arm. Jamie thanked Saphora for helping Tobias find allies in Oriental. "After your speech, we had so many calls. People even sent baskets of food and flowers to our house."

Saphora did not want to show weepy eyes to the boys and got down to business with Jamie as she followed her out to her car. "Here's the map to the stadium. Sam the Hammer is expecting him before the game. Let me know all about it," said Saphora. "Take pictures and e-mail me a few."

"He'll be surprised as all get-out," said Jamie.

Tobias ran down the walk with Eddie in tow. "What surprise?" asked Tobias.

"Later," said Jamie. She led him down the walk.

Mario hugged Saphora. "I appreciate your offering me a refuge for the weekend. It gave me time to think. This whole fight has been half my fault. I'm going to ask Evie to try again."

"I smell trouble," said Gwennie.

"Ignore her," said Saphora. "If you love Evie, the two of you will work it out."

Mario wheeled his suitcase to the rental car. He kissed Gwennie good-bye at the edge of the driveway. She threw her arms around his neck and hugged him in return.

Saphora and Gwennie took coffee out on the deck after supper. Gwennie turned off her cell phone. "I'm sick to death of this case."

"You're too young to be sick of your job already," said Saphora.

"Not my job. Just this client's headaches."

"You can't have a job without them," said Saphora.

"He's truly a victim, and we're fighting an uphill battle. Do the good guys ever win?"

"Maybe."

"I thought practicing law would be looking out for the weak." Time spent traveling had left Gwennie looking road weary.

"You're not a savior."

"So I'm finding out. I feel so helpless sometimes."

"The light's come on at Luke's place," said Saphora.

Gwennie turned around to see. "His patio light. Probably that cheerleader letting the cat out."

"Lifeguard."

"Whatever."

"Then don't let him go."

"Who?"

"Luke."

"I don't chase after men." Gwennie's voice was showing exasperation with her mother.

"I didn't say *chase*."

Gwennie sat up, surprised. "Is that the top of Luke's head?" she asked. She stayed in her chair but turned completely around to peer through the low-hanging branches.

"Might as well be neighborly," said Saphora. "Luke, over here!"

"Don't," Gwennie begged.

"He's going back into his house," said Saphora.

Gwennie came up out of the patio chair. She waited to see if Luke was coming out. But his patio light went off. His backyard was dark.

"Something's not right," said Gwennie.

"I don't understand you. Why don't you just go over there?" asked Saphora.

"He hasn't called me all weekend."

"You were brushing him off." She could not stand seeing Gwennie look so miserable. "Men need encouragement."

"I don't know."

"Go over."

Gwennie finally got up and went inside and left Saphora out on the deck alone.

∾

Saphora retreated to the deck upstairs outside her bedroom. It was fully dark now. Up here, Gwennie would not be so likely to accuse her of spying on Luke. She even left off her own bedroom light to cloak her presence. But her curiosity about him lured her to look over that fence. Johnson stretched from the patio up against the screen door, her feline coat luminescent in the glow of the porch light. Three wee velvet shadows huddled at her flank.

Gwennie's bedroom light filtered onto the lawn beneath Saphora. She was dressing for bed, talking to someone from New York most likely. That was what Gwennie did to protect herself from her racing thoughts. She retreated to the phone or her earbuds. She was like so many her age, not comfortable with solitude.

Saphora, however, had laid aside the hope for solitude. The splendor of the quiet house on the Neuse River was a dream. She had thought of nothing else during the days leading up to the *Southern Living* photo shoot. She wiled away the time imagining a quiet house all to herself along the Outer Banks. She was in love with the idea of hearing an old house creaking. There was something romantic about being alone and watching the sky die over the Neuse night after night, she had told herself. Ha! What a joke! She had planned a life no longer dictated by the hours between breakfast, lunch, and dinner. Instead it would be sunrise and sunset and all of the quiet hours in between those two predictable pages. But there had been few hours spent in solitude. Bender's escape into the netherworld of a coma had left her in between a dream of a life without him and the life of worrying about him in a continual mental exercise of breathing life back into him.

She wondered if he was dreaming in his comatose state. Was he remembering her when they danced in Charlotte? His journal indicated that he remembered the night Turner was born. But could he recall that night or the spring afternoon when Gwennie rode her first bike?

To her surprise, Gwennie's light went out. She was a notorious night owl, making her the ideal candidate for law school. But life in the busy world of law in the city had turned her back into a conformist.

With the lights out on either side of the house, Saphora's eyes got amazingly heavy. She decided to head for bed herself. But then she heard the gate latch squeak open. Luke did not turn on his patio light—something he had always done when he went outside, with or without his shovel. Even in the dark, he was visible due to the moon overhead. He padded into and out of his garage. He made several trips back and forth, finally flipping on a flashlight.

The last time he slammed his garage door shut. Then he pushed open the gate. Saphora did not know whether to run inside or just wait and see what he was doing. The flashlight waved back and forth across her lawn. He walked past the tree and out into the open. Then his flashlight came right up into Saphora's face. She was startled but tried to keep her comportment about her.

"Mrs. Warren, did you happen to notice my shovel?"

She had completely forgotten that she had taken it out of his yard. "How did you know I was up here?"

"I can see you from my patio."

"I put it in my shed."

"Do you need it?"

"I was going to replace it for you. It was a surprise. It's very rusted."

"I don't mind the rust. May I get it?"

"Are you all right? You don't sound the same, Luke."

The light came on below in Gwennie's room.

"Could we hurry?" he asked.

"I didn't lock the shed. Help yourself," said Saphora. "I apologize you had to look for it." She read his attitude as frustration with her. Whether or not it was true, he did not acknowledge her apology. He walked in the dark as lost in his thoughts as the first night she found him digging.

"I hope I didn't trouble you," she said.

Luke turned and walked away in a hurry. He was not trying to see Gwennie or tell her about his trip. He was making no efforts to make his presence known. He got the shovel out of the shed and then disappeared behind his fence.

Gwennie came out into the yard below. She looked toward Luke's house and then up at her mother.

"Luke was just here," said Saphora.

"I heard him. I got dressed." Her hair was pulled up on her head in a ponytail, splaying in several directions.

"He needed his shovel."

"From here?"

"I took it by accident."

Gwennie wore a tank top and gym shorts. She folded her arms across her stomach. The night air was somewhat damp and slightly chilly. She kept watching the gate for any more signs of Luke. Finally she sighed and walked back into the house.

Saphora went inside too. She got into bed and turned off the lamp. It was a good half hour before Luke started his shoveling.

18

Thirsty hearts are those whose longings have
been wakened by the touch of God within them.

A.W. TOZER

Marcy had finally come back to Saphora. Saphora met her at the airport. She was slender and glowing. She wore a lightly embroidered
belt that made her waist look like an ant's. It matched her wide-
brimmed summer hat.

"Saphora! Goodness, my, you look good enough to eat!" Marcy
dragged a set of floral luggage while juggling a tote bag stuffed full.
Being a wholesale buyer overseas, Marcy had to carry more luggage
than she'd like.

Saphora hugged Marcy so hard she could feel her rib cage.
"Marcy, you've got to eat. Thin is thin, but you know what I mean."

"I've been too busy to eat," she said. Her face had a rosy quality.
Her sunglasses were the kind worn by celebrities in Los Angeles. She
had the best of everything at her fingertips since traveling was part of
her job. She paid half what her friends paid with her handy whole-
saler's card in hand.

"I'm so jealous. You're dressed fit to kill," said Saphora. She
touched the small cornrows behind Marcy's ears. Marcy had left behind the dark African black hair color she was born with and colored
her hair red. With Marcy's skin the color of tawny peaches, Saphora
liked the red on her. "That's a perfect color."

"Does it work? I don't know. I'm still thinking about it."

"I'm telling you, it's you. And here I am plunking around in my old things. I haven't had a minute to shop this entire summer."

"It's no wonder your wardrobe's waning, what with you stuck down in that little lagoon of a place." She slapped her hands on her thighs. "I want to see Bender."

"He's not the same, Marcy. Bender's drifted from us. He's in a coma," said Saphora. She could cry easily in front of Marcy, but she held it in. She hated airport scenes.

"I won't stand for that. Take me to that man of yours. I'll bring him back. My grandmother used to say the women in our line had the resurrection power."

"We'll go to Duke then," said Saphora. Even in the shadow of death, Marcy could make her laugh.

Marcy talked incessantly while Saphora drove them to the hospital. She had found a man in a Tibetan village who wove silk rugs sought after by the Queen Mother herself. "He cut me a deal. If things keep going this way, I'll be at the top of my sales team by year's end," said Marcy. "I've shipped you a rug. You're going to die when you see it."

"No! I can't wait."

"Tell me about my godchild. Is Gwennie still in town?"

"You'll see her when we get back to the house," said Saphora.

"Has she got a man?"

"Not yet. But she teeters on the possibility." Saphora was feeling wrung out from the drive to the airport. "I'll tell you later. It's a story, like everything with Gwennie." She felt especially heavy for Luke and Gwennie this morning because she felt responsible for tampering with the natural order of things. When she got up, Gwennie was sitting on the back deck drinking coffee and half sleeping in her big-rimmed sunglasses. But Luke never came out to talk to her. Somehow her little maneuver had backfired.

"Nothing comes easy with that girl. She's got to make it big and splashy even if it's to her ruination," said Marcy. "The last time I saw her, she was teaching herself to water-ski off the family dock, bare feet and all."

"I forgot about that," said Saphora.

"She nearly wrenched her back. But there she was back up the next week leading her soccer team to the championship."

"She's not changed much," said Saphora. "Just a little older. But you've seen her since then, haven't you?"

"My divorce was seven years ago, Saphora."

"How has time slipped away? Where has my mind gone?"

"You always take care of everyone around you, Saphora. You don't notice life passing you by."

As usual, Marcy knew her all too well. "The life that is lived for others doesn't realize its own potential," said Saphora.

"Not necessarily."

"What do you mean?"

"Sometimes the things we do for others out of our selflessness complete us. We just have to remember to give in moderation. That way our candle doesn't burn down to the base before its time."

"You always were the smartest between us, Marcy."

"I'm glad you noticed." She laughed, playing at being smug when Saphora knew her to be humble. "Did you say Gwennie's here? That's rare for me to show up the same weekend as her."

"Gwennie's coming around more. Her hair's grown out. I think I like it. It's red like yours."

"She was always cutting it in some style, trying to look like the older girls. She was a little fashion plate."

"That's why she loves you so much, Marcy," said Saphora, finding a parking place as close to the hospital elevator as possible. "She's more like you than me."

"That's my Gwennie."

"I'll get us coffee. Then we'll go up and see Bender. He was next door to a senator. But that entourage has all come and gone. It was exciting for a week around Duke."

Once inside the tube, Marcy got worried about losing her cell phone signal. "I'm going to step outside and leave my boss a message. Can I meet you up in Bender's room?"

"I'll get the coffee. Take the elevator up to H, then veer right until you find 1221. Stop at the nurse's station if you get lost."

"Skim vanilla latte, decaf, if you don't mind," said Marcy. "Same as you."

"You remembered." Saphora let the elevator door close between them. Since her phone signal would not work anyway, she shut it off to save the charge. Six people were already inside the elevator. Saphora got off on the cafeteria and shop floor. She took her time. She picked up a gardening magazine, some extra mints. Then she ordered their coffees and walked back across the waxed black and green tiles to the padded waiting area in front of the elevator. A nice orderly helped her with the buttons, and she took the elevator up to Bender's floor. The door opened and there was the Chilean nurse who had made Gwennie mad.

"Mrs. Warren, I thought this was your day to be here. Your friend is in the room."

"She beat me here. Marcy can find her way around any place," said Saphora.

"Marcy? I thought her name was Evelyn."

"Marcy."

"This is your family friend, Evelyn. She's been here to see the doctor several times."

The nurse annoyed her. "I don't know any Evelyn."

Saphora walked around her, holding out the coffee cups as if she was in a hurry to set them down. She politely spoke to some of the visitors she passed in the hallway, people becoming sadly familiar to her. Then she backed into Bender's hospital room, pushing the door open. "I can't believe you beat me here," she said.

Marcy did not answer. Saphora parted the curtains and smiled. "They did have vanilla latte, you'll be glad to know."

But it was not Marcy smiling back at her. Truth be told, the frail woman sitting where Saphora normally sat at Bender's side, even holding Bender's hand, was not smiling. She wiped her eyes and sat up, flummoxed, her quiet moment invaded.

Saphora glanced at her husband to be sure she was in the right room. "Do I know you?" she asked.

"I'm so sorry. I didn't mean to intrude on your time, ma'am." She got up, the roots around her scalp showing silvery threads in the light as she moved quickly out of the chair. She hurried to get up and retrieve her purse. She was going to bolt for the door, but Saphora said, "Won't you tell me your name?"

"Evelyn."

When she spoke her name "Evelyn," Saphora's mind flashed back that instant to the boat moored at their home dock on Lake Norman. The *Evelyn* had been a greater source of pride for Bender than his golfing membership. Bender had told her he had named the boat after Evelyn, a great-aunt in his family who had loved him so much that when she died he wanted to memorialize her memory.

She studied the slight lines around the woman's very blue eyes.

With a little makeup, she might be pretty. Probably was a babe in her younger days. "Are you a patient of my husband's?"

"Many years ago."

"You live here in Raleigh?"

"Wilmington."

"My husband has flown to Wilmington often for fishing trips," said Saphora pointedly.

"I should go," said Evelyn. She made a wide arc around Saphora.

"I'd rather you stay. If you're a friend of Bender's," said Saphora, not trying to hide the tension growing inside her. She set the coffees on the tray at the foot of the bed.

Evelyn had almost made it to the door when Saphora saw a small book in the chair where she had just sat holding Bender's hand. She picked it up, opened it, and read out loud, "To my darling Evelyn, from Bender, Your Tiger Boy." She closed up the book of poetry. "It's dated 1987. Did you want this?"

Evelyn's very pale hand came to her mouth. "This is horrible."

"I agree, but why leave now? The cat's jumped out of the bag already." Saphora was shaking, she was so angry and hurt.

Evelyn stepped back as the door came open.

Marcy looked relieved to see Saphora. "Good grief, Saphora, I've been on every floor trying to find you. Thank the good Lord I finally did." She had stopped off at the gift shop and bought a vase with a rose in it.

"I'll leave you two." Evelyn looked into Saphora's eyes as if taking a breath might break her in two. "I'm so sorry." She sidestepped Marcy and slipped past her and out into the hallway.

"Who's she?" asked Marcy.

Saphora opened the poetry book. "Evelyn Yeats." She closed the book and slipped it into her pocketbook. She was too weak to explain the awkward incident of the last few minutes.

Marcy was still anxious from getting lost. "This place is a city, Saphora. Don't let me leave your side. You'd never see me again." She looked down at Bender, who slept with his lips slightly parted, his newly grown lashes resting like a child's upon his face. "I guess this rose is for you, you poor guy," she said. "Saphora, what is that in your eyes? You're going to cry. It's all right, baby." She put down the vase and opened her arms wide to Saphora. She held her while she cried. "You've earned your tears." She did not try to be funny the rest of their time at the hospital.

ᕙ

Marcy took a turn driving. She talked quietly about her travels outside America. "The last thing I would expect is that it would change me so much, seeing how other people live. I've met families who have built a small business out of, say, rug making. The husband and wife weave while their kids keep the household going. You'd not believe these children, the way they keep up the household chores and start the family meals. Not just girls, but little boys sweeping their mama's kitchen, shucking corn. Makes me feel less guilty about making my son learn to cook and do for himself. The more he looks after himself and does for his wife, the more I realize I did right making him figure out things for himself."

"Turner is helpless without frozen meals," said Saphora.

"Will I see him?" she asked.

"Just left this afternoon. He and his son, Eddie, only had a day to come and see us and then Bender on their way out."

"But Turner can't be completely helpless. Being a daddy grows them up fast," said Marcy.

"Some days, yes. Others, no. It's my fault. First we had Annie and then Tabitha to clean up after us. I would tell the kids they had to make their own beds. But after a while they would wind their way into Tabitha's sympathy. I'd find them sitting in front of the TV while Tabitha dusted and cleaned their rooms. She would tell me, 'Ain't no use giving them chores. I have to do it over anyway.' "

"Mmm." She seemed reflective. "If I may ask, who was the woman leaving as I came in?" asked Marcy.

Saphora let out what seemed an endless sigh and then finally gave in, since Marcy was annoyingly perceptive and relentless. She answered, "She's an old patient. I don't know her."

"She looked affected, that's for sure."

"I'd rather hear about Tibet."

Marcy gave her a moment of respectful silence. Then she said, "She had something in her heart. A woman can't hide that from her eyes."

"Since you're not going to get off the subject, she's an old flame."

She shook her head. "I knew that. Come back to see Dr. Warren? Seems like she'd know better. From college?"

"Much later. After marriage."

"That's not right. It's good I didn't know. I would have given her what-for," said Marcy. She drove into Durham. "I know of a tea room. You'll like it." She drove them straight there. Once they were seated, she would not let Saphora pay for midafternoon scones, berries, and hot tea.

"I didn't know this place was here," said Saphora.

"I service a big store here in Raleigh-Durham. This is my favorite place. Just a little of this and that to tide you over. This French tea is very nice." She poured hot water over the tea infuser clogged with leaves. Still looking into Saphora's cup, she said, "Why men cheat is beyond me."

Saphora pressed her spoon against the tea leaves over the cup. She did not know what to say, so she responded with an example of the one good man who came to mind. "I've been sitting out on the upper deck these past few weeks watching a grieving young man pine for his wife. She was a lucky lady."

"Not all men act like ours, that's for certain."

"The thing I don't understand about Bender is why he thinks I'm not enough."

"It's not you, just like it wasn't me."

"But look at you, Marcy. I've never seen you happier."

"I've had my nights. Don't think I haven't." She tried a chocolate-dipped strawberry. She closed her eyes and savored the taste. "But the whole time I was trying to hold my marriage together, I walked a tightrope of perfection. I thought if I did everything right to please him, then we would make it. But I'm free now in that I'm not subjected to his covert abuse of me."

"Covert, as in?"

"One minute loving me, the next sabotaging my hopes and dreams."

"Do they cheat because they're afraid of getting old?"

"Or maybe they're imagining being James Dean," said Marcy.

"Riding the highways, no ties. Just living a dream."

"For themselves, though," said Marcy, without a hint of bitterness. "A selfish dream. It won't give them happiness."

Bender had been trapped in his dreams now for a week. She wondered how that was going for him. "I was just letting myself love him again."

"You know, it's not like he asked her to come." Marcy loved Bender, so it was like her to give him the benefit of the doubt.

"She's been coming, the nurse said, several times this week."

"What gets into people?"

They took the rest of the afternoon to get back to Oriental. By the time they pulled into the driveway, Saphora was laughing so hard she was crying. "I'm so glad you came, Marcy. Laughing feels like rain on my soul."

The front door opened. Gwennie ran down the walk and met Saphora as she climbed out of the Lexus. "Your phone's turned off, Mama." She looked perplexed, arms stiff at her sides.

"Oh, I forgot," Saphora said, laughing. "I got distracted. I forgot to turn it back on." But Gwennie did not laugh with her.

"I've been calling you all afternoon," said Gwennie. She was pale.

"Did the hospital call?" asked Saphora.

"Yes. Two hours ago."

Her heart skipped a beat or two. "Your daddy?"

"No." Gwennie brought her fingertips to her mouth, composing herself. "Not a call from Duke. I'm sorry. I've been so worried trying to reach you. It's Tobias."

"Don't say that," said Saphora.

"He didn't know who else to call."

"Oh, so he's fine." Saphora was about to panic.

"Not fine, Mama. It's Jamie. There's been an accident." She was shouldering her oversized purse and slipping on her sunglasses, as usual, taking charge. "They're at New Hanover in Wilmington. If you don't mind, Marcy, I'll drive. You go with us, though."

Saphora turned on her phone and found twenty-three messages from Gwennie.

"Lord, run alongside us today," said Marcy. Her prayers rose up from the backseat all the way into Wilmington.

∾

Saphora realized halfway to Wilmington that she had been driving to hospitals all day. Normally she would be enjoying the ride down the coast, the sudden appearance of a sea gull overhead. But all she could do was imagine what Jamie was going through. All Tobias had told Gwennie was that his mother had been in an accident. He was crying from the ER lobby. A nurse was there with him trying to help him locate his daddy. Finally, the nurse took the phone and gave Gwennie a few sketchy details, as much as she could say legally.

"What exactly did Tobias tell you?" asked Saphora.

"They were in Kinston." Gwennie drove craning her neck and checking the tracking monitor. "What was Jamie doing up in Kinston anyway?"

"I sent her there on an errand," said Saphora. "It was a surprise for Tobias."

"They were at a baseball stadium," said Gwennie. "I thought they had gone home to Wilmington."

"No."

"Isn't that home for a minor league? Kinston?" asked Gwennie.

"Yes, it's how minors become majors, though. Tobias wanted to meet Sam the Hammer."

"Oh, Sam! That's right. Daddy plays golf with that guy. He was cute, if I remember right," said Gwennie.

"Pitched bullets, according to Bender," said Saphora.

"I've heard of Sam the Hammer," said Marcy.

"The Cleveland Indians scouted him. Anyway, Tobias wanted to get his new baseball card before he was too famous to get," said Saphora. "I called Sam on Bender's phone. He invited Tobias up for batting practice. Jamie just could not stop talking about what a surprise it was going to be. Is that where they had the accident? Was Jamie driving?"

"It wasn't a car accident. But Tobias was crying so hard I couldn't figure out what happened," said Gwennie. She was quieter than usual. "The nurse said they needed a friend of the family to come as soon as possible. I'm afraid for him."

"Gwennie, is Jamie all right?" asked Saphora.

"They wouldn't let him in to see her. He wanted us to come and make them take him to her," said Gwennie.

"What about the boy's daddy?" asked Marcy. "I didn't understand that part."

"Tobias couldn't get him on the phone," said Gwennie.

"That doesn't sound right," said Marcy.

It took a couple of hours, but they finally made it to the hospital. New Hanover Regional Medical Center was in the middle of everything—Shipyard Boulevard, the canal, downtown Wilmington. Gwennie found parking, though, close to the trauma center. A nurse directed them to a waiting room.

Tobias sat in a corner, his hands pressed between his knees. Next to him sat a social worker. When he saw Saphora he was on his feet and running. She knelt so that he easily collapsed against her. "Mom's still not out of the emergency room," he said.

"Tobias, what's going on?" asked Saphora.

The social worker, a middle-aged female, spoke. "I'm sorry, ma'am, but I need to ask who you are."

"I'm his mother's good friend," Saphora said without taking her eyes off Tobias. "Mrs. Saphora Warren. I can show you ID if you need it."

"That's not necessary at the moment. However, I'm still trying to reach Tobias's father," said the social worker. "Mrs. Warren, can you sit with him?"

"I'll take responsibility for him while he waits for Mel," said Saphora.

"Tobias, you need to stay with Mrs. Warren until your father arrives, all right?" she said.

Tobias nodded. His eyes were racing from Saphora to the ER check-in station.

"Have you talked to your daddy at all?" asked Saphora.

"No. But they told me he left a message at the nurse's station. He's coming."

"He'll make it all right," said Saphora. Mel was not around much in Oriental, but Jamie made him sound like a good dad.

"He won't," said Tobias.

"You're just upset," said Saphora.

"You don't know," said Tobias. "He doesn't know I know."

"What?"

"He and mom separated. He thinks I don't know. But I know."

Saphora had no idea and did not know what to say. Jamie had not divulged the news to her. "He'll make things right, Tobias," said Saphora. "This is different."

"How?"

"Tobias?" Mel was being directed into the waiting area by a nurse.

"Daddy," Tobias said, his eyes sullen. He looked at Mel with a pained sense of helplessness. "They won't let me see her."

"Saphora," said Mel, acknowledging her.

"Tobias has been so anxious to see you," said Saphora.

Mel took her aside. "I'd like to talk to you."

Gwennie said, "I'll go for coffee. Marcy, go with me."

"Tobias, let the grownups talk," said Mel.

"He's waited for you a long time, Mel," said Saphora. She hoped he would at least offer some comfort, hold Tobias or something. But there he stood as if lost and not present.

"I know," he said, and then he turned and walked out as if he expected Saphora to follow. The sliding doors closed behind him.

"I hate him," said Tobias, quietly, but standing erect and not taking his eyes off the door between him and his daddy.

"Don't say that. I'll talk to him," said Saphora.

"He won't change," said Tobias. "I heard my mom say that."

Gwennie and Marcy had stopped a few feet away. "Want to come with us, Tobias?"

"Good idea. I'll join you all in a few minutes," said Saphora, rising and grateful to Gwennie for intervening.

"You won't get anywhere with him," he said.

She hated that Tobias knew more than a kid his age should know.

He left to catch up with Gwennie and Marcy. He did not turn to look back at Mel but disappeared through the doors down the next hallway.

Saphora met Mel out in the lobby near the nurse's station. The trauma center was in an upheaval. A semi loaded with chemicals had overturned along U.S. 17. Cops hurriedly shuffled into the center. They were all over the place, talking into phones and passing along the facts of the accident. An ambulance parked outside along the curving entry was still flashing red echoes into the trauma ward.

"Saphora, I can't believe you're here. You've meant so much to Jamie," said Mel. He looked down for a second and then back at Saphora.

"Mel, what's going on?" she asked.

"Jamie didn't make it," he said. That was when he broke down, sobbing.

"I don't believe it!" The words were coming at her too fast. She surely misunderstood him. She leaned back against the hospital wall, her hands covering her mouth.

"It was some loose wire in the concrete, or some such thing. New construction. You know how things get neglected. There's a lawsuit in it for Tobias, I'm sure."

"Mel, I don't care about a lawsuit."

"I'm just so angry, is all."

"Why hasn't Tobias been told? He thinks she's in the ER getting patched up, good as new," said Saphora.

"They wanted me to tell him. But I can't."

"You have to."

"Will you tell him?"

"It's not my place, Mel. You're his father." Saphora was seeing Mel for someone other than the man Jamie had painted.

"Tobias and I, we've not done well together. He loves you. It'll be easier if he hears it from you."

"It won't be easy coming from anyone, Mel. This is the time for you to step up and be his father. I won't tell him."

"I'm stepping out for a smoke. I got to clear my head."

"It can wait."

He left Saphora standing in the middle of the cops and the ambulance attendants. He turned and glanced through the plate glass door and then at the ground. It seemed he was well practiced at avoiding eye contact.

Gwennie walked up empty-handed. "Mama, what's going on? Why is Mr. Linker standing outside?"

"Where's Tobias?"

"Marcy's got him back at the drink machine," said Gwennie. "There's a waiting area there."

Saphora put her arms around Gwennie. She was crying as she said, "Jamie didn't make it."

Gwennie responded at first with silent shock. Then her emotions gave way and she sobbed, holding on to her mother.

"Mel won't tell Tobias. His mother is down in the hospital morgue and no one will tell him," said Saphora.

"None of this makes sense," said Gwennie through the tears.

"I'm going to march out there and make that man do his duty, that's what!" said Saphora.

"Mama, what is wrong with Mel?" asked Gwennie. "Why won't he talk to his own son?"

Mel slumped against an outside pillar a few feet from the automatic doors. His eyes were closed. He blew out a white stream of smoke, coughed, and took another draw on his cigarette.

The ambulance pulled away from the curb, the lights going off. The emergency room lobby was still as a funeral home, the activity of the highway accident having poured into other parts and places.

"You tell Tobias, Mama. I'll go with you," said Gwennie.

Marcy came through the door from the hallway holding Tobias's hand. She saw the two of them crying. "Oh no," said Marcy, taking two steps back. She closed her eyes. "God, give this woman some strength," she whispered.

Saphora had trouble focusing. She imagined Mel running in, realizing his mistake. She watched her imaginary Mel telling Tobias the truth about Jamie. She watched Tobias throw his arms around his father. The love between them was flooded with relief at the thought.

"Mama?" Gwennie sounded concerned.

"Miss Saphora, what's going on?" asked Tobias. He juggled the canned drink back and forth nervously.

Saphora opened her eyes and saw Mel walk away from the automatic doors. He put out his cigarette. He looked around as if he could not remember where he parked, shoved his hands into his pockets. He took off, slowly ambling down the sidewalk, eyes to the ground.

"Tobias, let's go back down the hallway to that waiting area," said Saphora.

Gwennie opened the door for her. Marcy was right behind her.

"Where's my dad?" asked Tobias.

"He went to be with your mama," said Saphora, lying.

"Why didn't he take me with him?" He looked as if he might bolt.

Saphora sat on one of the plastic-covered padded bench seats. "Tobias, tell me what happened back at Kinston."

Tobias was more settled than before, maybe because his daddy was gone. Or Marcy had worked her comfort over him. "Mom took me to Kinston to meet Sam the Hammer. She said he's friends with Dr. Warren."

Saphora hid the regret welling up in her throat.

"We decided to walk around. They were building a new concession stand. Then I saw Sam the Hammer out pitching. I yelled out his name, you know, like we were friends and all. Mom said he had invited me to his pitching practice so it was okay. I turned away from her. It was just a second. She touched some pole holding up the overhang. They said the wiring wasn't grounded."

"Who said that?"

"A man. He looked like a janitor. He was so scared. There were men running everywhere. Sam, he came running up. But I didn't care about him anymore. I just wanted Mom to get up. They wouldn't let me touch her. The janitor put sawhorses all around her until the cops came."

"How awful," said Gwennie, still struggling to keep her composure. Marcy was humming a hymn, her eyes closed.

"They took us up in a helicopter," said Tobias. "I nearly threw up. I always thought I'd want to go up in one, but I was sick. Mom was so white. She didn't look like Mom. But the ambulance man and lady, they wouldn't give up. I wouldn't let them."

"They worked hard to save her," said Saphora.

"But they didn't, did they?" he asked, finally at the end of his words. The tears in his eyes were bigger than anything that ever fell from the sky. His head fell back. The first sob was slow in coming. Then he cried long and hard, like a baby animal lost in the woods.

"I'm sorry," said Saphora.

"I want to go to her," said Tobias. He pressed his face into her, crying.

"I'll work it out," said Saphora. She and Marcy locked eyes, and she wished for once that she was anywhere but here.

❧

The next morning Saphora got Mel's number from Tobias, who had slept on a hotel cot in their room—Jamie's family would need to be called. After spending the night in a nearby La Quinta, Saphora rang Mel's doorbell precisely at ten o'clock, the time he had asked her to drop by. He answered the door wearing a shirt not buttoned, his belt hanging open. He gave Saphora a set of keys to the house, explaining each one.

"We thought we would make calls for your family, if that helps," said Saphora. Jamie had mentioned a sister.

"I called her sister, Dora." There was a tone to his voice. Jamie had mentioned Dora was a welfare mother.

Saphora thought Jamie's mother and father were still living but Mel said no.

Gwennie turned on her managerial magic. Marcy was right beside her with a pad and pen. Between the two of them, they sat in Jamie's kitchen calling every relative from Myrtle Beach to Oregon.

Jamie's kitchen was just like her, small but inviting. Tobias's red Pomeranian, Fang, kept running in and out of the kitchen, so Tobias threw the dog a ball. But Fang only lay down and whimpered. "He's looking for Mom," said Tobias.

Jamie had put an oversized black dining room table right at the edge of the galley of cabinets. Even though there was a formal dining room, it seemed all of the household activity was done around that table. Jamie had organized Tobias's life so that he could live as well as any boy. She had tacked a calendar to the wall scheduling his meds and activities. He had baseball practice on Saturdays. There was a photograph of the baseball team seated around the black table. They were eating cake. Tobias took trumpet lessons. Jamie apparently seated him at the table to practice while she cooked his supper because there was his little music stand and book. There was a math book and a book of kitchen science experiments. Saphora could visualize Jamie counting out his meds at that table.

Mel crossed the kitchen, buttoning the peach-colored shirt. A van load of relatives pulled up, and he went out to meet them. From the look of things, they were Jamie's family.

Neighbors had brought over casseroles and honey-baked ham,

filling up Jamie's refrigerator. Saphora got out bread and sandwich meat to save the covered dishes for the evening meals.

A woman pushed through the back kitchen door as if she had come through it a thousand times. "Are you Saphora?" she asked.

"You must be Dora, Jamie's sister," said Saphora.

"You women are awfully nice to call everyone," she said. "I don't have the energy." Two thin teenage boys followed her into the kitchen. "This is Tom and his younger brother Stu. That wild animal coming through the door is Little Paul. Named after my ex."

"I'm making sandwiches," said Saphora.

"Good. My youngest, Mary, is driving me nuts. She's a bottomless pit, that one," said Dora.

The only girl among the brothers was a pudgy kid, her blond hair cropped right beneath her ears. She said in a voice wise beyond her years, "You didn't make breakfast, Mama."

"Now don't start with me, you hear? I'm too worn out, kid." Dora slid into the chair next to Gwennie. "Go and help your brothers unload the suitcases. I put your things in a grocery bag. Don't scatter the stuff all over the yard neither." She dragged a ponytail holder out of her yellow overprocessed hair and finger-styled the long, wavy strands back into the holder. "Mel, got an extra cigarette?" she asked.

Mel left the kitchen to fetch a carton.

"My mother's car—we forgot it," said Tobias.

Saphora said to Tom, "Do you drive?"

"Sure, ma'am. Been driving since I was fourteen," said Tom.

"He drove us here from Myrtle," said Dora. "He does all the driving for me now."

"Jamie's car is still in Kinston," said Saphora.

Tom and his brother Stu took on the job dutifully. Tobias followed them out the door. Saphora did not think it was a good idea for him to go along, considering he'd be revisiting the scene of the accident, but he insisted.

"He'll feel like he's done something important," said Marcy after the boys took off.

"I usually stay overnight here in Jamie's guest room," said Dora.

"You should," said Saphora. "We're just friends helping out."

"I saw a nice inn on the way over," said Gwennie. "I'll get us rooms."

"Just one night. Please call your brothers so they know we're here," said Saphora.

Mel brought a pack of cigarettes to Dora and then left them to handle the chores. "I'm calling business friends to let them know what's going on. I'll be in the den if you need me," he said to Saphora. He left her alone with Dora.

Dora lowered her voice. "You know the two of them was separated, didn't you?"

"I just found that out," said Saphora.

"Mel, he never gave two cents for Tobias. He just thought adoption would give Jamie some purpose. He never liked staying around the house much." She tamped another cigarette out of a red pack and mouthed, "He's impotent."

"I don't need to know," said Saphora. She put out the paper plates. "Sandwiches are ready. Mary, Little Paul, come and eat."

"Tobias has AIDS," said Mary.

"Shush!" said Dora. "These kids have ears bigger than Texas and mouths to match."

"Mel will finally get to know Tobias," said Marcy. "That's the good that will come of all this." She was trying to bring her usual cheer to an otherwise bleak situation.

Mel was closing up his phone when he came into the kitchen. "Sandwiches, just in time. I'm starved. You're a good woman, Saphora." He picked up a ham and cheddar. "They need me to come and pick out a casket." He surveyed all the females assembled in Jamie's kitchen. "Who's good at that?"

Gwennie looked at Saphora. "Sandwiches and funerals. My mother is the one to ask." She let Fang jump into her lap. "I'll look after the dog."

Saphora thought about making a Gwennie-sized gag.

Marcy turned the page on her list and dialed another number. "We're all doing our thing, Saphora. You go and do yours." Her back was to Mel, so he could not see her bat her eyes at Saphora.

Mel said, "Sure, you'd be the best one to do it." He asked Saphora to ride with him to Mickelson's Funeral Home.

The weather had turned hotter than all the rest of the days that summer. Saphora stood out on the driveway while Mel cooled down the Audi. Finally he waved her inside.

"You like your Lexus?" he asked.

"It's one of Bender's cars. I drive a different car," she said.

"I guess a surgeon can drive anything he wants." He put a cigarette to his lips.

"Can you help me out? I can't tolerate smoking in a car."

"I'm sorry." He brought down the cigarette.

A box of tissues was on the floorboard, the box decorated with little boys playing baseball. Saphora pulled out a tissue. The radio station was turned to a light pop station. Mel turned it off.

"Everything will remind you of her," said Saphora.

"I'm doing okay."

"Tobias has a lot going on. You think you'll be able to keep up with him?"

"He's always been hers. We couldn't have kids. Tobias satisfied a lot of feminine urges for her."

"Feminine urges?"

"Women have a need to look after others."

"We do?"

"You know you do. I know what women think, that they're like men, want to work like men, talk like men. But you're made to raise kids. Me, I could never keep up with Tobias like Jamie. She was born to do it. Matter of fact, she lived to chase after Tobias."

"I think it's been hard on her."

"My work is hard, but I love it."

"You have it all categorized."

"It's not rocket science."

"What will happen to Tobias then?"

"Dora, she's got lots of kids. Tobias likes his cousins. It'd be like instant siblings."

"You don't mean to send Tobias back with Dora?"

"I can't deny I've been thinking about it, what time I've had to think, that is."

"Dora wants Tobias?"

"I haven't asked her. But she loved Jamie."

"Dora's nothing like Jamie." Jamie barely tolerated Dora, of that she was certain.

"I'm not saying the deal's set in stone. I'm in shock. You know?" He coughed into one hand, holding the unlit cigarette in the other.

"Yes, but you could find support and rear him on your own."

He did not answer but just stared out the front windshield.

"Mel, you can't mean you'd do that to Tobias. Jamie's provided him a good life. You can't send him into Dora's world. It'd be cruel."

"Dora's not a bad person. She's just got low expectations. But Tobias, he's disabled. He can't do much better anyway."

"Dora's not a good mother, Mel. You can't say she is."

"Aren't you judgmental?"

"It is what it is," said Saphora.

The remaining mile to Mickelson's Funeral Home was quiet, the sun bearing down on the black car.

Mel turned the radio back on.

৶৹

Casket shopping was the last thing Saphora had counted on doing that day.

Mickelson's chauffeur smoked outside the main entry under the overhang where guests were dropped off. He opened the door for Saphora and said to Mel, "I'm sorry for your loss, Mr. Linker."

"Tommy, you still here after all these years?"

"Work's steady," said Tommy. "How's the software biz?"

"Up and down," said Mel.

"Mr. Mickelson's asked me to walk you to the Agatha room," said Tommy. He dropped the cigarette into the ashtray. A rock song played in a viewing room as they passed.

"Teenager," said Tommy. "His mother wanted the kid's favorite band playing when she comes to approve the deceased."

Saphora fell behind Mel a couple of steps.

"Funny. I don't think Jamie had a favorite song," said Mel.

" 'Both Sides Now,' " said Saphora.

"She told you that?" he asked. He stopped in the middle of the reception area.

"She liked Joni Mitchell," said Saphora.

"Joni Mitchell we got," said Tommy. "Everyone picks her."

"It's all people our age who are dying," said Saphora.

" 'Both Sides Now.' She never said that to me," said Mel. "It's one of those feel-good songs."

"Joni Mitchell? Not likely," said Tommy.

"It's about the uncertainty of life," said Saphora. "You look at it one way when you're young. But another way when you get older."

"That's the song then," said Mel. "She'd want it."

The Mickelson brothers had staged a big, expensive display inside a glass case. A polished wood casket was covered with silk irises. A woman's painting hung suspended over the casket. A nameplate read "In Memory of Our Mother, Agatha Mickelson." The remaining caskets lined the walls and inner walkway of the selection room.

"I'll leave you to decide. Gerry Mickelson will be in to help you with your arrangements," said Tommy.

Saphora stared too long at the polished wood caskets. Mel called her down to the blue and pink colored metal models. "Saphora, you're going to have to do this. I'm feeling dizzy. I think I'm getting hives."

"What's your budget?"

"There's some insurance. And I'm coming into some money. We can do it right."

"Do you have a preference?" she asked.

"Women like pink."

"Not all women."

"Like I said, you pick it," said Mel.

She was torn between a mahogany or an oak stain.

"The mahogany, I think," said Mel. "The angel on the inside, she'd like it."

"That's good." She was feeling the need to go out for air but reconsidered since it was best to help Mel bring these matters to a close.

"What's next?" he asked.

"They'll want to know about the vault and all."

"I had to bury my dad. He wanted a vault. He was scared to death of floating away," said Mel.

"It's up to you," she said. "Not everyone buys them."

The door opened at the opposite end of the sales floor. A man dressed in a brown suit poked his head into the casket room. "Mr. Linker, do you need more time?" asked Gerry Mickelson. He forced the door open a little wider. The door was sticking on a plush red carpet runner.

"He's decided," said Saphora. "The mahogany one with the angel embroidery."

"Such a beautiful choice, Mr. Linker. If you'll come down this way, I've got a room where you can rest your feet and finish up," said Mickelson.

Saphora lingered over the mahogany casket. Mel nearly made it to the door left open by Gerry Mickelson when he staggered and then fainted onto the plush carpet.

19

My island selects for me people who are very
different from me—the stranger who turns
out to be, in the frame of sufficient time and
space, invariably interesting and enriching.

ANNE MORROW LINDBERGH, *Gift from the Sea*

Gwennie sat scribbling in a legal document the size of a phone book.
She was lying on her stomach on the antique bed. She had checked
them into an inn. "Tell me again. When Mel passed out, did the un-
dertaker yell?"

Saphora slipped into a pair of yoga pants and walked on her
knees across the other bed, carefully so as not to cause Marcy to spill
her tea. But Marcy was laughing anyway, so tea dripped down her
chin. Marcy put down the drink and fell over laughing.

"I'm not telling it again. That poor man is suffering more than
he wants to let on."

"He's just such a big man and kind of a chauvinist. I'm trying to
see it all like you did," said Marcy. "I hope his head is healed up before the funeral."

Gwennie was shaking as she held in laughter. She leaned over the
transcript, holding her eyeglasses on her face.

"I'm glad the two of you weren't there," said Saphora. "Mr.
Mickelson was yelling for an ambulance. I just knelt down and talked

until Mel opened his eyes. He kept saying a name over and over," said Saphora.

"What name?" asked Marcy.

"It sounded like Francis. I don't remember Jamie mentioning a Francis," said Saphora. "But then he got hold of himself and asked me where we had parked."

"He was ready to get out of there, I guess," said Marcy.

"He still had not finished up with the funeral home director. But that's not the worst of it," said Saphora. "The doctor in the emergency room said he was experiencing anxiety. He told Mel he needed to take some time off and then went to have him discharged. That was when Mel told me for certain he was not equipped to take care of Tobias."

"I knew it," said Marcy.

"He's Tobias's legal father," said Gwennie. "He'll be all right in a day or so. It's just the stress of losing Jamie so quickly. I've seen it before."

"Gwennie, he wanted me to ask you if you could help with the legality of giving him up," said Saphora.

"Don't tell me that," said Marcy.

"Who would take him? Not that crazy Dora?" asked Gwennie.

"He's already talked to her, I'll bet," said Marcy.

"What makes you think that?" asked Saphora. She knew; she just wondered how Marcy knew.

"I heard her griping over the phone to some trash friend up the coast about taking in another mouth to feed," said Marcy.

"Tobias would not do well with that woman," said Gwennie. "Mel needs to give himself some time. He'll start taking him to ball games and school. They'll figure it out as they go."

"He seemed to believe that Tobias and Jamie were destined for each other. To hear him tell it, this was his way of exiting the relationship," said Saphora.

"He's got a child, and he'll have to deal with him now," said Gwennie. "Surely he knows Dora can't deal with her own kids. They live in a tiny trailer in an RV park. It's not even a real home. I heard her daughter complaining about it."

"From the looks of their house here and the one you said they own in Oriental," said Marcy, "Mel's got all kinds of money. He can hire someone to help cart that boy around to his games and such. Anything is better than dumping him off on Dora."

"He just can't picture himself rearing Tobias," said Saphora.

"I'll give him until the funeral to come around," said Marcy. "Then I'm having a talk with that man."

ᏺ

Finally Wednesday rolled around, and Saphora woke up with the dread of paying her last respects to her beautiful friend.

She called Turner. "Please take tomorrow off and go see your daddy. The nurse says there's no change, but I can't stand the thought of him lying there without one of us nearby." Truth be told, she wanted to chase off that Evelyn. She would be surprised if she showed her face again but did not want to risk her returning.

"Mama, it's time to go," said Gwennie, opening the bedroom door of the inn they had been staying in so they could keep an eye on Tobias. Gwennie had dressed in the black top and pants she had bought yesterday when Marcy had marshaled them into a local retail shop to buy clothes for the service.

Saphora imagined Dora and her children piling into the family limousine, sandwiching Tobias into the middle of her brood, while Mel ducked into the front seat so as not to have to look at Tobias.

Half of Wilmington must have known Jamie Linker. The large donated church sanctuary was crowded, full nearly to the last row of seats.

Mel had saved a row of chairs for Jamie's friends. Just as Saphora was leading Gwennie and Marcy down a row in the back, Tobias ran to fetch them. "You're supposed to sit behind me," he said to Saphora. Bluish circles under his eyes hinted that he had not slept. Saphora followed him up the church aisle, stepping into the line of Jamie's friends in the row behind the family. Saphora sat square behind Tobias. She leaned forward and said to him, "You're supposed to come in the door from the side with your daddy. Did they not tell you?"

"I didn't want to," said Tobias. He never turned around but faced forward, sitting between his young cousins Mary and Little Paul.

Marcy cut eyes at Saphora and mouthed, "He knows."

Just as an usher was leading Mel from the side waiting room, a minister walked briskly at his side holding a Bible in one hand and a small box in the other. "That's Pastor Mims," said Saphora to Marcy. "How appropriate. He's Jamie's pastor. He's our pastor too."

"I didn't know you had a pastor," Marcy replied. She seemed pleased to know.

Gwennie whispered to Saphora, "Look, Luke's across the aisle."

Saphora turned and saw that Luke was one aisle away from the family seating. "That's so sweet of him to come. He was tender toward Tobias."

Every so often Gwennie would turn and glance toward Luke. But he kept his eyes forward, fixated, it seemed, on Pastor John.

Gwennie pulled out her phone. Saphora assumed it was to see if

Luke had left her a message. But only messages with New York area codes filled up the screen.

"Go and talk to him after church, for goodness' sake," Saphora whispered.

Gwennie had not taken off her black sunglasses. She kept them on even after John Mims made the opening statement and prayed. So New York of her.

Pastor John was wearing the same dark blue suit he wore when Bender collapsed.

Three women climbed the blue carpeted steps to the platform. Each of them read handwritten stories about how Jamie had affected them. One lady started sobbing, unable to be consoled. Her son had played baseball with Tobias. The other two had worked alongside Jamie in a children's AIDS charity called the Secret Angels.

After they had finished, John read Jamie's eulogy. He was luminescent in the gleam of the stained glass behind him, like angels were waiting in the windows for him to talk. He said, "There was a man who brought his bride to a little house along the Neuse River. The bride loved the house so much that she buried a possession in the backyard, she said, to bless her marriage to her one true love. But she contracted cancer and died two years later. That husband loved her so much that he went back to the house, bought it, and spent his evenings digging up the backyard until he found this." John held up the small wooden box. He took off the top and then held up the object.

Gwennie was frozen. She could not take her eyes off Luke.

"I know this story," said Saphora.

"Listen," said Marcy. "I want to hear."

"It's Luke's story," said Gwennie.

"This is a simple wooden cross," said John. "The bride was given this trinket as a young girl. She had come to my church with her mother, who was vacationing in Oriental. I remember the morning that I invited the children forward for a children's story. I told them the story from Matthew 13:44. It's a simple one-verse story. A man discovered some treasure buried on a piece of land. It was so valuable that he reburied the treasure. Overjoyed at his find, he sold everything he had to return and buy that land. It was a simple story, but it made an impression on young Mabel Anne Birch, the child who grew up to marry her true love, Luke Weston."

"He loved her so much," said Marcy.

"Hush, hush," said Gwennie.

John continued, "As we honor a life well lived today, the life of Jamie Sheree Sondheim Linker, it seems fitting to talk about the things in life she taught us about treasure."

Saphora felt Gwennie's hand come around hers.

John laid the wooden cross on the lectern. "Jamie Linker was a special woman. She married Mel Linker and prayed every night for God to give her a child. When she was unable to have children, fate, it seemed, brought a boy to her threshold. Would she take him?"

Tobias sat on the edge of his chair.

"Tobias has given me permission to tell you that he was born HIV-positive. A virus embedded in his frail body at birth mutated and took over his DNA so that it could duplicate and make more virus cells. But Jamie saw past Tobias's attacked DNA. She saw instead the treasure she had been looking for her whole life, a boy to call her own. She told me a few Sundays ago that when her eyes fell on Tobias, she knew instantly that he was hers. She said, 'It was like his soul was inviting me to participate in his journey.'" John paused for a moment, maybe to contemplate or else to swallow the lump in his throat. "She said, 'How could I turn down such an invitation?' "

Saphora could not hold back the tears that she had not allowed herself in the stress and clamor of looking after Jamie's funeral arrangements.

"I'm in need of tissues, sisters," said Marcy.

Gwennie dug a pack of tissues from her handbag and handed the whole thing to Marcy, who took two and passed them to Saphora.

John closed his Bible. "There is a place in the gospels where a woman sits at Christ's feet. She is so involved in expressing her love for him that she can't stop washing his feet with her tears and hair. She is criticized for such outlandish worship. Jamie Linker's life has been like both of these characters—the treasure seeker and the woman crying onto Christ's feet. We understand her and yet are confused by her mode of worship—that of loving what life has overlooked.

"Jesus was himself both adored and misunderstood. He offers a continual invitation to us to follow him. He loved us enough to allow our DNA to become embedded in his. He took on our disease of sin. But like Jamie, who accepted Tobias's invitation to join him on his journey, Jesus invites you. He knows your life is going to be difficult, that you'll stumble, that you'll know shame, dishonor, abuse. But God also knows that, with a little help, you'll learn to love. That's the part he highly anticipates for you, that moment when, like Jamie, you say yes to the journey."

Saphora stopped listening to Gwennie sniffling. She even took her eyes off Tobias.

When John Mims offered a chance to pray, she bowed right then, without waiting, just like he said to do.

﹏

Jamie's family members, the Sondheims, had been buried in Oakdale Cemetery dating back to the Civil War. Saphora followed the funeral processional through the cemetery gates.

"The reverend did a good job. It had to be hard to preach a funeral like that," said Marcy.

Gwennie was quiet. She had gone straight from the church to the car. If Luke had come out looking for her, he would not have found her.

"I had no idea what Luke was digging for. Did you, Gwennie?" asked Saphora.

"He never told me. I just thought he was this quirky guy looking for some buried treasure. All along, it was grief driving him," said Gwennie. "He still loves her."

"Of course he should," said Marcy. "But I didn't know he was the one you were holding out for. I don't blame you for that. He's a peach of a man, that one."

"He's not holding out for me, Marcy." She dug through her purse. "Not that I care."

"I know it hurts. But it's not the end, Gwennie," said Saphora.

"I really don't care," said Gwennie.

"He found Mabel's cross. It's part of the process," said Saphora.

"Mabel. You don't hear that name on a young woman anymore," said Marcy.

"Mabel was beautiful. I saw her picture in his living room," said Gwennie.

"He's got good tastes. So what?" asked Saphora.

"Mama, if I didn't know better, I'd say you're really pushing this thing with Luke. But you're the only one," said Gwennie, lowering her voice until it was thin as hopelessness.

Saphora parked behind the family limousine. She waved at Luke, who was standing a few feet away from the Lexus. "Then that's a mirage out there waving at us."

"Luke," said Gwennie. She popped open her door.

Saphora waited in the car for a moment. Marcy took her cue and waited as Gwennie ran to meet Luke.

"I don't understand romance anymore," said Saphora. "They like each other, but no one's supposed to admit it."

"He's a nice-looking man," said Marcy.

"Good dancer." She thought how different Luke was from Bender. But, yes, he could dance.

"There's Tobias standing next to his mother's casket," said Marcy. "Mel is not even looking at him. How does he expect that boy to go on all alone?"

"We should go to Tobias. Bring him with us for lunch. Then I'm going to talk with Mel and help him get his mind straight," said Saphora.

⁓

After the service, Luke walked Gwennie across the cemetery. Saphora stayed back several steps. She was not about to mess things up again. She had not meant to do that in the first place.

"That was a beautiful thing you did," said Gwennie, "sharing Mabel's cross with Pastor John."

"He knew about my little treasure hunt all along. When I found it, I went straight to his office. I was sitting across from him when he got the call about Jamie's accident," said Luke.

"Who called him?" asked Gwennie.

"Mel. He said that Tobias was falling apart. Pastor John and I left straight for Wilmington."

"You came here? I didn't know," said Gwennie.

"I didn't know you were here. I wish I had known."

"You do?"

"Are you going back to New York?"

"Thursday."

"That's tomorrow." They walked quietly for a few more paces. Finally he asked, "Gwennie, I have to know. Are you seeing that man I saw you with out on the driveway?"

"Mario? He's just a friend," said Gwennie.

"But you kissed him."

"You were home?"

"I had come back but parked my car in the garage. I wanted to give you your space."

"It wasn't that kind of kiss. Only good-bye and good luck. He was going back to New York to make up with his girlfriend. I was just a shoulder to cry on."

"Gwennie," he said.

"Yes, Luke?"

He put his arms around her and said, "This is hello." He kissed her right on the cemetery lawn. Then he opened the car door for her. She climbed in, looking stunned. After he closed the door, he turned and jogged up the road and got into his car.

"He's such an odd man," said Gwennie, touching her lips where Luke had just kissed her.

Saphora was standing with her door open.

Gwennie's phone rang. It was Luke. She answered it. Then she sat wiping her eyes. "Yes, tonight is good. Coffee is good. Sure, dinner is good. Anything you want, Luke."

Tobias was the last to leave Jamie's burial plot. Saphora walked back to the funeral tent and said to him, "See if your daddy will let you ride back with us ladies." She did not want him to wait too long and see the casket being lowered.

"He doesn't care," said Tobias. "I'll ride with you." He turned and waved good-bye to Mel, who nodded and gave him a manly thumbs-up.

Saphora caught Dora by the arm before she headed for the limousine. "Dora, we're kidnapping Tobias. But we'll bring him right back."

"Whatever you'd like," said Dora, distracted by her own children. She told Tom to herd Little Paul back to the road. He was loping across the cemetery like a calf.

Saphora kept holding on to Tobias's shoulders. He walked so stiffly that Saphora thought it might have been due to his new dress pants. "You can change as soon as we get you home." She helped him into the backseat, where Gwennie pulled out his seat belt.

"If I bought lunch, where would you like to eat, Tobias?" asked Marcy.

He shrugged.

"He might like the bistro I saw when we left the church," said Gwennie, but it was a ploy.

"Not that. Girl food," said Tobias.

"How about a buffet? I know I saw one someplace," said Marcy.

"I'd go for that," said Tobias. "Can we go to the Golden Corral?"

"Done!" said Marcy. "You'll have to show me."

"You'll turn up there by the Krispy Kreme."

"Tobias, here's something I've been meaning to give you," said Gwennie. She pulled out the satin throw pillow Bender had given her for her high school graduation.

"This is your favorite, isn't it?" asked Tobias.

"That's your 'Love is forever' pillow," said Marcy. "Tobias, you really rate now."

"It's kept me through many a long night, Tobias. You're the bravest boy I've ever met. But also the most loved boy I've ever met. Everyone who meets you loves you, especially me," said Gwennie.

"Thank you, Gwennie," said Tobias, cradling the pillow against his chest.

Saphora drove past several streets before Marcy yelled, "I see it!"

Once inside, they got trays and teas. Tobias went straight for the steak and the macaroni bar.

Saphora selected a table near a window. She could see cars passing. Gwennie sat on one side of her and Marcy on the other. "It feels odd when you lose someone. I count the minutes in the day until I have to say good-bye. Every minute passes so fast, but I feel like I'm trying to slow them down."

"I know what you mean," said Marcy.

"Time's sacred, isn't it?"

"But the cars just keep passing, people keep living."

"Luke and I are going to date," said Gwennie.

"I could see it coming," said Marcy.

"I'm so glad for you, darling," said Saphora. She was glad, for she was retiring her matchmaker hat for good.

Saphora was still looking out the window. Tobias came back with macaroni and cheese and mashed potatoes mounded around his steak.

"That's a lot of carbs, young man," said Gwennie.

"Let him go," said Saphora. "Tobias, eat anything you want today."

"I can't eat anything I want," he said.

"I forgot. You know what to eat, so eat as much as you want of it, minding your diet," said Saphora. "And speaking of being mindful, I should tell your daddy where we've stolen you away to." She tried to call but he was not answering. She did notice there was a message from Turner. She relayed the message to Gwennie. "Your brother's at Duke with Daddy."

Marcy said, "Tell me about your batting average."

"Not good lately, but it's improving," said Gwennie.

"I don't mean you, Gwennie. I mean you, Tobias," said Marcy.

"I'm giving up baseball," said Tobias.

"You're not," said Saphora.

"It's my fault. She never would have died if I hadn't asked for Sam Hammersley's autograph."

"Then it's my fault for setting it up," said Saphora. "Tobias, don't you think that's keeping me awake too?"

"You're not sleeping either?" he asked.

"Not more than an hour or two."

"I lie there seeing it all over again. Then I just get up and look at her picture," he said.

"Baby, I'm so sorry," said Saphora, soothing him in a way she was unable to soothe herself.

"Daddy wants me to go live with Dora," he said.

"What did you tell him?" asked Saphora.

"I said I wouldn't," he said.

"Good for you," said Gwennie.

"Stand your ground, Tobias," said Marcy.

Saphora appreciated all the bravado but wondered how a little boy might stand up under the weight of such a decision. "Maybe just give your father some time to get his bearings. He's still in shock," she suggested.

"He means it," said Tobias. His lip quivered slightly. "Forever. Daddy doesn't want to deal with my problems. But who would?"

"Don't let it ruin your lunch," said Saphora, feeling her own dam about to break forth. "I'll talk to him. He'll come around."

They talked about other things the rest of lunch.

Gwennie helped Tobias back into the car. She shut the door and then said to Saphora, still standing in the parking lot fishing for keys, "What if Mel won't drop this stupid idea? Maybe we're not helping Tobias by telling him it will all turn out."

"Gwennie, you're as negative as an old woman. Tobias needs hope, so that's what we'll give him." She got into the car. Tobias closed his eyes and put his head on Gwennie's satin pillow. He slept for the ten-minute drive back to his house.

ରୁ

"Here comes your cousin. Let's get moving." Dora herded all four of her children from the house to the van. "Get your things out of the house. We've got to go," she said, seemingly in a hurry to get them packed up.

Tobias stood in the doorway watching his cousins load up their belongings.

Dora thanked Saphora. "I know you all have to get on the road, what with your husband in the hospital. But you've been a world of help."

"Sure. Where is Mel?" asked Saphora.

"He took off for some rest," said Dora.

"To Oriental?" asked Gwennie.

"A friend invited him onto their yacht."

Tobias walked away from them in a huff. He stood beside Gwennie.

"Then why the hurry to leave?" asked Saphora.

She said to Saphora in a whisper, "This is going to be hard, so you may want to take your friends on out of here."

"Do you mean hard on Tobias?" asked Saphora coolly.

Tobias came walking toward them. "What's going on? Why did my dad leave me here?"

Dora answered, "Tobias, you're going to spend a few days with your little cousins. And I packed some of your things from your room. Your daddy showed me."

"I have school," said Tobias. "It starts in two days."

"His school is very rigid," said Saphora. She was in disbelief.

"I told Mel I wouldn't be no good at this. All right, I'll spill it. Tobias, you're going to live with us for a bit till your daddy gets his head on straight."

"Uncle Mel's paying Mama for it," said Mary.

"Shut up, Mary, and get your fanny back out to the car!" said Dora.

"Under the table, whatever that means," said Mary. "And the social services will pay her too." She made a face at her mother.

"I'm not going with you, Aunt Dora," said Tobias. "I'll call Daddy. I told him I wouldn't go with you."

"The last thing I need is you flapping your gums," said Dora. "I don't spoil kids like Jamie. That's one thing we'll get straight."

"Dora, Mel will be home later. We'll just stay with Tobias until he gets back," said Saphora.

"Look, lady, I'm an attorney. You don't just take off with a man's child without proper legal work," said Gwennie, even though she knew Mel's intent. She must have been playing ignorant to buy time.

"He signed on the dotted line," said Dora. She held out a document. "It's been authorized. I signed it and he signed it in front of his attorney." Dora was now on the defensive.

"Let me see it," said Gwennie.

Dora handed it to her.

Gwennie read it carefully. She told Saphora, "It's a letter stating that he gives Dora temporary custody throughout his time of bereavement," said Gwennie. "It is signed by both of them on a letterhead from an attorney's office."

"I didn't sign it," said Tobias.

Gwennie was engrossed in the document. "Robert Melvin Linker."

"Temporary custody," said Saphora. "That's not as bad as we thought." She could only make a promise at this point. "Tobias, I'll find your daddy. Give him a few days."

"You keep saying that, Mrs. Warren, like he's a good man. He was leaving Mom and me. He's not going to change his mind," said Tobias.

"If you ladies don't mind, this is a family affair," said Dora. "I'd like to ask you all to vacate the premises. I'm on the verge of a breakdown anyway, what with losing my sister."

Saphora then remembered what Jamie had said about Dora, that she had never known the meaning of love. "We'll go. But, Tobias, you contact me as soon as you get back to your aunt's place."

Tobias turned and ran up the hallway. He was calling for Fang.

Dora waited for him to go into his bedroom and slam the door. "That dog disappeared this morning. I let it out to do its business, and it never came back."

"Smart dog," said Gwennie.

20

Our deepest wishes are whispers of our
authentic selves. We must learn to respect
them. We must learn to listen.

SARAH BAN BREATHNACH, *Simple Abundance*

Marcy stoked up the coffee right at bedtime. "Gwennie looked so pretty tonight. Luke too," she said.

"She's doing the right thing. Luke's the best thing that's come her way in a long time," said Saphora.

"Want to watch a movie?"

"Maybe I'll just go to bed."

"That Dora, she's a piece of work, isn't she?"

"As I was pulling out of the drive, the curtains opened upstairs. Tobias stared at me as if I was abandoning him," said Saphora.

"He's a smart boy. He'll rise above Dora and her gypsy life. Don't you take that on."

"Tobias didn't just come out of a bad home into a worse one. Jamie was giving him a future. The only future Dora thinks about is the next boyfriend she'll snag," said Saphora.

"You got that right."

"I hated to agree with Tobias. I'm supposed to give him grown-up answers, but everything he said about Mel was right."

Saphora excused herself. She went upstairs and dressed in her pajamas. She turned and saw herself in the mirror. The pajamas had faded and frayed at the hem. She was thicker around the middle, having gained some pounds over the summer. She did not care about the pounds or the frayed pajamas. But the thought of crawling into her empty bed made her want to eat. She went outside to brood on the deck.

Johnson squeezed through the gate and ran down the length of the yard in a midnight chase. She caught the mouse at the river's edge. She must have killed it right away, for she crept into the bushes and disappeared. The moon was flattened, as if pressed between the glass of fog and universe, hazy at the edges. The only light was the den light from below where Marcy sat up watching a movie.

Luke would not be digging in the backyard again. It made sense now why he had been so driven to dig up every square inch of lawn. But when she first found him digging like a maniac, she thought he was a little crazy. Crazy and in love might be close kin, though, now that she thought about it. But she felt so much better about Luke being with Gwennie. If she fell in love with him, it would be like falling in love with her best friend. Gwennie needed Luke's friendship maybe even more than she needed to fall in love.

Saphora herself needed friends, but the kind who call and check on you when your husband is dying. She knew that tonight Jamie would call and check on her if she could call from heaven. John Mims called her to make sure she was all right. Marcy knew exactly when she needed her. There was only one Marcy in the world though.

She could hear a song beating through the air, soft as moths circulating, and then realized she had left her telephone on the nightstand. She went inside and answered the phone. It was Turner.

"Mama, you've got to come to the hospital right now. Bring Gwennie," he said.

Her heart seemed to leave her and fly away to where Jamie had gone. "Turner, tell me what's wrong."

"Not wrong, Mama. Dad's come awake."

Saphora ran downstairs but did not remember dressing all over again. But there she was back in jeans and a cotton blouse. "Marcy, Marcy, get up. Get up!" Marcy had fallen asleep on the sofa.

"What on earth?"

"Turner called. It's Bender. He woke up," said Saphora.

"Are you sure?"

"He was so sure, Marcy. Excited sure."

"This is a resurrection. I prayed that power down on him."

"Whatever it is, I just can't believe it. My head's spinning. I can't wait to see my husband, Marcy."

"That's a whole 'nother resurrection. Did you call Gwennie?"

"I'm calling now. They're out somewhere on a date. Probably down by the marina."

As it happened, Gwennie and Luke were at the Marina Bistro. They drove and met them at the edge of town. Saphora turned on the inside car light and brought down the window. "Who's going?" she asked. Gwennie kissed Luke good night and joined her mother and Marcy.

Saphora felt as if she drove in slow motion. She checked the time again as Marcy said, "Slow down or you'll get a speeding ticket."

By the time they congregated around Bender's bed, Turner was holding his hand and Eddie was seated in a chair next to his grandpa's bed. Bender's eyes were closed just like before. Saphora felt herself holding back. Maybe since Turner had called he had already slipped into the coma again.

"Daddy," said Turner, "wake up and see your family."

Bender opened his eyes. "Saphora." He took a moment to take her in. "You were the first person I wanted to see," he said. "Come close."

Turner changed places with Saphora. She took Bender's hand. "I can't believe it" was all she could think to say.

"Turner said I collapsed in church," he said.

"You did. It was a big scene with the ambulance, Pastor John clearing out the lobby. He's a good man, John Mims."

"He is. Can I talk to my wife?" he said to the others without taking his eyes off her.

"Turner, let's go outside," said Gwennie. She was on the other side of her daddy's bed. She kissed him on the cheek. She held her hand out to Eddie. "Come outside and tell Aunt Gwennie when you're going back to school. Mama, we'll come back in a few. I'll call Ramsey."

"Mama, the nurse says dad's doctor, Jim Pennington, has been called," said Turner. "He's on his way here."

Marcy followed them out the door too. Eddie was smiling at his grandpa and was the last to go out the door.

Bender squeezed Saphora's hand. "I'm as weak as a little girl. But you feel good, Saphora."

"You've come back to us," she said. "I still can't believe you're looking at me and talking."

"I've lost time."

"I'll catch you up," she said. But she would not tell him about Jamie or Tobias just yet.

"I mean that I've lost time with you, and I don't want to lose anymore," he said. "Saphora, I've not done right by you."

"You don't have to say that." But she knew he did.

"There are days I can look back on and say that I was no good to any soul on earth."

She waited.

"I'd guess there have not been a lot of people coming by to see me. While I was in the coma I was keenly aware of two things. One was when you were here, and the other was when my children or grandchildren stopped by my bed."

She did not ask him about Evelyn.

"You should have left me a long time ago."

"Bender, don't say that."

"But you didn't."

"Bender, don't paint me with such broad strokes. The day you came home to tell me about your cancer, my suitcase was packed."

"Where were you going?"

"Oriental, I thought."

He closed his eyes again.

"Bender, I'll admit that I've struggled about us. But love is not a feeling. It's the actions you take whether or not you feel like it."

"That's what I wish for. To show you I love you. I kept praying like I thought Mims would. I kept willing my eyes to open. Then I came awake, and there was Eddie running a car down the side of my bed."

Saphora laughed at him.

"But it was great. I mean, the sounds that a boy makes at that age are sacred. I have a new list, Saphora."

"You do?"

"Bender's list of sacred things."

"Like what?"

"Mistakes."

"Mistakes?"

"They're a wonder. We try so hard not to make them. But our

lives are puddled up with them, like mud holes that kids are drawn to after a rain. And then there's the everyday chatter of people. You think I'm kidding. I became aware of nurses in the room talking. They were talking about unimportant things. I never knew how important it was to observe mindless chatter. It's how we know one another."

"It's a good list." She liked him like this, confessional and thoughtful.

"And a woman's lips on your hand."

"What woman?"

"You, Saphora. Your lips. You would come in and before you left you would kiss my hand. You're so tender. The seconds that it took to be aware of a parting kiss taught me a lot about you."

"Like what?"

"The way you exercise care for everyone around you. The vigil you keep over all of us, our kids and grandkids. When you didn't want to love me anymore, you just kept doing it."

"Like this," she said, lifting his hand and kissing it.

"Yes." Bender closed his eyes. The slight turning up of his mouth looked a good deal better than the emotionless pallor that had darkened his face during the coma.

Saphora got up out of her chair. She kissed the side of his face.

Bender moaned. It was the kind of moan a man might make who was buried and had finally broken through to the oxygen.

She twisted the top off a bottle of peppermint lotion. She massaged the lotion into his arms.

Tears ran down his face. "Don't know why I can't stop crying," he said.

She cleaned him up and massaged his neck, around his ears. Then she put her mouth very near his face and said, "I love you, Bender Warren."

A small sob came up from inside of him. It both pained and delighted Saphora to no end. Now he was making her cry. She wiped her eyes. Then she came up onto the bed and laid her head on his chest, but facing him so he could see her. "Make the time stop so we stay like this for a long time."

"I will ask God just for you, my Saphora."

Jim Pennington stuck his head into the room. "Okay if I come in?"

"Jim, you're a sight for sore eyes," said Bender.

Saphora lifted up and said to Jim, "It's a miracle."

Jim sat in Gwennie's place. "Wonders of the brain, old man," he said. He checked his chart and then examined him. Saphora did not let go of Bender's hand the entire time.

Jim sat back in the chair, dropping the stethoscope. He clasped his hands and looked somewhat pensive. "This happens sometimes with terminally ill patients. They'll suddenly just wake up and be very lucid."

"Jim, you don't sound very hopeful," said Saphora.

"I'm sorry. Consider this time a gift. Bender, you know what I'm talking about," he said. "Just make the most of this time. Saphora, if you'd like, I'll step out and invite your kids back in."

"Yes, please," she said.

Jim excused himself.

Saphora bent over and pressed her lips into Bender's hand, still holding tightly to hers. "Don't leave me again."

"I don't know how to stay, Saphora," he said. "I'm not in charge. This I know."

෧෨

Gwennie and Marcy split the cost and stayed overnight in a hotel. Saphora slept all night on the lounge chair next to Bender's bed. She would wake up to listen to the heart monitor and then drift back into sleep. She decided hospitals were too cold for real sleeping. It felt like she was watching herself sleep without ever actually entering the deep abandonment of real rest. She woke up and Bender was looking at her.

"You look terrible. Ask Jim to order my release. Take me home, Saphora."

"To Davidson."

"Oriental. I want to sit with you by the Neuse. I'm running behind on my quota of sunrises."

"You're right. Let's go," said Saphora. She called for the nurse, Kew.

The Asian nurse came in, smiling. "Nice to see you again, Dr. Warren."

Saphora asked, "Kew, could you help us run down Dr. Pennington?"

"Glad to. I'll find him," she said.

Jim bustled in about ten minutes later. Bender made his request known. Jim, although very forward thinking, was old school enough that he balked at first at Bender's request. But he finally acquiesced since there was no point in arguing with Bender Warren. He signed the release orders. "As long as you ride to Oriental in an ambulance," he told him.

Marcy drove Bender's Lexus, keeping up pretty well with the ambulance. Gwennie rode shotgun with Marcy. Turner and Eddie drove behind them, bringing up the rear of the procession.

When the ambulance pulled into the driveway, Luke was pacing up and down, his phone to his ear. He closed up his phone and threw open the ambulance door and also his arms. "Welcome home, Dr. Warren."

An Asian neighbor woman one driveway down from Luke sidled up the street in tiny inching steps, as if Saphora might run her off. Even though Saphora had never met her, she offered a steaming dish spicing the air around it, colors and swirls of vegetables that Saphora would not have the imagination to plait together. "For you and your family tonight. Pork, cabbage, and Chinese vegetables. It's good for you, Dr. Warren." She gave her casserole dish to Gwennie.

"Will you come back and have coffee?" asked Saphora.

"You say when," she said. "I'm Liu." Gwennie wrote her number on her daddy's discharge papers.

By the time the sky was so thin on the horizon that every hue created a whole new collage by the second, Ramsey and Celeste barreled through the front door. Liam skittered across Saphora's rug like a tadpole just finding its legs. He said to the adults, "Where is everybody?" as if the adults did not count.

"Eddie's upstairs, Liam. But go outside and see your grandpa first," said Saphora. Gwennie had walked her daddy outside so he could sit in the chair he liked best, the big, blue dolphin deck chair. Bender was weak, as if when he fell into his coma, he left the most robust parts of himself back in the dark crevices of that quiet world. He came out of the darkness part Bender and part the newly bewildered man causing his children and grandchildren to talk about him in whispered corners of the room.

He stole a bucket from under the deck, keeping it close by in case he was struck by the nausea that flooded his esophagus. He was too queasy, he said, for even a single lusty draw on a Cuban stogie.

ᏩᎥ

The new routine was to get him out of bed for the sunrise since he meant what he said about seeing as many as possible. Turner helped his mama and, between the two of them, they dressed Bender in a morning jacket, khaki trousers, and blue trouser socks. By the time the sun came up, Saphora wanted to go back to bed. But she sat with him for three mornings. She noticed him slipping away the third morning. She asked if he wanted a bacon omelet, to which he answered, "Wa-melon," meaning, she thought, watermelon.

The sun was nearly fully up. The cool of the morning put him in a more amiable and stable attitude. He had taken to avoiding the hot afternoons baking in the deck chair.

Saphora talked to him about Eddie and Liam and the twins, not expecting him to answer. She said, "Have you thought about heaven and what it's like over there?" Jamie was in her thoughts, but the kids had discussed the whole Jamie and Tobias debacle and decided their daddy best not know what none of them could change. "I've just been thinking about it."

Bender lifted his hand. He pointed at the sun. "Light."

"Did you like talking to Pastor John?"

"Toad."

"Frog?"

"To-ad me good," said Bender.

She took it to mean that Pastor John had told him good things.

Gwennie and Celeste burned a pancake. Gwennie had decided she should stay over and had called her office to rearrange her schedule. They opened the doors to air out the house. "The house phone's been ringing. Are you answering the phone today?" asked Gwennie.

"Go ahead," said Saphora. But the phone did not ring again. In the middle of helping Bender squeeze his walker across the door stoop into the den, the local sheriff came to call. It wasn't even eight o'clock.

He was a big man, name of Cole Langford. Saphora had heard

about him. He acted as both the town dogcatcher and horse doctor and kept the homeless guys off the streets at night. "Mrs. Warren, can I talk with you?" he asked.

Saphora followed him out onto the walk.

"Wilmington cops called me this morning about a runaway kid. You know Tobias Linker?" he asked.

"I know him. He's my grandson's friend."

"He was staying with an aunt at an RV park along the coast."

"Dora, yes, she took him in when his mama passed on. He ran away?"

"She thought you might know something of his whereabouts. Mind if I take a look around?"

"Of course not, come inside," she said, although she was somewhat resentful Dora would sic the sheriff on her.

Sheriff Langford walked into the house but, seeing the Warrens collected around the kitchen table for breakfast, excused himself. "Sorry to bother you."

"What's this?" asked Gwennie.

"Tobias has run away," said Saphora.

"That boy's got lots of medicines to take," said Marcy. "This is some serious business, I hope you know."

"Look, Sheriff, Tobias has not been in a good home. That Dora is not looking out for him like she ought," said Gwennie, taking the opportunity to get in her legal digs on the woman.

"I'm not here to patch up family disputes. Just following a lead on a runaway." He walked around the house. Satisfied that they were surprised at the boy's disappearance, he gave Saphora his card. "Call me if he shows up, ma'am."

"Will you take him back to Dora?" asked Saphora.

"Social services says he's got to be returned to his legal guardian," said Langford.

Saphora saw him out the door.

Gwennie was already running to dress. "I'll get Luke. We'll go out and look for him," she said.

"Tobias might come out of hiding if he saw you," said Saphora. "But Marcy's spot-on. He can't go long without his meds." She tried to call Mel three times. But he did not pick up the phone.

ᘒ

Ramsey and Celeste stayed one more night. The next morning they loaded up the boys after they had each kissed their grandpa good-bye.

Eddie walked down the street, pushing his bike. He scarcely waved good-bye to his cousins as they pulled out of the neighborhood. Every few yards, he yelled, "Tobias! It's Eddie! It's safe to come out!"

Saphora could see him through the front-window sheers. Aunt Celeste had cut the legs off a pair of his jeans for his sudden beach wardrobe. He wiped his eyes with the back of his arm.

Turner walked Bender to the sofa and turned on an Eagles' reunion tour on public television. Saphora checked his pulse as Jim had told her to do. When she looked up from his wrist, he was looking straight into her eyes. "Ja-mie. Tell," he said.

"Not now," she said.

"Now."

"There was an accident," she said. "Jamie didn't make it. Tobias's daddy sent him to live with Jamie's sister, Dora. Now Tobias has run off, and we don't know where he is."

Bender turned his eyes on the Eagles. "Sad. Boy."

"He's very sad," she said. She dabbed her eyes as it was painful telling Bender. He was still so aware of details even if he could not fully express himself.

The police looked for Tobias for two days. Saphora called the sheriff's office once in the morning and again at the end of the day. But he would tell her only one thing: "You are not family. I can't tell you anything. But if there were any news, I'd tell you at least that, Mrs. Warren. There's no news about Tobias Linker." She was put out with the man who had come asking for her help.

Gwennie came wheeling her suitcase out of the guest room. "I'm sorry I have to leave, Daddy. It's my job," she said to her father. "I've got a very important lead on my case that I've got to hunt down."

"Call me when you land in New York," said Saphora.

"I will." She set aside her luggage and said, "Mama, when Luke and I drove out to Dora's place, we found them all living in squalor in an RV. Not even a mobile home where they would at least have room. When I say she lives in a vacation park, I mean the kind where old people go. Her children run up and down the beach all day because they can't stand to be cramped up in that orange juice can of a trailer," she said, threading a colored ribbon through her suitcase handle.

"Where does Tobias sleep?" asked Saphora.

"Little Paul had a bed made from the kitchen table. It drops down into a makeshift bed. Tobias had to share it with him."

"What was she like? Dora, I mean?"

"She's Dora, you know. I think she thought she had to put on for the police. And—" She stopped. "Mama, is that Dora on TV?"

Saphora looked toward the television. "Oh my!" she said, turning up the sound.

Dora was looking straight into the camera. "This is the child of my dead sister. This is killing us. We can't even make ends meet as it is and now this." Dora's face was contorted. She looked up at the sky. "God, help us."

"She's appealing for sympathy," said Gwennie. "Like she's asking for donations. What an exploiter that woman is!" She gathered up her things. "Keep me up on things, Mama." She kissed her mother. Then she put her arms around her daddy. "I'll be back next weekend."

Saphora walked her to the door and exchanged I-love-yous with Gwennie.

Gwennie said, "You keep your prayers going up. Something's got to break soon."

"God hears," said Bender, surprising them both.

That was a surprise.

21

There is no such thing as a simple act
of compassion or an inconsequential act
of service. Everything we do for another
person has infinite consequences.

CAROLINE MYSS

A shipping box arrived just as Saphora made coffee the next morning
for Bender. It was a small, flat parcel. The label was handwritten by
Sherry. She had forwarded it from Davidson. Abigail Weed's name was
taped in the upper left corner—the journalist from *Southern Living*.

Saphora opened the package and pulled out the fall issue. Abigail
had stuck a note to the magazine that read, *You made the cover! Congrats, Abigail.*

Bender lay in the hospital bed in the library. She walked in to
show him the magazine. She opened the blinds. Sunlight turned the
tree bark red like cinnamon. "Bender, we made the cover of *SL*.
Look. You have to see this!"

Bender was still and his face the color of shale.

"Bender? Beloved, wake up and see," she said. She felt his hands.
"You're cold." She bent and kissed his cheek. His eyes opened. "Look
and see," she said. She pulled the magazine wide open to the lawn
party spread. Most of the photographs were of Sherry's food or the
gardens. But there was one picture of Saphora and some of the guests.

"Saphora," he said.

"Yes, it's me and Vicki, Bernie Mae, and Pansy. We're on the dock with our feet in the water. Isn't that fun?"

"Saphora," he said, pointing to her.

"It's all of us," she said.

"My. Love," said Bender.

It took an hour to get him out of the bed and dressed in his khakis and a pullover shirt.

"Out," he said.

"Out on the deck. I know," she said.

"River," said Bender.

She figured that meant he wanted his chair moved close to the riverbank. "I'll get Turner up. He'll move it for us."

Turner and Eddie were sleeping in the same bed. She cajoled her son awake. "Your daddy has need of you," she said.

Turner walked barefoot onto the deck, one side of his hair sticking out like a cat had licked it. It did not take long for Turner to hoist the blue dolphin chair down to the riverbank. He came back grinning. "I'm getting Eddie up to fish," he told Saphora. "A trout as big as my arm's hiding out in the marsh grass."

"That's Big Indifferent. Eddie tried to catch him before," she said. "There's a reason he's gotten so big."

"Funny name, Mama. But me and Eddie, we'll catch him."

Turner got under his daddy's right arm and lifted him up. "Let's go down to the river, Daddy. We'll catch ol' Indifferent."

Bender groaned. He was saying, "No. Not," but Turner just kept walking him until he put him into his blue chair.

"Mama, coffee?" asked Turner.

"Of course," she said, noticing how much Turner looked like his daddy.

Turner went inside to dress and wake up Eddie.

"How about I make some eggs? You take Daddy his coffee."

He had lost some weight and looked young again, like when he was seventeen and on the tennis team, complaining how it ate into his social calendar.

"I'm glad you came back," she said.

He would rather use up his accrued leave, he said, while he still had his daddy.

"We'll stay through Sunday," he said. He went upstairs to raise Eddie out of bed.

Saphora got the coffee for Bender. She kept it black like he liked it. Then she opened the *SL* magazine. She saw the women that she had decidedly hated since the morning she had packed her suitcase. Vicki had her arm around Saphora's neck. There was admiration in her eyes. Bernie Mae and Pansy were laughing. But now none of them looked the same to Saphora. Maybe they had had designs on her husband, but he did not belong to them.

Bender would need a table for his coffee. She put his coffee on a tray she had bought once when she imagined the two of them having breakfast in bed. She put a rolled copy of the morning news-paper on the side as if he would read it. The texture and smell of the newspaper was enough for him. He would close his eyes, and the familiarity of it might draw him back into the comfort of a simple remembrance. Saphora backed out through the french door. She turned around and saw Bender in his chair, holding something. He was laughing. She set the tray on the table. "Bender?"

He kept laughing, throwing back his head.

She came off the deck and ran down the lawn to the riverbank. She could see him better. He had his arms around a boy who was holding on to him.

"Tobias?" she said, not trusting her own eyes.

There was a school bag next to Bender's chair.

"Mrs. Warren, I found him. He's here," said Tobias. "That Dora said he had died and you had gone back to Davidson. But he's here." He could not stop giggling. "I found you!"

Bender took to Tobias's cuddling so fondly that he was still laughing out loud. Tobias held on to his neck. He pressed his face into Bender's chest.

"Tobias!" Saphora shouted toward the house. "Turner! Eddie! Come see!" She ran to meet him and he threw his arms around her.

"I couldn't stay at Dora's," he said.

"I know, honey, I know. I haven't slept since you took off. What happened?" she asked.

"I made a plan and worked it, just like Dr. Warren taught me. I took my pills with water from the bottle Eddie gave me. The pillow from Gwennie, it helped me sleep. I prayed like Pastor John said, to keep the rain from coming. Dr. Warren was right. You can live off oranges and apples for a few days." He pulled out Mabel's wooden cross. "Luke gave me this. He said it would bless my way."

Saphora must have held her breath the whole time he talked. She let it out slowly when he got to the end of his words as if she could slow down time and make it stand still right then.

"Don't send me back to Dora," said Tobias. "She doesn't know how to love."

"That's a shame," said Saphora. "You're so easy to love."

❧

To Saphora's great relief, it took Sheriff Langford three days to realize she had stopped calling him. Turner and Eddie had just left for

Charlotte. Tobias sat on the floor playing his video game using both player devices; he could be the monster and kill it at the same time.

The doorbell rang.

Saphora said, "Tobias, go upstairs."

"Mrs. Warren, I'm not going with those cops. They believe everything Dora says."

"Wait upstairs."

Sheriff Langford was examining the bicycle propped against the side of the house. "Have you had company, Mrs. Warren?"

"My grandson Eddie, as you well know, Sheriff. His daddy just took him back to Charlotte."

"Mind if I come in, look around?"

"Might as well," she said.

"You've stopped calling me."

"There's no need," she told him. "You informed me you couldn't tell me anything." She opened the door for him.

He looked beyond her, seeing Bender out on the deck, his eyes closed.

"Glad to see Dr. Warren's on the mend," he said.

"Would you have some coffee?" she asked.

"None for me."

A soft thud came from overhead.

"Sounds like your company's still here," he said.

"Can't you just go on and act like you didn't see me?" she asked.

"That would be a crime," he said.

"Sending him back to Dora's is the crime," she said.

"I don't know the woman. But Melvin Linker's signed temporary guardianship over to Dora Flaherty."

"She just wants the money."

"She's made an emotional plea in the public arena. She'll get her money. Mrs. Warren, harboring a runaway's also a crime."

"You take him and it's back to hell. Give us one day."

"If I come back here tomorrow and he's gone, I'm arresting you."

"I'll make sure he's here."

She showed Langford out. She had a headache coming on when she got back to the den.

Tobias had come downstairs. "What do we do now?" he asked.

"You prayed back the rain, Tobias. Do you have a prayer left in you?"

෨

Saphora tried all afternoon to reach Gwennie. She watched as Tobias stayed with Bender into the afternoon, sitting at his side under the umbrella shade. He talked to him as if Bender might start spouting back his funny sayings and advice. He even made him a sandwich. Bender looked at it as if he did not quite know what to make of it.

Saphora had stepped into the library to tidy up when Tobias ran into the house saying, "Mrs. Warren, Dr. Warren's messed himself." He ran and got Bender's robe, then raced past Saphora going in the other direction. "It's all right, Dr. Warren. I do that all the time," said Tobias. He got him up on his walker and put his robe around him.

Saphora knew the task was too adult for Tobias to handle. She said, "Tobias, you go and play in the tree house. I'll take care of it."

"I know what to do," he said. He took down Bender's pants and helped him step out of them. "Off to the shower," he said. "Not a big deal, Dr. Warren."

Tobias walked Bender back into the library. He pulled out the latex gloves from the box on the nightstand. Then he got the shower water warmed up so he could walk Bender into it. "Just go in, walker and all," said Tobias. He followed him in, guiding him to turn his backside to the warm water. Tobias walked right in wearing his flip-flops.

"You're getting soaked," said Saphora. She laughed at Tobias standing in the shower in his shirt and denim shorts next to naked Bender.

"You get to wash all these clothes," said Tobias.

"Like you said, no big deal," said Saphora, still laughing. Together, she and Tobias helped Bender shower and then dress into lounging clothes.

By nightfall, Saphora had gotten in touch with Ramsey. "Ramsey, you'll never guess who's here. It's Tobias."

Ramsey told her she should take him back to his daddy and be done with it. Ramsey did not understand Mel's tendency to stick his head in the sand. Next she called Turner, who she knew to be sympathetic.

Eddie had gone back to his mother's house. School was in session. Turner said, "He wanted Tobias to come and live with him." He was going off break so had to end the call.

Tobias was happy to sleep in Eddie's room. He told Saphora, "Aunt Dora was making me sleep on a kitchen table. She doesn't know that's not how you put kids to bed."

Saphora stood at the bedroom door with her hand on the light switch. She knew that time was passing too fast and that tomorrow would bring another round of sorrow down on Tobias's sweet head. "I'm so glad you're here. You get some rest." She turned off the light, fearing the pain of his situation might show in her face.

She went downstairs to check on Bender. The light was on in the kitchen. To her surprise, he was standing in the kitchen with his walker. "Honey, what are you doing? You could fall and then what would I do with Turner already gone?"

He was holding a small book in his hands. She looked and there was her tote bag dropped onto the floor. She had left it there probably the entire time since coming back from the hospital, what with having to come and go so much, running back and forth from the pharmacy.

Bender was holding the book out, the pages flopping open. At first she thought he had gone and gotten his Bible. Then she saw that it was the poetry book Evelyn had left in his hospital room. She'd forgotten it in her tote bag all this time. "You don't need that," she said, irritated with what he had done. Her keys were on the floor along with the checkbook and other items that had all spilled onto the floor.

Bender was crying. "Sorrow," he said. "Saphora. Sorrow."

She took the poetry book from his hand and said, "Yes, sorrow, Bender. I understand." Her anger was subsiding. Even with his limited vocabulary, he sounded so contrite.

He grasped her arm and squeezed it. "Saphora. Forgive."

Bender had come out of his coma sorry for the life he had made for them. That had been a sort of blanket apology. But this was specific.

"I forgive you, Bender." She took the book and dropped it into the garbage bin. "Completely." She helped him back to bed and turned out the lights.

She was just getting back to her room when Gwennie called. She told her mother, "I'm flying back tomorrow morning. Don't let Sheriff Langford take Tobias."

Tobias came out of Eddie's room sometime in the night. He made a bed in the lounge chair next to Bender in the library, and that was how Saphora found him the next morning. He was still asleep when the doorbell rang. She closed the door behind her, not quite ready to rouse them both.

Saphora let Sheriff Langford into the house. She had a speech ready but did not get to give it. Two Wilmington cops came in the door right behind Langford.

"I've not gotten Tobias up yet," she said.

"We've got orders," said one of the cops.

"I know this is hard, ma'am," said the other cop. "It's good the boy trusted you enough to come here."

"If you will, Mrs. Warren, it's time to bring him out," said Langford.

"Give them a moment," the benevolent policeman told Langford. "We'll take some coffee. When you're ready to bring him out, we'll escort him back to his aunt."

"Has his daddy been called?" asked Saphora.

Langford exhaled in obvious impatience. "The last time we talked to him he was firm that the boy should live with his aunt."

"When was that?"

"Yesterday afternoon."

Saphora showed them where to find coffee mugs. She pushed open the library door.

Tobias stood next to Bender's bed. He was crying.

"I'm sorry, Tobias. I guess you heard from in here. The police have come to take you back."

"It's Dr. Warren, ma'am. He's passed."

Bender lay still, his hands on his chest.

"Tobias, are you sure?" Saphora rushed into the room. "Bender."

"He's dead, Mrs. Warren. I know. I've seen it."

"Oh, my love. You can't leave me," she said.

"Should we do something?" he asked.

Saphora checked his pulse. She pulled the covers back. There was the Bible Pastor John had given him.

"He wanted it," said Tobias. "It took me awhile to figure out his words. First I got him his socks and then his heating pad. But finally I got him what he wanted."

Saphora stood over Bender's bed. She did not know how long she stood over him. She remembered how Luke had said the soul travels south after death. She imagined him walking right out onto the Neuse with the sun coming up, going south until he could catch a boat skyward. She kept taking Bender's hand, cupping it as if she could keep the warmth intact. Then she wiped her eyes. She cried and called out to him as if he were still walking on the river. She could only imagine Jamie's surprise when he came through the gate.

Finally the nice-faced cop appeared at the library door. "We need to go."

Saphora said, "My husband, Bender, has just passed on."

The cop was so surprised that he opened the door all the way. He told the other officers, "We've got a situation here."

First the coroner was called. Saphora got in touch with Jim Pennington. He was down fishing and told her it would only take him forty-five minutes to get there. He asked her to put the sheriff on the phone.

Whatever Jim told the sheriff stalled the police for the time it took Gwennie to show up.

Her hair was pulled back, and she had not put on any makeup.

She was wearing a disheveled knit shirt and flip-flops. "I got Mr. Linker to sign new papers," she said. "I flew in to Wilmington on the red-eye. I was up with him hours on end, but finally he agreed Dora was not the one to raise Tobias."

The cop took the papers from Gwennie and read them.

Gwennie saw Tobias standing in the library door. "Where's Daddy?" she asked him.

Tobias looked sadder than he had since losing his mother.

"I'm sorry, honey," said Saphora. "We've lost Bender."

"Daddy?" she cried, and Tobias put his arms around her.

Saphora asked the police to excuse them. She followed Tobias back inside the library and closed the door behind Gwennie.

"When did he die?" asked Gwennie.

"Not too long ago," said Saphora. "Tobias slept beside him all night. He's been such a comfort to your daddy."

"I think he was trying to save me," said Tobias. "He threw the cops off my trail this morning."

Saphora held on to Gwennie and let her have her cry.

The sheriff knocked at the door. "Mrs. Warren, we need to ask you some questions about the child."

Saphora was opening the door just as the coroner came in. Jim Pennington followed right behind. He greeted her and kissed her cheek. "I can't believe he's gone. My best friend, ever."

"Mine too," said Saphora.

Jim promised to see her through Bender's arrangements in the coming days. He told the coroner, "I'm Dr. Warren's doctor." He followed him into the library.

Tobias and Gwennie came out into the den.

Sheriff Langford said, "Mrs. Warren, this document, signed by Mr. Linker, gives you temporary guardianship."

"Me?" she asked.

"I meant to ask," said Gwennie. "But nothing's gone exactly like I thought it would. When I saw Mel Linker's full name on the custody agreement, I suspected it was more than a coincidence."

"What coincidence?" asked Saphora.

"He's the one suing my client, Francis Pierce. Mel Linker is Robert Melvin Linker. Francis was Mel's best friend. He trusted Mel, telling him about his software program. Mel found out my client had never filed for a patent. Mel took advantage."

"So he stole it?" asked Saphora.

"I heard my mom fighting with him about it," said Tobias. "She was mad and told Daddy he was a thief and a backstabber."

"When I told my client about Tobias, he said to offer Mel a settlement to buy back his own patent. But on the condition that he sign custody to you, Mama," said Gwennie.

Tobias hugged her. "I love you, Gwennie. You're a rock star."

Saphora had not thought of much else the past few days other than Tobias's fate at the hands of Dora. It was a lot to think about. All at once she remembered the quiet afternoon she stood on the landing with her suitcase packed. She had planned to come and live alone in her house by the Neuse River.

"Give her time," said the cop.

"I don't need time," said Saphora.

22

We find again some of the joy in the now,
some of the peace in the here, some of the
love in me and thee which go to make up
the kingdom of heaven on earth.

ANNE MORROW LINDBERGH, *Gift From the Sea*

Davidson Prep had planned an outdoor ceremony for the senior
graduation. Black thunderheads grew from south of Lake Norman.
They grumbled like hungry bellies. Five hundred parents and grand-
parents grabbed seats on the folding chairs in rows along the front
lawn. Some of the parents pulled out plastic rain parkas, maybe because the air smelled like rain. But right overhead was a triangle of
blue, the shape of a pool ball rack.

Saphora saved six seats beside her. Even though it was May, the
air was chilly. She buttoned her yellow sweater. She sat only one row
behind the graduation candidates.

Gwennie yelled across the school lawn, "Here we are!"

Saphora got up and waved at Gwennie's two girls running in
sundresses and sweaters. Finally girls in the Warren clan had balanced
out the loud boys congregating in the summer house at Oriental.
Luke blamed the female progeny on his gene pool. Gigi and Evanley
hugged Saphora and then climbed into chairs on either side of her.
Gwennie carried a gift wrapped in Davidson Prep blue.

"Luke's parking. He drove us round and round until I was going nuts, so I told him to drop us off," said Gwennie.

Turner walked alongside Eddie, who had grown taller than his daddy. He had to bend his knees to kiss his Nana. Eddie sat beside his Aunt Gwennie. Turner was still arguing over Eddie's not having gotten a haircut.

"I like his hair," said Saphora. It was blond and curled around his shoulders. "We've got a minute to spare," she said. "I don't see Tobias."

"The Ws are seated right in front of us. He should be there somewhere," said Gwennie.

Saphora counted the boys in front of her, the boys she had gotten to know the past few years because they seemed to congregate in her basement and around her refrigerator.

Andrew Watson, Jeffrey Warlick, Matthew Wade, all the boys who either played baseball with Tobias or had come to the games for the past few summers. Andrew Watson had won a baseball scholarship. Tobias had brooded over it but then found the character to congratulate him.

"I made it," said Luke. He picked Evanley up and sat down with her in his lap.

The school's dean made opening comments and a minister prayed. The valedictorian was slated to make her speech. But the dean took the podium again and said, "Davidson Prep has a longstanding tradition of honoring its scholars. As I name the following scholarship awards, I would ask the students receiving them to take the platform."

Saphora was beginning to worry. Tobias still struggled with the unpredictable consequences of his illness.

The dean named seven scholars. Each student came from the

front row and took the platform. As they did, they were handed a gold tassel that they each affixed to their graduation caps. The dean said, "There was one scholarship awarded yesterday. It was given to a Davidson Prep student for outstanding achievement in science. Tobias Jefferson Warren is the recipient of this award at Elon University, where he will take studies in medical research."

The parents came to their feet. Saphora gasped. Tobias was standing slightly shorter than his peers but holding the gold tassel over his head.

"Mama, did you know?" asked Gwennie.

"He didn't tell me," said Saphora. She was near to bursting with joy.

"All right," said Eddie. "That's my man."

The scholars filed down the aisle, taking their seats alphabetically. Tobias walked past his friends along the back row, each of them giving him a high-five.

The salutatorian read her winning essay and then introduced the valedictorian. She was a funny girl who gave a speech for which all the students cheered.

The crowd was seated as the front row of graduates stood to receive their diplomas.

Tobias handed the cap back to Saphora. "Can you put the tassel on for me, Mom?" he asked.

"I can, but it's not a hard thing to do," she said.

"I wouldn't have gotten it without you," he said.

"Tobias, you are a surprise," she said.

ᕙ

Tobias asked to leave flowers on Bender's grave before heading off to the senior parties that would end with a sleepover back at his house.

Saphora drove him to Mt. Zion where Bender had been interred back in that fall season when Saphora had decided not to run away from home. He laid flowers from Saphora's garden on the grave. He'd tied blue and white ribbons around it, his school colors.

Saphora took him home where he changed before Andrew picked him up. The house was going to be very quiet come August when Tobias headed off to Elon. There was not much summer ahead when she thought like that.

Sherry had opened the patio door drapes full-blown. The sun warmed the potted begonias setting outside on her green garden cart. The light filtered into the living room that she had repainted the color of olives, a tint that she could nearly taste.

She might sell the house. Luke had finally sold his house in Oriental since Gwennie had been taken on as a partner in a Charlotte law firm. She had been nagging Saphora about moving into one of those upscale condominiums in uptown. Saphora tried to imagine herself in a place where the views glistened with car windshields, not a rippling lake.

She could live like Marcy, but then Marcy was seldom home. She imagined the quiet was difficult, an enveloping kind of silence that echoed with past conversations that had been taken for granted. She would decide when the thought of it no longer made her feel suffocated.

Tobias had delayed her season of solitude the summer that Bender died. Now he was going away. The tide of those days had beckoned in so welcome a manner, as if she could dance in the elation of escaping her life on the lake. She was holding it out now in front of her, seeing all of it as if her past were a long, mellifluous skein of silk—the night Bender held her, whispering to her while they danced on the street; the first time she told him "we're pregnant," the way her breasts ached and yet gave her such pleasure to feed a baby from her own body; Gwennie standing in a French shop holding up the blue coverlet, now worn, and how her eyes emoted elation at having passed the bar; Turner holding Eddie for the first time and Ramsey marrying the girl who would eventually bear him children. She could see Bender standing in the entry telling her about his cancer, Eddie coming to stay with them that summer in Oriental, Tobias meeting them on the beach, Jamie kissing her good-bye for the last time, Gwennie falling in love with Luke, Mel losing his way.

Last of all, she could see Bender apologizing in a language so affected by wilting neurons that he might have been misunderstood. But she comprehended.

There was no pain capable of erasing the moments that she had lived in the manner she had chosen. Her life was not ruined by Bender's lapses. Nor was it halted, but the minutes kept unfolding, awakening, disappointing and astonishing.

Turner was dating a woman he had met at the hospital. She had been a patient, and she taught school in Matthews. Over dinner last Friday night, he looked smitten with her. She was as red headed as Gwennie.

Tobias ran across the tiled lobby and slid in his socks. He pulled on his sneakers that had been parked by the door and kissed Saphora. "I'll be back tonight, Mom."

"Sherry will have the food ready," she said.

"You are the best woman in the world," said Tobias.

"Tobias, you make me feel loved." She hugged him and then said, "See you later on."

Sherry came up from the basement into the kitchen. She was leaving some food upstairs for the parent chaperones who would arrive in two hours. "What are you thinking about, Miss Saphora? You look lost in your thoughts."

"I'm fine, Sherry," she said.

"You're about to have the house all to yourself finally," she said. "You won't be needing me around here."

"I do need you, Sherry. I've needed every person the good Lord's put in my life."

"I'm glad to hear it. I didn't want to go looking for a job in this crazy job market. The only skills I have are looking after you. I don't even know how to explain that in a résumé." She brought a box of books and magazines for Saphora to go through. "These are from the house in Oriental. You asked me to clean things out before you all headed down there for the summer," she said. She pulled out a magazine. "Look what I found. You thought it was lost."

It was the copy of *Southern Living* with her gardens on the cover.

"You are a miracle woman," said Saphora.

Sherry went back downstairs to put out more food for Tobias's graduation party.

Saphora went through the box. There were the medical journals that Bender had pored over searching for a cure for brain cancer. Tobias would want those. He had claimed a lot of Bender's books for his own over the past few years. She had found a good use for the library after all. Tobias swore he could smell the man in the pages who was almost his daddy.

Then she found Mabel's small wooden cross. She would keep that for sure. Every time she looked at it, she could see Luke digging in the backyard for treasure. The *Southern Living* she would keep to remember what she almost threw away but found along the way.

She dropped the magazine into the rack with the other periodicals.

It would be nice to pull out and remember every now and then, to see the black-eyed Susans open faced when winter set in.

The doorbell sounded.

"I'll get it, Sherry," she said. She half expected Marcy to be standing there. But she was surprised.

"Saphora, I'm so sorry. I missed the whole graduation ceremony." John Mims looked apologetic. He was robust, though, dressed out of church in jeans. Hair the color of snow curled behind his ears. He held a bouquet of flowers in his good hand; a gift bag dangled from his wrist. "I got Tobias's invitation and had to come. I've enjoyed watching him grow over the summers."

"I didn't know you were coming." To her recollection, he had not returned the response card. "His party's here tonight. You haven't missed him entirely," said Saphora.

"I'm glad. I did leave soon enough. But there was an accident on the Interstate."

"Traffic gets so backed up."

"I saw it happen. So I sat with the lady until the ambulance showed up."

"How awful."

"She's going to be fine," he said. "You look good."

"As do you." She enjoyed his attention. "Can you come in?"

John came inside. He commented about how he was still wrestling over missing the commencement ceremony. He handed her the bouquet. "I'll bet Tobias looked good in his cap and gown."

Saphora led him into the living room. He put the gift bag on the coffee table.

"Your house is beautiful. It looks like you."

"Thank you, John. Did your charity drive go well?"

"It did. Thank you for the check." He took a seat on the sofa so Saphora sat across in the overstuffed chair. "Sherry must be cooking," he said. "Smells familiar."

"Yes, she's cooking for the party."

"I hope I'm not interrupting your plans."

"You know me."

"I do know you," he said. "I just don't want to get in the way."

"Tobias will be thrilled to see you. Besides, the other parents will stay upstairs with me. We'll watch a movie while the kids meet downstairs in the basement." She felt surprised at how eager she was for his company. "So, will you stay?"

"I'd hoped you would ask."

She made John hot tea, lemon only. She was able to take a few cookies hot from the pan before Sherry came back upstairs. She realized that she had not asked him how he wanted his tea. At the summer house, he had paid numerous visits, so she had come to know how he liked his tea, his steak, and his salad with spinach leaves and red onion slices.

She looked up from the kitchen bar. He sat facing toward the big picture window, looking out over the lake. Then he picked up a framed photograph of her. He held it in his lap. He looked at it for a good amount of time.

"Hot cookies?" she asked.

He put back the photograph as if he'd been caught. Then she remembered how he had been caught in the act of stealing oysters the first time she met him. It came to her that she had been so busy with Bender and then with grief and then with rearing Tobias that she had not noticed how she had been collecting common details from the life of John Mims. There sat John on the periphery of her memories, tending to Bender's soul but never far away and always observant of how she lived.

John got up from his seat. "I'll have a few," he said. A sailboat was gliding across the lake.

"I'm glad you came," she said.

"Will you come and sit with me?" he asked. "I want to hear all about your life this year. You always catch me up in the summer. But this year I didn't want to have to wait for you to come back to Oriental."

"John?"

"Yes, Saphora?"

"It's so thoughtful that you've come to see Tobias."

"I'll confess it was more than Tobias," he said. "I'd hoped you'd agree we cultivated more than the conventional friendship, Saphora." He took her by the hand and led her back to the sofa.

"I guess that's true." She sat next to him.

He helped her set the plate on the table but kept holding her hand. "Tell me everything that I've missed this year."

"First, I'd rather you tell me everything that has happened to you this year," she said.

"I insist. You first."

"What's to tell? I adopted a boy and he loved me and my life is full."

"Stole him, actually."

"As you know, I'm a pirate."

"It's called finding 'the better part.'"

"You helped me find fullness, John." It had taken the passing years to understand what a clergyman meant by abundant living.

"Saphora, you're the most interesting woman I've ever met. I've noticed when you're around, everyone pulls out all the stops. You make others want to be better people."

She was drawn to his compliments. He never said anything unless he meant it. "You see me," she said.

"Even when I'm sleeping."

"How did I miss that?" Now he was surprising the fool out of her.

"The life you lead is hard to see from inside."

"Why can't I see it like you do?"

"What?"

"My life."

He took her hand in his. "Sometimes even I can't take you all in."

"You have been waiting all this time, John Mims, for me to learn these things, haven't you?"

"You needed time to pass, Saphora."

"I've never met a man like you." She looked out across the lake. The sailboat had anchored in the greening cove beyond her dock.

Saphora did as John asked. She could have told him about all that had happened since the last time she saw him at the summer house, last summer in Oriental. Tobias's last year of high school was full of the trials and victories of a young man coming of age, and that meant she stayed busy keeping up with him. But she started back only as far as the few weeks leading up to Tobias's graduation. She was in a hurry to get on with knowing John Mims. It was time to start saying hello instead of good-bye.

ACKNOWLEDGMENTS

I would like to express my gratitude to Lissa Halls Johnson, my editor, for your tireless attention to our shaping of this story through your skills and wisdom. Thank you also to Pam Shoup, my production editor, who contributed greatly to the things we might have missed, but your keen eye caught. Thank you to Captain Chris Daniels of the Oriental's School of Sailing. You were very patient and helpful as I gathered sailing facts for this story's Outer Banks setting. Thank you to adoptive mom Beverly Mitzel for your careful reading of this story regarding the care of a child with HIV/AIDS. You deserve a medal for your commitment and compassion for special needs adoptions. I also want to thank the art department for this gorgeous book jacket. A very special thanks to the Random House/WaterBrook Press staff whose work often goes unnoticed—Shannon Marchese, Allison O'Hara, Steve Herron, the staff assistants, sales team, marketing team, and publicity staff who support your novelists behind-the-scenes. Jessica Barnes, you find answers and hunt people down and are a calming influence in the midst of a harried schedule. Thank you, WB staff, for your tenacity and patience. It takes a small army to put out a high-quality novel, and I'm so honored to have you all in my camp.

I would also like to send encouragement to the brave women and children I've come to know through the Secret Angels Project. To help a mom or child affected by HIV, please visit www.secretangels project.com.

READERS GUIDE

1. A writer friend recently said to me that if she were Bender's wife she would tell him to go and convalesce alone. But a marriage of three decades has complicated Saphora's choices. Why do you think she stayed with Bender?

2. Saphora's strongest desire at the outset seems to be to run away from home. But in the end, we discover there were hidden desires realized in Saphora's story. What other intrinsic desires were driving her?

3. The *Southern Living* party frames the story. What was different about Saphora from the day of the party to the day the finished *SL* issue arrived?

4. The women who attend the *Southern Living* party make only a brief appearance, but it is evident they have each played a role that causes Saphora great and inexpressible pain. How did time shift her attitude toward these women? Does that mean she was condoning that type of behavior?

5. Saphora's desire to get away from her family obligations was thwarted in more than one way. Suddenly throwing her grandson Eddie into the mix only added to her frustration. But Eddie's presence drew another person into

her life. If she had gotten her way, how different would
her life have been?

6. Saphora's fantasy about an Outer Banks life was reduced
   to short ruminations in the midst of the clamor of caring
   for Bender's cancer and the guests filing into and out of
   their house on the Neuse River. What part did these fan-
   tasies play in her acceptance of her circumstances?

7. Luke is a mysterious part of Saphora's Outer Banks journey. What qualities did Luke possess that drew Saphora
   into his strange quest?

8. Gwennie is equal parts Saphora and Bender, although
   Saphora only sees her husband's qualities in her daughter.
   How does their alliance affect the story's outcome? How
   are these two women strengthened by their relationship?

9. What symbolism unfolds through the metaphor of the
   Pirate Queen?

10. Pastor Mims is benevolent, but in what ways does he
    assert himself into the Warren family? Whether or not
    you are a person of religious faith, how did you respond
    to the way he engaged their predicament?

11. Tobias has learned to live with survival strengths that
    benefit him later and in unexpected ways. Bender's care
    for him is eventually reciprocated. What bond was
    formed through these acts of compassion?

12. The class distinctions and domestic responses between the Warrens and the Linker family are more fully realized after Jamie's accident. How did you respond to Saphora's involvement in this family's bereavement process? How different was Mel Linker's response to illness and grief from Saphora's?

13. John Mims makes a surprising move at the end of the story. Why might he have waited so long to respond to Saphora romantically?